The Virgin Romance Novelist

MEGHAN QUINN

Copyright © 2015 Hot-Lanta Publishing, LLC

bookmark: Copyright
Published by Hot-Lanta Publishing, LLC
Copyright 2015
Cover by Meghan Quinn

All rights reserved.

ISBN: 1508829500
ISBN-13: 978-1508829508

CHAPTER 1
"The Briar Patch"

Her bosom heaved at an alarming rate as his rough hand found its way down to her soft, yet wiry briar patch...

"Briar patch? What the hell are you writing?"

"Jesus!" I screamed, as I slammed my computer screen of my laptop shut. "Henry, you can't just walk up on me and start reading my stories."

"Stories?" he asked, while creasing his brow. "Bosom, briar patch? Are you writing a sex scene?"

"Why, yes. In fact, I am," I said, while sticking my chin up in the air.

He crossed his arms over his chest and said, "What the hell are you referring to as a briar patch?"

Feeling the heat of his question start to show on my face, I turned from him in my chair and stacked up my notes so they were neatly put together. Briar patch was a well-respected term to use to refer to a lady's' private area, at least that's what my mother taught me.

"Rosie, what were you referring to?"

Clearing my throat and with my chest puffed out, I looked him in the eyes and said, "Not that it's any of your business, but I was referring to a lady's peaceful pleasure garden."

I watched as Henry carefully studied me with those blue green eyes of his that have spent the last six years studying me and my eccentricities. He was my first ever true friend, and he accepted me for who I was the first day we met: a homeschooled, sheltered, naïve girl being thrown into her first day of college.

Finally, he threw his head back and laughed, causing me to tense immediately; even though we were best friends, I still felt self-conscious about my lack of "modern verbiage."

"What's so funny?" I asked, while holding my notebook close to my chest.

"Rosie, please tell me you don't call a lady's vagina her pleasure garden."

"Henry," I hushed him.

That garnered another laugh from him as he wrapped his arm around my shoulders and walked me out of my room of the apartment we shared together with our other roommate, Delaney.

"Rosie, if you can't say vagina out loud, then there is no way you will be able to write about throbbing penises and aroused nipples."

Heat washed through me at the mention of a throbbing penis, something I've never experienced firsthand. The only penises I've seen were courtesy of Tumblr and some careful Googling. I would rather study one in person, because from what I could see from the Internet and what I've read in other romance novels, they had a mind of their own…twitching and rising when aroused. I was fascinated to see an actual boner take place. What would happen if I touched it? That was a question that was constantly on my mind.

Growing up, I was very much sheltered by my parents. I was homeschooled and spent many days on the beach or in my room reading. Anything written by Jane Austen was my go-to book, until I found one of my mother's dirty novels in her night stand. We didn't talk about sex, ever, so it fascinated me to read a book about heaving breasts and thick bulges. I couldn't help it; I was hooked.

Ever since then, I've been reading romance novels. When I was young, I would only read in the library, so I was never caught by my mom, and I got away with it. During college, I focused on my school work, so it wasn't until I graduated that I started reading again, feeding the passion for romance inside of me.

"Hey, are you even listening to what I'm saying?" Delaney, my best friend and roommate asked as she looked at me with her hand on her robe-covered hip and her hair tucked up into a towel.

"Umm, no," I said with an innocent smile. When did Delaney even show up? "What were you saying?"

Rolling her eyes, Delaney repeated herself, "Have you started writing your romance novel again?"

The way Delaney said romance novel in her haughty voice was a little frustrating. I had known Henry and Delaney since my freshman year in college, where we met at freshman orientation and found out we were all majoring in English. For those four years, we had the same classes, same schedules and same housing. We moved off campus after our freshman year and lived in a small three bedroom apartment in Brooklyn, where we currently still live.

Unluckily for me, the walls are thin, the space is tight, and I unfortunately get to know every single person my roommates bring home on an intimate level. Henry was a ladies' man, no surprise there, given his tanned skin, blue-green eyes and brown hair that was styled just right. Delaney, on the other hand, had a couple of relationships throughout college, but was now serious with her latest boo, Derk. Yes, Derk. Hideous name, especially when it's screamed at the top of Delaney's lungs as her headboard slams against my wall.

Now that we've graduated, we're still living together, but going our separate ways in the work force. Henry got a job with one of the top marketing firms, Bentley Marketing, editing ads, and

Delaney is working as a freelance writer for *Cosmopolitan*. She started writing articles about anything from haircuts for the summer to how to maximize your orgasm count in a night. I had that article saved in my notebook, as research.

Me, well, I wasn't as lucky when it came to the job force and was unfortunately offered a job at *Friendly Felines,* where I write about the new and upcoming clumping formulas in cat litter. Our offices are located in Manhattan, but in the smallest of buildings, where my boss insists upon having a gaggle of unneutered and randy cats, who seem to be in heat every day. Have you ever listened to a cat whine from needing a little attention when in heat? Yeah, sounds like its dying. Try writing in an environment like that. I'm a walking fur ball when I leave work.

To keep myself from ending up as a crazy cat lady who doesn't mind when she eats thirty percent cat hair with each meal, I decided to write a romance novel. I'm the girl who lives in fantasies where love always prevails and a hero is just waiting around the corner to swoop in on his white horse to save you. Given my love for love and my ability to get lost in my writing, I didn't think it would be so hard to write my first romance, given the fact that it's my favorite genre, but I forgot about one little speed bump in that plan. I was still a virgin.

Answering Delaney's question, I said, "Yes, I've started writing it again. I felt like it was time to revisit Fabio and Mayberry."

"Please tell me you did not actually name your character Fabio," Henry said with a snort, while he went to the fridge and pulled out three beers.

"What's wrong with Fabio?" I asked, slightly offended. "I will have you know, Fabio was a well to do name in the eighties and nineties for the romance genre. He's the king of all romance. You just can't go wrong with a name like that."

"Rosie, you know I love you, but I think you need to get your head out of your books for a few hours and realize we're not living in the eighties and nineties anymore. We're living in an age of

Christian Grey and Jett Colby, dominant men with kinky sides. Stop reading that heaving bosom shit and get your head in the here and now," Delaney chastised me.

"There is nothing wrong with a heaving bosom," I defended, thinking about what I was just writing. What else would bosoms do in the heat of passion? Jiggle? Jiggling reminded me of my Aunt Emily and her Jell-O salad, not two passionate humans rubbing bodies together.

"There sure is," Henry said, as he handed Delaney and I each a beer. "When I have a girl writhing under me, I'm not thinking, damn look at her heaving bosom. I'm thinking, shit, her tits are jiggling so damn fast from my thrusts that I'm going to blow it all in a second." Of course, he would say jiggling.

"Eck, Henry. You're so crude," I responded.

"Hey, I'm just telling you how a guy thinks, might do you some good."

"No, what will do her some good is actually losing her virginity," Delaney said, while taking a sip of her beer.

Embarrassment quickly rushed through my body as I awaited Henry's response; he had no idea of my sexual experience, I kept that to myself...and my loud mouth friend, Delaney.

"What?!" Henry said while looking at me wide-eyed and almost a little hurt. "You're a virgin? How did I not know this? How come you didn't tell me?"

"Delaney," I gritted out, feeling completely mortified. Being a virgin wasn't something I made public, given the fact that I was now twenty-three and only had two kisses under my belt of sexual proactivity.

"Sorry," Delaney said with an innocent smile. "It just slipped."

I didn't believe her one bit.

"You're seriously a virgin?" Henry asked again, still dumbfounded from the news.

"Well, if you must know. I am. I just haven't found the right guy, yet," I said, while staring down at my beer bottle, starting to feel slightly sorry for myself.

"I can't believe that. I'm, I…" Henry stuttered, trying to find the words to express his shock. I didn't blame him; we told each other everything. I'm surprised he wasn't madder at me for holding back such vital information.

"It's not like I haven't tried," I defended. "I just, I don't know…"

"You haven't tried," Delaney said with a pointed look. "Don't lie. Marcus and Dwayne don't count. You barely poked your head out of your books long enough to kiss them on the cheek. You're living through your characters when you need to be living in real life."

"I'm not living in my books; they're just my friends," I replied softly. Any serious reader would know what I'm talking about.

"Don't say that," Delaney said, pointing at me. "We talked about this, Rosie. Mr. Darcy and Elizabeth are not your friends."

"*Pride and Prejudice* is a fine example of literature and romance," I shot back.

"You need to get fucked," Delaney shouted. "You need to drop the books, spread your legs, and get fucked, Rosie. If you have any chance of writing that book of yours, you need to experience the sensations firsthand."

Eeep!

"Ha, firsthand," Henry chuckled to himself.

"What does that mean?" I asked confused.

They both looked at me and shook their heads.

"Masturbation," Delaney eluded.

"Oh, gross. I would never do that."

"Wait, hold up," Henry said, while standing up and pointing his beer bottle at me. "So, not only are you a virgin, but you're also telling me you've never even masturbated?"

Gulping, I said, "You mean, touching myself?"

"Damn, Rosie," Henry said in disbelief. "How come I've known you for six years and I've never known about your sex life, or lack thereof?"

"Maybe because you were too busy banging your way through the English department," I said in a snide tone, starting to get irritated at Delaney and Henry ganging up on me.

"Hey, got good grades, didn't I?" he smirked.

"You're irritating," I said, while trudging back to my room.

"Hold it right there, missy," Delaney said, as she got up and pulled on my arms. "You know I love you, right?" Her voice softened.

"I thought you did."

"Don't get all salty on us; we're only trying to understand you. You want to write a romance novel because you want to have a future other than writing about the latest and greatest shit scooper, right?"

"Yes," I answered, exasperated. "I also just love the idea of making my own love story, making two people fall in love who've been living through such different circumstances. It's all about the find when it comes to love, the moment when you meet the one person in your life you can't possibly live without, that was what intrigued me."

"Agreed, but you know sex sells, correct?"

"Yes, I know that firsthand. I like books that have a little friskiness in them." Although, the books I read were slightly outdated, things still happened in them, things that made my entire body heat up.

"It's called sex, Rosie" Delaney corrected. Fucking, fornicating, poking the donut, making milk, smushing."

"Porking," Henry cut in. "Slapping the ham, knocking boots, dick twerking."

"Riding the bologna pony, getting some stank on the hang down…"

Henry cut a look over at Delaney and said, "Getting some stank on the hang down? You're better than that, Delaney."

She shrugged her shoulders and was about to start up again when I said, "I get it. Sex, see I can say it." Even though it felt like I had cotton in my mouth.

"Try saying it without developing a light sheen on your upper lip."

Instantly, I started wiping at my upper lip, feeling mortified.

"There was no sheen," I defended.

"Oh, yes, there was."

I waved my hand in the air, trying to erase the conversation and said, "Just get back to your point before I storm off."

"Fine," Delaney continued. "Sex sells, so if you want to write a book that's going to turn on all the lady folds around the damn country, then you're going to have to put yourself out there and experience what it's like to have an orgasm, to have a man squeeze that hard little nipple of yours, to know what a dick feels like in your hands, in your mouth, in your pussy…"

"Okay," I held up my hand. "I get it. I need to have sex. How do you suggest I go about doing that without paying someone on the corner?"

"Tinder," Henry suggested.

Delaney seemed to consider his option for a second, but then shook her head. "Tinder is too aggressive. I think she would wilt under the pressure. She needs to be taken out on a date first, not meet up at the closest motel. We need someone who's going to take it easy on her."

"You're right," Henry agreed.

"What's Tinder?" I asked, feeling a little curious.

Smiling brightly, Henry pulled out his phone from his pocket and nodded his head at me to come closer. I sat on the armrest of the couch with him and looked at his phone as he pulled up an app.

"Tinder is a hookup app. It shows you all the girls or men, in your case, who are in the area and are using Tinder. You can look through the different profiles and see if you're interested in them or not with one swipe of your finger."

"Really?" I asked, while looking at his phone in fascination.

Once the app was open, a picture of a female came up on his phone. She was wearing a bikini and had some of the biggest breasts I had ever seen.

"Oh, my God," I said. "Is she one of your girls?"

"No," he laughed. "But if I swipe saying I like her, and she says the same about me, then it's a match, and we can communicate with each other through the app...send text messages, possibly hook up."

"Yeah, I don't think I'm ready for that."

"You're definitely not," he smiled, while texting on his phone.

"Are you writing her? What happened to Tasha, your college sweetheart?"

Sweetheart was far from the truth. Henry had never really had a relationship. The closest thing he ever had that came close to a relationship was Tasha, and they were off and on between all his other random hookups.

"Tasha is out. She got too clingy, plus, it was a match with this girl, and I'm down for some big jugs."

"Ugh, you're a pig." I turned to Delaney as Henry laughed and said, "What's my next option?"

With a giant smile on her face, Delaney said, "Online dating."

"Yes!" Henry fist-pumped the air while finishing up his texting. He grabbed his tablet off of the coffee table, the man had money, and started typing away. "Minglingsingles.com here we come."

"Oh, good pick," Delaney praised. "She won't get too many creepers on that website."

"That's exactly what I was thinking," Henry said, as he started typing away. It seemed like Henry's displeasure with me not confiding in him had worn off, because he was in full-on Henry helping mode. Typical Henry, it was one of the many reasons why I love him.

Within minutes, he had a profile up and ready for me to fill out with a picture of me from our graduation. I was wearing a red polka dot dress, my red glasses and black heels, blowing a kiss at the camera.

"Don't use that picture," I said, trying to grab the tablet from him, but he was too quick and spun away. "Guys will get the wrong idea from that picture," I stated.

"And what idea would that be?" he asked with a snarky smile.

"That I'm loose…" the minute the words left my mouth, I realized what I was saying. "Ugh, never mind. Do what you need to do to get me, um...some action."

If I was going to do this, if I was going to try to fulfill my dream of writing a romance novel, then I was going to have to start becoming more comfortable with talking about sex…and that started today.

"That a girl!" Delaney said, while nudging my shoulder. "Before you know it, you're going to be going at it just like Derk and me."

"Yeah, by the way, can you keep the screams to a minimum?" Henry said, while typing away on his tablet, not looking up. "I don't need a boner over hearing you having sex."

"Awww," Delaney dragged out, while clearly pleased; I wrinkled my nose in disgust.

"Gross, you get boners from hearing Delaney have sex?"

He shrugged his shoulders as if it was nothing. "It just happens. Doesn't mean I want Delaney, no offense," he said apologetically. "I'm a guy, I get a boner over side boob…anything can turn me on, really."

"Interesting," I thought to myself. I really needed to start reading more erotic, modern novels because the fluffy stories my mom introduced me to were not teaching me half the stuff I needed to know. I needed a Kindle.

"Alright, you're all set. Your username is your email and your password is 'takemyflower' all one word."

"Clever," I said sarcastically, as I took the tablet from him and looked over my profile. "What now?"

"The system will match you up with someone and you can talk online. If you find enough interests, you can start going on dates. Pretty simple," Henry explained.

"Do I search for guys?"

"They will come to you," Henry laughed. Just relax for now and let things happen.

"This will be great," Delaney clapped her hands together. "Make sure to keep a journal of everything you go through, all your feelings, because you're going to want to refer back to your experiences. Oooh, this is like an experiment," Delaney said with a little too much excitement in her voice.

"Glad I can entertain you, but if you two don't mind, I think I'm going to get back to my writing."

Henry cringed and said, "Hold off on the briar patch for now."

"Do we need to go over lady-scaping?" Delaney asked with a brow raised.

"No, I've got that handled ever since freshman year when you called me out in the gym." Another disservice my mother did to me.

"Well, don't be sporting a bush…"

"Delaney, please!" I pleaded, while Henry laughed.

"Ah, Rosie, I love you," he said, while pulling me into his chest and kissing me on the head. "Those traditional parents of yours really did a number on you. Do they still sleep in separate beds?"

I nodded as I thought about my parents who were stuck in the fifties. They had separate beds still, believed in the man providing for the family and the women tending to the home, as well as not ever speaking of intercourse; hence my disconnect with the whole concept. Although, my mom was very fond of matchmaking.

The only reason I have a fascination with the genre of books I read was because of my mom and her secret novels she kept under her bed. They used words like "sex" to describe a lady's genitals and "sword" for a man's penis. Those novels were my only window to the crazy world of sex.

Feeling energized and apprehensive at the same time, I said good night to my roommates and took off for my room, hoping someone on the website would find me attractive enough to take out to dinner. Even though I was inexperienced with the opposite sex, I still craved the feel of a relationship, of a man's touch, of a kiss. It was an aspect of my life that I was sorely missing, and Delaney and Henry were right, maybe once I experienced the real deal, I would be able to put all my emotions into my writing and actually make a name for myself, other than Cat Crap Extraordinaire.

CHAPTER 2
"The Virgin Bullet"

"I swear to God, if you don't stop licking yourself, I'm going to take that sand paper tongue of yours and snip it off with a pair of scissors, and you know what? I'll enjoy doing it, too!" I shouted to Sir Licks-a-Lot, the orange tabby who insists upon hanging out in my office around one every day for his daily bath regimen.

"What did I tell you about talking to the cats?" Jenny, my co-worker, asked as she stood in my doorway. "It's not healthy, Rosie."

"Nothing about this office is healthy," I said, while I had a stare down with Sir Licks-a-Lot. "Stop staring at me with your tongue half out; it's creepy!"

As if he owned my office and everything in it, he sat up straight while maintaining eye contact with me, puffed his chest out, and then yacked up a hair ball, right on my desk.

"Eck, gross!" I screamed, as I backed away from the orange puke ball.

With a smarmy look on his face, he lifted his paw, wiped

his mouth, and then jumped off my desk.

"Did you see that?" I asked Jenny, who was on the floor laughing at me. "I think he gave me the middle finger while wiping his mouth."

"Cat's don't have fingers," Jenny corrected in between giggles.

"Middle claw then, he gave me something, that's for sure."

"Are you going to clean that up?" Jenny asked, while pulling herself off the floor and into one of the cat scratched chairs that sat in front of my desk.

"Nope, planned on saving it for dinner," I stated sarcastically.

"You're disgusting."

I grabbed a wet nap from my desk; I kept a stock pile of them in there for this very reason, cleaned up the hair ball, and threw it into my trash can, hating every aspect of my life in the process.

Deflated, I leaned back in my chair and said, "Don't you get tired of being in this office? The cats are starting to drive me insane. This can't be sanitary."

"Hey, just be happy you're not an intern whose duties are feeding the cats, grooming the cats and making sure the litter boxes are always clean in the shit room."

The shit room.

I've only been in there once, and it was because it was my first day and I was getting a tour of the office. The offensive cat pee smell was so awful that I have yet to even go near the room since. The shit room was where all of the litter boxes were held, and I'm not talking about the little tray litter boxes, I'm talking litter boxes the size of a ship from *BattleStar Galactica*. They were perched on different shelves and different levels of the room. It was an intern's nightmare.

"How do we even hold interns for so long?"

"Desperate college students," Jenny replied, while looking down at her nails. "They will do anything to get an in with a print magazine these days, even if it means being a walking scratching post."

"That reminds me, did a shipment of Cat Emery Boards come

in for me? I'm supposed to do some kind of exposé on them, but have yet to receive the box."

"Not that I know of, but you can ask Susan up front; she's the one who handles all the UPS shipments, which, by the way, did you see her outfit the other day? She was in full on slutty Grandma mode."

Susan was our receptionist, certifiable crazy cat lady herself, who had a major crush on the UPS man. Whenever she knew he was coming in, she donned her red lipstick that always wound up on her teeth, her blue eye shadow, which was sixty years too young for her, and a low cut top that always seemed to wreak havoc with her old lady bras.

"I didn't; I was interviewing a shelter downtown. What was she wearing?"

Jenny leaned forward and looked over her shoulder at Susan who was picking at her teeth with a toothpick. In a hushed voice she said, "She had on a Hannah Montana shirt with a low cut neckline that she must have created herself and a pair of purple pleather pants."

"I don't think I can believe you right now," I said, trying to hold in my laughter.

With a smirk on her face, Jenny pulled out her phone and showed me a candid picture she took of Susan talking to the UPS man with her belly hanging out the front of her Hannah Montana shirt and purple pants.

"Oh, my God," I said, while covering my mouth. "That is the greatest thing I've ever seen."

I was about to grab the phone for a closer look when Sir Licks-A-Lot jumped on my desk and started using my keyboard as a scratching post.

"Eh, get out of here. Pssst!" I tried to shoo him away.

He scrambled off of my desk, but not before popping off the "d" on my keyboard and taking it with him.

"That little bastard!" I yelled, as he scurried out the door, but not before smiling back at me with the "d" in his mouth. "He now has my d and my e. How the hell am I supposed to write up and coming cat articles in an environment like this?"

Shaking her head and laughing, Jenny said, "He only hates you, you know that right?"

"I stepped on his tail once, by accident. Is he going to hold that against me for my entire life?"

"Pretty sure he is. Hey, what do you suppose he's trying to spell?"

"What do you mean?" I asked.

"Well, he has your d and e, he must be trying to spell something."

"Probably 'die, bitch, die,'" I joked, mainly joked.

"He would need too many i's for that."

"Well, let me know if you see other keyboards being scratched to death, we can try to break his code before he acts."

"Will do," Jenny said with a smile. "So, I came in here to ask you something."

"Oh, no. I don't like that look on your face."

Jenny held up her hand and said, "Before you say no, please just hear me out. I know you're not into the whole blind date thing, but I know this guy who would be perfect for you."

"Jenny…" I drawled out.

I dated, but I never blind dated. I wasn't really into the possible awkward moment scene where you meet the blind date and see that not only is he a foot shorter than you were told, but he also had a pet mole on his chin that winked at you every time he smiled.

"Hold on, before you say no. I have to tell you that he's not like Marcus."

Marcus was the last guy she set me up with, the chin mole winker.

"He's Drew's friend and is new to town. We said we would take him out to have some fun and thought that you would want to go with us. We're going swing dancing…"

Damn her, damn her to hell! She knew I loved a good swing

dance and it was very rare that I got to go because I never could find a partner, one that was semi-decent, anyway.

"He knows how to swing dance?"

"Some call him Fred Astaire," Jenny said, while wiggling her eyebrows.

"You thought Marcus looked like Andy Garcia, when in real life he looked like PeeWee Herman, so excuse me if I can't fully trust your opinion."

"I told you, I was drunk when I first met Marcus, okay? I had my tequila goggles on. I apologized for that, can we move on now?"

"Fine. When do you want to go out?" I asked, feeling apprehensive, but somewhat excited about a possible date.

"This Friday," she squealed while clapping her hands.

Thinking about my options, I nodded my head and pointed my finger at her before she got too excited. "Don't make this a big deal. I'm only going because I haven't been swing dancing in a while."

"Eeeeee!" she squealed again, while clapping and bouncing her feet up and down. "You're going on a date!"

"You exhaust me," I said, while pointing for her to leave. "I have to finish this article if I want to get out of here at a decent hour, and before Sir Licks-a-Lot comes back to plot my death."

Nodding, she got up and clasped her hands by her chest. "You're going to love Atticus!"

"Atticus?" I asked, but she left before she could answer my question.

Just from his name I was already starting to feel nervous about Friday and who this Atticus might be. Jenny, bless her heart, had great intentions, but her blind dates were usually picked up from the corner of Creepy Court and Loser Lane, but that was because they were usually her boyfriend's friends, who he himself wasn't much of a winner, not that I could judge much. I had pretty much been on a handful of dates my entire life. I'm the friend, never the girlfriend, and I was okay with that until I realized I'm twenty-three, still a virgin, and as sexually inexperienced as a tween with Justin Bieber posters covering her walls.

I finished up my work, avoided the stares of Sir Licks-a-Lot and his posse, who seemed to be crowding in the corner, writing a game plan on the wall with their nails, while passing around a ball of catnip. I instantly felt nervous for my keyboard and just prayed it made it through the night.

As I took the subway home, I thought about my life situation. I was currently being bullied by a twenty pound tabby cat with the devil in his eyes; my job, which paid the bills, was horrifying to have on my resume as a real life job, and my sex life was non-existent. I needed a change and big time.

I'm in my twenties, I should be out perusing the sexual dating pot of overeager gentlemen and horny homies that New York City has to offer, instead of dating my book boyfriends, even though they were the only kind of men who could truly satisfy me. They were perfect.

The eclectic people of the subway flowed in and out of the train, listening to music on their phones, texting, and some were even making out in the corner. Being the pervert I was, I watched the couple making out with fascination, how their hands ran up and down each other's bodies, how they barely came up to breathe...

I want that! I want to know what it was like to stick my tongue down a guy's throat. I want to know what it looks like to see a boner in live action, instead of just reading about it. If I'm going to get out of the crazy cat lady life I'm living and finally write the romance novel I've been working on for years, then I need to experience life; I need to have sex!

With renewed vigor, I walked off the subway, up to my apartment, and into my room. I was going to make a game plan on how to lose my virginity. Delaney was right, I needed to start experimenting, getting myself out there and taking notes, because when I was finally ready to have a man bee pollinate my flower, I wanted to remember everything about it.

Dropping my purse on the side table, I grabbed some water from the fridge and went to my bedroom, where there was a little gift bag sitting on my bed with a note. I closed my door and flopped on my bed, wondering what one of my roommates had left me. I opened the card and read it out loud.

"Time to find your big 'O'. Love you, Henry."

Confused, I dug through the bag and pulled out a little pink nugget the size of a bullet and a kindle that had a note on it saying it was fully stocked. My heart fluttered at the gift of books, but then observed the nugget, wondering what it was.

"What the hell?"

I twisted it in my hand and it immediately started vibrating, sending the searing color of red to my face.

Henry got me a vibrator. A vibrator! What the hell was I supposed to do with a vibrator?

"Henry?" I called out to the apartment with the bullet in my hand, looking around for my roommates, but no one was home. I went to Henry's room, where there was a note hanging on the door.

Rosie – won't be home until late tonight, turn down the lights, get naked and have some fun. Love you – Henry P.S. I hope I loaded some good books; I picked all the ones with half naked men on the front. Thought those would be inspiring.

"Oh, my God, I hate him," I said, as I stormed off to my bedroom and slammed my door shut.

I tossed the bullet back in the bag, but left the Kindle on my nightstand, still giddy about that gift but irritated about the other. I went to my desk, where I pulled out a fresh notebook and wrote, "My Sex Diary" on the front. Feeling already accomplished with my progress, I opened the notebook and started writing.

June 2, 2014

I saw a couple making out on the subway today...

For at least five minutes, I sat and stared at my first journal entry, not knowing what else to write. I was so lame. If this wasn't an indication of how much I needed to venture out of my comfort zone, then I didn't know what was. My annoyance with Henry started to wear off as I realized I might just need the unwarranted help he was offering. I could feel the gift bag on my bed begging to be opened again, to be played with. Damn it.

I eyed the bag, thinking that it might not be a bad thing to try; it was a new experience, it could help clue me in on what to expect of what's to come.

Taking a deep breath, I set my pen down, went to my door and called out to my roommates once again; no one responded, indicating that I was home alone. I shut the door and turned toward my bed, eyeing the bag once again.

I can do this, I told myself, as I went over to the bag and pulled out the little vibrator, wondering why Henry got such a small one. The only conclusion I could come to was because I was a virgin and didn't have much experience with longer man items.

The wool of my skirt was rather itchy, so I decided in order to test my sexuality, I had to be comfortable. With that solid idea, I tore off my skirt and tucked in button up shirt and put on a long, oversized shirt that had a giant cat on the front. Yeah, I liked a free shirt from work; I was okay with it. Shucking my underwear, I tossed it into my hamper with the skillful deft of my big toe and fist pumped the air while I made my way to the bed.

The bed squeaked as I sat down and got into position, which basically was me flopping around on my bed like a whale until I was comfortable. I scooted the gift bag onto the floor and grabbed the vibrator in my right hand, thinking I would use it more skillfully with my dominant hand.

Carefully, I examined the little mechanism and turned it on. It shook in my hand, making me giggle at how powerful the actual thing was for being so small.

"I guess size really doesn't matter," I said to myself, as I closed my eyes and brought the bullet down to my vagina. I hovered over my lady area for a good couple of minutes, wondering if the bullet was going to turn off from no action.

"I can do this," I said as I took a deep breath and spread my legs wide on the bed so they were almost hanging off each side. The wider the better, I suppose.

"I can't believe I'm doing this," I spoke to no one, as my other hand rested on my forehead. "Just do it," I chastised.

Gritting my teeth, I gripped the bullet with my index finger and thumb and inserted the bullet into my vagina. Thank God for tampons, because I was easily able to locate the hole. Vibrations instantly ran through my lower half, making me squeal.

"Oh God, this is weird," I spoke to no one, as I made little in and out thrusts with the bullet. "This should really be bigger; I can barely get it in there."

I continued to make little insertions. I could only think about what my vagina must be thinking right now, as if I was trying to play whack a mole with it. I started to giggle as I thought about winning the game against my vagina.

I found it easier to insert as the vibrations started to grow on me. I wondered if it was because I was starting to get turned on. Was I wet downstairs? It was quite slick, was I turning myself on? The mere thought made me shudder. I'd never masturbated before, so I had no clue what to expect when it came to feeling up my own vagina. Was I doing it right?

I didn't think I was because the bullet barely went inside.

I wonder...

Taking a deep breath, I pressed the bullet all the way inside of my vagina, until I felt it was fully inserted. Instantly a sweat started to break out along my skin from the vibration inside my vaginal canal.

"Oh, sweet Jesus," I said, as my hands started to grip my bed sheets.

The bullet not only vibrated continuously, but it also pulsed in different patterns that my vagina was starting to memorize and tense up with each shock from the bullet, to the point that I started to feel uncomfortable.

Wanting to go back to my mini thrusts, I went to grab the bullet from my vagina, but was stopped when I couldn't even feel it because it was too far up.

"Oh, my God!" I sat up in fear as my vagina started to contract from the sensations.

Panic washed over me as I went to try to grab it again, this time, trying to push it out using my vaginal muscles, but all that happened was a threat of pushing something else out, so I stopped immediately and looked around my room for something to help me.

On my desk, next to my bed, was a ruler which I grabbed and eyed the sharp edges. No, I wasn't ready to gouge the damn thing out, so I put down the ruler and looked around my room some more, all the while continuing to panic over the lodged vibrator in my pleasure hole.

Maybe there were forceps in the gift bag or instructions, I thought, as I reached down just as a pulse ran up my spine from the bullet.

"Mother of pearl!" I screeched as I fell to the floor, scrambling around for the bag. I tipped it upside down, but nothing came out. "Damn it," I swore as another pulse shook my entire uterus.

Sweat continued to form on my skin, as I thought about the consequences of having a vibrator stuck in my vagina; this could not be happening. I was not about to go to the doctor to have him pull a vibrator out of me, so I stood up, lifted my shirt up so I could look at what I was doing and spread my legs like a Sumo wrestler.

"Come on, you little bitch," I swore, as I jumped up and down in my squatted position, trying to spread my legs as much as possible, wishing my vagina would stop contracting around the damn thing.

"Please come out!" I said, as I jumped harder while staring

down into my southern region wishing for the damn thing to release.

More sweat trickled down my back while the sensation of the pulses kept running through me, while the pure fear of having a permanent vibrator stuck in my vag crossed my mind.

Just as I was making one last giant jump, my door flew open and Delaney walked in.

"What the hell are you doing in here?" she asked, as she stopped in the doorway and looked at me with shock.

I stood in the middle of my room, my shirt up around my waist and my naked torso shown for all to see. I was about to yell at her to get out of my room when the bullet that was once lodged in my vagina clunked to the floor and rolled toward Delaney, thanks to the old uneven floor only a New York City apartment could offer.

We stood in silence as Delaney stopped the bullet with her shoe and then looked back up at me.

Her lips twitched as she studied the scene unfolding in front of her. "Was that stuck in your vagina?"

I quickly put my shirt down and smoothed it out so I was properly covered before I began speaking.

"It's rude to enter someone's room without knocking."

"Excuse me for wondering what kind of elephant stampede you had going on in here. If only I had known you were trying to remove a vibrator from your vagina, I would have given you more privacy."

Heated embarrassment went straight to my face, turning it completely red.

"It's Henry's fault," I blamed. "He didn't give me a long enough one."

"What are you talking about?" Delaney asked, as she grabbed a tissue off of my dresser and picked up the vibrator. "He gave you a bullet."

"Because I'm a virgin, I know," I said, rolling my eyes.

"What? No. Do you know what a bullet vibrator is, Rosie?"

I was about to answer, when I closed my mouth and thought about it for a second. I actually didn't know what it was. I just guessed.

"A vibrator for someone who hasn't broken their hymen yet?"

A twisted look of disgust crossed Delaney's face as she studied me.

"You can say hymen, but pussy is disgusting to you?"

"It's a medical term, the p word is slang."

Shaking her head at me, Delaney said, "I love you, Rosie, but you can be so naïve at times. A bullet is a clit stimulator, it doesn't go in your vagina, it just plays between your valley."

"You mean...it plays in my sweet lady folds?"

"Jesus, yes!" Delaney answered, while tossing the bullet on my bed. She started laughing and said, "I can't believe you got it stuck in your vagina." As if she just realized what she walked in on, she started laughing hysterically while gripping the doorway to my room. "You got it stuck in your vagina and were jumping up and down to get it out." She slid to the ground and wiped tears from her eyes, while I folded my arms across my chest and waited for her to be done.

"How was I supposed to know?" I defended myself. "There were no instructions. Henry just told me to find my O. Who knew there was such a thing as a clit stimulator?"

"You would know if you ever went to sex shops with me."

"Did you know those places are covered in semen? You know those sex video booths in the back? Yeah, they don't have hand sanitizer. There is no way I would go in one of those places. You can practically get pregnant from sniffing the air."

"Yes, I did read that in the headlines the other day. Sexually charged woman gets pregnant from breathing in too much sex shop."

I studied Delaney for a second and said, "You and I both know that title is way too long for a headline."

Delany got off the ground while laughing and shaking her head. "Seriously, Rosie, I'm proud of you for trying, but maybe ask next time before you start sticking things in your vagina. Could you imagine if we had to go to the hospital to get that thing removed, sitting in the hospital while you're constantly getting vibrated? God, can you actually stick it back up there so we can see what happens in the waiting room. That would just make my night."

"You can leave now," I pointed.

"Alright, she held up her hands, but said before leaving, "By the way, I'm calling my wax specialist tomorrow; we're getting you a Brazilian, girl, because that bush is not the least bit flattering."

"Hey, I trim," I said, while clenching my legs together.

"We want smooth, Rosie, not trimmed. Believe me, when you finally get a guy down there, you want to make sure things are as clean as possible."

Another wave of embarrassment flashed through me at the thought of a guy being so intimate with me.

"And stop flushing every time I talk about sex. You have to own it, girl, be a sexual being. Start watching porn…that might help."

"Okay, goodbye, Delaney."

"Bye, Rosie. Make me proud and masturbate the right way, one hand on the tit and one on the clit."

I shut my door on her as she laughed all the way to her room. I looked at the tissue wrapped bullet on my bed and sneered at it. The damn thing knew exactly what I was doing and took advantage of me. I wouldn't be going near that thing for a while. Stupid Henry.

Grabbing my notebook, I sat back down at my desk and continued to write in my journal.

June 2, 2014

I saw a couple making out on the subway today…Note to self, google sex toy objects before using them. Such rash actions may cause bodily harm and embarrassing trips to the hospital without the proper research being conducted first.

On another note, vibrators are not sized due to your sexual experience.

Bullet vibrators are for clitoral stimulation, not virgins who still need to be deflowered. Also, Virginia, aka my vagina, enjoyed the pulse option on the bullet, but did not like being viciously attacked by said stuck bullet, aka, the mini machine.

CHAPTER 3
"Porn is Science"

"Rosie, come on, please come here," Henry said, calling me over to the couch. "I didn't know you were going to get the vibrator stuck in your vagina," he laughed on the last word.

"Why did you take the instructions?" I asked, while I reluctantly sat on the couch next to him and let him pull me into his embrace. I rested my head on him as his arm wrapped round my shoulders. "Oh, my God, was it used before?" I asked, looking up at him.

Laughing, he shook his head no, and said, "It came in plastic packaging, you know the kind you can never get open, and I knew if you saw it, you would never even attempt to open it, so I did that for you. It didn't dawn on me to actually include the instructions. I just thought you already knew."

"I know nothing," I said, with shame in my voice.

"Chin up, Rosie. You'll get there," he squeezed me tighter.

"Thank you for the Kindle, though. I can't wait to start reading."

"Of course. I wish you would have told me about all this

earlier. I would have been flaunting you all over school and at parties; we would have hooked you up."

"I don't think I could have handled a one night stand back then. I'm not as sexually charged as you and Delaney. I'm not comfortable in my skin like you two. I mean, you two walk outside and people just start humping your legs."

"That's not quite accurate, but I appreciate the compliment," he said with a smile in his voice.

"Do you think I need to change my hair or clothes?"

Pulling away, he looked down at me and shook his head as he studied me with those pretty eyes of his.

"You're perfect, Rosie. Don't change a thing. You just need to have more confidence in yourself. Instead of cowering behind your books, maybe unbutton your top button and thrust your chest out, flip your hair to the side, and do a little flirting. You're beautiful and you know it; own it, Rosie."

"Thanks, Henry, but it's harder for me."

"Oh, I see, playing hard to get." He nudged me, making me laugh.

"Yes, that's it. I'm playing hard to get with every man on the planet for the past twenty three years."

"Ambitious," he laughed.

"Go big or go home," I shrugged. We sat in silence for a second before I said, "I have a date on Friday."

Squeezing my side, he said, "Seriously, that's great. With who? Is it from the dating website?"

"No, I haven't even looked at that thing yet. Do you remember Jenny from my office?"

"The one who's dating that douche nugget, Drew?"

"Yeah, that's her."

"She could do so much better."

I pulled away and studied him. "Are you saying you would want to get it on with Jenny?"

Laughing, Henry shook his head. "Get it on? You're adorable, and no, she annoys the crap out of me. She's gorgeous, though, but you know I like the little brunettes. I'm just holding out for you."

"Are you trying to teach me how to flirt?"

"Is it working?" he winked.

"No," I laughed, as I wrapped my arm back around his waist and snuggled closer. "Anyway, Drew has a friend named Atticus."

"Atticus? Like from *To Kill a Mockingbird*?"

I paused as I thought about it. "You know, I never connected his name with a book. That makes it so much better."

"Jesus," he shook his head. "I should have kept my mouth shut."

"Anyway," I dragged on. "We're all going swing dancing on Friday. I'm excited because I haven't been swing dancing since college, but also a little nervous about actually going on a blind date."

"You know I will go swing dancing with you. I am the best partner you will ever have. Remember the time I flipped you over my head and you lost your balance and landed ass first in the punch bowl?"

"How could I forget? My butt was stained red for days."

"I miss swing dance club," he said with a forlorn voice.

"Funny you say that, because our senior year you ditched me for your late night Friday booty calls, and that was the end of swing dancing for me."

"Well, I was a dick back then," he admitted. "If you ever want to go, just ask me."

"Come on, Henry. You're too busy on Friday nights to take me swing dancing."

He genuinely made me look him in the eyes and said, "Rosie, you know I'm never too busy for you."

He was my best friend, but he could still make my heart flutter; it was common when I was around him.

Giving him a side smile, I said, "Thanks, Henry, but I think this blind date might be good for me. Get me out there…and who knows where it might lead?"

"You looking for sex on the first night?" he asked, a bit

astonished.

"Oh, my God, no. I think that would be a huge mistake, especially given my lodging of a vibrator in my vagina today." That's right, I said vagina. "I need to study up a bit before I jump right into it with a stranger. The only sex I know of is from books, and they make it seem so easy and wonderful. Is it really like that?"

"Depends," Henry answered honestly. "You have to be with the right person who knows what they're doing first. Some guys like to just plow you to get what they want, but a real man will make sure you're satisfied before he is."

"Does that come straight from the *Henry Playboy Bible*?"

"Damn straight," he said, while leaning forward and grabbing the soda we were sharing from the coffee table. "You have to realize that your first time is going to be awkward; you won't know where to put your hands or what to do when the sock that he's trying to take off just won't let up, so you wait for him to take it off while you lay there naked." He handed me the soda and I finished it up, handing it back to him to set on the coffee table. "It's going to hurt, Rosie. I won't lie about that, and you're going to bleed."

"Wow, sounds like a pleasurable experience; I can't believe I waited this long to participate."

I knew sex wasn't going to be great right off the bat, but now, thanks to Henry, I was really dreading it. What the hell was I supposed to tell the person who finally took my virginity? Sorry for the bloody mess, but did I forget to tell you I was a virgin? The whole process seemed overwhelming.

"Maybe I should wait until I'm in a serious relationship," I thought out loud. "It seems like if I'm with someone, actually dating them, they would be more sensitive to my condition."

"It's not like you're diseased or anything," Henry laughed. "You're a virgin, not a leper. Any guy in his right mind would respect the fact that you've saved yourself and would treat you with respect."

"You really think so?"

"Yes, you just have to find the right guy first."

"So, you think one night stands are out of the question right now?"

He cringed as he thought about my question. "Do I want you to be a virgin forever, now that I know you are? Well, yes, because that means you're still innocent, you're untouched, my sweet Rosie, but if you must go to the dirty side," he flashed me a grin, "Then I would prefer for you to be in a relationship."

"And when did you become my dad?" I teased.

"Not your dad, just an overprotective and concerned best friend." He ran his hand through his hair and said, "I don't know, Rosie. Ever since Delaney said you were a virgin, I can't stop thinking about how innocent you really are, and it's pulled at my heartstrings. I love you the way you are; I don't want you to change. I don't want some dickhead coming in here and corrupting you. I like you for you who are now, just perfect." It was cute how distraught he was. He gripped my chin and spoke earnestly as my pulse picked up at his proximity. Why did he have to smell so damn good? "You're just so damn perfect," he repeated.

Taking a steady breath, I said, "Thank you, Henry, but a part of me doesn't like who I am. You and Delaney have these great jobs, and I'm stuck dodging hair balls and feral cats every day at work, wondering whether I'm going to get sprayed and claimed by Sir Licks-a-Lot. Ever since I can remember, I've been writing stories, and now that I'm out of college and have a chance to make something of myself, I'm not doing it. I want to write this book, finish it, and be proud of myself, but I'm kind of stuck when it comes to the whole sex part."

"Then, why do you have to have sex in the book? It's not a requirement."

"No, it's not, but when I read a book without sex, I feel like I'm missing that connection between the characters…call me a pervert, but I think sex in a book is not just about getting all hot and steamy. It's about seeing the characters form this bond that is undeniable, you know?"

"I do, and believe me, the last thing I would call you is a

pervert. Why don't you try reading some of the new contemporary books I added to your kindle, rather than the stale ones your mom has sent your way?"

"I'll start one tonight, but I still feel like I need to know what an orgasm feels like. What a penis looks like in real life in order to really do my books justice, you know? Writing from experience is always so much easier."

"You haven't even seen a real life dick?" he asked, perplexed by me.

Blushing, I shook my head. "Nope. I've only seen…" I cleared my throat and said, "Ones on the Internet."

As if I just told Henry my nipples popped off at night and performed their own burlesque show, his mouth hung open in shock.

"You've watched porn?" Henry's voice broke at the end of his sentence.

"No, just seen some things."

"Wait. So you've never watched porn, you haven't seen a dick in real life, and you haven't even as much as touched one outside a pair of jeans?"

"No," I confirmed, while shaking my head.

"Well, shit. Do you want to see mine?" he said, while grabbing the waistband of his sweats.

"Henry! No!" I squealed, while covering my eyes. Heat raced up my back from the near exposure from my best friend.

Laughing, he said, "If you haven't even seen a real penis, how do you expect to describe one in a book?"

"I'm working on it," I answered quickly, still feeling the heat in my body from Henry's fake out with his waistband.

Silence fell upon us as I saw the inner workings of Henry's mind turning. It was never good when he started thinking about things.

"I don't mind showing you my dick, Rosie. It could be for experimental purposes. Science. Although, it wouldn't be very fair to all the other men you will probably see, since I'm so big and girthy."

"A snort escaped my nose. "Full of yourself much?"

"Not full of myself if it's the truth."

"I'm not going to look at your dick for science," I giggled and shook my head.

"Well, at least let me show you some porn. I can walk you through it, like a football player and his coach. We can pause and I can talk about positions, erections, and all the erogenous zones you should be aware of. We can watch on my tablet."

"Why am I even considering this right now?" I said from the curiosity I felt come upon me.

"Yes!" Henry leaned over, kissed the top of my head and said, "Be right back, love."

I watched his well-defined backside run off to his room, while convincing myself it was okay to check out your friends. I'd caught him doing the same thing to me on multiple occasions. He was back in the living room, seconds later, holding his tablet in his hand and sporting a huge smile on his face.

"I subscribe to a classier porn site that won't be too bad to watch for a newbie like you."

"You have a subscription?" I asked, a little dumbfounded. "Why? You have a girl with you almost every night."

Absentmindedly, he shrugged his shoulders and said, "Some girls like to watch porn while we have sex, so I thought it might be nice to just have a subscription rather than search the internet for something while in the heat of the moment."

"Women actually like to have sex while watching porn?" I gulped, thinking I didn't ever believe I would be one of those women.

"You'd be shocked, Rosie. You might even like it."

"Doubt it," I said like a snob, hating myself.

Henry leaned against the couch arm rest as he sat down and placed his one leg behind me, so I had to lean against his chest.

"Come here; I'll hold the tablet in front of us while we watch."

Always loving a good Henry snuggle, I leaned against his chest and propped my knees up so he could rest the tablet on them while he held it steady. He leaned into my ear and spoke softly.

"Student teacher porn or businessman secretary?"

"Secretary," I said quickly. "Don't know about the student teacher thing."

"Don't knock it; it's hot. You'll open up more, trust me. Once you get your fingers wet….oh, wait, you already did that today," he laughed.

"Henry!" I elbowed him in the stomach, causing him to buckle over slightly. "Can we please drop it?"

"Your vagina sure did."

"I hate you."

His chest rose and fell as I felt him laugh against my back.

"I'm sorry. I just wish I was there while you were jumping up and down trying to get the damn thing out of you."

"Did you ever consider the fact that I was severely terrified that I would have it stuck up me forever?"

"Were you?" he asked, his voice softening a little.

"More embarrassed than anything."

"You live and you learn, love. Now, let's get down to business." He opened up an app that was on his tablet and started searching for a video for us to watch."

"There's an app for your porn?"

"Yeah, makes it so much easier to watch."

Of course it was easier, I thought to myself, as I watched Henry look for the video he wanted. Any porn website would want to make it easier for people to watch. It was actually kind of genius, to have an app for porn, and the tricky designers didn't even make the icon for the app seem like it was porn. It was just a movie reel, clever.

"Oh, the girl is hot in this one."

"What about the guy?" I asked, finally feeling a little comfortable, thanks to Henry's warm embrace. I wouldn't want to be watching porn with anyone else. Henry made it easy.

"He has a good sized dick for you to learn from."

"Oh, lovely."

"Now, lean back and relax. We're going to have a little lesson in the art of fucking."

The screen went black and music started to play. The camera zoomed in on a skyline of New York, making it almost seem like the actual flick was classy, that was until the CEO, main character, popped on screen with a naked lady on his desk.

"Oh, they just get right into it, don't they?"

Chuckling, Henry said closely to my ear, "Were you expecting a little romance before?"

"Well, it would have been nice."

"I can romance you later, love," he spoke ever so softly as his lips caressed my ear, his voice completely genuine. It threw me off.

The way he said love, made my toes tingle. Ever since freshman year in college, I'd always harbored a little crush on Henry. I mean, how could I not? He's the most handsome man I've ever met, and my infatuation soon became a crush, which turned into a real friendship. His nickname for me was love, because he knew that's what I believed in. Everything about me revolved around love. I was a romantic at heart and loved love, simple as that.

But the semi-intimate setting we had going on right now had me second guessing the way he said my name, which was crazy, because out of all the women Henry dated, I would be the last on his list. I by no means thought I was ugly, because I knew genetically I wasn't, but I was of the shorter brand of women with some slight curves and a retro style that was more *I love Lucy* rather than skanky club sex kitten, the typical girl Henry went for.

"Are you paying attention?" Henry asked, disrupting my thoughts.

"Yup, looks like he's about to do her. Wow, look at her nipples."

They were like torpedoes lifting off of her chest. I had never seen anything like them. I had good-sized breasts, but my nipples weren't poking people in the eyes when I was cold.

"What's wrong with them?" he asked, confused.

"They're so big. I guess I'm just used to my nipples, which are significantly smaller than those, those, tweeters."

"Tweeters?" he paused the video and laughed a deep laugh.

"They're the size of my Chap stick. Seriously, look at them."

"And what do your nipples look like?"

"You know," I said, while I held up my hand and made a small circle with my forefinger and thumb.

Henry inspected my fingers for a decent amount of time and then said, "Rosie, that's hot. You've got small little nipples. Let me see them."

"No!" I swatted him from behind as he continued to laugh.

"Tit for tat?"

"Can we just watch the film?"

"Porno is more like it," he said, while pulling me in closer, snuggling up. "Now, pay attention. This is a learning experience."

The porno started up again and the CEO started walking around the table, surveying the woman who was spread naked across his desk with her torpedo nipples sticking straight in the air. Corny music played in the background, fulfilling all my expectations and generalizations I had about porn.

The minute the man walked all the way around the desk, his lower half came into view, and that's when I saw his massive boner.

"Oh, my God, is that a boner?"

Containing his laughter, he paused the film again and circled the man's dick with his finger. "You see this, love? This is called an erection, and this right here," he circled the lady's vagina. "This is where he will be sticking that erection."

"Henry, I'm not an idiot," I chastised.

"Alright, just wanted to make sure. In my defense, you did get a vibrator stuck in your vagina today."

"Drop it," I scolded, but then laughed a little.

The porno continued, and I watched in fascination how the

man slowly took off his clothes while rubbing the silk of his tie against the woman's body. It was actually kind of hot to watch, to see the way the woman reacted to the man's small touches and the way the man was completely satisfied with how he was making his woman feel. I started to get hot just from watching everything play out. I was so entranced in the man taking off his boxers that I groaned when Henry pressed pause again.

"What are you doing?" I asked, while looking over my shoulder.

"Just thought you needed a water break. Pretty sure your tongue was hanging out."

"It was not," I said, while wiping my face just to make sure.

"Alright, love. Are you ready for this next step? Things are going to get pretty serious."

"Just play it; I can handle what happens next."

"Okay, but if you get scared, you can always wrap your little arms around me. I wouldn't mind one bit."

"Noted, now continue."

He pressed play and we both watched as the man turned around and took his boxers off, giving the camera a great display of his ass, which was actually pretty nice to look at. I always considered porn stars to be quite nasty to observe, but this guy was kind of hot.

Within seconds, his ass was switched with a full frontal of him jerking off.

"Sweet molasses monks," I mumbled, as I leaned forward for a better look. "Are dicks really that big?"

"Not for an average man, but for us gifted ones, yes."

I gave him a pointed look, and then turned back around. Men, that was one thing I did know about them…they were always bragging about their dicks. That was something I actually wanted to find out about, why men were so proud of their members. It wasn't like ladies went around purposefully giving themselves camel toes to show off how big their lady folds were. Yuck, the mere thought of prancing camel toes gallivanting the streets of New York had me dry heaving. No matter who you were, no one could pull off a camel toe.

I drew my attention back to the tablet, where the man continued to jerk off.

"Is that normal? For a guy to fondle himself in front of a woman?"

"Sure, why not? It's usually a turn on for a girl, to see a guy get off just from looking at her naked body."

"Hmmm, I guess that could be reassuring, to know that the guy thinks you're attractive. Yeah, that is kind of hot."

"That a girl, love, getting into the spirit of things. Next thing you know, you'll be twiddling that twat of yours to one of these clips."

"Don't count on it."

Yawning, I covered my mouth as I leaned my head against Henry's shoulder.

"You tired?" he asked, lips barely caressing my ear.

"Yeah, just a little."

Pausing the film and setting his tablet to the side, he wrapped his arms around me and said, "That's enough learning and sexual experiences for you today. How about we pick this up another night? We tangoed with foreplay, how about another night we actually tackle insertion?"

"What an odd thing to say, but sounds like a plan."

Reluctantly, I pulled away from Henry's warm embrace and got up from the couch. I pulled up my hot pink sweat pants and pulled down my oversized t-shirt with a cat on it. I adjusted my glasses and looked down at Henry, who literally looked like perfection with his styled hair and tan that no man should have living in the city.

"God, I look like a trash bag compared to you."

"You look adorable." He got up off the couch and pulled me into a hug. "Don't let anyone tell you differently." He paused and then said, sincerely, "Sorry your vibrator got stuck in your vag today."

"Sorry you missed me jumping up and down in a sumo squat to get it out."

"You're forgiven," he chuckled and kissed the top of my head. "See you in the morning, love."

"Don't forget to make the coffee. I'm going to need it."

While I got ready for bed, I thought about the new adventure I was embarking on. I was already starting to feel a little randy, maybe soon enough I would be able to say the P word out loud without blushing and look at a man's penis without giggling like a little school girl. I could start to feel maturity setting in. Hopefully, my date Friday night would be the beginning of a new relationship. It had potential. The guy liked swing dancing; he had to be nice if he didn't mind dancing all night with a stranger. At least that's what I hoped.

When I got in bed, I saw that my phone had a text message. It was from Delaney.

Delaney: Wax appointment, tomorrow after work. Time to mow down the bush, babe.

Oh, hell.

There was one thing I had to be grateful for. Even though it was mortifying, I was glad my friends were trying to help me in my endeavors to de-virginize myself. If I was on my own, who knows who I would be seeing and what I might be sticking up my vagina. Without them, I might very well still be making out on my arm to the thought of my latest book boyfriend while casually thrusting my hips into my mattress, just hoping that a penis would sprout up for me to hump against.

What the hell kind of thought was that?

Shaking my head, I lay down and told myself to sleep. I think the porn was starting to get to me.

CHAPTER 4
"The Red Brick Road"

Fabio was lying across the bed waiting for his medieval mistress to release her chastity belt and finally let him claim Mayberry's flower from the garden she had beautifully prepared for him. He watched as she walked toward him while shedding her clothes, starting with her white cotton bra. He noticed her breasts were significantly different sizes, but he shook the revelation from his head and focused on the belt she was loosening around her waist. She dropped her underwear to reveal a silky patch of bright red curls that matched the same curls on her head. Fabio started to drool over the idea of being able to get lost in the curls on her head and in her magical garden…

"No, you can't write about curtains matching the drapes. Are you insane?" Delaney asked from over my shoulder, scaring the ever loving crap out of me.

"You guys can't keep doing that," I yelled, while covering my computer screen with my hand.

"Medieval mistress? You're better than that, Rosie."

"I know I am," I said, deflated. "To be honest, I don't even know if I want to do a medieval book anymore. The sex seems so clumsy with all that armor and whatnot. I mean, where does he put his sword? Just throw it to the side?"

"No, he sticks it in her pussy, duh."

Rolling my eyes, I shut my computer and grabbed my purse. "I'm not talking about his pork sword."

"Wow," Delaney laughed. "Henry told me you watched porn last night, but I didn't think he rubbed off on you that much."

"I can be sassy if I want," I responded with my head held high.

We walked out of the apartment and headed down the stairs, where we ran into Henry who was carrying a box of pizza and a six pack of beer. The man could eat and drink anything he wanted and not gain a pound; how was that fair?

"Dinner, ladies?" he offered.

"Sorry, we have an appointment," I said quickly, as I tried to pass him, but was stopped of course by that smile on his face.

"What kind of appointment?"

"Time to pluck the bush out of the 'lady garden,'" Delaney said, while using air quotes. "Shredding the weeds."

Henry raised an eyebrow at me, and then glanced down at my crotch.

"You all natural down there, love?"

Covering my crotch with my hands, as if I wasn't wearing pants, I said, "Don't stare, and no. I'm trimmed."

"So then, what's the problem?"

"She's getting a wax," Delaney stated.

Cringing, he looked at me with pity. "Damn, have fun with that. Show me later?" he wiggled his eyebrows, always a tease.

"Get out of here," I pushed him to the side and exited our apartment building.

As Delaney and I walked to the subway, she talked about her

day at *Cosmo* and having to test out different kinds of tampons...at least it wasn't cat poop scoopers. I would rather fondle a tampon any day over a certified shit sifter.

"So, Henry seems to be interested in your new endeavors," Delaney said while we were on the subway heading to the salon.

"Doesn't seem different to me," I shrugged my shoulders and checked my Instagram feed.

"Oh, come on, he's clearly interested in taking your virginity."

"What?!" I said, while choking on my own saliva.

There was no way Henry was interested in having sex with me. We've been friends since freshman year, practically brother and sister. The thought that he was even semi-interested in me was actually kind of hilarious. The man saw me through my overall days my freshman year in college, definitely not interested.

"He's all over you. I saw the way he was looking at you in the hallway and the porn date last night, not to mention the vibrator and Kindle. He wants in your pants."

"That is so not true, and stop talking about it. I don't want to feel uncomfortable around him. We're just friends. That would be like you saying you want to get in my pants."

Delaney looked me up and down and smirked. "I'd tap that."

"Flattering, but no."

We got off the subway and headed up the pee covered stairs of the subway underground to our destination. The stench of the New York subways was something I would never get over. If anything, pee on the subway tracks, not on the stairs. My biggest fear was tripping while climbing them and catching myself in a puddle of pee; I wouldn't be able to handle living my life after such a traumatic event.

"You know he's a virgin chaser, right?"

"Who?" I asked, still thinking about the subway stairs.

"Henry. He loves welcoming virgins into the world of sex."

"That's not true," I said, actually not knowing if I was right or not. It didn't seem like Henry. Yes, he liked to bring women back to the apartment, but he was a genuine guy, sweet, kind...there wasn't a mean or manipulative bone in his body...that was why I loved him so much.

He was a ladies' man, though. The majority of women Henry brought back to the apartment looked more like two cent hookers rather than chastity belt wearing nuns, so to say he was a cherry chaser was news to me.

"Think what you want, but he loves a virgin."

Not wanting to talk about Henry behind his back, I dropped the subject the moment we walked in the salon. It was a soothing environment, which was surprising, given what was going on in the back rooms. The walls were a neutral tan color with green hues and bamboo surrounding the room, giving off an almost serene feeling. Maybe the waxing wasn't going to be so terrible. Nothing terrible could go on in a place like this...where waterfalls winked at you and the sweet scent of tenderness greeted you at the door.

"Miss Bloom," the receptionist greeted me with a smile. "Right this way."

Before walking away, I turned and gave Delaney a nervous look, and in return she squeezed my hand with a wink and said, "Don't scream too loud."

That wasn't all too reassuring.

The receptionist spoke to me as she led me down the dark, yet soothing, hallway that was filtered with soft lighting and calming music. When we passed doors on either side of me, I would occasionally hear a yelp or the sound of what seemed like Velcro being pulled off magnetic fabric. Fear started to tickle down my back, as I tried to think about what Delaney had gotten me into.

"You'll be with Marta; she's one of our best technicians. I informed Marta this was your first time, so she is aware to be gentle with you."

As opposed to rough, I thought, as she escorted me into the room. Why wouldn't you be gentle when you were pulling out every last hair from your most sensitive lady bits?

"Marta will be with you in a moment," the receptionist continued. "For now, take off your pants and panties. You can place them in the dresser over there, and then lay on the table with that cloth over your lap for privacy. Would you like any tea?"

"I'm good," I gulped, as I looked around the room. It looked like a relaxing place, but I knew sadist things occurred in here; the walls were talking to me, telling me to run, run like hell. Before I could say I wasn't quite ready, the receptionist shut the door and left me to strip down.

Giving myself a pep talk, I peeked into my pants and told my vagina that even though what was about to happen to her was construed by the devil himself, I still loved her and hopefully, such actions would bring great rewards in the future.

With all the bravado I had, I took my pants off, folded them gently into the dresser, which was an odd thing to me, but I wasn't going to focus on it, and then took off my boy shorts. I owned thongs and only wore them when absolutely necessary. I lived in boy shorts my whole life and didn't plan on changing, even if I wanted some action.

After everything was tucked away, I hopped up on the table and placed the cloth over my lap, which seemed completely useless, given the fact that Marta would soon be spreading hot wax all over my vagina in a couple of minutes.

Waiting for Marta to appear was pure torture. The music in the room was just loud enough that it drowned out the shrill cries from the rooms next to me, but I could still vaguely hear the pain coming from every woman in the salon. I could feel the crying vaginas, calling out to all other vaginas in the vicinity to clam up, to turn inside out and run for their damn lives, to never show fold in a salon like this again.

Pictures of trees and meadows scoured the walls, trying to distract me from what was about to happen, but I saw right through their tactics, because all my mind was focused on was the wax that was heating up to the side, and the strips waiting to be stuck to my milky white skin.

That's right...milky white!

"What am I doing?" I asked myself, as I pressed my

fingers to my eyebrows.

I was seconds from getting up and putting my pants back on when the door to my room opened and in walked an oversized, uni-brow sporting, perverse looking she-man wearing an ill-fitting dress, knee high white stockings, and her hair in two pig tail buns. Her uni-brow snarled at me as she drew closer, and I could hear my vagina weep from a far distance. I tried to do some keegles, sending her a Morse code that I was gravely sorry for what was about to happen, but the damn bitch gave me the old middle clit and told me to fuck off by instantly turning into a world of itch.

Uncomfortable in so many ways, I shifted on the table, trying to look nervous, but instead, aimed to scratch that unscratchable itch that only a finger to the vag would get.

"You look ill; you okay?" Marta said in a heavy accent that I could only assume was Hungarian.

"Just nervous," I admitted, while I continued to shift.

"No need to be nervous. Marta knows what to do."

She better, I thought, as she pulled a rolling table full of wax and strips close to me. A light sheen of sweat broke out on my skin as Marta whipped off my cloth and placed her hands on my knees and spread my legs as wide as they could go.

Mary Magdalene!

Her head lowered down and studied my most private of areas. My gynecologist wasn't even this thorough when examining me, and she sure as hell wasn't this close. I swear, I felt Marta snort into my valley of wonders.

"Whatcha looking for down there?" I asked, wishing her nose wasn't so close to my vagina.

"Want to see what kind of thickness I will be working with. Looks like I will need to use more wax than expected."

"What? Why?"

"Your hair is thick. It's like rain forest. Too many heavy vines, especially in the dark areas," Marta said without sugar coating it.

"Dark areas?"

"Yes, inside of vagina and around anus, but we will get to that."

"I'm sorry, did you say anus?"

Marta was mixing the wax as she spoke, "Yes, your anus, it's the hole between the two butt cheeks."

"I know what an anus is, Marta," I said, exasperated. "I'm just wondering why you're talking about it."

"You are signed up for Brazilian, no?"

"And your point?" I asked, growing sweatier by the second.

"Hole to hole," Marta said, while picking up a thick Popsicle stick and grabbing a thick coat of wax on it.

"Hole to...holy prepubescent hairs!" I yelled as Marta coated my vagina with some wax.

"Hold on," Marta said, as she placed a strip on my skin. There were bars on the side of the table that my hands went instinctively to, wondering what the hell was going to happen next. "Three, two, one..."

Rip!

Heavy black spots appeared in my vision as pain ricocheted over my skin.

"My clit, you tore my clit off," I screamed, as my hands went to my crotch, but were quickly swatted away by Marta, who set down another wax strip and then ripped it off in a matter of seconds.

My head flew back and I begged for her to stop, but the she-devil herself didn't listen as she continued to rip hair after hair right out of me. She tossed pubic covered wax strips to the side, and I searched them for signs of my lady folds. I swore to the heavens above they were attached to them, because I was almost one hundred percent positive they were no longer attached to my body.

"I'm bleeding, I know I am. Just tell me. Am I bleeding? Sometimes I have a hard time clotting, does it look like that?"

"You're fine," Marta said, matter-of-factly, as she placed a strip right over my vagina. "Three…"

"No, Marta, please, leave Virginia alone."

"Two…"

"Marta, I thought we were friends. Leave the vagina alone."

"One…"

"I'll do anything you want," desperation laced my voice. "Just don't…"

Rip!

"Captain Cunt Ripper," I screamed, as tears fell from my eyes. "You're a cunt ripper," I said, startling myself with the menacing tone in my voice. I looked up at Marta to apologize, but the she-devil just laughed. She laughed at me!

She was a barbarian.

She brought out the potty mouth in me, and I hated her for it. Never once had I ever say the C-word out loud, but with Marta at the helm of my vagina, inappropriate words just flowed right out of me.

"On all fours," she said, while tapping my legs shut.

"What?" I asked, too delirious from pain to process anything.

"Get on all fours and spread your legs wide." I paused, not wanting to do what she said until her uni-brow got angry and practically started barking at me. "Now."

Eeep!

Quickly, I turned over and got up on all fours, sticking my ass in the air.

Without warning, she spread wax over my anus and applied a wax strip. There were handles at the top of the table that I took advantage of, and in one smooth motion, Marta ripped my butthole right off my body to join my other lady bits in the graveyard of broken and torn private parts.

"Demon, you're a demon," I muttered, as Marta placed both of her hands on my butt cheeks and spread them wide. I could feel her face close in, and at that moment, I prayed to the flatus gods that they would award me with a prize winning toot that would curl her eyebrow right into a fro, but was I ever that lucky? No.

Instead, Marta said, "We will bleach too."

"Bleach what? You're removing all the hair."

"Bleach the anus," she said, as she placed another strip of paper on me.

"What? Ahhh, cock sucking sadist," I called out, as my forehead found the cushion of the table.

"One more, and then we will do the bleaching."

"Wait, why are we bleach…bouncing beluga whales, I hate you," I cried out, after she pulled one last strip.

"All done," she tapped my ass as I tried to catch my breath from the onslaught of the uni-brow waxing beast.

"We will do light bleach; just stay like that."

I felt too abused to even stop her, so I just curled up against the bed with my ass in the air, trying to find my happy place where unicorns frolicked in glitter fields of donuts and cherry trees.

It wasn't until I actually got home and sat on my bed that I finally came out of the fog that I was in, that Marta put me under.

The comfort of my room encased me as I stared down at the ground, wondering if I would ever feel my nether regions again. I was too scared to even look at what Marta did to me, and to say I was on fire down below was an understatement.

Taking a deep breath, I walked over to my dresser, grabbed a pair of short shorts and a big shirt and started to take off my clothes to get ready for an early bed. I was in no mood to talk to my roommates.

Henry tried to talk to us when we got back but I just went straight to my room and shut my door, not even talking to Delaney. I've never felt so torn apart in my life, so openly massacred from the waist down. There had to be skin missing; there was no doubt in my mind that I would be needing some extra vitamins to repair whatever damage was caused down below. If Delaney wanted to prolong my virginity, she hit the mark, because right now, nothing was even getting close to my vagina with a ten foot pole.

Taking a deep breath, I pulled down my pants and then my boy shorts. My eyes lifted to the mirror that was standing in front of me, and I nearly screamed at the sight that I saw in the reflection.

I was completely bare, but in place of hair, there were a million red bumps all over my skin. I squatted to the ground, spread my legs and looked in the mirror. From my belly button to my ass was a line of red bumps caressing my skin that led to a rather white looking asshole.

"Holy fuck," I said, not caring about my language one bit.

"Rosie? You in there?" Delaney called out, knocking this time.

"Don't come in here," I yelled back.

"Rosie, I have some cream for you to put on your vagina, it should help with the pain."

I put my shorts on quickly, and then went to the door. I whipped it open and gave Delaney my best death glare.

"You have cream to help with the pain? Do you happen to have any cream to help with the giant red brick road I have that will take you to the wizard of bleached white assholes?"

Delaney's mouth dropped open as she glanced down at my crotch.

"You bleached your asshole?"

"Yeah, and it looks like fucking Saturn in the middle of a red colored meteor shower. What the hell, Delaney?"

A small smile tried to peek past her lips, but she was wise enough to tamp it down before I slapped it right off her face.

"I never told you to bleach your asshole."

"You got your asshole bleached?" Henry asked as he walked by, stopping mid-stride when he heard bleach and asshole in the same sentence.

"I didn't want to. Marta made me."

"Who's Marta?"

"The she-devil who did this to me," I stated while pulling my shorts down, just enough to show some of the red bumps.

"Oh, my God," Delaney said, while Henry cringed in the background and took off for his room, clearly knowing when he wasn't needed. "You must have had an allergic reaction to the wax."

"You think?" I asked, while everything in my nether regions continued to burn. "What do I do?"

"Sit on ice?" Delaney shrugged.

I pointed at her before closing my door and said, "I don't like you right now."

"Fair enough," she said, while the door closed on her face. "You'll thank me in a couple of days…"

"That's if I don't murder you in your sleep," I threatened.

I walked over to my bed and plugged in my phone. Thank her, was she serious? I nearly lost every sexual organ off my body today and I was supposed to thank her? Pretty sure Marta almost ripped out my uterus at one point; there was no way I would be thanking Delaney.

I grabbed my journal and started writing.

June 3, 2014

Don't trust anyone named Marta, especially if they wear knee-high stockings and spread your legs as if it's second nature. If only she accidently got a little wax on that uni-brow of hers that seemed to have a mind of its own. The damn thing held its little uni-brow stomach and cackled at me with each rip and tear of my labia.

Brazilian wax, more like fuck you in the ass wax, because that's what it felt like, not that I would know, but I assume that's what it felt like. There was no way what happened to me was legal, and there's a reason they keep those rooms dark and full of music, because they don't want you to really get a good look at the technicians or hear what they're saying. It's all a conspiracy. There's probably some lab in the back where they turn pubic hair into some kind of black market drug. It's the only explanation I can come up with as to why these ladies take pride in ripping sensitive hair right off a woman.

I understand you're supposed to present a pretty muffin to your man, but is a Brazilian really necessary? Why isn't a trim sufficient enough?

Note to self, see what it takes to become a wax technician. Payback is a bitch, Marta, and I'm coming after you.

I set my notebook to the side and got under my covers, just as I received a text on my phone. I grabbed it and saw that it was from Henry.

Henry: Sorry about your red brick road, love. At least you have the great and powerful asshole sitting between your two cheeks; that's something to be proud of. There's no place like between your legs, there's no place like between your legs. (Said while clicking your pussy lips together)

Shaking my head and laughing, I sent a text back to my very nosy best friend.

Rosie: Have I told you how much I hate you?

Henry: Don't lie, love. You love me and you know it. Feel better. You have to get better for swing dancing on Friday. Big date night!

Rosie: Yeah, let's just see if I can make it through the night without clawing my vagina off from it itching so much.

Henry: Your vagina actually just sent me a text. It said I should come over and rub some soothing lotion on it.

Rosie: Would that be with your dick?"

Henry: Whoa! Randy Rosie, I like it! Offer still stands if you need it. Love you, Rosie.

Rosie: Love you, Henry. Now leave me alone.

CHAPTER 5
"The Backdoor Ball Sac"

"I'm almost there. I'll be sure to let you know how giant a Maine Coon really is," I reassured Jenny, who wanted nothing more than to be working on assignment with me.

"You know that's not what I want to know. I want to know what it's like working with Lance. God, he's gorgeous. You're so lucky."

"Now you want the Maine Coon piece, not my fault you turned it down," I said, while opening up the door to the studio where the photo shoot would be taking place. I had to conduct an interview with a family who owns the now popular, Baboo, who is a YouTube sensation, and since no one else wanted to interview the family, I was stuck with the duties. But once Jenny found out that Lance, the photographer, would be taking the pictures for the magazine, she did everything possible to "ease the burden" the article was giving me. I didn't believe her for a second. Even though she was with Drew, she still had a wandering eye for Lance, not that she would do anything. She was all about looking and never touching.

"I didn't know Lance was going to be there," she whined.

"Not my problem, and don't forget about Drew; he's a nice guy."

"Trust me, I won't forget about Drew. Take a picture at least for me."

"I'm not taking a picture of La..."

"Hi Rosie," a deep male voice said from behind me.

"Oh, my God, that's him, isn't it?" Jenny squealed like a tween meeting a member of One Direction.

"Got to go," I said, while hanging up. Taking a deep breath, I turned around and came face to face with Lance McCarthy.

The thick black rim of his glasses framed his deep blue eyes and his light brown hair was styled with a little bit of gel, so you could see those tiny curls of his, making him drop dead gorgeous, not to mention the body on the guy. He was wearing a light blue shirt with a grey cardigan, a damn cardigan. It wasn't very often you saw a guy who could pull off a cardigan, especially not with muscles like his.

"Um, hi, Lance. How are you?"

"Good," he nodded, while looking around and then meeting my eyes again. "You look pretty today; are those new glasses?"

I thought of my purple glasses and nodded. "Yeah, I got them a couple of weeks ago."

"They make your blue eyes really stand out."

"Thanks," I said shyly.

I had only worked with Lance one other time, and I really didn't even think he took notice of me, since we didn't talk much at all. We did our jobs and then took off, so I was surprised when he noticed something small, like my glasses.

"You ready for this?" he asked with a smirk, nodding toward

the photo shoot.

"Taking pictures of a cat and asking it questions? Pretty sure I'll never be ready for this," I joked.

Laughing, he looked around and then leaned forward. "I'm glad you're on set with me today. Sometimes *Friendly Felines* sends over these stage five clingers that won't let me take my pictures and leave."

"I get what you're saying. You want to be in and out," I winked. Where did that come from?

Smiling brightly, he nodded. "You get me, Rosie. That's why I'm glad you're here, and also because I wanted to talk to you some more. I felt like last time we worked together, we barely had a chance to talk."

Mr. Professional Hot Pants wanted to talk to me? That was a new shift in my life.

"What photo shoot was that again?" I asked, trying to not show how out of my element I was. It was rare I talked to men, let alone casually flirted, if that's what was happening. I really couldn't tell, given my lack of experience and the sweat that was starting to pool in my armpits.

"The exposé on litter box best practices," he said with a smirk.

I shook my head and grasped my forehead with my hand. "God, I need a new job."

Laughing some more, he replied, "But then you wouldn't be able to meet up with me."

"True. Do you like doing these articles?"

He shrugged his shoulders. "These little photo shoots are alright, but I stay with my job because most of the time, I get to go to some pretty cool places, and if I have to take pictures of cats in litter boxes on occasion, it's worth it."

"Where do you get to go?"

"Lance, can we get some test shots?" one of the production assistants asked.

"Be right over," Lance called over his shoulder before

returning his gaze to me. "I want to talk some more. Go out with me Saturday?"

Was he serious right now? Go out with him? Jenny's boobs would flip inside out if I told her I had a date with Lance. He seemed way out of my league, but he was hot, sweet and talented; I would be stupid to say no, especially with my new goal in life.

"That sounds like fun," I replied.

A big smile crossed his face at my answer, as if he was relieved to know that I would go out with him.

"Don't leave this set without giving me your phone number, you hear me?"

"Don't worry," I smiled, as he pinched my chin with his index finger and thumb and then took off toward the set with his camera in his hand.

Sighing, I watched his jean-clad butt sway away. He really was beyond good looking. Needing to tell someone, I pulled out my phone and texted Delaney. I would be telling Jenny my news in person, just so I could relish the look on her face.

Rosie: Delaney!! I have a date on Saturday with this really hot photographer.

Her text back was almost instantaneous.

Delaney: Rosie, I love you, but what kind of hot photographer are you going to meet at a photo shoot for a cat that likes to lick his own crotch while balancing on a ball?

That was Baboo's number one trick. He was Baboo, the ball-licking balancer. Entertainment for the masses had really gone downhill.

Needing to prove that not only frumpy people, excluding me and Jenny of course, work for cat magazines, I pulled up my camera app on my phone and acted like I was texting, but secretly took a picture of Lance as proof that I wasn't crazy.

Like a dumbass, I forgot to turn off my camera's flash,

though, so when it flashed brightly at Lance and the assistant, I fumbled my phone and dropped it to the ground.

"You okay over there?" he asked with a smile that said he knew exactly what I was doing.

"Yup," I called out, while grabbing my phone and turning my back toward them so they couldn't see the crimson running through my cheeks.

When I looked down at my phone, I saw that the picture I had so secretly tried to take was of my thumb, because the minute the light flashed, I panicked and tried to stop it, resulting in my thumb being in the shot, but not Lance.

"If you wanted a pic, you could have just asked," Lance said next to my ear, making me jump.

"Christ! I, umm, I wasn't taking a picture of you."

"Liar," he said even closer, while he grabbed my phone and turned the camera back on. His long arm stretched out in front of me and his head lined up with mine. "Smile," he whispered, as he took a picture of us. "Now, send that one to your friends and let me know if they approve."

"Will do," I said like a dingus as Lance took off.

Avoiding all eye contact with the man, I kept my back turned away from him as I sent the picture to Delaney. I was mortified, but also happy that I had a picture of him.

Rosie: He's hot and we have a date for Saturday.

Delaney: Holy shit!! Rosie, you sure know how to pick them. He's gorgeous. Are his glasses real?

Rosie: I think so. Why wouldn't they be?

Delaney: Hipsters, their glasses are always an accessory not a necessity.

Rosie: Pretty sure they're real.

Delaney: Ask him.

Rosie: I'm not going to ask him, that would be such a stupid question, and I'm trying to keep my date for Saturday. I kind of like this guy.

Delaney: What about Atticus? Rosie Bloom, are you playing the field?

Was I? I guess I was. I didn't have any real commitments to anyone, and if I wanted to write a solid book, I was going to have to get a lot of experience with men, all different kinds, so why not have some fun while I could?

Rosie: I guess I am. P.S. That's a book title, Playing the Field. *Amazing series about some hot baseball players.*

Delaney: You're annoying.

"Rosie, we're ready for you," someone called out to me, while an excited couple and a less than excited Baboo walked out on set.

Pulling out my notebook and questions, I took a deep breath and walked over to the couple. They were wearing matching blue Baboo shirts, khaki pants, and smelled of tuna and cheese. Baboo looked like he was about to throat punch me with his paw; he wasn't having any of it. This was going to be one hell of an interview.

***

"Thank you so much for your time," I said to Baboo's people. "Baboo is such a friendly feline," I said, using the magazine's tagline. I gagged saying it, since it was a requirement. My boss thought it was a good way to connect with the owners of our "stars;" I thought it was a load of crap.

"We can't tell you how happy that makes us. I feel like we've been lifelong subscribers and can't believe that our little Baboo is finally going to be a featured friendly feline. I can literally die happy."

And I believed the woman who was staring at me with crazy in her eyes and rabid foam in the crease of her mouth. Only the cat people could really draw you in with their crazy, convincing you they were kind people, when in real life they just wanted to take you back to their place and use you as a scratching post. I wasn't falling for it.

"I'll be sure to email you the pictures and article for you to keep. We appreciate your time." I looked over at Baboo, whose ears were flattened and his lip quivering, as if saying, "If you don't get me out of here soon, I'm going to go feral feline on you."

"Safe ride home," I patted Baboo, who was seconds away from slitting his own throat with his claws.

The couple left, practically floating away on cloud nine. It always fascinated me how much people were obsessed with their animals. I liked a good four legged friend every now and then, but not to the point where I thought they were my child, and if I could, I would be breast feeding them three times a day…that's the impression I at least got from Baboo's parents.

As I packed up my notebook and recorder, I felt Lance's gaze land on me a few times while he packed up as well. He should have left a while ago, but he took a long time gathering all his things. He actually stayed and looked through the pictures with the couple, something he didn't do at our last shoot, but then again, it's not like he was going to share his pictures with the different sized litter boxes starring in the last article.

"Are you leaving now?" he called out to me as I swung my purse on my shoulder. "Without even giving me your number?"

"You didn't give me a chance," I said, as I turned and smiled at him.

He was sitting on one of his bins with a crooked smile on his face and his arms crossed over his expansive chest. He looked divine, and I wasn't sure if it was my newfound ambition or the fact that my vagina could now see past the cloud of curls, but I was starting to get all tingly inside just from an interaction with a man. Did this mean my sexual being had awakened? Was that even a thing?

I walked over to him and put out my hand. He looked at it in confusion, wondering if he was supposed to put his hand in mine.

"Hand it over."

"Hand what over?" he asked, still confused.

"Your phone, so I can put my number in it and you can do the same," I said, while holding out my phone.

"So, you're not a tease?"

"Why would you think that?" I asked, actually surprised he would consider me a tease.

He shrugged while he typed into my phone. "You have this whole pin-up girl vibe going on. I thought you might be just playing with me."

Pin-up girl? It took everything in me not to snort in laughter. Yes, I had a retro style, but I wasn't a pin-up girl. At least I didn't think I was.

"You've got that wrong," I said, while handing him his phone back. "I'm the farthest thing from a pin-up girl."

"You sure as hell don't look like it. You're sexy, Rosie. You have some amazing curves, and your eyes…I just can't stop looking at them."

Okay, so I could see a clam from a mile away. I wasn't that dense when it came to men, but right now, looking into Lance's eyes, he spoke sincerely, and it actually blew me away. I wasn't an ugly, rabid beast by any means, but I wasn't supermodel perfect, which I knew was the kind of woman Lance dated.

But I wasn't going to overthink it; if he thought I was pretty, I was going to accept the compliment because hell, I was pretty, and just because I didn't get much male attraction, since I was always the friend, never the lover, I was going to soak up this moment. It was time I started appreciating my curvy body, my muted brown hair, and my unorthodox style. If I wanted Virginia, my vagina, to get some love, then I needed to love myself first.

"Thank you," I accepted his compliment, feeling good about myself. "I guess I'll see you Saturday?"

He nodded, while giving me a devilish look. "Do you like bowling, Rosie?"

"Sure, not very good at it, though."

"You don't need to be. A group of my friends goes cosmic bowling on Saturday nights. I know what you're thinking, total teenage hangout, but I promise, you'll have a good time."

"I'm in. Should I wear white?"

"Ah, girl after my own heart. Yes, wear white. I'll text you the details."

"Sounds good, I'll see you then, Lance."

"Bye, Rosie," he smiled as I walked away. Even though I thought I might possibly break a hip from not really knowing what I was doing, I put an extra sway in my hip as I retreated away from him, hoping I didn't trip and fall over all the cables in the room.

I rushed back to the office, making sure to ignore all of Jenny's text messages that were begging for details. I wanted nothing more than to talk to her face to face, because she would never believe what I had to tell her.

When I got to my office, I was instantly greeted by Sir Licks-a-Lot, who was sitting in my chair, cleaning his paw, and looking less than thrilled that I'd showed up.

"Get out of here," I said, while waving my purse in front of him. Instead of moving from the oh so scary purse wave, he sighed and licked his other paw.

"Pssssst!" I hissed, trying to get him to move, but all that did was cause him to stretch and then scratch my white leather chair.

"Stop," I cried, as I pounced at him. Like a ninja, he jumped up, launched off of my head, and flew to the top of my filing cabinet, where he perched himself and sneered down at me, as if I was a mere peasant, disturbing his excellency's private time.

"Don't you have better things to do than hide out in my office? Maybe go torment someone else," I said, while I dropped my things and sat down in my chair. I shook my mouse and woke up my computer, but when I went to type in my password, I noticed the B on my keyboard was missing.

Holy crap, he really was trying to say, "Die bitch, die."

Growing angry, I turned toward him, and right there, sitting on my filing cabinet was Sir Licks-a-Lot with the B in his mouth and a look of satisfaction in his eyes.

"You son of a bitch," I said, while getting up, but I was too slow as he jumped off the filing cabinet, bounced off my chest, and ran out the door. The force of his weight against me had me flying backwards into my chair and into the bookcase behind me. A couple of books fell down on me, as well as a dried-up furry lump, which landed in my lap.

"What the hell?" I asked, as I lifted it up.

The minute I saw a beady eye peak out from the fur, I screamed and tossed it clear across my room, where Sir Licks-a-Lot popped out of nowhere, caught the damn thing in his mouth, and ran off without missing a beat.

"That cat be crazy," Jenny said in my doorway, as she watched Sir Licks-a-Lot jumping off of other humans, like we were his personal trampoline zone.

"I hate that cat. He hid a mouse in my bookshelf, a dead mouse, Jenny!"

"Hey, he must like you. He hid a pigeon's wing in the boss's office a month ago, and we know how much they get along. Look at that, he feels safe in your office."

"No, he's just messing with me, I know it. And he took my B."

Jenny peeked over my desk and looked at my keyboard. "Yeah, maybe he really is plotting your death. Hard to tell with that one, but enough about the demon cat; tell me all about Lance."

"Well, he asked me out on a date."

Jenny slammed her hands on the desk and looked me dead in the eyes.

"No, he did not."

Nodding, I replied, "He did. We have a date planned for

Saturday."

"Holy shit! Oh, my God, I'm so jealous. You know how hot he is, right?"

"Jenny, I have eyes. I can see."

"Just making sure. Oh, my God, I can't believe this. You have to have sex with him."

"What?" I said, blushing to my toes. The only people who knew I was a virgin were Delaney and Henry, so for Jenny to say such a thing had me turning bright red. "I'm not going to just have sex with him, Jenny."

"Why the hell not?"

I was about to open my mouth, when I realized I didn't have an answer. Why the hell not? Maybe because he didn't look like the kind of guy who wanted to have a fumbling girl trying to undo the button of his jeans and then just stare at his penis, wondering what she was supposed to do next.

"Um, I don't like to jump into things so fast."

"Oh, who cares about that? You're going out with Lance McCarthy; you need to give it up."

"Maybe," I said, not really meaning it.

"Hey, what about Atticus?" Jenny asked.

"What about him? I still plan on going out with him on Friday."

"Oooh, I like this new side of you, Rosie. Playing the field, I like it."

"*Playing the Field*, that's the name of one of my favorite books, it's about these amazingly hot baseball players who live in Atlanta. The main character is Brady, oh my God, Jenny you have to…"

The look on her face told me she could care less about the book I was talking about, just like Delaney. Didn't anyone share the same passion for books that I did?

"There's the Rosie I know," she smiled. "I'm glad you're putting your Kindle aside for a little bit and going on a couple of dates. I'm proud of you. Do you need me to take you shopping?"

"No, I'm good," I replied, realizing that maybe I did spend too much time reading, if Jenny even noticed. The more I thought about it, the more I thought that notion was crazy. I didn't spend too much time reading; there was no such thing. I just needed to make more time for a social life, that's all.

"I guess I'll see you tomorrow. Date night!"

"Woo hoo," I cheered with her, feeling a little anxious, but excited in general.

***

When I got home that night, I was walking up the stairs to my apartment when I ran into an impeccably dressed and divine smelling Henry. He really set the standard for men. Just at the sight of him, all the thoughts of Delaney talking about Henry wanting to have sex with me came to the forefront of my mind, making my entire body heat up. Damn her.

"Hey, love," he greeted me with that charming smirk of his.

"Hey, Henry. Date?" I asked, trying to forget the sexual thoughts running through my mind and the sincere eyes Henry was giving me, as if I was the only girl he wanted to talk to.

"Yup, a blonde I met on the subway." He acted as if it was no big deal.

"Picking girls up on public transportation is kind of below you, Henry."

Smirking, he leaned over and said, "Not when her tits are hanging out for the world to see."

"Ugh, Henry."

"What?" You know I like a good rack, and can't help myself when I see one."

"You could try. What if she's a psycho killer?"

"She's not, I already Googled her after she told me her whole name. She works at a fashion company in Soho. She has that whole bohemian style and doesn't mind showing off her assets." He wiggled his eyebrows while tickling my side.

"Stop," I laughed while pulling away. "Please excuse me, I

need to go pick out some outfits for the two dates I have coming up."

"Two dates?" his eyebrows shot up.

"Yes, I have swing dancing tomorrow and bowling on Saturday with a guy I met today."

"Bowling? Uh, that's lame."

"No, it's cute," I said, while raising in my chin.

"Okay, but you will be giving me his information before you take off. I don't trust any man who takes a girl on a bowling date."

"You're so weird," I chuckled. I was about to take off when I stopped myself and pressed my hand against Henry's chest to stop him. Thoughts of what Jenny said to me earlier about giving it up to Lance ran through my mind. "Henry, what does a guy like when it comes to a blow job?"

"What?" he shook his head as if he didn't hear me correctly.

"A blow job, what do you like?"

Clearing his throat and shifting in place, he said, "Rosie, this is not a conversation to have in a stairwell, I would rather show you in the privacy of our own home where I can really teach you."

"If you're talking about me practicing on you, you can think again."

"It's education," he laughed, while lacing my hand with his. Always a flirt.

"I'm serious, Henry."

Running his hand through his hair, he looked at his watch and then took me upstairs.

"I have ten minutes; sit down and be quiet," he said, while he forced me on the couch and went to the kitchen. When he returned, he had a banana in his hand and a concerned look on his face.

He sat down next to me and held out the banana, but I didn't pay attention to that; I, instead, studied the crease in his brow.

"What's going on?" I asked, rubbing out the crease with my fingers.

"I don't like this."

"Like what?" I asked.

"You, blow jobs. I don't want you to be handing out blow jobs. I know I've been teasing you a lot lately, but this seems so real. I don't like it."

"So, you're saying I shouldn't be giving guys blow jobs?"

"Guys? Rosie, please tell me you aren't about to hand these out as a parting gift after each of your dates."

I sat back and studied Henry closer. "I don't get you. One minute you're encouraging me, helping me learn about sex, and the next you're restricting what I'm allowed to do. I don't think you have the right to tell me what I can and can't do."

"You're right," he shook his head. "It's just getting real now. I like you all innocent."

"You're holding a banana in your hand and about to tell me about the art of a blow job. I would hardly call that real."

"True," he chuckled and then took a deep breath. "Alright, hold this and pretend it's a dick."

"Are they really this big?" I asked, looking down at the banana and feeling intimidated.

"Yes, Rosie, when erect, the penis can be that big and sometimes even bigger."

"Dear God, where do you guys stuff them?"

"We just tape them down to our legs."

"Seriously?" I asked, as my gaze swung up to his.

"No! Jesus, let's just get this over with. There are three basic things a guy wants in a blow job. Number one…"

"Wait, let me get a notebook, so I can write this down."

"No, you're not writing this down, just pay attention. Be in the moment, Rosie."

"Fine," I succumbed.

I looked down at the dick…well, banana and studied it while Henry spoke.

"Number one, flick your tongue on the underside of his cock. It's so fucking sensitive under there, you will have him ready in seconds."

"Got it, underside of cock."

"Two, play with his balls, the head of his cock, and perineum."

"Perineum?"

"Yes, it's the spot right behind his nut sac. I'm telling you, a guy will scream like a girl if you do it right."

"Okay, back door ball sac, got it."

He chuckled while shaking his head. "Finally, give him a hummer."

"What's a hummer?" I asked, while looking down at the banana.

"A hummer is when you have his cock in your mouth and you hum lightly. The vibrations will jolt all the way down to his balls, and it will cause an amazing sensation to stir inside of him."

"Interesting. Should I hum show tunes?" I teased.

"Not recommended. Whatever you do, apply pressure, use your hands and mouth at the same time, and just go for it, but for the love of God, do not use your teeth, even if magazines say guys like a little graze of the teeth, they're lying. Anytime a girl busts out her chompers, I instantly start to panic that she's going to bite down on me. I just can't handle the unknown like that, so keep them tucked like a granny."

"Granny, check," I said, while tucking my teeth under my lips.

"Perfect," he smiled softly and then looked at his watch. "Shit, I have to go. Practice on the banana, especially the no teeth thing. Have fun."

"Thanks, Henry."

"Anything for you, love, but just promise me you'll be careful."

"Promise."

He placed both of his hands on my face and studied my eyes for just a brief moment before he kissed my forehead ever so softly. When he pulled away, he smiled lightly, as if he wanted to say something, but then shook his head to himself and took off.

Weird.

Once he was gone, I went back to my room and stared at the banana while trying to gain the courage to give a blow job to a phallic shaped fruit. Instead of wrapping my mouth around it, I wrapped my hand around it and started moving it up and down in a steady rhythm.

"Oh, yeah, you like that banana? Are you going to turn into banana pudding soon? You going to lose your peel?"

"There is something seriously wrong with you," Delaney said as I was mid-stroke.

"Shut my door!" I called out, as I tossed the molested banana to the side. Damn roommates.

I pulled out my notebook and started making notes for the day.

June 4, 2014

Flick, granny teeth, backdoor balls, and hum your life away: the keys to the perfect blowjob. Men like to be hummed to when getting blowjobs, interesting. I wonder if it's some kind of lullaby for their penis. I would want to see the scientific research on that.

And who decided that playing with a man's pern-en-whoozy-whatty was something that would make him explode faster? I need to Google what that is and where it is, because I was a little confused on the placement of that little hidden orgasm button.

I can understand the granny teeth thing. I doubt a ravenous woman showing her dick-eating fangs is very comforting to a man. I could imagine the libido factor dropping down a few notches after seeing fresh teeth waiting to take in the man's most sensitive member.

Flicking your tongue. How do you flick a tongue? As I sit here and write, I'm practicing the flick motion, and I'm wondering how effective it really is on a man. After just grabbing my banana and flicking my tongue across it, I can see the aPEEL. God, I'm so funny.

After my blowjob crash course, I feel like I can tackle the world, one penis at a time...hopefully.

CHAPTER 6
"The Smoking Vaginator"

"Are you ready?" Delaney asked, as she was perched on my bed with her hands under her chin and her feet in the air.

No, I thought to myself as I stared in the mirror. I was wearing a polka dot dress that came to my knees and a pair of red heels. My lipstick matched my shoes, and my hair was up in a ponytail with a big pinned curl in the front that was being held tall with a decent amount of hairspray. To top the outfit off, I placed a red flower in my hair with some bobby pins to make sure it stayed tight. I was ready, at least appearance wise; my heart, on the other hand, was beating drastically against my chest.

"As ready as I'll ever be," I responded.

"Well, you look fantastic, seriously Rosie, I'm stunned."

"Thanks, Delaney. You sure my boobs aren't showing too much?"

"No, they look great, and your waist looks impossibly tiny in that dress."

Surprising, since I wasn't as small as Delaney by any means.

"Thanks. Where's Henry? I thought he was going to be here."

"No clue. I sent him a text, but he never responded."

"Alright, well, I don't want to be late. Thanks for all the help, Delaney. I really appreciate it."

"Anything for my girl. Go have fun and don't think about the whole sex part of the night. Just relax, enjoy the company, and if he kisses you, he kisses you."

I nodded and then looked around my room. "Do you see my mini bottle of baby powder?"

"What do you need that for?" she asked, as she looked around with me. "Here it is."

"Thanks. Ever since that wax, I've been really itchy and I found the baby powder helps. I don't think I will ever get waxed again."

"You just had a bad reaction, no big deal."

"It's a big deal when all I want to do is spread my legs and act like a damn ape scratching his balls on a hot day."

"Do apes do that?" she asked with a quizzical eyebrow.

"In my head they do. Okay, got to go." I leaned over and gave Delaney a kiss on the cheek. "I'll text you later."

"Have fun." She waved at me and then clapped her hands together.

The subway ride over to the club was nerve racking, especially since I looked so out of place. Then again, it was New York City, no one looked normal. The city was an eclectic melting pot of weirdoes, but I was proud to be one of them. It wasn't very often you could live in a place where everyone was so vastly different from the person next to them. I loved every bit of it.

Jenny said Atticus wanted to pick me up at my apartment, but I thought that was silly, since we would have to take the subway to the club anyway. Plus, I wasn't quite ready to be alone with him, especially since I've never met the guy, so that was why I was riding by myself. I thought it was awfully considerate; Jenny and Delaney had other thoughts.

Once I got off the subway and walked the couple of blocks to the club, all my nerves vanished when I saw a bunch of people dressed up just like me and looking more than excited for the night to come.

Jenny, Drew, and Atticus were all standing on the sidewalk talking when I walked up to them.

"Hi guys."

"Rosie, you made it," Jenny gave me a big hug, while I chanced a glimpse at Atticus.

He fit right in with the times by wearing cuffed grey tweed pants, shoes that matched his pants, and a white shirt with red suspenders and a red bow tie. His hair was slicked to the side and his brown eyes looked warm and inviting.

"Rosie, meet Atticus," Jenny said, as she pulled away from me in her brown dress and white gloves. She looked adorable.

"Atticus, it's great to finally meet you," I said, holding out my hand.

"Likewise. Jenny has told me so much about you."

"Well, I hope I live up to what she's said," I said shyly.

"You do," he smiled kindly at me.

I could hear the silent squee in Jenny's mind as she looped her hand around Drew's arm and walked into the club, while Atticus and I followed closely behind. He offered his arm to me like a gentlemen, and I took it, letting him guide me inside.

The club instantly brought me back to the era of swing. The club was covered in plush red and gold colors with intricate details. There was old school New York décor flanking every corner of the room, adding a bit of nostalgia to the ambiance. A giant chandelier graced the ceiling of the dance floor, where couples were swinging already and having a great time. I couldn't be more excited.

"You look beautiful, by the way," Atticus said into my ear as we followed Jenny and Drew to a table. "I'm sorry I didn't say it right away. I'm kind of rusty when it comes to this dating thing."

"That's okay. I am too, and you look very handsome."

"Thank you," he smiled down at me and pulled me in a little

closer. I already was starting to like Atticus. He was soft spoken and sweet…right up my alley.

"Will this be alright?" Jenny asked about the booth they started to sit down in.

"Looks good to me," I said, as I sat down next to her and Atticus sat right next to me.

His arm wrapped around behind me on the cushioned bench seat as he looked out at the dance floor, surveying the dancers and band.

"Wow, there are some amazing dancers out there tonight."

"Do you come here often?" I asked, silently agreeing with him.

"I try to. It's been tough lately. My dad's been in the hospital with cancer, so I haven't had much time to come out."

"Oh no, I'm so sorry."

"It's okay, he's in remission right now, so things are looking up. When Jenny and Drew said they were going out tonight and had a pretty friend I could dance with, I couldn't help but agree to come out. I needed the release, you know?"

"I do. I'm glad you met up with us," I said, while touching his thigh instinctively. The movement shocked him for a second, but then he softened toward me and tugged on my shoulder.

I sat frozen as I wondered what the hell possessed me to touch his thigh. It was a rather bold move, one I'd never done before, so now I sat there contemplating what to do next. Did I remove my hand and place it in my lap? Did I stroke his thigh? No, don't stroke his thigh, I warned my hand, who seemed to have a mind of its own. Stroking of the thigh would be way too bold and beyond creepy after only knowing the guy for two minutes. Instead, I lifted my hand, not making any stroking motion and quickly grabbed my purse that was on the table. I was starting to feel itchy and needed to head to the bathroom. The nerves were starting to get to me.

"Excuse me, do you mind if I go to the ladies room real quick?"

"Not at all," he said, while getting up. "When you get back, do you want to head out on the dance floor?" The vulnerability in his eyes cut to my very core as I nodded.

"I would love that."

I turned from the booth and headed to the bathroom, where there was a short line.

"One holer," the lady in front of me called out with a seriously dark smoker's voice.

"I'm sorry?" I asked, not quite understanding what she meant.

"There's only one shitter in there, one holer. It's going to be a while, toots."

"Oh," I said while I shifted in place, casually pressing my purse against my itchy crotch to scratch it. It was better than my ape hand getting all down and crazy on my red brick road.

"Fancy meeting you here," a familiar voice said in my ear. I turned to see my handsome best friend standing next to me.

"Henry, what are you doing here?" I asked, while pulling him into a hug.

"Thought I would do a little swing dancing. Care to dance with me?"

"I can't. I'm on a date, Henry, and I have to umm…throw some fairy dust on the red brick road."

He looked down at my crotch in confusion, so I pulled out my baby powder from my purse and he nodded in understanding. He looked around and then pulled me by the hand out of line and straight into the men's room.

He locked the door behind us and said, "Go ahead, do your business."

I covered my mouth and nose and said, "Oh, it smells like pee in here."

"Good job, love. You recognize we're in a small room with a pisser, now let's do your business and get out of here."

"I can't when you're looking at me."

"Fine," he turned and put his hands in his pockets, giving me limited privacy.

For a moment, I took in his appearance. He was wearing tight fitted grey khaki pants that were folded at the bottom, a pair of saddle shoes, and a checkered shirt with a black tie. He looked beyond handsome, like always.

"Nice outfit," I said, while I pulled up my skirt and started squirting baby powder in my underpants, the more the better.

"Thanks. I must say, Rosie, you look spectacular. Your tits are amazing in that dress."

Rolling my eyes, I said, "Thanks, I guess."

Laughing, he said, "In all seriousness, you look beautiful, love." I gulped at his compliment. The softness of his voice shot straight through me, making me wonder if he was starting to look at me in a different light.

Silence fell between us, and an unsettling tension formed between us. Was I crazy for thinking Henry actually might find me attractive? He was just being a friend, right?

I was so damn confused.

Clearing his throat, Henry asked, "You about done?"

"Yeah," I replied, while twisting the cap of the baby powder shut and stuffing it back in my purse.

He turned around and held out his hand. I took it with mine and let him pull me closer. He lifted my chin and said, "Seriously, you took my breath away when I saw you, Rosie. I'm sure Atticus is head over heels infatuated with you already."

"Thank you," I replied, not knowing what else to say. Wanting to change the subject so I stopped sweating in my best friend's arms, I asked, "Did you see him?"

A small frown marred Henry's face for a second before he answered, "Not yet, but I will be sure to give you my rating later tonight, and if he starts to get handsy, you can bet that pretty little butt of yours that I will be stepping in."

"Don't you dare!"

"Can't help it, I'm protective."

"Is that why you came here?" I asked as we exited the bathroom, avoiding sneers from all the women in the long line, waiting for the one holer. "To spy on me, make sure Atticus wasn't getting handsy?"

"If I said yes, would you be mad at me?"

"You're impossible," I shook my head and stepped away. "I'll be fine, Henry, but thank you for your concern…"

"Henry," a shrill came from the side of the room as a blonde Jessica Rabbit came strolling up next to Henry. Her breasts looked like they were going to fall out of her dress at any moment, and her voice rivaled that of Fran Dresher's. "There ya are. I've been lookin' all over for ya," she said, while chewing what seemed like a wad of gum.

I cringed at the heavy accent coming from the elegant-looking lady, sans breasts.

"Just helping out my best friend here," he said, while blatantly staring at her breasts. Some people never changed. She noticed his perusal and puffed her chest out some more.

"Nice to meet you," I said, lying, since I actually didn't meet her. I turned to Henry, who was able to take his eyes off of his date's nippleloons for more than two seconds. "Have a good night, Henry. I'll talk to you later."

He pulled me into a hug and whispered in my ear. "I'm here for you if you need anything."

"I'll be fine," I said back. "Enjoy your friend and her giant moo mammies."

Chuckling softly, he hugged me tightly and pulled away, giving me that little wink of his.

I headed back to my booth full of energy. I had a date to attend to.

As I approached the table, Jenny gave me a look of utter confusion as she stared down at me. Atticus came up beside me and asked if I was ready to dance. I was, but the look Jenny gave me was concerning, so I told Atticus "one second" and beckoned Jenny over to me, who was already on her way to talk to me.

"What's going on?" I asked in a hushed tone.

"You're smoking."

"Oh, why thank you," I accepted her compliment. "But why are you giving me a weird look."

"No, I mean you're smoking."

"What are you talking about?"

"Every time you move, there is this cloud of smoke coming out from under your dress."

"Cloud of smoke? Are you high?"

"Is your vagina high? Because it's smoking something under that dress of yours."

"Jenny, you're losing it…" as I said the words, her accusation clicked in my head, just as Atticus grabbed my hand.

"I love this song, come on."

He pulled me out on the dance floor with a trail of puffed baby powder following in our wake. He whipped me around the dance floor, jitterbugging, bouncing up and down and pulling me into him. With every movement, I could see the puff of baby powder come up from under my skirt. Mortification ran through my veins, and I stiffly moved across the dance floor with Atticus.

Desperate for help, I looked over at Jenny who had her hand over her mouth, looking at me in disbelief. I knew she had to be convinced my vagina was on fire. She was no help.

Thank God Atticus was completely oblivious as he jigged about, but I couldn't say that for everyone else around us as the lights shone down on Atticus and me, picking up the film of baby powder excreting from my panties. The lights made it that much more obvious.

Humiliation set in deeper and deeper with each passing moment, with each puff from my panties, and with each itch the diminishing powder left the little red brick road.

"You're a good dancer," Atticus said above the music as he twirled his finger in the air to the beat of the music. He really was cute, I had to admit it.

"You are too," I complimented.

"It's foggy in here," Atticus called out as he brushed the baby powder cloud out of our space.

"Yeah, weird," I laughed nervously, as I tried to avoid eye contact with everyone who thought I was smoking a plate of pork loins in my vagina.

"Do you want to try a flip?" he asked, while shuffling his legs and twisting my hips by directing my arms.

Did I want to try a flip? And risk all the baby powder gathered in my panties to fall directly on Atticus' head, yeah, no way in hell.

"Maybe not right now." Not until I cleaned out my underpants.

I chanced a glance at the bathroom and noticed the line was non-existent, so I would be able to take care of my private lady puffs that kept floating out from me, but my only concern was, if I told Atticus I had to go to the bathroom again, he might think I was having some kind of bowel movement issue, or that I was a coke addict needing to get my fix. Both options were not flattering, so I tried for option number three, female telepathy.

While dancing, I tried getting Jenny's attention to see if she could sense my distress, but for the first time since I'd been out on the dance floor, Jenny had vanished, probably to make out with Drew. They were known for heavy petting in public; I was just grateful they stepped aside this go around instead of doing it right in front of everyone.

"Where did you learn to dance?" Atticus asked, as he spun me out wide and then back into him again. The minute my body connected with his, a puff of baby powder sprayed up between us, like the damn tide of an ocean, but instead of water, it was my—I hate to say it, but—it was my pussy powder.

"College," I answered, trying to play it cool, even though I could feel sweat start to trickle down my back from embarrassment.

"I wonder if people are smoking in here," Atticus said, as he surveyed the room. "Wow, we must be good partners, everyone seems to be watching us."

"Well, you're good at leading," I complimented, even though I wanted to tell him, "No, Atticus, it's your partner's panty pollution that's affecting the air."

I continued to fill the air with every move I made, and it got to the point where I grew almost too stiff to move, and Atticus noticed.

"Is something wrong?"

Needing to take care of the situation, I said, "Don't think I'm a drug addict or anything, but I have to go to the bathroom again; the line was long last time and I really didn't get to go. I swear, I'm not doing drugs or anything, since it looks like it, given the fact that I have to go to the bathroom again."

I was rambling, and by the look on Atticus' face, I wasn't doing a good job, because I could see in his eyes, the "whoa, this girl is showing her crazy" look.

"Sure, I'll meet you back at the booth."

Defeated but determined, I took off for the bathroom and quickly locked myself in the stall. I pulled down my underpants, took them off completely and dumped all of the baby powder that I so stupidly accumulated in there and put it down the toilet. Powder flew everywhere, making me sneeze uncontrollably.

After I controlled myself, I wiped my nose with my hand and then took some toilet paper to my lady parts to get rid of any excess; I would just have to be an itchy beast. Better itchy than smoking vagina girl. I put my panties back on and flushed. I washed my hands as quickly as possible and practically ran back to the booth where Jenny, Drew and Atticus were waiting for me.

"Sorry about that," I sniffed, as I felt some powder still linger from my sneeze attack.

"What's under your nose?" Jenny asked, looking at me funny.

"What do you mean?" I asked, wiping my nose, feeling self-conscious in front of my date.

"It's white."

Atticus' eyes shot open as I wiped away the evidence.

"Not sure, is it gone?"

"Yeah..." Jenny drawled out, as they all stared at me.

I fidgeted in my stance, trying to contain the itch that started to develop down below. I knew I looked crazy as my legs spasmed about, trying to casually rub together to relieve the prickling down below.

"Umm, it's getting late," Atticus said, while looking at his watch. "I should be going."

He got up and waved bye to Jenny and Drew. He took one look at me and shook his head as he started to walk away.

I was so confused as to why he was leaving so abruptly, and then it hit me. The white substance under my nose, the erratic leg movements, the bathroom trips…holy shit, he thought I was high.

"Atticus, wait," I called out, as I grabbed his shoulder and turned him around. "I can explain."

"Rosie, I like you, but I'm not someone who can be strong enough to deal with an addiction."

"That's what I can explain," I pressed my hands to my eyes and grimaced. "It's baby powder. I was…umm, chafing before I came, so I decided to use some baby powder to help. I apparently used too much, and that's what all the fog was around us, the baby powder kicking up. I went back to the bathroom to relieve some of it from its duties."

Mortified was the only way to describe the way I was feeling, but I liked him and I didn't want him to just leave without explanation, especially since he thought I was some kind of druggie. So, I put on my big girl pants and explained everything; I only hoped he didn't judge me.

"Baby powder?" he asked, eyeing me suspiciously.

"Yes," I pulled the little bottle out of my clutch and showed him. "See?"

He nodded his head as he looked at it.

"You can smell it, if you don't believe me."

"I believe you," he said, his voice softening a little.

We stood there in silence for a second before I said, "I just have to tell you this is probably the most embarrassing thing that has ever happened to me." Besides getting a vibrator stuck in my vag, but I wasn't about to tell him that.

He chuckled and said, "Well, it's an interesting story, that's for sure. How about we start over, get back out on the dance floor?"

"I would love that," I said, as I shifted my legs together, trying to ease the itch.

Damn you, Marta, damn you!

Like a gentleman, Atticus led me out on the dance floor and started twisting me all over, but this time, I wasn't steaming out my rear end. He smiled brightly at me while he snapped his fingers to the side and his feet floated seamlessly across the dance floor.

He was adorable with every kick of his foot and twist of his arm, pulling me into his chest and then sugar-pushing me away. I snapped along with him and matched his moves step for step.

When Jenny asked me to go swing dancing, I had no clue I was actually going to be set up with a good dance partner; I might even admit that he was better than Henry, who was standing to the side, hovering over his girl with the giant tatas while watching me with a careful eye. His date pulled at his shirt, but his gaze never truly lifted from me, so I smiled and waved to let him know that I was having a good time. He nodded, but that was it.

"Who is that?" Atticus asked, as he pulled me in close and started twisting me with his body in short but quick movements.

"My friend, Henry. He was actually my swing partner in college."

"Really? Is he jealous?" Atticus asked with a smile.

"I don't think so. He's just protective, that's all."

"Shall we show him he has nothing to worry about?" Atticus asked, while wiggling his eyebrows.

"I think we shall," I said, just as Atticus pushed me out and then pulled me back in, only to push me back out on the other side. I felt my feet fly across the ground as the music picked up and we switched from east coast swing to the classic Lindy Hop, my favorite.

With every movement, I tried to rub my legs together, to relieve the itch that kept building up, but nothing was soothing the tickling between my legs; it was almost torturous because I was having such a fantastic time with Atticus, but I felt like I couldn't truly enjoy it.

I was twisting low with my arm out to my side, right when someone else grabbed my hand and pulled me into their chest, leading me up and down the dance floor.

"Henry," I said breathlessly, as he picked me up and tossed me over his back in one smooth motion, without missing a beat. "What are you doing?"

"Having a little fun with my good time gal."

"I'm on a date," I said, as I passed him and then flew right into Atticus' grasp.

He twirled me a couple of times and then started bouncing his feet and twirling around with me in circles while shifting our feet back and forth. He pushed me out and Henry grabbed my hand again.

I looked over at Atticus, who was actually smiling, enjoying the back and forth.

"Hold on, love," Henry said, as he picked me up and tossed me in the air in a twist. I luckily landed on my feet and kicked my leg up to the beat. The minute my leg moved up, the itch that was eating away at me was slightly relieved from the friction of my leg against my panties.

Sweet Jesus, it was a little relief, but relief at that.

"Come here," Atticus said, as he pulled me away and picked me up, drove me to the ground so I slid under his legs, turned around quickly and picked me back up. At this point, the crowd had formed a circle and was hooting and hollering with every move the boys made. I was just the pawn in their little game, and to say I was getting dizzy was an understatement. I flung my arms and legs about as I kept up with the fast-paced music, trying to concentrate on what was happening next.

"Time for the grand finale, love," Henry said, as he pulled me into his grasp and swung me around. He grabbed me by the waist, pulled me into him so my legs wrapped around his hips, and then he lifted me over his head and I flipped down his back, landing behind him just so he could pull me between his legs and shoot me back up in front of him. The crowd around us cheered and Henry spun me in circles while releasing my hand. I kicked my legs forward, not really paying attention to where I was going, relishing in the itch relief the movement provided for me, until my leg connected directly with something soft.

I looked up to find Atticus lying on the ground, holding his crotch and grimacing in pain. I realized what I did, not from the poor man in front of me, crouching in a fetal position, but because of the crowd's collective "oof" as they watched me kick my date dead on in the nuts.

At that moment, I was pretty sure I would have taken the cocaine looking mishap over the fallen man in front of me.

"Should have twisted instead of kicked," Henry said next to me, as he stood with his hands on his hips while we both looked down at Atticus.

"You think?" I said sarcastically, hating myself.

June 5, 2014

Note to self, excessive amounts of baby powder can lead to a smoking vaginator if not applied properly. Also, one swift kick to the balls can end a date in point two seconds. Next time, keep all extremities to self and avoid the family jewels at all times. Also, possibly invest in multiple sizes of cups to hand out to dates, just in case runaway legs get away from you again. Better safe than sorry, and boy, was I sorry.

CHAPTER 7
"The Magnificent Pencil Holder"

Embarrassment from last night kept me from rising early and working out like I normally did. Instead, I rested in my bed and stared up at my ceiling as Delaney's kitchen singing floated under my door. It was waffle Saturday, and I could smell her homemade treats filter in to my bedroom, tempting me, but not enough for me to drag my sorry carcass out of bed.

Last night was so perfect in the fact that Atticus was a brilliant dance partner and a real joy to be with. He was cute, sweet, and had some really good moves. He didn't mind dancing, which was always a turn on, and the guy could smile to the point that I felt myself melting every time he cheesed it in my direction.

I really thought we had something going for us, until my leg spasmed and connected directly with his unsuspecting crotch. I watched in distress as Drew helped Atticus off the ground and escorted him out of the club, while the poor guy crouched in a fetal position and shuffled away. I found out later that night from Jenny that Atticus lost his cookies outside of the club from the pain and was too embarrassed and in pain to come back in the club, and that was the end to my date.

A soft knock played at my door, as Henry's smooth voice flowed through.

"Rosie, come have breakfast, love."

"I'm not moving from this bed," I called out, as I placed my pillow over my head.

Henry let himself in my bedroom and sat next to me. He pulled my pillow away and looked down at me with soft eyes. He was shirtless, like usual on Saturday mornings, and was wearing a thin pair of grey sweatpants that sat low on his hips. His hair was messed and pushed to the side, while there was a light five o'clock shadow gracing his jaw.

It was unfair to have such a hot roommate.

"You can't stay in here all day. Come have breakfast with us, love."

"I can't. I'm too mortified to do anything."

"It wasn't that bad, Rosie."

"Not that bad?" I replied, as I sat up and looked Henry in the eyes. "Henry, I kicked my date in the balls, to the point where he had to step outside to throw up from how hard I kicked him. I reverted his balls back to undescended testicles."

Chuckling and not caring to hide it, Henry said, "Don't give yourself that much credit; you weren't kicking that hard." Trying to sweetly console me, he rubbed my back as I beat myself up about last night.

"He turned green!" I admitted.

"That is invalid information. There was no way in that lighting you could see his face turn green; it's practically impossible to make such an assessment. We have to scratch that statement from the record," he joked, trying to bring light to the situation.

"I hate that you're enjoying this."

"I'm not enjoying it," Henry softened some more and grabbed my hand. "I'm just trying to show you it's not the end of the world."

"It is! I actually liked him, Henry. I felt like maybe we could have had something."

"You still could," he tried to encourage me.

"Henry, pretty sure I burned that bridge the minute my foot connected with his nut sac."

"You never know; he might have liked it…"

"There is something wrong with you," I said, as I threw my blankets off of me and put on my slippers as I headed out toward the kitchen, where Delaney was spinning around. Derk sat at the bar and watched Delaney with dreamy eyes. They would be getting married at some point in time; it was obvious by the way he admired her. If only I had someone like Derk, minus the hideous name.

"There's our little nutcracker," Delaney called out, while pointing at me with her spatula.

"Ha, ha, very funny." I slumped on a stool next to Derk, who put his arm around me in consolation.

"Don't sweat it, Bloom; I'm sure the guy has already forgotten about it."

"Would you have forgotten about a girl with powder coming out of her privates who kicked innocent balls?"

He thought about it for a second and then shook his head no. "I would be posting that on my Facebook any chance I got."

"Derk," Delaney scolded him, but laughed at the same time. What a friend.

"It's going to blow over," Henry cut in, as he poured me a glass of orange juice. "You need to let it go, because you have a date tonight, don't you? With that cat photographer?"

"Oooh, a cat photographer, that seems exciting," Derk cooed next to me.

"He's not just a cat photographer," I corrected everyone. "He occasionally shoots pieces for us. He likes to spend his time traveling and doing photo shoots for travel magazines and has even had some of his photos in *National Geographic*. He helps us out on occasion, just for some easy money."

"World traveler, seems interesting. Is he hot?" Derk asked, while forking a couple of waffles onto an empty plate. He was a giant of a man, like a six-five kind of giant, and he ate like it. He could inhale one waffle in two bites, and by the look of his plate, those weren't his first waffles.

"He's hot," I said, while thinking about Lance. "He's got this whole Justin Timberlake vibe to him, you know, post Ramen Noodle hair."

"Don't knock the noodles; you know it was hot back then," Delaney warned.

I held up my hands in defense, "Just wanted to be clear, that's all."

"They're going bowling," Henry said over the lip of his coffee mug. "Don't you think bowling sounds fun tonight?" he asked Delaney and Derk, whose ears perked up.

"It does. I think it's time we dust off our bowling shoes, don't you think, sweetie?" Delaney asked, while putting some waffles on a plate for me.

"Don't you three even dare."

"Why not?" Henry asked, looking a little hurt.

"I don't need you guys peeking over the ball shelf, staring at me, watching my every move. I already have to deal with meeting his friends; I don't need to think about you three watching me as well."

"We'd be there to help," Henry offered.

"Yeah, a lot of help you were last night."

After drenching my waffles in strawberry syrup, my favorite, I cut them up in small pieces like a child and started eating them, ignoring the glare Henry was giving me. I knew he was just trying to help last night, but all he did was make matters worse once he started the dance-off with Atticus.

Oh, poor Atticus and his balls. I really hoped he was okay and I didn't do any permanent damage.

"Are you mad at me?" Henry asked, as he pulled up a stool

next to me; his warm hand went straight to my thigh.

"No," I sighed. "It's not your fault. It was just bad luck and a need to itch the godforsaken red brick road."

"Is it still bothering you?" Delaney asked, now sitting down with us to chow down on some waffles.

"Not as bad as last night."

"Well, that's a good sign; you should be clearing up soon. Happened to me when I first got waxed too. Remember that, Derk?"

"Yeah, looked like a fucking ant farm grew on her crotch. Couldn't touch her for days."

"Thanks," she admonished. As she chewed on some waffles, she asked, "Any interest from the online site?"

"Oh, I don't know. I forgot about it," I admitted.

With all the action between Atticus and Lance, I completely forgot about Henry's attempt at getting me into the dating world. I hated to admit it, but I was just a tiny bit curious whether men thought I was interesting or not.

"Well, let's see," Delaney said, while grabbing Henry's tablet off the counter. "What was her password again?"

"Take my flower," Henry said with a mouth full of syrupy waffle.

"Oh, that's awesome," Derk laughed. I assumed he knew about my little chastity belt because whatever Delaney knew, Derk knew. It was some kind of couple's code; they knew everything. It was a BOGO when handing out information, you tell one, the other is going to know. I was okay with it, since Derk was a nice guy.

"Oh, my God, sixty-seven responses."

"Are you serious?" I asked, almost choking on my last bite of waffle.

"Yes."

She turned the tablet in my direction, and sure enough, there were sixty-seven requests just waiting for me to read.

"How can I even filter through those?"

"Don't worry. I'm already on it," she said, while scrolling through the requests and deleting the ones she apparently didn't like for me. "Bald, ugly, fat, mole face, sporadic facial hair, bald, loves Nickelback—go bury your head in a hole." She looked up from the tablet and stated, "No friend of mine is going to date someone who listens to Nickelback. No way in hell."

"Agreed," Henry said, while raising his fork to the sky.

"What's wrong with Nickelback?" Derk asked.

All three of us turned our heads and stared Derk down. Delaney took a deep breath and said, "Sweetie, I think for the sake of our relationship, you should rephrase that question."

Derk's eyes bounced back and forth as he looked at all three of us. Finally, he said, "Uh...fuck Nickelback?"

"Yeah!" we all cheered, confusing the hell out of Derk, but instead of pushing his luck, he just shrugged his shoulders and picked at the fruit that was in the middle of the counter.

"So, any good prospects?" Henry asked, while looking over at the tablet in Delaney's hands.

"There is this one guy. His name is Alejandro and seems to be really nice. Look, a picture with his little sister, how sweet."

"Alejandro, that rolls right off the tongue nicely," Derk approved.

"Let me see this guy."

Looking irritated, Henry pulled the tablet away from Delaney and started looking at Alejandro's profile. His brow creased as he read all about my potential date.

"It says here that his job is an artist...that's a hobby not a job, can't trust those guys. Oh, and look, he has a pet iguana...that's stupid."

"There is nothing wrong with a pet iguana," Delaney countered. "He would be perfect for Rosie. Clearly, the guy is handsome, with that thick black hair of his and dark eyes. You know he would romance our girl, and that's what she needs. His Latin love would spice up her life."

"I don't like him," Henry disapproved.

"Well, thankfully, it's not up to you; it's up to Rosie."

Without warning, Delaney snatched the tablet from Henry and handed it to me.

"See for yourself, he's handsome, he looks fun, and you know he would be able to melt the panties right off of you. You would have no problem relaxing around him."

The profile picture on the screen showed a man who seemed to be in his later twenties, wearing a bright teal tank top, showing off his muscles, and a pair of sunglasses on top of his head. The background seemed to be some foreign coastline, where the water was just as blue as his shirt. His smile reached cheek to cheek, and I realized that he could possibly be one of the prettier men I had ever seen. He wasn't rugged; he was more suave.

"He's attractive," I mumbled, as I looked through his profile. I was kind of shocked that such a pretty man was interested in me, but I was flattered to say the least. There was a message in my inbox from him, so I decided to take a look at it.

Hi Rosie,

I couldn't help but write to you after seeing your profile picture. Your red glasses caught my eye, along with those beautiful blue eyes of yours.

After further stalking, I saw that you love tacos, making you a girl after my own heart. I can't get enough of tacos; they are my one and only addiction. If you're not too busy, maybe I could take you out for some amazing tacos not too far from my apartment. I promise you, they are the best tacos in New York City.

What do you say?

Awaiting your reply – Alejandro

"Well, he seems sweet," I blushed.

"He wants to take you out for tacos," Henry admonished.

"How is that sweet?"

"He wants to eat your taco," Derk chuckled to himself.

"Watch it," Henry warned uncharacteristically. "I don't like Alejandro; I don't trust him."

"You don't even know him," Delaney countered, while she gathered everyone's empty plates. "Write him back, Rosie. Set up a date."

I studied Alejandro's profile some more, while Derk cleaned up for Delaney, like the dutiful boyfriend he was.

He seemed nice, like a genuine guy, but what could you really tell from the Internet? He could be a psycho killer in real life, but his profile could say he knitted sweaters for nuns at Christmas time. Should I really give him a chance? And why was Henry so against Alejandro? Was he seeing something I wasn't?

"Why don't you like Alejandro?" I asked, cutting the silence that had fallen in the kitchen.

"He seems…too experienced. I don't want him taking advantage of you," Henry replied.

"You don't think I can handle myself with an experienced person?"

Henry gave me a pointed look and said, "Love, you kicked a guy in the crotch last night, not sure how well you will do under a very nerve-racking situation."

Insulted, I sat back on my stool and looked at Henry. Hurt crossed me as I thought about his words. Yes, I wasn't experienced, but I was pretty sure I could handle myself when put in a situation that I wanted for myself.

"You're an ass," I finally said, as I got up and took Henry's tablet back to my room with me. Alejandro was going to be getting a message.

The minute I walked through my doorway, I shut the door behind me to gain some privacy, but it was stopped by Henry's hand.

"Leave," I said, not bothering to turn around.

"Rosie, I'm sorry. I didn't mean to insult you. I'm just

worried."

"Well, stop worrying, Henry. I can handle myself; I'm not a child."

He took a deep breath and ran his hands through his hair, clearly flustered. "I know you're not a child, I just...God, Rosie, I care about you."

Finally turning around, I set the tablet on my bed and walked toward him. I placed both my hands on his shoulders and said, "I appreciate your concern, but I want a friend, not a big brother. I want you to help teach me what I need to know, not be my knight in shining armor."

"But I like being your knight," he smiled sheepishly.

"I know, but it's time you step back, Henry. I can't have you there for me forever; you're going to move on at some point, maybe with that big breasted lady from last night."

"Charlene? No, she's just fuckable. No substance to her."

"See, that's what I want. Maybe Alejandro is just fuckable, maybe he will be fun enough where I can let loose and gain some experience. I need experience, Henry, because right now, my book is about as dry as my vagina."

Henry's lip twisted in a smile. "I told you I could do something about that for you."

"Get real," I pushed him away, but he grabbed my arms and pulled me into a hug, making my stomach flutter all over again from being so close to him.

"Do you forgive me?" he whispered softly against my hair. How could I not?

"Always." I squeezed him tightly, pressing my cheek to his bare chest.

"Are you really going to write him back?"

"I am."

"Will you tell me where you go at least?"

"Do you promise not to watch me through the window?"

"I can make no such promise, but I can try."

Laughing, I said, "I guess that's the best I can ask for."

Once Henry let go of me, I grabbed his tablet and we sat down on my bed together and wrote Alejandro back.

Alejandro,

You had me at tacos. Let me know when and where.

Ready to munch – Rosie

"You sure it's not too lame?" I asked before sending. It wasn't a very poetic message, but it got the point across.

"No, it's perfect."

"Don't you think munch sounds a bit sexual?"

"Yes, and that's the point," Henry cringed. "Not that I really want you giving out sexual innuendos, but as a friend giving advice, this is perfect."

"Okay, good."

With confidence, I pressed send and just hoped I didn't sound too cheesy.

"I'm proud of you," Henry said.

"Why's that?" I asked, as I walked to my desk and opened up my laptop to the dating website to scope out the other messages.

Henry adjusted his seat on my unmade bed and played with the blankets.

"For putting yourself out there, it's very brave."

"It's all for research," I smirked.

"How is the book coming along?"

"Scratched the whole thing. I don't know if a medieval romance is something I can write."

"Why's that?"

"Well, since I've started this new journey, I've been reading some more contemporary romance and I have to be honest with you, I love it. Contemporary romance is so much different than historical romance. It's a little more edgy, the slang is more up to date and the sex, holy crap, Henry, you should read some of these sex scenes."

"Really?" he asked, looking really intrigued. "Like soft porn?"

"More like hard porn." I leaned forward and spoke animatedly. "The girls like it hard, they like their panties to be ripped off, and they tell the guy they're with when they're going to…" I looked around and whispered, "come, like straight up shout it to the rooftops."

A bellow of a laugh escaped Henry as he held his stomach.

"What's so funny? It's true. And you should read some of the things these girls do. Henry, I read one book where the girl let the guy stick a pencil in her butt hole."

Henry's laughing seized and one of his eyebrows rose in question.

"Rosie, what the hell are you reading? I don't remember downloading any book like that for you."

"It's a teacher/student romance. I know I had mixed feelings about that kind of story, but I just went for it. It seemed interesting, but then things got a little out of control…but still it's fascinating. She liked the pencil in her butt hole; she was holding it for him while he graded her physique. She got an A plus, of course, but still, just fascinating."

"Rosie, you know she could have just held the pencil with her hands, he didn't have to stick it in her butt hole…that seems kind of odd."

"Wait," I stopped him with my hand up and said, "That's not a regular thing?"

"Sticking pencils in people's assholes? No, Rosie, that is not normal."

I sat back in my seat and thought about it for a second. It seemed so normal in the book…there was no hesitation. It was like, oh you're sticking that pencil in my ass, perfect! Like the woman knew her ass was the perfect pencil holder and should be modeled as the modern day pencil holder.

"Well, that seems a little disturbing then. Why would the author write that?"

"How the hell would I know?" Henry laughed. "Do I need to start screening what you read, and honestly Rosie, are you that naive? You know I love you, but a pencil in the ass?"

"I don't know," I shrugged and laughed. "I just learned how to suck a dick on a banana the other day. How am I supposed to know that people aren't supposed to stick things in butt holes?"

"Oh, things can go in butt holes, just not pencils."

"Oh! Like anal plugs!" I said with pride. "She had an anal plug in her butt before she had the pencil. And, you know, I was thinking the other day, when he pulled out the anal plug to replace it with the pencil, do you think it made a popping sound? Like when you pull a cork out of a wine bottle? I'm trying to envision this so called plug and all I can think about is a wine cork."

Visions of corks in butts ran through my mind while I turned and saw Henry running his hands up and down his face, like he was in pain.

"Rosie, you know how to Google, why didn't you just Google what an anal plug looks like?"

"So, it's not a wine cork?"

"For fuck's sake, no, Rosie," he laughed. "An anal plug is thin on one side and thicker on the other, and they come in all colors and sizes."

"Glow in the dark?"

"Probably. I've never used one."

"Oh, so they're not just for girls?"

"No, anyone can stick an anal plug in their ass."

"Interesting," I pondered for a moment, thinking if I could incorporate an anal plug in my book...they seemed interesting.

"Don't even think about it," Henry stopped me. "You're not writing about anal plugs."

"And why not?" I asked defiantly.

"Because you don't even know what a dick looks like in person. You can't go from virgin to anal plug stuffing romance writer. Work your way in, Rosie. Write about stuff you know."

"I know nothing," I said, a little frustrated. "I know that when you kick a man in the crotch, he won't want to see you again."

"That's not true. Atticus may want to call you."

"I made him throw up, Henry."

He nodded and I saw a small smirk spread across his face. I despised him at that moment.

"Yeah, we might want to cut our losses with Atticus and move on. Your date tonight, focus on that and the taco man."

"His name is Alejandro," I corrected, just as a ping went off on my computer, causing me to turn around and see what the noise was.

A picture of Alejandro popped up on my screen along with a message from him.

Hi Rosie,

I'm so glad you wrote me back. How does Monday sound? We can meet at the restaurant.

Alejandro

"Alejandro wrote me back," I squealed. "He wants to go out Monday night. What should I say back?"

A long exhale came out of Henry as he got off my bed and stepped up behind me. His hands rested on my shoulders and he read the message off of my computer.

"For the record, I don't like this guy. He seems too excited."

"And that's a bad thing?" I looked up at him over my shoulder.

"No, but I just don't like him."

"That's very mature of you," I teased. "So, what should I say?"

"Do you want to meet him on Monday?"

"Should I? I don't want to sound desperate?" Henry gave me a pointed look, so I pinched his stomach, making him step back. "I'm not desperate, just…intrigued. So Monday, then?"

"Sure, but you will be telling me where this taco place is, because hell if I'm going to let you go out with this Alejandro and have me not know about it."

"You're too protective," I said, while writing Alejandro back and letting him know Monday worked perfectly.

"Just don't want to see you get hurt." He paused for a second and then spun me around in my chair. He knelt in front of me and held my hands. He took a deep breath and said softly, "You know, Rosie, if you wanted, I could just show you everything myself."

My heart stopped beating in my chest as I tried to comprehend Henry's offer. Was he serious?

"What do you mean?" I asked, my voice breaking.

His brow creased as he thought about his words. He cleared his throat and stood up, putting distance between us.

"Never mind." He shook his head, as if what he was about to say was crazy. Unsure of what to do, he stumbled a bit and said, "I have to go, but make sure you say bye to me before your date tonight. I want to wish you good luck."

With that, Henry left my room, leaving me completely and utterly confused. Did he just offer to show me everything, as in, have sex with me?

Delaney's words of Henry being a cherry chaser kept running through my head; there was no way he was a cherry chaser, and even if he was, he wouldn't want to be with me just because I was a virgin. He wouldn't want to ruin our friendship like that; it was impossible.

I shook the thoughts from my head and went back to my bed where I pulled my Kindle off of my nightstand and started reading about the magnificent pencil holder and her kinky man.

CHAPTER 8
"The North Star"

"I'm telling you, I'm terrible at bowling," I laughed, as Lance and I both looked at the TV that held our scores. I was at a measly fifty-two, and Lance was bowling a one-eighty, which was quite impressive to me.

"At least you look adorable doing it," Lance pinched my chin, making me melt in place.

I was nervous coming into this date, because I honestly didn't know what to expect. I had only met Lance once before, and we barely held a conversation, so to see this fun side of him was different for me; it was intriguing.

We met at the bowling alley, and I was instantly intimidated to see he was with four of his friends, who were all dressed up for cosmic bowling, thankfully, since I wore my tight white shirt, jeans and neon green bra. I fit in with the crowd, perfectly actually, but outside of the bowling alley, I looked like a teenager who spent her spare time hanging out by the light post of the local gas station. Real classy, top notch.

Lance loved my outfit, though, and I had to admit, he looked beyond handsome in his dark jeans and white V-neck shirt. It was simple, yet classic.

"Want to take a break?" Lance asked, as his hand found the small of my back.

"That might be a good idea. My thumb is starting to hurt."

"Aw, you have bowler's thumb." Lance grabbed my thumb and brought it to his lips, where he lightly kissed it.

At that moment, I felt like one of those cartoon characters who started floating in the air while their legs kicked about and hearts sprouted from their heads. A little kiss on the thumb from Lance had me wanting to dance around and fist bump anyone with a hand.

I hated that I was so caught up in the little things…that a small gesture from a man had me shaking and quaking in my shoes, but I've never been romanced. I never really went on dates and never really put myself out there, so it was nice to see I could garner some male attention. I rather enjoyed it.

Lance grabbed my hand, entwined our fingers, and led me to the bowling alley bar, where he helped me up on the barstool. I wasn't someone who frequented bowling alleys very often, but a bowling alley in the city was much different than one in a smaller town. It was fancy and kind of posh, with white leather seating and exposed brick.

Luckily, Lance gave me a heads up that usually the bowling alley had a strict dress code, but once a month they had cosmic bowling night and encouraged bowlers to wear fun colors and white shirts to add to the atmosphere. Otherwise, there was a no athletic wear and white shirt policy. When did bowling alleys become judgmental snobs of a white shirt? Hello, have they seen the classic bowling shirt? Uh, tacky!

"What can I get you?" he asked, while calling the bartender over to us.

"Um, how about a margarita? Can they make one of those?"

"I'm sure they can." When the bartender came over, Lance grabbed my hand and said, "Margarita on the rocks for this little lady, and a Stella on tap for me, thanks."

"Big beer drinker?" I asked, trying to make conversation.

"Love beer. Different craft beers are my favorite. I love traveling around and finding local breweries, little holes in the wall where they make their own brews. I've had some pretty stellar beers from local breweries," he crinkled his nose and continued, "And I've had some real donkey piss too."

A genuine laugh escaped me from the look on his face. "Oh no, that bad?"

He nodded as the bartender set our drinks in front of us. Lance grabbed his beer and took a swig, while turning in his seat to face me better.

"I was in Milwaukee for a sailing boat photo shoot during the summer…"

"There are sailing boats in Milwaukee?" I asked, a little dumbfounded at finding that out. I always pictured Milwaukee as a frigid metropolis, where snowmen and polar bears play friendly games of ice hockey. Apparently not.

"Oh, yeah. Summer in Milwaukee is huge. The city sits right on Lake Michigan, so sailing and speed boats are big during the summer season, as well as music festivals. It's quite a lively city in the summer; if you ever get a chance, I suggest you go. And if you go, I suggest you don't go to the brewery I went to. I can't remember what it's called, but I know exactly where it was because when I was walking downtown, I saw a homeless person peeing on the corner of Michigan Avenue. Instead of passing him and risking the possibility of getting pee all over me, I went into the brewery on the corner to get a drink. Little did I know, the homeless person was most likely helping to make the beer."

"Eck, gross. Did they at least serve pretzels?"

"No," Lance said with outrage. "You would think there would be some sort of pretzel, but there were none. Can you believe that?"

"I can't," I giggled. "So, have you traveled a lot?"

He nodded as he sipped on his beer. "I've been all over the

U.S., and then, of course, outside the states."

"Really? Where?"

"Let's see, I've been to Europe, stuck my head up the center of the Eiffel Tower; I've been to the coastlines of Italy and Greece, as well as saluted the Queen of England. I've also been lucky to travel to Africa, South Africa mainly, and Australia, both very long flights."

"I can imagine. What's been your favorite place?"

He paused and thought about the question, something I admired about him. He really took his time and put thought into his answers.

"I would have to say Greece, there is something about the contrast of the blue of the coast up against the white of the buildings. It is a true photographer's dream being out there. Plus, the culture is exciting. The families are intense, and I like that. I have a close-knit family, so being over there made me think of home."

"It sounds amazing. I wish I could go there someday. I have a passport, but no stamps yet."

"No? Maybe other countries aren't ready for you just yet," Lance said with a wink.

"That or I just haven't had the money saved up for it, but I will. I'll get that stamp."

"Where do you want to go, once you do?"

I took a sip of my margarita that I was really starting to enjoy and said, "Promise you won't make fun of me?"

"Promise," he said, and grabbed my leg to give it a light squeeze. My lady bits shivered from his touch.

"I really want to go to the Icelandic coast. I've always been fascinated with the Northern Lights, and trips up to Iceland are actually quite affordable. I think it would be such a beautiful and fun trip."

"Now, why would I make fun of you for picking Iceland? My buddy went up there for a week and when he came back, he showed me all the pictures he took, and I couldn't have been more jealous. It's gorgeous there."

"It really is, at least from what I've seen from my Googling."

"Now, tell me why you thought I would make fun of you?" his hand went to my hair and started twisting it absentmindedly. Good God, he was pulling out all the stops tonight, touching me in every way possible, and damn if I wasn't falling for it, every single one of them.

"I feel like when you usually ask someone where they want to go, anywhere in the world, they answer someplace exotic. Not many people want to go up to Iceland."

"True," he chuckled. "But that's what makes you so unique; you're not like everyone else, Rosie."

The way he said his statement made it seem like he'd known me for a while, when in fact, we really didn't know each other at all.

"Can I ask you a question?"

"You can ask me anything." He grabbed my hand and brought it up to his lips, lightly kissing my knuckles. His gestures were sweet and sucking me in every time he made one.

"Why did you want to ask me out? I feel like we don't know each other at all, and this date came out of the blue, not that it's a bad thing. I guess I'm just curious is all."

"I can understand that," he answered with a devilish grin. "To be honest, I'm kind of shy, so when I first met you, I brushed you off because I was too damn nervous to go up to you. If you haven't noticed, Rosie, you're drop dead gorgeous, and the first time I ever saw you, I was hooked. Ever since then, I've been trying to get put on another photo shoot with you. It's been a challenge, but once I found out about you writing up the Maine Coon interview, I made sure to be there."

"Really?" I asked, feeling a little flabbergasted.

"Really. I like you Rosie, a lot, and since I'm putting myself out there, I have to tell you, I've read all of your cat articles." An adoring look crossed his face, making me laugh.

"What fine literature you've chosen to read."

"I know more about cats than I would prefer, but I think

you're great at writing, even if some articles are about the most effective ways to clean hairballs."

"Yeah, the pictures for that article were a little intense for my liking."

"They were a bit rough," he nodded and smiled.

Sincerely, I said, "Thank you for reading my articles, even if they are not the most riveting literature ever."

"Hey, I learned something," he shrugged. "Do you want to work somewhere else?"

Starting to grow nervous, since I hadn't really talked about my life aspirations with anyone but Delaney and Henry, I contemplated telling him what I really wanted to do. He seemed like he would be cool with me being a romance novelist.

Sometimes, I was worried what people would think if I told them, told them I was interested in writing sex, writing romance, writing about that all-consuming power called love. I feel like there is a stereotype in the world for people who read romance novels, people depict them as sad ladies sitting in a corner of their house, wearing a torn up sweater while eating chocolates and petting their cats, but that's not the case at all. There is a whole community out there who loves love, who loves romance, and I'm one of them. It's a world I love living in, where there are happily ever afters, the odd girl gets the good looking guy, and where chivalry isn't lost. I know it can't all be true, that life isn't as grand as some novels make it out to be, but I still love every single story because it's an escape from reality, a moment in time where you can daydream of the impossible, where there is a chance of watching true love unfold right in front of you.

Sigh.

"Rosie?"

"Oh, sorry," I shook my head. "I actually am writing a romance novel, well trying to."

"Wow, really? That's pretty cool. Does your hero have glasses and take pictures of cats?"

"Something like that," I laughed, while I finished off my

margarita. "Want to go back to bowling?" I told him I was writing a book, but I didn't think I was comfortable enough to get into the fine details of my riveting novel, because I could see the look in his eyes, he was curious. I was afraid he was going to start talking about sex, and I wasn't prepared for such a thing. I could barely talk about sex with Henry, let alone a guy I was interested in.

"Sure. Do you need some tips to keep your ball from staying out of the gutter?" he teased.

"Probably. I've never really been athletic. I'm surprised I can even pick up the ball."

"It's six pounds," he laughed.

"That's why my arm is tired."

Shaking his head at me, he wrapped his arm around my shoulder and led me back to our lane, where his friends were no longer lounging. They seemed to have dispersed, which was nice because I was enjoying my time with just Lance. When it was all of his friends, I felt quite intimidated.

Like a weirdo, I was fascinated with the white leather seats, which were pristine, and I really wondered how they kept them so clean. They must Scotch Guard the crap out of the seats because there were too many drinks just dying to be spilled all over them. I took note to possibly ask the manager; I wanted their secret.

"Ladies first, Rosie," Lance gestured.

"Alright, I got this."

I walked up to the ball holder and grabbed my bright pink, six pound ball, stuck my thumb in and walked up to the line. I was about to start to walk up to the front of the lane when I felt Lance stand behind me and speak softly in my ear. His voice had chills running up and down my skin.

"Can I give you a pointer?"

"Please," I said a little too breathlessly.

His hands were splayed on my shoulders and his mouth was practically kissing my ear. Gah, Virginia was awakening.

"Do you see those little arrows on the alley? You want to line up your hand with those arrows and make sure your hand flows straight through them. Think you can do that?"

"Seems simple," I replied with some confidence.

"Good. You got this, Rosie." He leaned in more and placed a gentle kiss on my cheek before pulling away. What a flirt!

My entire lady region was alive and awake, letting me know she still existed, and in fact she had a well working libido, which was now spiked, thanks to Lance's little intimate act. Hell, I would be lying if I said I didn't like it. I wanted to actually toss my ball down the alley and run into his arms. I wanted more kisses…and not just on my cheek.

Concentrating on what Lance said to me, rather than dry humping his leg, I brought my arm back and walked up to the edge of the alley. With a strong thrust, I threw my arm forward and released the ball. I watched with my hands linked together as the ball went straight into the gutter.

"Damn."

I turned to look at Lance, who had a giant grin on his face, but was shaking his head as well. He walked up to me and lifted my chin while pulling me into his chest. My hands went instinctively to his hips, where I could feel myself start to shake from the close contact. I wish I could be one of those girls who wasn't affected by close intimacy, but I wasn't. I was nervous, one hundred percent, a sweaty hot mess of nerves.

"That was a good try."

"It was kind of pathetic."

"It kind of was," he chuckled. "You got this next one, though. Remember, straight arm and get lower to the ground…that might help."

"Got it, straight arm and low to the floor."

He rubbed my cheek with his thumb and then pulled away. I wanted to cry and tell him to come back, but I held on to my self-respect, turned around and got my ball, which was just spit out by the crazy ball returning thing. That contraption was scary, visions of my head getting stuck in it frightened me every time I went near it.

With confidence, I got in my stance, looked at the arrows and then started walking toward the alley as my arm started to swing back. I squatted down and threw the ball forward just as I heard a loud rip and a gush of air go straight up to Virginia.

I froze in place as I tried to will time to rewind, because I was pretty sure I'd just split my pants from Virginia to the Great and Powerful Asshole.

Some onlookers might have thought I was freezing my bowling pose by the frozen stature I immediately adopted, but little did they know, I was trying to mentally call up Scotty to beam me the hell out of the bowling alley.

Too bad Scotty was retired now, the bastard.

What the hell was I supposed to do? Did I get up? If I got up, I would have to explain what the hell just happened, and I wasn't sure I was ready for that, but then again, I was wearing a thong and right now, I was squatting, meaning…

Holy shit.

I stood straight as a rod and turned around quickly, hiding my butt from Lance, so only the pins could see the mess that was my backside.

Out of all the days to choose to wear a thong. It was my punishment, it had to be.

There are moments in a person's life where you really think if you died, the situation in front of you wouldn't be better, and that's how I was feeling, because all I could think about was the bleached asshole I had and it lighting up like the damn North Star under the black lights. Wasn't sure if it was possible, but if it was, it would happen to me. With my luck, three kings would be walking through the door any minute now with presents for Virginia, and a camel would be harnessed outside chewing on a bale of hay.

"You got two pins!" Lance cheered as he walked toward me, causing me to walk backward. He couldn't come close to me. How the hell was I going to get out of this? "What's wrong?" Lance asked, concerned. "Careful!" he called out as I continued to back up.

With one wrong step, I felt the grip of my shoe seize and slip on the grease from the alley.

My legs twisted under me, and right when I thought things couldn't get worse, my legs flew out from under me and I fell backward, legs spread and up in the air, exposing my ripped crotch and matching neon green thong.

To hold on that last ounce of self-respect I had left, I clenched my ass cheeks tightly together, just in case the Great and Powerful tried to peek through.

"Oh, shit," Lance said, while grabbing my arms and pulling me into his chest. He walked me over to the seats and crouched in front of me.

I clenched my legs tight and buried my head in my hands.

"I split my pants," I muttered in mortification.

"It's okay," he rubbed the top of my thighs. "Believe me, I've done it too, right in the middle of a photo shoot, where everyone saw my package fall right out of my jeans."

"Your balls?" I asked, peeking through my hands.

Laughing, he nodded. "Yes, my balls. I don't tend to wear underwear, so when I split my pants, everyone got a great view of the hanging twins."

A small smile spread across my face, but I was still mortified. This was something I wouldn't get over easily. I split my pants in front of my date.

"Here, take my cardigan, wrap it around your waist, and we'll get you home so you can change. How does that sound?"

I just nodded my head as I took his cardigan and wrapped it around my waist, wanting to wilt and just sit in a dark hole all by myself.

The date was over. I didn't talk much as we took a cab back to my apartment. I just stared out the window, completely removing myself from the present. There was nothing I could really say; I was mortified for many reasons.

When we pulled up in front of my apartment, Lance kindly told the cabbie to wait as he walked me to my door.

We reached the front of the door and I started pulling off his cardigan, but he stopped me.

"Give it back to me on our next date."

"You want another date?"

"Of course. Do you think a tear in the pants is going to deter me? Come on, Rosie. I'm better than that. I like you, a lot. I kind of think it's cute what happened."

"How is that cute? You saw my Virginia."

Throwing his head back and laughing, he said, "Your Virginia? Oh, that's amazing. And, no, I didn't see your Virginia. I did see a pretty hot piece of underwear, though."

He gathered me closer and pressed his hands on my lower back, bringing me into his chest. One of his hands ran up to my cheek, where he ran his thumb gently.

"See me again?"

"No more bowling?" I asked with a slight smile, warming up from his touch.

"No bowling," he agreed.

I watched as he pulled me in closer and my breath caught in my chest as his head lowered to mine. I quickly wet my lips and pressed my hands against his chest as his lips connected with mine. The hand which was on my back now ran up my neck and into my hair, making every single nerve ending in my body stand on end.

His soft lips played with mine, providing me with confidence, so I ran my hands up his chest and linked my hands together behind his neck to hold on better. I felt him moving me backward and let him as he pressed me against the side of my building and deepened our kiss.

So, I've been kissed before, but nothing like this, nothing that made my toes curl, that made Virginia cry out in joy, that had me wanting to rip the man's clothes off. Was this what it felt like to feel randy? To feel completely out of control? To need a man so badly that you were going to claw his clothes right off?

It was.

Welcome to the real world, Rosie. This was what all those

books I read were talking about, all-consuming passion.

Just when I was settling in for a long night of lips locked on the stoop of my apartment building, Lance pulled away, looking a little dazed...a look I was most likely sporting as well.

He touched my cheek again and said, "I'll call you, Rosie."

I just nodded and watched him walk away, while Virginia squealed with delight. I was so glad she approved.

Once the cab took off, I ran upstairs, into my room and shut my door. I needed to write in my journal, and talking to my friends was something I wanted to avoid at the moment.

I was on such a high, I really didn't want to rehash everything, I just wanted to revel in the kiss I just shared on the stoop of my apartment while I stood under the stars with an incredibly sexy man with...my pants ripped.

June 6, 2014

Pretty sure I almost had an orgasm today just from Lance's kiss. He is so sexy and understanding and sweet. There has to be something wrong with him, because there is no way a guy that amazing could be that perfect, but for now, I won't dwell on what could be wrong because HOLY CRAP, I was just kissed senseless. That kiss made up for an almost shining appearance from the North Star.

Note to self: check pants longevity before wearing them on dates, because they are bound to rip if they are old. Plus, never get asshole bleached again, bad decisions all around.

CHAPTER 9
"Man Milk Mutilator"

    I was able to avoid my roommates all night last night, but now that it was Sunday morning and they were starting to trickle out of their rooms from their slumbers, avoidance was impossible. Henry was wearing a pair of plaid pajama pants...and that was it. His hair was pushed to the side from his pillow, creating a rather hilarious bed head effect. Delaney walked out of her room wearing a long shirt and her pink slippers.

    Together, they traveled like zombies straight to the coffee maker, where there was some fresh brew waiting for them. I was that nice.

    I sat on one of the kitchen stools, watching them while sipping on my own cup of coffee. I waited for the caffeine to touch their lips to see them light up and realize I was in the kitchen, waiting for their questions.

    As usual, Henry was the first one to perk up, since it always took Delaney longer. He rubbed the side of his head and gave me a lazy smile.

"Good morning, love. How was the date? I tried asking you last night, but you were already asleep. I hope everything went well."

I shrugged my shoulders and smiled over my coffee cup.

Henry stopped in his tracks, mug half way to his mouth when he said, "Did you lose your virginity?"

"No! Really, Henry? On the first date?" I laughed at the look on his face.

Relief flashed through his eyes as he settled in next to me.

"From the look in your eyes, you can't blame me for asking. So, what happened?"

"He kissed me," I said with a bright smile, still remembering how it felt to be held by Lance, to have his lips on mine, demanding more.

"Did he kiss your pussy?" Delaney asked from where she was perched on the counter. Her voice sounded like a seventy year old smoker. She had the most amazing morning voice ever. Sometimes, when we were all drunk, Henry and I would try to imitate it, but Derk was the only one who came close to doing justice to the impersonation.

"No, why would you ask that?"

"Just wondering. Didn't know if there were more juicy details than just a kiss."

"It wasn't just a kiss," I replied. "He was sweet and tender…"

"Don't say tender," Delaney held up her hand. "God, I hate that word. And moist. When you're writing, please make sure never to say his tender hands ran up my moist lady folds. God, I gag just thinking about it."

"Okay," I dragged out. "Moist and tender are stricken from my vocabulary. Henry, would you like me to remove any words as well?"

"Choad, that word is nasty."

"Why would I ever use that word?"

"Who knows? You're a loose cannon."

That was true, especially since I was so easily influenced by the books I read. For heaven's sake, before my conversation with Henry, I was thinking about what other things could be held in a woman's butt hole.

"So, anything else happen?" Delaney asked, changing the subject back to the date.

I grimaced as I set my coffee cup down.

"The night was going fantastic…"

"Was going? Uh oh, what happened?" Henry interrupted.

"Let her tell the story," Delaney said, while smacking his shoulder and sitting on the counter next to me, snuggling up for story time.

"The night was going fantastic," I repeated. "I bowled terribly, and he was great, of course." Henry rolled his eyes. "We had a nice conversation at the bar for a bit, talking about traveling and where we would want to go."

"Iceland," Henry said while pointing at me.

"Henry, let her talk," Delaney reprimanded.

"Yes, I told him about Iceland and he didn't judge me. He actually had a friend who went to Iceland and said it was gorgeous. Anyway, we decided to bowl again. Since I was so bad, he thought it would be helpful to give me some pointers…"

"Classic move to get close to you," Henry interrupted again.

"I will cut your balls off if you get in the way of this story one more time," Delaney warned, causing Henry to back off.

Don't mess with Delaney when she was ripe out of bed.

"Coffee," Derk mumbled, as he shuffled out of Delaney's room and into the kitchen.

"Shh!" Delaney said, while pointing to the pot that was already made. Derk wasn't looking much better than Delaney; they must have gone out clubbing, one of their favorite things to do. Right about now, they could win best mug shot if put up against the wall in the police station.

"He was giving you pointers…" Delaney helped lead me on.

"Yes, so I decided to take them, and the first one I tossed landed right in the gutter. I wasn't very successful. I think it's because my thumb was hurting…the ball was kind of small for me, the holes that is. So, he encouraged me some more, stood behind me and waited for me to throw the ball again."

"Holy shit, you threw the ball backwards and tossed it right into his nut sac, didn't you?" Henry said with a giant grin.

"No!" I defended myself.

"Henry!" Delaney said, as she flew across the counter holding up a pen as a weapon.

Laughing, Henry backed up and asked me to continue.

"I didn't throw the bowling ball into his crotch."

"Sorry, but it would only make sense after your date on Friday. You're a ball crusher."

"Semen smasher," Derk chimed in, looking livelier.

"Jiz jostler."

"Man milk mutilator."

"Good one," Henry said, while giving Derk a fist bump.

"Do you want to hear the story or not?" I asked, now getting frustrated.

"Sorry, please proceed, love," Henry said with an endearing look. Frustrating man!

"So, I was throwing the ball forward, and as I bent down to release, my pants ripped from crotch to ass, right on the seam."

My friends sat silent and stared at me, not making a move to say anything, so that's when I showed them my pants that were folded on the counter. I shook them out and stuck my hand through the gaping hole in the crotch to prove my point.

Delaney was the first to crack as she busted out in laughter, followed by Derk and Henry, who grabbed the jeans from me and inspected them.

"Only you," Henry shook his head while examining the crotch. "What did you do?" he asked, clearly concerned, but with a little amusement still left in his voice.

"Well, clearly, I was mortified and stood there for a second, bent over, hoping nothing was showing, and that's when I remembered I was in a black light situation with a freshly bleached butthole…"

"Wait, what?" Derk asked, while looking over at Delaney. "You made her bleach her butthole? Why would you do that?"

Delaney looked down at her nails and said, "There is too much butthole talk in this apartment. Honestly, can't we be adults and talk about something else?"

"No," Derk said, matter-of-factly. "Why did she get her butthole bleached?"

"I didn't tell her to do it; Marta did."

Derk shook his head and took a drink from his coffee. "I can't wrap my head around that right now. Bloom, tell us why it mattered about your bleached ass."

"Duh, I didn't want it lighting up for the world to see under the black lights."

It made perfect sense to me, but apparently Henry, Delaney and Derk thought I was joking, because at the same time, they all threw their heads back and roared with laughter while grabbing onto their stomachs.

"Please don't tell me you think the black lights would have made that thing glow," Delaney offered.

"I don't know. They might have."

"Rosie, your asshole was bleached, not dipped in radioactive materials. That is the most ludicrous thing I've ever heard. Please don't tell me you actually believed that."

I just shrugged my shoulders, because frankly, I was deathly scared of things lighting up down there from the black lights. I had no clue what Marta did to me. For all I knew, she could have pierced the damn thing; I wouldn't have felt it, not after the ass ripping she gave me right before.

"That's beside the point," Henry cut in. "I want to know what you did."

Taking a deep breath, I continued. "Lance noticed something was wrong immediately, so he started to come toward me, which I didn't want, given my predicament, so I backed up into the alley and slipped on the grease they use to help the balls roll, falling straight on my ass and exposing my ripped jeans for Lance. Gave him a front row seat actually."

"Oh, Jesus," Henry shook his head, while Delaney and Derk tried to contain their smirks.

"Yeah, he was pretty sweet about it, though. He told me about a time he split his pants and then he gave me his cardigan so I could walk out of the bowling alley with a shred of dignity. He brought me back here, and that's when he kissed me outside our apartment. It was fantastic."

"Besides the jeans ripping and exposing Virginia to Lance on the first night, I would say you had a good date," Henry said.

"We did. He asked me to go out again."

"Do you want to see him again?" Delaney asked, while Derk sidled up next to her to place a hand on her bare thigh.

"I do," I admitted, wanting what Delaney had with Derk. "I'm just nervous for two reasons. First of all, I have that date with Alejandro tomorrow. Do I cancel it or do I still go on it?"

"You have no commitment to Lance, you aren't exclusive, so I say still go on the date," Delaney said. "Right, Henry?"

Henry was looking down at his coffee mug as if he was in serious thought.

"What?"

Rolling her eyes, Delaney repeated herself. "Rosie can still go on a date with Alejandro tomorrow."

"Ehhh, no. I don't think that's a good…"

"Shut up," Delaney cut him off. "You're only saying that because you don't like Alejandro, which is just so weird, since you were the one who set up her online dating account. You really only have yourself to blame." She turned to me and said, "You're going out with Alejandro tomorrow. What's the second issue?"

Feeling a little awkward, especially since Derk was in the room and Henry was being weird, I shifted in my seat and finished my coffee before continuing.

"Things got pretty heated with us last night. He was very touchy. I liked it, don't get me wrong, but I feel like if I go on another date with him, he's going to want to step it up a notch."

"Don't you want that?" Henry asked.

"Yes, but I don't know if I'm ready. I mean, what if he pulls his pants down?"

"What do you mean?" Henry asked. "Do you think guys just enter a room and pull their pants down?"

"Maybe," I shrugged. "I started this new book and the guy walks in the room all the time with his pants off. What if that happens to me? What if he pulls his pants down and starts pelvic thrusting in my direction. What do I do? Do I just open my mouth? Or do I spread my legs?"

"Jesus," Henry said, while running his hands through his hair. Shamelessly, I watched as his torso flexed with his movements. He was my friend, but I was still allowed to admire. "Love, listen to me closely. If Lance walks in the room and just pulls his pants down, you need to leave, because what dude just pulls his pants off? That's fucking weird. And, do you open your mouth? Seriously?"

Laughing, I said, "I just want to make sure I do the right thing."

"Do not open your mouth if a dick comes flying at your face."

"But you told me guys like blow jobs."

"They do," he responded, "But you only give him a blow job if you want to, not because he's tapping you on the cheek with his dick. Jesus, you were so sheltered."

"Okay, so let's say he pulls his pants down and I want to give him a blow job. How do I know if I'm doing it right?"

"We went over this the other day," Henry said, while grabbing another banana and flipping it at me. "Show us what you've got."

"I'm not sucking on this banana in front of all of you to judge me," I stood my ground; I had my limits.

"I'll help," Delaney said, while getting off of the counter and grabbing a matching banana. "This will be easy, given the size of this. It doesn't even come close to my man, right babe?"

Derk winked at her and said, "You've got that right, gorgeous."

"Derk, come over here; let's hold the bananas for the girls, so they can fully use their hands. Grab the base like this," Henry said. "Love, pretend my fist is the balls, okay?"

"This is so ridiculous."

"Just imagine," Henry continued. "Once you master the blow job, you will be able to write a blow job into your book without even thinking; it will come, no pun intended, so naturally. Don't you want that, love?" His voice was joking, but I knew he was trying to help, and that's what I loved about him, he was always trying to help, no matter what the task was.

"Fine, but I swear to God, if something ever happens with one of these guys, you keep your mouths shut. I don't want them knowing I practiced on a banana."

"Promise, this stays between us, right you guys?" Henry asked.

"Yes," both Delaney and Derk answered together.

"Okay, where should I start?" I asked, while looking down at the banana Henry was clutching.

"Taking your shirts off would be job one," Derk said, while staring down at Delaney.

"Dude," Henry chastised him. "No, shirts stay on." Henry turned toward me and said, "Remember what we talked about? Start there."

Leaning forward, I looked at the banana and shook my head in disbelief. Was I really about to suck off a banana? I wanted to learn, and if I was put in a situation where I was with Lance or even Alejandro, I didn't want to fumble around. I wanted to have at least a small piece of confidence, so that was why I found my lips wrapped around a banana while pretending Henry's fist was the balls.

"That's perfect," Henry said. I looked over at Delaney and noticed her and Derk were lost in their own little world while she pleasured the banana and looked up at Derk, enticing him.

"We're done with this," Derk said, tossing the banana aside

and grabbing ahold of Delaney. He led her out of the kitchen and back to her bedroom with Delaney giggling the entire time.

I pulled away and looked up at Henry. "This is so ridiculous. People don't practice on bananas."

"You can practice on me," Henry wiggled his eyebrows.

"You keep offering, Henry, when are you going to realize it's never going to happen?"

"You'll say yes one day, love."

"Okay," I rolled my eyes. "Back to the banana. What about a condom? I read that the guys like it when the girls put the condom on for them. Is that true?"

"Are we done with sucking the banana?"

"I don't know, just seems weird."

"Just do it real quick, and then we'll talk about condoms."

"Fine," I grabbed ahold of Henry's fist and started to lightly massage it, while I ran my tongue along the ridge of the banana and then down the underneath of the banana until I hit Henry's fist. I licked his finger while laughing, and then went back up just like Henry said. Once I returned to the tip of the banana, I pulled the circumference of it into my mouth and started sucking. I looked up at Henry who had hazy eyes, and that's when I glanced down at his crotch to see that he was excited. Henry, my Henry, was excited. He caught my eyes and pulled away, but not ashamed.

Shrugging his shoulders, he said, "That was hot."

A small smile crossed my face while I tried to avoid eye contact with his arousal. "I didn't get to the humming part."

God, I felt so awkward, and I hated, absolutely hated the fact that Henry was so comfortable with his sexuality that he could just sit there, aroused, and be okay with it.

"I'm sure when you hum, you will be just fine. There's nothing to it." He winked and then left for his bedroom, while shifting his pants around a little. When he returned shortly after, I couldn't help but glance down at his crotch, and to my dismay, he was already settled down by the time he came back out. I apparently got him excited, but not that excited, not that I was trying. It just would have been nice to see him harder for longer.

What the hell was I saying? No, I didn't want to see him hard at all. Good Lord. I needed to start getting a grip. All the new romance novels in my life and sex talk had my mind wandering.

"Here," Henry said while handing me a small packet that said magnum on it. I wasn't completely dense, I knew what a magnum condom was...I watched TV. The fact that Henry just handed me one made me think he must be...

"Stop staring at my dick," Henry said, catching me off guard.

"Sorry," I said, embarrassed all to hell. "It's just, this is a magnum condom," I practically whispered, making Henry chuckle and whisper back.

"I know. I wear them all the time."

I just stared at him, because just about now, things got personal. Yeah, I sucked a banana while he held it, something I would block out of my memory, but right now, I was holding his condom and that was more personal than anything we had done together. It almost felt like I was holding his penis in my hands, which I knew wasn't true, but still, I couldn't help but think of it that way.

"Rosie, it's a condom, not a bomb you have to dismantle. Unwrap it and put it on the banana."

"Why can't guys just do this themselves?" I mumbled, as the packaged proved to be a little harder to open than I expected. "They should make these easier to open," I struggled.

Just as I tore open the package, the condom flew in the air and landed right in Henry's coffee, which was sitting on the counter.

I smiled up at Henry and said, "Good thing we aren't using this for real, or else you'd be having a coffee cock."

I giggled too much at my lame joke. Henry just studied me with that questioning look of his, as if he was trying to read me. I didn't like that look; it always made me nervous.

He plucked the condom out of the coffee and wiped it off on his pants. He gave it to me and then looked down at the banana.

Carefully, he showed me how to roll it on and told me all about the process and how to make it fun for the guy as well by teasing him slowly. He also told me if I become really experienced, I could roll it on with my mouth while taking in the guy's length, but that seemed too intense.

All I could envision was getting the condom stuck in the back of my throat and dying from choking on said condom. I could see my tombstone now. Rosie Bloom, died from affixation of a condom. Her last words were, "watch me put this on."

Yeah, not the way I wanted to go, so I thought I'd steer clear of the old mouth trick.

"That seems pretty easy."

"It is. Just roll it down," Henry confirmed. "Now, a guy should be well-trimmed downstairs, but if he isn't, make sure you avoid getting the rubber all up in his pubes. That shit would hurt."

"Wait, so I go and get waxed to hell, but a guy can show up with hairy berries and that's okay?"

"It's not okay. That shit is nasty, but yeah, some guys think it's manly to have hair protruding from every wrinkle of their nut sacs."

"Eck, gross. Doesn't it get sweaty down there?"

"Yeah, massively sweaty sometimes, so if a guy has a bush, I would consider moving on; you don't want to deal with that."

Noted, I thought. What if Lance had a bush? Maybe that was his flaw. If that was the one and only flaw he had, I was pretty sure I could deal with it, because all he would need was a little feminine encouragement.

"Do you have hair down there?" I asked Henry. "You have this little happy trail," I pointed out. "So, does that mean you don't trim?"

Henry gave me a pointed look and said, "Love, does it look like I would be a guy carrying around a massive pile of burnt spaghetti with my balls?"

"No, but sometimes people surprise you."

With a smirk, he grabbed his waistband and pulled it down so

I saw the very top of his pubic region, and it was completely clean. The only hair he had was a well-trimmed happy trail, which I thought was incredibly sexy.

"No hair, love, and don't tempt me, because I will show you the goods if you keep peeking at me like that."

The room started to grow thick once again with this unannounced sexual tension between Henry and me as he lowered his waistband to the danger zone. My heart rate picked up, and I found it hard to breathe as I took in everything he had to offer. His chest rose and fell as he watched me stare at him. I felt the need to throw myself at him, to run my hands down his chest and past his waistband. I've never felt such a strong urge to take Henry in my hands before, but I'd be damned if I didn't want him right there and then.

"Not necessary," I cleared my throat and turned around, trying to shake my naughty thoughts away. "I should probably get in the shower and get some writing done today. I have some things I want to test out. Wish me luck?"

Looking deflated, Henry gave me a soft smile and said, "Good luck, love. If you need help, let me know. You can use my dick as your model." Always trying to lighten the mood.

"That's okay, but thank you, Henry. Your undying willingness to help has not gone unnoticed."

"Anything for you, love." Henry pulled me into his chest and I instinctively wrapped my arms around him, while resting my cheek on his bare skin. His back muscles flexed under my hands, and I loved the way his taut chest muscles felt against me.

I was really losing it.

He kissed the top of my head and said, "You know, you really don't have to go out with Alejandro…"

"Stop," I laughed. "I'm going, so get over it."

"You're telling me where those tacos are." He pulled away and pointed at me.

"Keep this up and you will know nothing!"

"Watch it, young lady. I'm not opposed to tying you up and

keeping you here so you can't go."

"Will you spank me if I get sassy?" The moment the words left my lips, I covered my mouth in shock.

Henry chuckled and shook his head. "Those books are starting to have an influence on you. I like it. In all seriousness, I'm glad you had a good time last night and was able to recover from the pants ripping."

"Me too. Thanks, Henry."

"Anything for my red brick road, man milk mutilator, pants splitting girl."

CHAPTER 10
"The Pussy Cat Posse"

"Do you know where you're going yet?" Henry asked into the phone.

"No, Henry, I don't, and I'm busy right now. If I have any chance of making this date tonight, I have to finish this article."

"What's it about?" he asked casually, as if I didn't just tell him I was on a deadline.

Blowing out a frustrated breath, I answered him, "It's about secrets your cats want you to know."

A short snort came out of Henry. I couldn't blame him, reading into a cat's psyche and trying to write a well-respected article about it was next to impossible.

"Tell me one secret."

"Well, cat's don't see us as a different species; they see us as larger, useless cats."

"Like cats aren't useless themselves," Henry chuckled.

"They, of course, think they are superior and consider us

humans to be inadequate when it comes to our cat abilities. That's why they lick us with their sandpaper tongues."

"God, I love your job," Henry said with amusement.

Someone spoke to him in the background, something unintelligible, but I knew what was coming next.

"I've got to go, love. Promise me you will tell me where you're going."

"Yes, now go do your professional work. I have some cat hair to gather and braid into a rug over here."

We said our good byes and hung up. Talking to Henry on the phone during the workday always helped reenergize me, especially when I felt a writer's block coming along.

For the article I was writing, I had to note fifteen secrets, and at the moment, I only had ten. I had two hours to write five more before I had to leave for my date. I would be working late, but as long as I got everything done before my date, then it didn't matter.

I was curious as to why I hadn't heard from Alejandro yet, made me wonder if he had another date. I still hadn't heard from Lance, which terrified me, because he said he would call me, but Henry told me he was doing the typical guy thing and waiting a couple of days to contact me. According to Henry, he was playing it cool. I would prefer for Lance not to play it cool, since I split my pants right in front of him.

Because I was so nervous about the date being cancelled, I decided to check my dating profile to see if he left me a message. Last night, I spent a good portion of my time weeding out all the creepers who messaged me, Henry looking over my shoulder every step of the way, naturally.

His reasoning was he was the one who got me involved in the website, so he wanted to make sure I was picking respectable men to take me out on dates. There was one guy on there that caught my eye, his name was Greg and was very sweet when he messaged me. He talked about his dog and how he loved to take him on walks in the park across the street. Henry thought the guy was a "cheesedick" as he called him, but I thought he was sweet, so secretly, I messaged him back last night.

Did I feel like a bit of a floozy messaging multiple men? Just a little, but I told myself I was keeping my options open. It was better to have options, and to be honest, I didn't have a commitment to any of them, and it wasn't like I was sleeping with all of them. I'd only kissed one and kicked one in the crotch; I would hardly call that getting around. More like taking out the male population, one kick to the crotch at a time.

I opened up my dating profile and saw four messages in my inbox. Like a giddy schoolgirl, I opened up the message portion of the website and saw messages from Alejandro, Greg, and two new guys. One was in a completely different language, so I deleted that one, and the other message was from a guy named Kyle. The subject was titled, "Hey, Baby Boo."

I snorted and opened the message. The computer took a second to upload the message, but when it did, Kyle's massive dick popped up on the screen with a bow wrapped around the base of his cock. There was a message attached.

Rosie,

Wrapped up a present for you. What do you think? This dick could be yours with one little yes.

Kyle

"Eeep!" I screamed, just as Jenny walked in my office.

"Watcha looking at?"

"Nothing," I practically flew out of my chair, trying to cover everything up that was on my screen. I wasn't much of a looky-loo when it came to the male genitalia, but recently, I'd taken a second to study the phallic member on occasion. For research, of course.

"Oh, you're so looking at something," Jenny said, while coming around my desk and moving my hands. "Holy crap, what the hell kind of porn are you looking at? That cock is big!"

"It's not a porn site, and can you please lower your voice? I don't want Gladys coming in here with her cane and bashing my head in for having a cock in her office."

Gladys was our esteemed leader at the magazine, glorified cat lady, and possible lesbian because not one man worked in the office, and if we even spoke of the male species, she got all huffy around us. The only males allowed in the office were the cats, and Sir Licks-a-Lot was the ringleader.

"Well, share, what's with the dick?"

"Some guy sent me a picture of himself on this dating website. Clearly, I won't be responding."

"Why not? He looks yummy."

"Jenny, all you can see is his penis."

"Exactly, what else do you need to see?"

"You're impossible. It's a no for this guy," I said, while taking one last look at the throbby looking meat sword. I deleted his message and wondered, did all dicks look that veiny up close? It seemed like his dick was being stretched to its limit. Was that really what a boner was like?

"You're missing the dick, aren't you?" she asked, mistaking my thinking for longing.

"No, that thing was too much." Wanting to change the subject, I asked, "Is there something you need?"

"No," she shook her head. "Just wanted to see how you were since the whole kick to the crotch situation."

"I'm fine. I actually went on a date Saturday night and have a date tonight. I feel bad for Atticus, but I can understand why he wouldn't call me back. I don't hold it against him."

"He had a good time. He said he was going to call you," Jenny said with a cringe.

"It's alright, Jenny, you don't have to lie to me. I know the boy is in hiding. He wants nothing to do with me."

"That's not entirely true. He's out of town right now. But I think he planned on calling you when he got back."

"Sure," I rolled my eyes and looked back at my computer. I

opened up Greg's email and smiled to myself when a picture of him and his dog popped up. Greg had blonde hair and brown eyes, almost had a Bradley Cooper type feel to him. He was quite attractive and his dog was some kind of Australian Shepherd.

"I can see you're busy, just wanted to make sure you were okay after what happened Friday night."

"Thanks, Jenny. I'm okay. I have a date tonight that I'm looking forward to, so it makes up for my rampant feet."

"Are you done with that article?" Gladys croaked from the hallway as she walked by with her limp and strangely grey hair.

"Almost," I called back.

"Good, have it on my desk no later than six."

With a cough that almost sounded like the clearing of a hair ball, she thumped back to her office while holding a cat to her side, Mr. Wigglebottom.

"These are terrible working conditions," Jenny whispered to me before leaving me, making me laugh.

It was true. There were too many cats, Gladys was a loose cannon, just carrying cats around the office by their scruff. And then there was the bullying, the fact that we were all tortured and abused by Sir Lick-a-Lot and his posse. The urge to write my book became more prevalent with each passing day. I felt comfortable with my plot. It was a going to be a New Adult story about two college friends who fall in love with each other after they graduate, kind of an ode to my relationship with Henry, minus the falling in love part.

Before I went to finish my article, I took a quick look at Greg's message and then Alejandro's.

Hey Rosie,

Here is Bear and me at the beach in Delaware. It's gorgeous there. Bear loves running up and down the beach with his favorite Frisbee in his mouth. It's not often he gets to have free range, since we live in the city, but when we have the space, I let him run free. He's always good about coming back, so no need to worry.

  I see that you work at a cat magazine. Does that mean you're a cat person? I really hope not. I don't hate cats, but come on, how could you not love a dog better? They would do anything for you.

  I know it's kind of early, but I would love to meet you in person. Are you free Friday night? If I'm too abrupt, just let me know. We can talk more about the small things until you're comfortable.

  Hope you're having a great day, Rosie.

Greg

  God, he was so cute. I wrote him a quick note back, letting him know I was free Friday. Might as well tack on one more date, since I hadn't heard from Lance, and Atticus was out of the picture.

  After quickly sending the message to Greg, I clicked over to Alejandro's message, where he gave me the directions for where to meet. We had a date for six, and if I was going to make it, I had to bust ass and get this article done. Thankfully, I brought a change of clothes in case I didn't have time to make it back to my apartment, which was what seemed to be happening.

  I spent the next hour and a half writing and rewriting the last five secrets a cat keeps from you. The whole time I refrained from swearing and talking to my walls about what a stupid article it was, but I powered through and was able to print out a copy and put it on Gladys's desk, who was passed out at the moment with a cat sleeping on her rather large breasts.

  I tiptoed out of her office and went back to mine, where I grabbed my bag of clothes to change into and went into the bathroom down the hall from my office.

  Delaney had helped picked out an outfit for me. She said Alejandro would probably want to see me in something sexy and red, so we went with a pair of tight black skinny jeans, black heels, and a red tank that was cut low on my chest.

  Changing in record time, I grabbed my items and checked

myself out in the mirror. My hair was already curled, so I just added a black headband and touched up my makeup. I also added a pop of red lipstick to go with my shirt. The overall look was perfect. I was pretty sure Alejandro was going to be impressed. Now I just had to get out of the office without getting cat hair all over my pants.

I gathered my items and opened the bathroom door to leave, but stopped in my tracks when I spotted Sir Licks-a-Lot with his pussy cat posse sitting behind him, just staring at me.

Instantly, I was transported to West Side Story, where the Jets walked the streets and snapped their fingers as they scared people away.

I swear I saw Sir Licks-a-Lot lift his paw and start snapping as he stared me down, eying the black of my pants.

"Don't you even think about it," I warned. "I have a date, and I can't have cat hair all over my pants; I didn't bring a lint roller."

Sir Licks-a-Lot lifted his paw at me while letting out a hideous meow. Pretty sure he just flipped me off, just before he started walking toward me with the pussy cat posse following closely behind.

"Don't," I grew panicky as the walls of the hallway started to close in. Was I really this terrified of a cat?

Considering the look in Sir Licks-a-Lot's eyes, I was; I was deathly terrified of what the crazed feline might do.

"Psssst," I started saying, while swinging my bag back and forth and walking forward. I repeatedly told myself to show no weakness. He could smell weakness. "Psssssst! Shoo, get out of here, you demon."

"Meow, rarara," Sir Licks-a-Lot responded, while crouching down in a hunting position.

"No!" I shrieked like a lunatic and took off running toward them, trying to use the element of surprise. The pussy cat posse scampered away, but Sir Licks-a-Lot held his ground and leapt in the air, right at my crotch with his claws out. With the best reflexes I had, I moved my bag in front of me, just in time to block Sir

Licks-a-Lot.

"Ha, nice try, you bastard," I said, while walking toward my office.

It wasn't until he clawed my hand that I realized he'd attached himself to my bag like a piece of Velcro and held on for his damn life.

"Ack, get," I yelled at him, while shaking my bag, but he held on strong. I didn't have time to fight with the beast, so I tossed the clothing bag to the side, with him attached, grabbed my purse from my desk, and sprinted toward the lobby, where I frantically pressed the elevator button. I turned toward my office and saw Sir Licks-a-Lot peek his head out of my doorway and spot me. Like a predator, he started walking toward me with only thoughts of spreading mounds and mounds of cat hair on my pants.

"Come on, come on," I spoke to the elevator as he drew closer.

The magical bing of the elevator door sounded off and the doors opened. Quickly, I got in and started pressing the lobby button as quickly as possible. The doors started to shut and that's when I called out to Sir Licks-a-Lot.

"Ha, ha, you little shit, nice try! You and your pussy cat posse can go to hell."

Just as the last words flew out of my mouth, the elevator doors closed and I rested against the wall.

"Interesting work environment," a deep voice sounded from the other side of the elevator, scaring the ever living piss right out of me.

My body flew against the side, and my hand held onto my chest, right where my heart was beating at a rapid pace.

"Oh, my goodness, I didn't see you there," I said to a dark-haired man wearing a suit and eyeing me suspiciously.

"Sorry, I suppose. Should I warn you next time you enter an elevator?"

"No, sorry, I was just distracted."

"By that terrifying cat? I can see why. I'm guessing you work at *Friendly Felines.*"

"I do, unfortunately," I admitted and shrugged my shoulders. "It pays the bills, but sometimes, like tonight, I wonder if I would be better off being a waitress. I wouldn't have to deal with demon-possessed cats."

"Yes, but you wouldn't be able to meet strange men in the elevator like me," he smiled a very bright white smile.

"Is that a pick up line?" I asked, slightly confused.

"Was it that bad?" he winced.

"No, I think I just might be dense," I laughed.

He held out his hand and said, "Phillip."

"Rosie," I replied, shaking his strong and very large hand.

"What a beautiful name, Rosie. How come I've never met you in the elevator before?"

"I normally don't work this late, but I had a deadline and procrastinated too much today. So, here I am, leaving the office late."

"Makes sense. Why were you running away from that cat? You seemed slightly crazy, yelling at it through the crack of the elevator doors."

Laughing, I replied, "I didn't want to get cat hair all over my black pants. I forgot my lint roller."

Normally, I would rather drop dead than talk to a guy in an elevator, only because I've been extremely shy my entire life when it came to the opposite sex, but with my new goal in life, I was feeling more confident. Hence, I was able to carry on a conversation without sweating a pool for the cats in the office to swim in.

Nodding in understanding, he eyed my pants, and then my entire outfit. His perusal sent a wave of heat through my body. He wasn't very subtle at all.

"Wouldn't want to ruin those pants."

What was I supposed to say to that? Instead of coming up with something intelligent to say, I giggled like an idiot and waited for the doors to open.

Once the doors opened, I looked back up at Phillip, smiled cordially, and then took off toward the subway.

I heard his steps following behind me, causing me to sweat instantly. I didn't like people I barely knew following me. Visions of him pulling me into a dark alley and having his way with me crossed through my mind. I went to reach for my phone when I realized I'd left it up in my office.

"Hey," Phillip called from behind me.

"Please don't steal me," I said, while cringing and putting my hands up.

"What?" he stopped in his tracks.

I peeked through my hands and noticed he was holding onto the piece of paper that held my directions.

"You, uh, dropped this."

Feeling like a complete moron, I took the paper and apologized. "I'm sorry. I just…I have an overactive imagination."

"So, you thought I was going to steal you? Do people even steal grown adults?"

"Maybe?" I asked.

A small smile spread across his face before he said, "Well, I'll keep an eye out for such a thing. Have a good time at Manny's. They have the best tacos."

"Thanks," I said, as I glanced down at the paper. "Any taco suggestions?"

"I'm a real man and go with the beef tacos, but I heard their fish tacos are good too. Watch out for their margaritas, though. They are good, but can knock you on your ass."

"Got it, thank you, Phillip, and sorry I'm such a freak."

"You're not a freak, Rosie. You're quite the opposite. Hope to see you around."

He waved a small good bye and then took off toward the curb and hailed a cab. He moved with such confidence, it was hard not to watch him. For some reason, I almost wished it was Phillip I was going to have tacos with, because he seemed like he would be good company, plus he was very attractive. I could see myself really liking him.

Shaking my thoughts, I followed the directions to Manny's. It didn't take too long, it was a quick ride and a couple of blocks' walk. I arrived just on time.

The restaurant was quite quaint. It had some twinkle lights hanging outside and the inside was vibrant with orange, yellow, and red gracing the walls. There was a bar, where the infamous margaritas were made, that was lined against one side of the wall and there were big string lights hanging from the ceiling, crisscrossing from wall to wall, providing a lovely ambiance.

In Alejandro's letter, he said he would be wearing a black sweater, so I looked around for the man I remembered from the profile picture sporting a black sweater.

"Hello, Rosie," a deep, very accented voice came from behind me. I turned to see Alejandro standing behind me, holding a single rose and wearing a black sweater. The V-neck of the sweater showed off some chest hair, but nothing that was too distracting, and his hair was slicked back, giving me a great view of his deep brown eyes. He was a Spanish dream.

"Alejandro?" I asked, while gulping. This man almost seemed too exotic for me, with his intoxicating after shave, deep sultry voice, and suave appeal.

"Yes, querida. Don't you recognize me?"

"I do. I just wasn't expecting for your voice to be so sexy."

Oh, my God, did I just say that?

A devastating smile crossed his face at my compliment.

"Come," he demanded as he grabbed my arm and led me to a table in the back, where there was plenty of privacy. His warm touch had me shivering in place as he guided me. His strong hand held on tightly, not applying too much pressure, just enough to let me know he was taking control.

"Here, querida, let me pull this chair out for you."

Like a gentleman, Alejandro pulled out my chair for me and helped me sit down. Once he was satisfied with my seating, he took his own seat across from me. My back was toward the front of the restaurant, so I could only focus on him. I wondered if he did this on purpose.

"I'm so honored you decided to come to dinner with me."

"Thank you for asking. This place is charming," I added, while looking around.

"Manny's is my favorite restaurant."

A very pretty waitress came up to us to take our order. Her hair was black and styled in a long French braid with a flower behind her ear. She was gorgeous, and when I turned to see how Alejandro was reacting to her, I was surprised to see his eyes were locked on mine.

"Can I get you two something to drink?"

"Two margaritas on the rocks with salt, please," Alejandro ordered without taking his eyes off of me. Once the waitress left, he asked me. "I hope you like margaritas."

"I do," I admitted, but felt a little leery about the order, since Phillip told me they hit you hard. I swore to myself that I would only be having one. I wanted experience in my life, but not drunken with a total stranger experience.

"Mind if I order us tacos as well?"

"By all means, you're the expert."

The waitress returned at a speedy rate with our margaritas, and I listened as Alejandro ordered out tacos in Spanish. The way the words rolled right off his tongue had me leaning on my hand and just staring at the dark and exotic man.

When the waitress left, Alejandro turned to me and said, "Tell me, Rosie, why is such a beautiful senorita as yourself on a dating website? I bet millions of men are lined up to date you."

Flattery, I knew it when I heard it, and damn if I didn't fall for it every time.

"It's hard to meet guys in New York," I lied. I didn't want him to know that a week ago I was a hermit living in my room and daydreaming about a man's touch rather than experiencing it.

"Si, this is true, no? The dating scene is a difficult one. I, myself, find it hard to meet a genuine woman, a real woman like yourself, Rosie. Now, tell me about these gatos."

"Gatos?" I asked, trying to understand his mix of English and Spanish.

"You know, gato. Eh, what's the word, I'm drawing a blank. You know, meow," he said in a cute voice, making me giggle.

"Oh, cats."

"Si, cats. The word escaped me. Tell me about the cats."

"Nothing really to say about them. They're annoying and take up my entire work life. I avoided a cat hair confrontation with the ringleader right before I got here. He was trying to make a mess of my pants, but I was able to outsmart him."

"It seems like you don't like these cats," he chuckled.

"No, they are not my favorite, but some of them are nice."

"So, there are cats in your office?"

Not the most romantic conversation I ever had, but I took a couple of sips of my margarita and proceeded.

"Yes, there are too many. Our boss, Gladys, thinks it's necessary to live in an environment of cats when writing about them."

"That must be…smelly at times," he cringed.

"Oh, there's a whole room for them to do their business. I stay as far away from that room as possible. The poor intern has to deal with it."

"Intern?"

"Yes, umm, they're usually students in college who volunteer their time for work experience. Something good to put on the resume."

"Ah, I see. So poop scoop is good for the resume," he teased, making me laugh.

"Sometimes, you have to take what you can get."

"I'm glad I'm not an intern then."

Sucking on my straw, I pulled away and said, "So what do you do, Alejandro?" I knew what he did; it was on his profile, but I was trying to stray away from cat talk.

He casually sipped his drink and maintained eye contact with me while he spoke; it was quite impressive, actually.

"I'm an artist. My loft apartment is actually right around the corner. If you're comfortable with me later on, I can show you some of my pieces."

Weirdly enough, I was comfortable with him, even though he could be abrupt at times.

"That sounds wonderful. What aesthetic do you work with mostly?"

"Oils, only oils. I find mixing the colors and working with the thick paint gives me more movement on the canvas."

"I'm sure your art is just dreamy."

Dreamy? I looked down at my drink and noticed I was almost finished with it. Phillip was right, they were good, but I could already feel it sneaking up on me. Time to slow down.

"I've never heard dreamy, but I do have a gallery in Soho."

"Do you? Wow, so you must be very good."

"I do the best I can," he said, being modest, obviously, if he had a gallery in Soho.

"So, where are you from? You're clearly not a New York native with that beautiful accent?"

He smiled at me and grabbed my hand so our fingers were linked together.

"Spain is where I originate from. My father wasn't too proud of my artistic abilities, so when I was eighteen, I decided to make a life of my own where I wouldn't have my father looking down on me. I was able to move to America, earn my citizenship, and provide for myself. I am quite proud."

"As you should be." I wanted to applaud him, but thought it might be too much, plus, our hands were linked and I was enjoying the light circles he was creating on the back of my hand.

"Here we are," the waitress said as she set down two plates of tacos.

Sitting on three small corn tortillas were fish tacos with a cream sauce, cabbage slaw, and lime. To the side was a little tortilla bowl of beans. It was fresh looking Mexican food, something I enjoyed immensely.

"This looks amazing."

"Yes, querida. These will be the best tacos ever to grace that bonita mouth of yours. You want me to show you how to eat them, yes?"

"Please," I gestured for him to continue.

Sadly, he released my hand and grabbed the lime from his plate. I watched his strong hands squeeze the lime juice over his tacos, and then with a quick roll, he picked up a taco and took a bite.

"Simple."

"I guess so."

Just like Alejandro, I grabbed my lime, squirted the juice over my tacos, and took a bite. The acid of the lime hit my tongue first, followed by the spice of the sauce and the cool flavor of the fish. Food-gasm hit me head on as I felt my eyes close in pleasure and a light moan escape my mouth.

"These are amazing," I admitted, once I swallowed.

"Watching you eat them is even better," he responded with heavy lids.

Oh, I was in trouble.

The rest of our dinner, we ate our tacos, talked lightly about our lives in New York City, and stole glances at each other every chance we could get. Delaney was right, Alejandro was a must to go out on a date with. Just from the way he looked at me, I could feel Virginia flapping in agreement and my breasts screaming, yes please.

Alejandro paid our bill, not bothering to acknowledge my offer of help. He stood up from his chair and held out his hand.

"Would you like to see some of my art, querida?"

"I would love that," I said, as I stood up and felt myself wobble. After one margarita, I was feeling it for sure.

With his hand gripping my elbow, he led me out of the restaurant, around the corner, and up a set of stairs. He wasn't kidding, he did live close.

I waited as he unlocked the door and led me to the second floor, where a big sliding metal door was locked. Once again, he unlocked the door, moved the door to the side, turned on some lights, and led me inside.

Color invaded my senses as I took in picture after picture of colorful, but very naked, women.

Oh, my God.

CHAPTER 11
"The Squirrel Tail"

"Do you like my art?" Alejandro asked, as he led me inside his apartment.

Big nipples, small nipples, square nipples, abstract nipples, vaginas with hair, vaginas completely bare, vaginas spread wide, vaginas with fingers in them...

"Wow," I said, as I took in the vast amount of naked woman gracing every inch of his walls. "I didn't know a vagina could be green."

He chuckled next to my ear and whispered in a deep, husky voice, "It's art, querida. A vagina can be any color you want it to be."

Nodding, I walked over to some of his smaller paintings to get a better look.

"Do you just paint naked woman?"

"No, I do self-portraits as well."

"You do?" I asked, interested and tipsy. I could feel myself swaying back and forth.

"Yes, would you like to see?"

"Please, I would love to see how you capture yourself."

"This way, querida," he guided me to the back of the loft, where there was a massive bed in the middle of the room with the fluffiest comforter I had ever seen.

"Wow, your bed looks comfortable. Can I jump on it?"

I heard myself say it, but still, I didn't care that I sounded like a teenager.

"You can do whatever you want on my bed."

I heard the innuendo in his voice, but chose to ignore it as I took my shoes off and hopped on his bed. Instantly, I was sucked into the plush confines of his comforter.

"Oh, I can't jump on this, it's too unbelievable. What kind of comforter is this? Goose down?"

"Not quite sure. I can look and see if you would like."

"No, I want to see your self-portraits."

Yes, the margarita was taking its effect. I told myself to be cool, but my brain was giving me the middle finger and did whatever it wanted.

Alejandro walked over to a chest and opened it with a click. His back flowed with his movements, and I was instantly aware of the fact that I was in a small loft with an extremely attractive man and laying on his bed. That was the farthest I had ever been with a man in all of my virgin years.

"Querida, are you watching?" he asked, staring at me.

I realized I had zoned out, so I shook my head clear and focused on the painting Alejandro was holding. The painted side was facing him, ready to be revealed.

"Yes," I said, while I sat on my knees and placed my hands on my thighs.

With a debonair look on his face, he turned the picture and revealed his self-portrait.

It took a second for my eyes to adjust, because I was

expecting to see a picture of his face, with his slicked black hair and maybe a shirt with some buttons undone, but instead, I was staring at a two foot, what I assumed was, a self-portrait of his penis.

"Oh, my," I studied. "Um, is that life size?"

Laughing, he shook his head, "No, that would be too much, querida but I appreciate your confidence in me."

The portrait was interesting. The background of it was just a swirl of colors, but the penis portion was most definitely a penis with a head, some veins, and a set of balls that lay next to a pair of legs. It was erotic, that was for sure, and after the initial shock, I was kind of digging the colors.

"You have a great eye for color," I praised.

"Thank you, I will show you more."

He went back to the chest and started taking out more pictures, all of his erect penis. As I perused each and every one of them, I thought to myself, how could someone paint this many pictures of one's penis? The pictures were nice, but he must think very highly of himself to have so many pictures of his dick. Growing more and more curious, I realized I had to see this penis; I had to see what the big deal was.

"How do you do the self-portraits?" I asked, curious.

"What do you mean, bonita?"

"I mean, do you umm, sit there with an erection and paint?"

"Why, yes. Is that strange to you?"

Is it strange to be sitting in a room with an erect penis and painting while looking down at it, uh yeah...that was weird.

"Not sure," I lied. "Just wondering about your process."

"I see. I usually sit down, naked and think of a bonita senorita, like yourself, Rosie, and lightly caress myself until I feel like I'm fully erect. That's when I take out my brush and start painting."

That could explain all the angles of the pictures, they were all angles from up top.

"Interesting," I said, while staring at his crotch.

"I see the way you stare at me, querida. Do you want to see the muse for my self-portraits?"

What a creepy thing to say to a woman, especially when you are speaking about a penis, but I found myself nodding my head. Yeah, that margarita had way too much tequila in it.

Taking in my request, Alejandro climbed on the bed and leaned against the pillows and head board. With precision, he started to undo his jeans, and I watched in fascination as he pulled them down slightly and allowed just the head of his cock to jut out from the confines of his pants.

Holy shit, I was looking at a real live dick. A dick!

I inched closer, curious to see if it really looked rubbery like in pictures, or if it was a different texture in real life.

"Your eyes are making me hard, Rosie. The way you look at me, I've never had a woman look at me like this before."

I just nodded, wanting to see more.

His hands went to the waist of his briefs and jeans, and in one smooth movement, he pulled his pants down fully, allowing his penis to spring free.

I was about to move even closer, until I caught a glance at everything that was sitting between his legs. I glanced back at a portrait and then back at the real life thing. To say his pictures didn't portray his model was an understatement, because sitting right in front of me was a long erect penis, displayed upon a wild set of curly hair covered balls. It looked like Chewbacca was staring up at me, winking and mewing his crazy ass sounds.

Henry warned me of such a thing, that men didn't necessary think they had to shave, and boy, was he right. Alejandro didn't even know what a razor was, according to the pubes I could start braiding.

"Nice, yes?" he asked.

"Yes," I nodded, feeling like even though there was a crop of hair on his balls, I was still interested in what he had going on.

"You can touch."

There are moments in your life where you wish you could have an out of body experience and see everything you were going through from above. This was one of those moments. I was slightly drunk, thank you margarita, but I knew what was happening was odd, not normal, not something I read in one of my romance novels.

Usually, when the man and woman started having a sexual encounter, it was more romantic, more smooth, more hot and heavy, but this felt like I was conducting a science experiment.

Going with the flow, I straddled his legs and leaned forward so I could inspect his penis a little closer. I was drunk. If he thought what I was doing was weird, then I would blame it on the booze, but from the way he stroked himself and he continued to grow, I could see that he didn't care what I was doing.

"Rosie, the way you look at me, it's too much...and your cleavage, it's just spectacular."

I looked down and saw that I was giving him a great view of the ladies, and frankly, I didn't care.

I lowered my head even further down, and surprisingly, opened my mouth and licked the side of his penis, but missed and licked the side of his leg. Damn margarita.

His chest heaved just from the one lick. What possessed me to do so, I would never know, but I liked the way he reacted to it, so I licked him again, but on the other leg, like I was trying to lick an ice cream cone.

"Oh, bonita, you tease me."

Was I teasing him? I wasn't quite sure. I thought about taking him in my mouth, but his hand was still wrapped around his cock, mostly at the head, so I decided to work the base of his penis, but was stopped by his hand that was now pumping harder. I stuck my tongue out again and licked his leg once more, since that was my go-to licking spot, but this time, he moaned out loud and got more comfortable on the bed.

Well, if anything, I was good at licking legs, something to put on the old sexual resume.

Rosie Bloom—still has a brand new hymen, but can lick a man's leg like it's her job.

Energy filled me and a new sense of purpose ran through my

mind as I eyed his entire "muse." I was going to do this, I was going to get down and dirty. Since his stick was occupied, I decided I was going to lick his balls.

I dipped my head down further, eyed the fur pie staring me in the eyes and stuck my tongue out once again. My tongue ran across the thick, coarse hair, and tried to find his actual nut sac, but was having a hard time with the tangled mess my tongue was trying to penetrate.

"Yes, yes, bonita. Lick my balls."

"I twying," I said with a mouth full of spit. Saliva ran down my tongue and into his pubic hairs, making the texture that much worse for me to experience.

Licking hairy balls was just as unappealing as it sounded; I learned that really quick. Noted.

I pulled my tongue back in to try again—never being a quitter—and that's when I felt a hair on my tongue. Knowing that one of Alejandro's ball sac pubes was sitting on my tongue had me dry heaving in seconds, but Alejandro didn't notice as he put his hand on my head and pushed me back down.

"Lick my balls, bonita. Don't tease me."

Coughing and trying to release the hair that was slowly traveling to the back of my throat, I pressed my tongue out again and tried to dive down into the squirrel tail that was covering his balls. The combination of the hair in the back of my throat and the wet texture of his ball hairs did it for me, I was gone.

I tried to pull away, but he wouldn't let up. Sweat coated my skin in a matter of seconds as I dry heaved over my date's hairy covered cherries.

"I ma troll up," I muttered, as my tongue collided again with his briar patch.

"Yes, hum on them," Alejandro said, as he pushed my head back down again.

My stomach revolted on me, the margarita roared with a vengeance, and in a matter of seconds, my belly convulsed and I found myself heaving all over my date's genitalia as screams of horror left his mouth.

I watched as the tacos I once thought were delicious, now sat on the once beautiful comforter and mixed into Alejandro's lap broccoli.

"What is wrong with you?" Alejandro yelled as he scampered across the loft, pants around his ankles, dong flying about and balls hanging low.

I didn't have to answer; I didn't need to answer. What I needed was to get the hell out of his apartment…and fast. Without looking back, I grabbed my purse, slipped on my shoes, and took off for his front door.

While in a hurry, I didn't see the self portrait of his penis lying on the floor, so in the midst of my run, I added insult to injury and accidently slammed my foot through one of his small paintings, dragging it along with me, all the way down the stairs of the loft and out to the street.

It wasn't until I hailed a cab, told him my address and took a second to gather myself that I pulled the picture off of my foot and set it to the side. My head rested against the cab window as the lights of New York passed me by.

I didn't think about what happened, how I just threw up on my date's private parts, how I had a pubic hair stuck in the back of my throat, or how I ruined yet another chance at being with a guy.

The ride to my apartment was longer than normal, thanks to traffic, but once I arrived, I paid the cab driver, grabbed the dick picture, and walked up to my apartment with a heavy heart and lighter stomach.

The apartment was dark, so I went straight to my room, realizing it was quite late. We must have spent a good amount of time at the restaurant for it to be so late already.

Once tipsy, I was now sobered up, thank you puke session, and ready to just crawl into bed.

I flipped my switch on and nearly screamed my life away when I saw Henry sitting on my bed with a sullen look on his face.

"Henry, what the hell are you doing sitting here in the dark?"

His eyes bore into me when he looked up, and for the first time since I'd known him, I saw that he was angry with me.

"Why didn't you tell me where you went?"

Shit, I forgot my phone at work and didn't text him because I was in such a hurry to get out of the office.

"I'm sorry, Henry. I forgot my phone at work."

"Do you know how worried I was? That this guy might have done something to you? I had no way of getting ahold of you, Rosie. No way of checking up on you."

"Henry, I'm a grown woman; I can take care of myself."

"That's not the point," he spoke sternly and stood up while running his hands through his hair. "I want to make sure you're okay, that no one is taking advantage of you."

"No need to worry about that," I said, while I tossed my purse and picture on the floor and went to my dresser to pull out my pajamas.

"Where are you going?" Henry asked, walking after me.

"To the bathroom, to change and wash my face. Do you mind? Or do I need to get your permission first?"

He stopped in his pursuit of me and asked, "What's your problem?"

"You, just leave me alone, Henry."

I walked into the bathroom and slammed the door shut, making sure to lock it, because knowing Henry, he would just let himself in.

Taking my time, I washed my face, brushed my teeth, went to the bathroom, and changed into a pair of short shorts and an oversized T-shirt with an American flag on it, all the while, having my puke session on replay in my head. As I dried off my face, I thought how impossible my luck was. Did that really happen to me tonight?

It did, and honestly, it wasn't entirely my fault. I wasn't the one forcing my head into his nut patch. He was forcing me; I gave him fair warning, but he wouldn't let up. Maybe it was a good thing I threw up on him, maybe that was my body's way of reacting to his pressure.

I applied lotion to my face and started to giggle from the retreating glance I had of Alejandro…his dick swinging about while he shuffled to the bathroom to clean it off. It was actually slightly comical. If I wasn't so ashamed, I would be in a full on belly laugh mode right now.

Satisfied with my nightly ritual, I walked out of the bathroom and into my bedroom, expecting to see Henry waiting for me, but my room was empty except for a small book that was on my nightstand. I went over to look at it and saw it was a book about sex, a small guide on intercourse. I opened it up and saw on the inside a note from Henry.

Love,

Thought this might help with your research. If you have questions, don't be afraid to ask.

Love you, Henry

Guilt washed over me. Henry could be a little too concerned at times, but he had good intentions. Taking a deep breath, I tamped my stubborn pride down and walked out of my bedroom and into Henry's, where his lights were off and his back was facing me in his bed.

"Henry?" I asked as I walked forward. "Henry, I'm sorry. I just had a bad night, and I took it out on you."

Without a word, Henry rolled over in bed and lifted up the covers, inviting me in. I followed suit and snuggled against his bare chest, something that wasn't foreign to me. During college, sometimes I would come to his bedroom to snuggle when I was feeling lonely or having a bad day. He would stroke my hair and talk to me quietly until I fell asleep; he didn't fail me with the same treatment tonight.

"What happened?" he asked, his voice now light, rather than

angry.

"I don't even know if I can tell you; it's too humiliating."

"Can't be that bad; I heard you giggling in the bathroom."

"You heard that?"

"Yeah," he said, while kissing the top of my head. "I was going to check on you and I heard you giggling, so I thought you were doing just fine."

"Not really fine, just thinking about how ridiculously insane my night was."

"Does this have anything to do with that naked picture of a painted penis you have in your room?"

"Oh, God, I forgot about that," I said, while covering my face. "Yes, it has everything to do with that."

"I take it Alejandro wasn't the man you were expecting him to be?"

"He was at first. We had such a good dinner, and he wasn't lying when he said those tacos were amazing. Their margaritas were even better."

"You drank? Did you get drunk?"

His hand combed through my hair, helping me relax into his chest.

"Yes, I only had one, but it was really strong. I mean, really strong. Next thing I knew, I was in his loft, looking at his art, which was all naked women in all different shapes and sizes. I saw so many different variations of nipples that I feel like I have a nipple fixation now, I need to see all nipples and study them."

"How do my nipples compare?" Henry joked, while puffing his chest.

"Well, they're not green."

"You saw green nipples?"

"Yes, and green vaginas, but that's beside the point. So, he says to me, 'Do you want to see my self-portrait?'" I used the best Spanish accent I had, making Henry chuckle. "So, of course, being the polite person I was, I said yes. But, Henry, these weren't self-portraits."

"What were they?" Henry asked, curious.

"They were portraits…of his penis."

A deep laugh came from Henry and my hand that was resting on his stomach felt the laughter flow in and out of his body.

"No way, he had portraits of his penis? Is that what that picture is?"

"Yes, a little memento from the night. I accidently stepped on it and stole the hideous thing during my attempt to flee his apartment as quickly as possible."

"Why were you fleeing his apartment?"

This was the part I didn't want to discuss, but knowing Henry, he was going to get it out of me at some point.

"Okay, you have to promise me you won't tell Delaney, because I don't think she would ever let me live it down."

"I promise," he kissed my forehead. "Your secret is safe with me, love."

"Okay, well, he decided to show me the real thing."

"The real thing?"

"Yes, his muse, the penis. The real life portrait, not the painted one."

"Like, he just pulled his pants down?"

"Yes."

"Fucking creep. Guys are so weird, sorry, love."

"It's okay, I was actually fascinated, to the point that I decided to, um, lick it. Well lick in that vicinity."

"Lick it?" Henry asked, surprised. "Love, you touched your first penis," he lightly cheered.

"Not really, more like just licked his legs, because his hand was wrapped around his cock, not giving me a chance to actually touch the muse. Once he fully pulled his pans down, that's when I realized there was a wooly mammoth staring back up at me. Henry, you were right, some guys don't care about shaving."

"Oh, shit, really?" he laughed.

"Yes, like a brillo pad."

"Fuck, that's nasty," he chuckled.

"Tell me about it, but I still licked it, though. I licked his nut sac. I'm going to blame it on the margarita and extreme curiosity."

"Let's just stick with the margarita."

I nodded and continued. "So, I licked it and drooled a lot because the hair was too much to handle, and when I pulled away for a breather, I got a pube stuck in the back of my throat."

"Oh, I'm going to dry heave."

"Tell me about it. I did the same thing, but Alejandro had the wrong idea and pushed my head back down to continue to lick him."

"He forced you," Henry tensed up, but I soothed him by rubbing his chest.

"He did, but I think he learned his lesson."

"How, did you bite his balls off?"

"No, just puked all over him."

Henry stilled and turned to look me in the eyes. "Are you serious?"

"Yes, I dry heaved so bad that my stomach said that was enough, and I puked all over his genitalia. I left him with a puked up penis."

Studying me for a second, Henry was silent, but then threw his head back and laughed a pure and genuine laugh. I joined him as I thought about the night I had. It was truly comical.

"That's my girl," he pulled me in close. "Fuck…that is so great. Fucker deserved it."

"Yeah, so, clearly, he yelled and went to go clean himself and I took off, punctured one of his pictures and dragged it out onto the streets of New York, where I hailed a cab."

Still chuckling, Henry started stroking my hair. "Even though you had a bad night, I'm glad that you were able to take care of yourself by throwing up on your date. What better way to tell him no than by throwing up all over his precious work of art."

"His muse."

"Exactly. I love it. Good job, love."

"Thanks, I guess," I chuckled.

We laid in silence as we stared up at the ceiling together. It was comforting, having Henry next to me, knowing even though I might have had a bad night, he would always be there for me.

"Thanks for the book and for tonight. I feel much better after talking to you."

"Of course. Maybe tomorrow night we can look over the book together. Learn some new things together. I'm always looking to educate myself on the subject of sex."

"That doesn't surprise me," I said, while nuzzling in closer. His grip tightened around me as he sighed in contentment, and we both slept like that, reveling in the company of each other.

CHAPTER 12

"The Hyena Call"

June 9, 2014

    I saw a real life penis for the first time last night. It was interesting. It was a little floppier than I expected it to be, like the kind of floppiness a soggy baguette would offer. I wish I was able to actually touch it, rather than lick around it, because my eyes really had no clue about texture. So, to confirm or deny my thoughts on how rubbery a dick was wasn't possible last night. Even though his penis was sitting on top of a patch of lap broccoli, I was still able to get a good look, and what fascinated me the most was how it was hard but still had loose-ish skin. What's with that? Does Virginia have extra skin?

    I tried giving her a good look earlier this morning with my compact mirror, but was startled when Henry banged on the door, causing me to drop my compact and break my powder. After that, I left Virginia alone and just assumed her skin was normal. She didn't feel loose down there.

    I started a new book today, and it jumped right into the sex. I've found reading some erotic novels were more about the sex and less about the storyline, and do you know what? For an interested girl like me, I rather enjoyed it. The only drawback was when I read at lunch, Sir Licks-a-Lot sat on his perch, aka my filing cabinet, and licked himself while keeping his eyes on me the whole time...his little leg stretched in the air as he licked his balls. It was rather uncomfortable, as if he was trying to tell me, this is how the sex really went down. So now when I read about a woman going down on a man, my first thought is of Sir Licks-a-Lot, and there is something entirely wrong with that image on many levels.

But, back to the erotic novels, I found that the authors describe the woman's vagina as, 1) their sex and 2) like a blossoming flower, opening up for the man's seed. Now, in my head, when I think about this, all I can picture is a giant vagina, opening its lady folds for the penis of its choice. This confused me more about the concept of extra skin in the vaginal area. I tried googling extra skin, vagina, and let's just say I won't be doing that again. Something about a blue waffle popped up, and I'm pretty sure I dry heaved for a half an hour after that.

I've written some more in my book, but I feel a little at a loss and I don't know if that's because my life is at a bit of a standstill. It's hard to write romance when it's completely lacking in your life. I mean, I like to think I know romance, but when it comes to me experiencing it, I get so close but fail at the end. Am I doomed to be lonely for the rest of my life? Am I going to turn into Gladys, who walks around with a cat clinging to the back of her sweater without her knowledge? I hope to God not.

"Rosie, are you coming? Pizza is here," Delaney called out from the living room.

"Be right there," I said, as I closed up my journal and stuffed it away.

I was feeling a bit melancholy today, because not only did Alejandro completely wipe me off of his dating radar—didn't blame the man—but Lance hadn't called me either, and I never heard back from Greg, so all dating prospects failed me. It seemed too good to be true.

After a long day at work, I crawled into a warm bath and read, trying to block out reality for a small portion of time, but that was short-lived when Delaney came banging on the door claiming she needed to go to the bathroom and she needed her privacy. It was the downfall of sharing an apartment with two other human beings; bathroom time wasn't quiet time, it was do your business and get out time.

That's when I went back to my room to read a little of the book Henry gave me and write in my journal.

"Pizza's getting cold," Delaney called out again, starting to get on my nerves.

I pulled a sweatshirt over my head and slipped on my Care Bear slippers, yeah, I was an eight year old girl.

"There she is," Derk said while slow clapping. "She decided to grace us with her presence."

Flipping him off, I sat down at one of the bar stools and grabbed a piece of pizza from the box containing broccoli and black olive pizza; it was my favorite.

"Where's Henry?" I asked, expecting to see him.

"He has a date tonight; pretty sure he won't be coming home."

For some reason, a small pang of jealousy ran through my body, but I tamped it down just as quickly as it showed up. I couldn't have Henry to myself every night. I relied on him a little too much.

Trying to seem interested, I asked, "Oh, with who? Do I know her?"

"Not sure. Her name is Rindy."

"Rindy?" I asked, already being able to picture her in my head. If she was anything like Henry's typical girl, she would be big-boobed and blonde. He claimed to love brunettes, but almost every girl he went out with was a blonde.

"Yup, don't know what she looks like, but he said she was a cheerleader for the New York Knicks. I think she's a model now, can't remember."

"Sounds like she's right up Henry's alley then. The boy doesn't know how to date a normal girl."

"He has great taste," Derk said, while chewing on his pizza

and looking at it as if it was a gift straight from the heavens.

"He has horrible taste," Delaney countered. "Do you remember that blonde with the 'beauty mark' on her face? I swear to God, that damn thing moved every time I saw her. Pretty sure it was on the tip of her nose at one point."

"Sweetie," Derk said lightly. "That's called exaggerating. We both know it wasn't on her nose."

"It was. Remember, she came stumbling out of the bathroom the night we went to that small rink a dink bar in the meat packing district? Her hair was all a mess and her beauty mark was on the tip of her nose."

"Babe, you were highly intoxicated that night. You thought my dick was sprouting out of my ear."

"Why are you taking her side? Do you like her? Have you been talking to her behind my back this whole time?" Delaney accused.

Derk threw his hands in the air and said, "I give up; she had her beauty mark on her nose."

Smiling with satisfaction, Delaney turned back toward me and said, "Works every time. Remember that when you have a solid man in your life, just keep pushing him until he gives in."

"Great advice, babe. Teaching her how to show a guy to an early grave. Real nice."

"Just trying to help a girl out," Delaney said with a wink. "So what happened with handsome Alejandro? Was it everything I thought it was going to be? That picture speaks for itself, I'm just wondering why it has a size seven heel print in it."

We all looked over to the mantle in our living room, where Henry had put the punctured canvas for all to see. It was our new artwork, and I couldn't help but giggle, just looking at the stupid thing.

"I wondered what that new artwork was," Derk said, studying it. "That dude is packing in that picture."

"Well, it's not very accurate" I mumbled.

"What?" Delaney said, while shoving my shoulder so I had to

look at her. "I'm sorry, but did I just hear you right, you saw his penis last night?"

"I did," I confirmed, making Delaney's jaw drop to the counter. "I don't want to get into it, but let's say I saw his penis and it was extremely hairy, so I left his apartment as quickly as possible."

"Ahh, come on," Derk said, sounding disgusted. "Guys who don't man-scape really give us a bad name. A little trim to the balls goes a long way, especially when your lady is keeping things clean."

"Thanks, babe," Delaney said, while kissing Derk on the lips. "He's right, if he wasn't shaved and trimmed up down below, I would never put his balls in my mouth, and I'm going to be honest with you, Rosie, I like man balls in my mouth."

Did she just say she liked man balls in her mouth? I didn't believe that was a sentence I would ever utter, because after my experience from last night, I didn't think I would be able to look at a set of balls without gagging.

"I'm sorry, but did you just say you liked balls in your mouth?"

"I did," Delaney confirmed casually. She spoke passionately and said, "There's something about having your man by the balls, being able to bite down on their most prized possession with one tick of your jaw…not that I would, but it's so powerful, plus I like running my tongue along Derk's scrotum; he practically purrs when I do it. It's fun."

"You know, babe, there are some things you can keep between us, it's okay to do that."

"Where's the fun in that?" Delaney countered. "Then I wouldn't be able to see how red your face gets when I talk about how you purr." Delaney turned toward me and continued. "He also likes it when I run my finger into the crevice of his thigh, right where his leg meets the juncture of his torso. He says it tickles him, but it actually makes him harder…"

"Babe, seriously. Enough," Derk reprimanded, looking an awful shade of red.

"Don't be so stuck up, Derk. We're sharing."

"Are we? Okay." Derk set his pizza down, brushed his hands off, and looked directly at me. "You know the noise that comes out of Delaney's mouth when we're doing it, the hyena sounding one?" I nodded my head, just as Delaney covered his mouth with her hand.

"Don't you dare fucking say a thing," she warned.

Well, now I was interested. Whenever Derk and Delaney were together in her room, it wasn't uncommon to hear a wild banshee sounding animal noise come from her room. I chalked it up to Delaney having a really good time with Derk, but now it seemed like she had some hidden sex secret, and I was intrigued.

Fighting off her arms, Derk pinned her against the counter and looked over her shoulder at me. With an evil grin, he divulged her secret.

"Your friend has a serious toe fetish, and if I do anything to her toes, she starts hissing and screaming like a hyena. If I want the girl to come, I just wiggle her big toe while I'm deep inside of her, and she's a goner."

He pulled away from Delaney, pleased with himself. Delaney brushed down her rumpled shirt and stuck her chin up as she turned around to face me.

"I've found that I enjoy a good toe wiggle during sex. There is nothing wrong with that. I just know what I like. I've made it easy for you," she said to Derk.

I tried to hold it in, but I couldn't. A snort escaped me, instantly making me cover my mouth. A sneer greeted me when I looked back up at Delaney.

"Just wait, once you have had sex a couple of times, you'll find out what pushes you over the edge, because as much as men like to think that pounding into you with their stiff rod does the trick, it's so much more than that. You have to rub a lady in the right way."

"Head, shoulders, knees and toes, right Delaney?" I asked with a smirk.

"Yup, laugh all you want. Just wait for your time, Rosie. After the initial massacre of a man taking your vagina to pleasure town, you'll start to find out what you like, and you'll rely on that. You know this?" Delaney said, while sticking her finger through a hole she made with her other hand. "That is called a man's best friend, but to us ladies, it's just some simple penetration, nothing to fawn over. What we like is a little rub on our clits."

"Wait," I stopped Delaney for a second. "So when a guy enters you, it's not pleasurable? Everything I've read begs to differ."

"I'm not saying it doesn't feel good, and yes, I've climaxed just from penetration, but if you want that toe curling orgasm, there has to be some clit action involved, or if the guy can reach your G-spot, now that, that's an orgasm. Mmm, just thinking about it has me hot."

Derk perked up as he eyed Delaney up and down while placing his hand on her back.

"Is that right, babe?"

"Yeah, maybe we can go to the bedroom?"

"Hello, I'm right here," I offered, but they both ignored me, tossed their crusts in the box, and took off toward her bedroom, leaving me once again by myself.

"Figures," I said, while boxing up the pizza and sticking it in the fridge. I should have expected that to happen. It was rare when Delaney and Derk weren't hanging out in her bedroom, getting it on.

Just like old times, when both my roommates were out on dates, I grabbed my laptop and sat on my bed. I logged onto my dating account and saw there was a message. Praying it was from Greg and not some random guy, I opened it up.

Luckily, it was from Greg, and there was a green circle next to his name, which I had no clue what that meant, but I started to read his message when an instant message box pulled up on my computer with a message from Greg.

Greg: Hey beautiful. I was hoping to catch you on here tonight.

I shouldn't be affected by him calling me beautiful. He probably called his sister beautiful, but I couldn't help but feel giddy about it.

Rosie: Hi, I didn't know this thing had instant messenger.

Greg: Me either until a lonely old man messaged me, looking for companionship. I thought it was nice until he sent me a picture of his wrinkled up nipples, asking if the mole on them seemed to be cancerous.

Rosie: No, he did not.

Greg: He did. To say that I will be hitting the gym more often is an understatement. Seeing old man boobs will do that to you.

Rosie: Do you go to the gym now?

Greg: I want to impress you and say all the time, I practically live there, but I think if we ever meet, you would know that was a lie. I'm fit, but I'm by no means a body builder.

I could see he was fit from his pictures. There was even a shirtless picture of him, and he was cut in all the right places, but like he said, not a body builder.

Rosie: I don't know, you seemed so bulky and manly in your pictures.

Greg: I'm reading that as sarcasm. Would I be right?

Rosie: Not at all ☺

Greg: Total sarcasm, but I will live with it. Tell me, Rosie Bloom, what did you have for dinner tonight?"

Rosie: Pizza with my roommates.

Greg: Pizza? My favorite meal. Where did you get it from? Wait, let me guess, was it deep dish, regular or thin crust?

Rosie: Regular.

Greg: Light sauce, or heavy? What about the cheese, was it on top of the toppings or under?

Rosie: Light sauce and the toppings were under the cheese.

Greg: Bingo! Boriellos, I'm right, aren't I?

I laughed to myself at Greg's enthusiasm. Weirdly, he was right. The man was right, he loved pizza, and after his questioning, I could see he knew it well.

Rosie: I'm impressed. Yes, we ordered Boriellos. Now to really impress me, you have to tell me what I ordered.

Greg: Hmm, that's hard, because I feel like I don't know you as well as I should, but if I had to guess, I'm going to say black olives and...broccoli.

Rosie: No way in hell you just guessed that. Are you stalking me?

Greg: LOL! No! But if I told you my buddy delivers for them and when I showed him a picture of you the other day, he said he delivers to your apartment often and that you are the only one who orders that pizza, would you believe me?

Rosie: Your friend is our delivery man? Does that mean he told you about all my embarrassing cat shirts I wear when I answer the door?

Greg: He might have mentioned a cat shirt or two…

Rosie: I get them for free! I work at a cat magazine, so I'm constantly snagging oversized cat shirts. What can I say? They're comfortable.

Greg: Hey, I can never pass up a free shirt, so I completely understand. Tell me, do they have rainbows on them, maybe a unicorn?

Rosie: A girl could only wish. No, they just have some real life cat on them. Usually cat of the month. My boss loves getting them put on shirts.

Greg: Your work sounds amazing, although, it would be better if it was with dogs, because they're so much cooler.

Rosie: Tell me, if you had a shirt with your dog's face on it, would you wear it in public?

Greg: You're kidding, right? If I had a picture of Bear on a shirt, I would wear that thing every day. In fact, Bear would have a matching shirt with my ugly mug on it.

Rosie: Haha, I would love to see that, and you don't have an ugly mug. You have a rather attractive mug.

Greg: Why, Rosie. You flatter me. How did I ever get so lucky?

Rosie: The Internet gods?

Greg: I think you're right about that. So, are we on for Friday?

After my conversation with him, I was definitely more than ready to go out with him. He seemed fun, intriguing, and I felt like we would have a good time, given the easy flow of our conversation.

Rosie: Yes, tell me when and where and I will be there.

Greg: Damn, Rosie, you just made my day. What do you like to do?

Rosie: Anything, really. Just don't take me to a movie. I want to be able to talk with you.

Greg: Movies are for making out, and I'm not about to stick my tongue down your throat on the first date, unless it's a requirement for you. Is it a requirement? I would be happy to oblige.

Rosie: Haha, nice try, but no, it's not. Sorry.

Greg: A guy's got to try. How about we go to this place where we get to make our own brick oven pizzas? We go somewhere to pay people so we can do all the work.

Rosie: Sounds intriguing. I'm in.

Greg: Perfect. Listen, I could hang out with you all night on this thing, but I'm currently getting my masters and have some reading to do before my class tomorrow night. Will you forgive me for jumping off of this thing too early?

Rosie: I suppose. Have a good night, Greg, I look forward to Friday.

Greg: Me too, Rosie. Have a good night.

 We both signed off and I set my computer to the side as I smiled about my date with Greg. I felt rejuvenated about my dating life after feeling quite low.
 Feeling thirsty, I walked back out to the kitchen where I heard Delaney and Derk going at it from their room. I giggled to myself as I heard a muffled hyena sound come from under her door. Clearly, she was trying to cover the fact that Derk was playing with her toes. What a weird thing, but to each their own.

The front door to our apartment opened quickly and was slammed shut, startling me. I turned to see Henry…angry and on a mission.

He walked right past me, went to the fridge and grabbed a beer. With a quick pop of the top, he started downing the liquid while he gripped onto the counter. He was tense, angry, and frankly, not the Henry I was used to. Plus, he was home early from his date; he was never home early when he went out on a date.

Once he put the bottle down, I stepped closer and asked, "Henry, are you okay?"

His gaze turned on me and said, "No, does it look like I'm okay?" The anger in his voice startled me.

"No, but you don't have to yell at me," I defended myself. I hated being the punching bag for someone else's problems, and I refused to be one for Henry.

"Don't I, though? Isn't this all your fault?"

"Excuse me?" I asked, while placing my hands on my hips.

Henry grabbed another beer and downed it in one long gulp.

Wiping his mouth, his eyes bore into mine as he spoke. "Your dating bad luck, it's transferred over to me. Before you started sharing, I was good, I was perfect actually. I was able to easily get pussy without even trying, but then you came along, and I can't even get it up."

"What?"

"You heard me," he said in a nasty tone. "I'm getting down with Rindy, one of the hottest pieces of ass I've seen in a long time, and what happens to me? Visions of you puking all over a guy's dick run through my mind, making it impossible for me to get it up."

"Wow," I said, feeling insulted. "So, because you have a problem controlling your thoughts, you're going to blame me? You're an ass, Henry."

"Come on, like you didn't tell me all those stories on purpose?" he said, as he walked after me. I was retreating to my bedroom; I didn't want to deal with his drunk ass. He was clearly intoxicated and not just from the two beers I witnessed him drinking.

"On purpose? I'm sorry, but I thought I was sharing with a friend. You asked me about them. Was I just supposed to tell you nothing? You would never let that happen."

"Believe me, if I didn't have to listen to your sad excuse of a dating life, I would be more than happy."

My heart split in two at the venom coming out of his mouth. I didn't quite understand why he was being so mean, why he was being so evil to me, but I didn't like it and I wouldn't put up with it.

"Then, just leave me alone. I didn't ask for you to be all up in my ass, so leave me the fuck alone," I said, letting anger take over me and swear words slip so easily.

"Fine," he threw his hands up in the air. "Easy, keep your bad luck to yourself."

"Leave," I yelled, pushing on Henry's chest so he would step away, but he grabbed my wrists and pulled me into his chest.

Alcohol riddled his breath as he breathed heavily and looked down at me. His eyes were glazed over and the real Henry was slowly starting to peek through as he matched my stare with his. His features softened as he brushed my face with the pad of his thumb. It was slightly startling how quickly his demeanor changed when I was in his arms.

Pain ran through his voice as he said, "Rosie, you're beautiful, you know that?"

"Get out of here, Henry," I said weakly, trying to push him away. "You're drunk, and you're being an ass. I don't want you near me."

Sighing, he turned his head away from me and mumbled, "Yeah, you never want me. Story of my life." He pushed me away and walked out my door, confusing me now more than ever.

CHAPTER 13

"The Gargling of Molasses"

It was only eleven in the morning and I wanted to claw my eyes out, or at least let Sir Licks-a-Lot do so. After I pushed Henry out of my room last night, I didn't get one ounce of sleep as I tried to figure out everything he said and why he was being so rude to me. I didn't think I had done anything wrong, but, clearly, he did.

I was able to get ready this morning, earlier than normal, and slip out of the apartment without interacting with him, which was for the best because I had no clue what I was going to say to him.

Delaney texted me earlier, asking if I was alright, since she heard Henry and I arguing, even over her hyena screaming. I let her know I was fine and Henry was drunk last night, saying things he probably didn't mean, especially him thinking I was beautiful. That was a drunken slip for sure. I've seen the girls he's taken out, they were far above my level of pretty. I was good looking, but like I've said, I'm curvier than others and have my own style that doesn't come close to rivaling the models Henry takes out.

I hated being sad, especially at work, because most of the time, work was awful with Gladys breathing down my neck, making sure I represented cats in the best way possible and trying to stay as far away from the pussy cat posse as I could, which was quite difficult given the space in our building.

The only thing that made me smile today was the picture of a cat flying in outer space with a pop tart body and a rainbow coming out of its ass that Jenny sent me. It was, by far, the weirdest thing I had ever seen, but it made me laugh. I even printed the picture out and put it on my bulletin board. I was just waiting for Gladys to see Pop-Tart cat and tell me what a bad depiction it was of our feline friends; until then, Pop-Tart cat was staying.

"Hey," a deep voice that I recognized instantly came from my door.

I looked up to see Henry propped up against my door frame with his hands in his pockets. He was wearing a navy blue suit and a white button up shirt with the top two buttons undone and a pair of brown shoes. He always dressed well for work.

Frankly, I was surprised to see him standing in my office doorframe, not just because of our spat last night, but because he never came to visit me at work for the simple reason that he hated cats, especially Sir Licks-a-Lot, who seemed to have a big crush on Henry and wouldn't leave him alone whenever he was around.

"What are you doing here?" I asked, looking away from my computer.

"Can we talk?"

"Don't you have work?"

"Took a long lunch. Please, Rosie?"

I sat back in my chair and crossed my hands over my chest as I said, "Fine, shut the door If you don't want Sir Licks-a-Lot to find you."

Henry quickly shut the door and took a seat in the chair across from me. He unbuttoned his suit jacket so he could sit down properly and positioned himself a little forward in his seat as he spoke to me.

"Rosie, I want to apologize for last night. I was way out of line, drunk, and a complete ass to you. I'm really sorry."

"Yes, you were, Henry. You said some pretty mean things to me."

He shook his head and looked down at his hands. "I know and I'm sorry. I was in a pissy mood and decided to blame everything on you, when none of it was your fault."

"So, you don't blame me for not being able to get it up?"

"No," he shook his head. "Not at all. That was my problem. Things have been different for me lately."

"What do you mean? How have things been different?"

Clearing his throat, he shifted in his seat as he adjusted his pant legs.

"I've been doing a lot of thinking recently, Rosie, and…"

Jenny knocked on my door and held up a vase with a box over the top. I waved her in with a questioning look.

"What's that?" I asked, as she set it on my desk.

"It's a little delivery that came in for you. Maybe it's from Atticus."

"The guy she kicked in the balls?" Henry asked, sounding skeptical.

"Yes, he said he liked her."

"It's not from Atticus, Jenny. Believe me, he's not going to call me again."

"Then, who is it from?" she asked, practically jumping up and down.

I shrugged and grabbed the box to pull the lid off. Inside was a bouquet of lint rollers. The sight of the set of five lint rollers made me laugh out loud. Nestled inside was a card that I read out loud.

"Just in case you aren't able to escape the cats so easily next time, Phillip."

"Oooh, he sounds dreamy."

"Who the hell is Phillip?" Henry asked, his demeanor completely changing.

"He's a guy I met in the elevator the other night before my date with Alejandro. He watched me dodge the cats and avoid cat hair central, which I was grateful for, since I didn't have a lint roller with me."

"So, he sent you lint rollers, how adorable," Jenny cooed, while she sat on my desk and started touching the "bouquet."

"Seems kind of lame," Henry said, while leaning back in his chair with a grumpy look on his face.

"It's not lame at all; you're just jealous you didn't think of it," Jenny countered.

The thing with Henry and Jenny was they never really got along. They've hung out a couple of times at the most and each time was a disaster. For some reason, they clashed, so I tried to keep them separated as much as possible. Since Henry never really came to my office, it wasn't that big of a deal, until now.

"Who the hell would I send lint rollers to?"

"Oh, I don't know, maybe the girl you've been crushing on for years now."

"What are you talking about?" Henry asked, venom spitting from his mouth.

"Don't play dumb with me; everyone knows you want Rosie."

"What?!" I asked, practically falling out of my seat. "Jenny, Henry and I are just friends."

A blank look crossed Henry's face as he took in my and Jenny's words. Once again, he cleared his throat and adjusted his jacket.

"Yes, just friends, Jenny, so drop it."

Henry and Jenny exchanged heated glares before Jenny rolled her eyes, got off the desk, and headed for the doorway.

"Whatever, live in denial. Rosie, Gladys wanted me to let you know she will be sending you her edits on your cat secret article. She wants more passion for cats in it."

I shook my head in confusion. "What does that even mean? Does she want me to lick the back of my hands and rub my hair as I write the article? Would that be showing more passion?"

"Possibly, try it," she smiled back and left, shutting the door behind her.

Once she was gone, Henry glared at me and said, "I don't like her, at all."

"I gathered that from the way you snarled at her the minute she walked in my office."

"She just thinks she knows everything when she doesn't."

"Taking the mature road today, I see," I said, while I moved the bouquet to the book shelf behind me. It was a perfect gift, but a little obstructive for my desk. I liked to keep things neat and orderly, just so Sir Licks-a-Lot could destroy them. There were many times where I walked in my office in the morning to find all the papers I organized in files strewn out along the floor because the cats thought it would be fun to knock everything off of my desk.

I've caught them many times doing so. They would sit on my desk, acting all innocent, but casually paw something until it fell, just to be jerks. Damn cats.

"Whatever, I'm going to get going."

"Wait, you were going to say something before Jenny came in."

"Forget it," Henry said, while getting up and brushing off his jacket.

"Why are you being so weird? I don't get you, Henry."

"Don't worry about it. Are we good?" he asked, a little concerned and less annoyed.

"I guess so. Please don't treat me like that again. You're my best friend, Henry, I don't want you mad at me or mean."

Blowing out a frustrated breath and running his fingers through his styled hair, he walked over to the side of my desk and sat on it while grabbing one of my hands.

"I'm sorry, Rosie. Truly, I am. I'm just going through some things right now, so I apologize if I took it out on you. It wasn't my intention to hurt you."

"What are you going through? You can talk to me, you

know?"

"I know, but it's nothing you need to worry about." Changing the subject, he added, "Want to watch *Indiana Jones* tonight? Maybe get some Chinese food? Unless, do you have other plans?"

I shook my head, no. "Not that I know of. I don't have anything planned."

"Then it's a date," Henry said, while pulling my hand to his mouth and kissing it. "Sorry again, Rosie. I never want to hurt you, ever."

"Thank you, Henry. I appreciate it."

"See you tonight?"

I was about to say yes, when there was a knock on my door. I looked up to see Phillip standing at the door with a smile on his face. I waved him in, feeling a little excited that he came down to visit me.

"I'm sorry, am I interrupting something?" Phillip asked, looking at Henry and me.

"No, not at all. Phillip, this is Henry, my friend. Henry, this is Phillip."

Henry nodded and shook Phillip's hand. "Ah, the lint roller guy."

"Yes," he smiled while sticking his chin up. "I see that you got them, I'm glad."

Henry and Phillip stared each other down in silence, sizing each other up. They were the same height and build; it would be an even match for sure, but my money was on Henry. He might look pretty at times, but he was a man's man and could hold his own, no doubt about it.

"Ahem," I cleared my throat. "Henry, weren't you just leaving?"

With one last stare, Henry turned toward me and said, "See you tonight, love?"

"Yes," I nodded, hating that he was acting all charming and sweet now, in front of Phillip, as if he was trying to mark his territory.

"Let me know if you need anything. I'll get the Chinese. Have a good day, love." With that, he pulled me in for a quick hug and then left, leaving me alone with Phillip.

He turned to me with a confused look on his face and then said, "You sure you're just friends? It seems like there may be more between you two."

"No, believe me, we're just friends. I'm not his type."

"Good thing, because I would have to fight him for a date with you if you were his type."

"You want to go on a date with me?"

He nodded and flashed that gorgeous smile of his. The man standing in front of me was unlike any other man I had ever met before. He was very cocky, very arrogant and confident in himself. It was actually kind of attractive, I could see why all the heroines in the books I've been reading fall for the dominant type man, because they were up front, knew what they wanted, and just took it.

That was Phillip. He had this air about him that I couldn't help but get sucked into. Maybe it was his bright white teeth, or how his suits were tailored specifically to his body. Whatever it was, I wanted to get to know him better, and even more, I wanted to get to know him in the bedroom.

God, I needed to put down the Kindle for a bit because my mind was getting dirtier by the second.

"Come to lunch with me," it was more of a demand than a question.

"Where would we go?" I asked, trying not to show how I was ready to jump on his back and giddy up down the hallway with him.

"There's a little café a block away; I promise we won't be too long. Don't want boss cat lady to be mad at you."

"No, we can't have that. Let me send this quick email, and then I can go."

"Okay, mind if I wait in your office?"

"Of course not. Have a seat if you'd like."

I shook my mouse to wake up my computer and pulled open a new email. I started typing a message to myself, reminding myself to take my vitamins when I got home. For some reason, I wanted to look important to Phillip, so in my head, sending out an email before lunch made it seem like I was at the same business level as him, rather than me working at a cat magazine where cats literally dictated my job.

Happy with my email, I sent it and then stood up.

"You ready?"

"Of course."

With his hand on my back, he led me to the elevator and out of our building, the whole time staying silent, which was a little awkward for me, since I didn't like awkward silences at all.

Once we were outside, Phillip turned to me and nodded in the direction he would like to go. "This way."

I followed him, all the while he had his hand on my back, guiding me through the streets of New York City where cars honked constantly, people on the streets tried to sell you fake handbags, and the smell of rotting something floated in and out of the air. I loved every second of it.

We turned the corner, and the sign for a little café that I walked by almost every single day came into view, but never once had I given it a thought.

"I see this place almost every single day, but have never been here."

"Really? Well, you're in for a surprise. They have the best cheddar broccoli soup you will ever have."

"Better than Panera?" I asked.

He gave me a funny look and then nodded his head. "Did you really just ask me that?"

"If I said no, would you believe me?"

Laughing, he shook his head and opened the door for me.

The café was quite small, just like every other place in New York, since realty was hard to come across. The floors were checkered black and white and the walls were a burnt orange.

There was a case of pastries lining one wall and another case of deli meats on the other side. It was a typical small café you would find in New York.

The one thing that did seem out of place was Philip. He seemed like a man who dined at the Loeb Boathouse in Central Park every day, not someone who looked forward to a cheddar broccoli soup from a local café.

"So, do you think you're going to go with the soup?" Phillip asked, close to my ear.

"Since you think it's the best, I believe I have to try it."

"That's what I like to hear," he smiled.

I watched as he ordered for both of us, adding in some waters and a cookie to share, all the while holding onto the strong, confident poise that screamed high society. He was a stark contrast to look at, to be around; it was rather fascinating, and it only made me even more curious to see how he was in bed. Not that I was ready to jump into one with him. I was just curious.

He guided me to a table in the corner of the café and set our tray down while handing out our food. It was sweet to see him take care of everything.

Once we were settled and eating our soup, Phillip lifted his eyes to mine and asked, "Tell me, Rosie, where did you go to school?"

Swallowing some soup, which actually was quite delicious, I said, "NYU with my two best friends who I live with now."

"You have roommates?" he asked, a bit surprised.

"Yes, unfortunately. As you know, it's expensive here, and living off of wages from *Friendly Felines* isn't going to be putting me up in a penthouse in Manhattan."

Laughing, he responded, "I can understand that. Do you have aspirations to work somewhere else?"

"I do; I actually am working on a book right now. I would love to be able to write my own things and not have to listen to a person dictate to me about what cat article I have to write for the day. Or how I need more meow in my stories."

"Meow? Seriously? Does your boss say that?"

"All the time," I laughed. "We have meetings every Monday morning, and you should hear some of the things she says. Meow is her favorite but she will also say things like purr-fect."

"She does not," he chuckled.

"She does, unfortunately. The lady is certifiable. Pretty sure she had a pillow made of cat hair."

"That's terrifying."

"Tell me about it," I laughed. "If I ever need a crazy ass lady in my story I'm writing, it will be based off of Gladys; she is perfect book material."

Nodding, he asked, "What kind of books do you want to write?"

Swallowing hard, I took a sip of water and said, "Um, romance novels."

A small grin spread across his face. "I was hoping you were going to say that."

"You were?" I asked, slightly confused.

"Yes. I think women who can write about romance, about sex, and describe it in vivid detail are one of a kind, exquisite creatures. I love a woman who is comfortable with her sexuality."

His eyes blazed right through me, lighting me up inside. Talk about flirting, damn, he was singing to my lady parts with just his eyes.

"I try my best," I lied, thinking about my last attempt at writing a sex scene, where I talked about pubic hairs and uneven breasts. Apparently, that stuff wasn't sexy, and I learned that from Delaney, who had zero filter when telling me when something was wrong.

"I'm not going to lie, Rosie...that makes me want you even more."

"Want me?" I gulped.

I felt like I was in one of those erotic romance novels, where one minute you're enjoying a fine meal and the next minute, you innocently lick your lips because they are seriously dry, but the alpha male sitting in front of you thinks you're licking your lips to show him how "pink" your tongue is and that's when things get out of control.

I was waiting for the moment where Phillip ordered me to bend over the table so he could take me from behind while slapping my ass and telling me to come on demand, something I was pretty sure I would never be able to do. Did women really orgasm from a man telling them to? When I had a vibrator stuck in Virginia, I tried to tell myself to come, thinking maybe the vaginal canal contractions would release the damn thing, but Virginia gave me the middle finger and held on tight to her mini friend.

"What are you thinking about that has you giving me that far off look," he asked in a deep voice, pulling the whole alpha male act on me, and damn if it wasn't working.

"Umm, nothing?" I asked in a question.

"Were you thinking about sex with me?"

Yup, this was a romance novel. No one was that abrupt when just meeting, right? Were you thinking about sex with me? I mean, I just met the man in an elevator and he was asking about sex?

"Yes," the word fell out of my mouth before I could take it back.

Who the hell just took over my body? I thought, as sheer mortification ran through me at my confession.

Patting his mouth dry with a napkin, he nodded his head and stood up while holding out his hand to me. I looked down at my half eaten soup and then to the heat in Phillip's gaze and decided to take his hand.

Was this really happening? I thought, as he led me back to our building and up the elevator, all the while keeping his hand on my back and not saying a word. We rode past my floor and up to the top floor, where I knew the fancy people worked.

The doors to the elevator opened, and with a hello from his secretary, he walked me past her and into a big corner office. The man was in some kind of high position, but I didn't have much time to think about it as he locked his door and turned toward me.

"Go sit on my desk and take off your pants."

He loosened his tie and took off his jacket in one smooth motion.

Umm, was he serious? Take my pants off, in broad daylight? I knew the red brick road was non-existent now, but still, couldn't he dim the sunlight? I was pretty sure the light would be harsh on my skin, casting a nasty glare on my curves.

"Rosie, don't make me repeat myself."

Holy crap! I wanted to say Yes, Sir, Mr. Grey, Sir and then bat my lashes like Anastasia, but decided to not role play, since I was pretty sure he wouldn't like it.

Coming to the conclusion that I was living out a scene from an erotic novel, I pushed away all my insecurities, my work obligations, and took off my pants, revealing the white panties I chose to wear that had a small heart on the front. Not the sexiest pair of underwear I had, but it hid the panty lines, and that was all I cared about.

"Take off that child's underwear," he demanded, while rolling up his sleeves with precision and examining me.

It wasn't children's underwear; I got it at Victoria's Secret, but I kept my mouth shut, took a deep breath, and pulled my underwear down, which he took from my hand and tossed in the trash.

Romance novelists were spot on when it came to alphas and underwear, they were as disposable to them as toilet paper was. I wanted to complain that underwear was five dollars, not some two cent tissue he could toss around, but once again, I kept my mouth shut.

"I want to taste you," he said, as he trapped me against his desk. "Ever since I saw you in the elevator, I wanted to know what that pussy tasted like."

Okay, when I first met Phillip, I thought he was attractive, strong and confident, but never did I think he had a dirty mouth.

Taste my pussy? Holy shit, guys really said that? This was a whole new experience. I wish I could ask him to slow down. If I could record what he said, maybe take notes for my future books and to compare to other erotic novels, because this little scene playing out was spot on!

With one lift, he had me sitting on his desk, bare from the waist down and legs spread.

"This won't do," he said, as he took my legs and brought them up to my chest, exposing every last inch of my lower half. I instantly turned red at the thought of what my vagina looked like next to my bleached asshole. I was just praying it wasn't a whole ebony and ivory situation down there.

"Rosie, your pussy pleases me. I didn't expect you to be a waxer, but I couldn't be happier."

My pussy pleased him? Well, thank the heavens for his approval, I thought sarcastically.

In one swift bow, his head was between my legs and his fingers were parting my lady folds. I couldn't help but think I was actually being touched in my most private parts by a man. If only I wasn't so spread open, I would feel more comfortable. He literally had my legs pinned against my chest and spread out as far as I could make them. If he wanted to conduct an exam, he would be able to do a bang up job.

When I thought he was going to just sit there, with his head between my legs, not doing anything, he dipped his tongue against my clit, making the most heinous sound come out of my mouth.

It sounded like I gargled a vat of molasses while being struck in the ass by a rattlesnake.

Pleasure ripped through me, just from one simple flick of his tongue.

Now I knew why women's bosoms heaved and their legs quivered, because with one flick, Phillip had me panting. Literally, I was panting, tongue hanging out, leg bouncing up and down, drool escaping my mouth as he licked just the right spot.

A complete stranger was licking me, licking Virginia, who, by the way, was by no means protesting. No, she was clapping her folds in joy, letting me know that my inappropriate and rash decisions were greatly appreciated.

His tongue dipped in and out of Virginia and then traveled up to my clit where he teased it, blew on it, and licked it again.

The torment he was giving me had my body lighting up, sweating profusely, and words like shit balls, fucking fairy magic, and thank you coming gods were at the tip of my tongue as this need, this burning need in the pit of my stomach started building at an alarming rate. My toes felt like they were no longer attached to my body, rather floating to the side, wiggling at me. My knees shook, as the center of my lady cactus started to hydrate, preparing for a monsoon.

My head fell back and I thrust my hips into his face. I could feel pressure building at my bottom, and with one flick of his tongue, by body relaxed all at once and a loud, very ugly sound escaped me, but as my mouth was closed, I realized, the sound didn't come from my mouth, rather…my ass.

Phillip pulled away, seizing all pleasure and scrunched his nose as he looked up at me through my legs.

Playing back the last couple of seconds, I had to think about what just happened. Did I really just fart while a man was licking Virginia? No, not possible, but the look of disgust that crossed his face made me believe it was true.

Panic set in as I tried to figure out what to say. There was only one thing that came to mind, so I voiced what was rolling through my head.

I looked down at Phillip and said, "Whoever smelt it, dealt it?"

From a far distance, I heard Virginia queef me a 'fuck you' and then felt her shrivel up to end all humiliation. The poor girl was never going to come out to play, ever again. I swore at my ass, wanting to take a cork to it and teach it a lesson.

I farted; I farted on the man's head. I farted on his chin, on his damn chin.

Without a word, Phillip pulled away and walked to a closed door, which I assumed was a private bathroom to wash off the flatus I imparted on him.

Not caring if I even zipped my fly, I threw my pants on and got the hell out of his office as quickly as possible, all the while keeping my head down and trying to avoid all eye contact with every human in the building.

On my elevator ride down to my office, I swore at all erotic romance novelists in the writing community, because not once did they ever mention the possibility of farting on a chin while being eaten out. Why was that?

Oh, I know, because it wasn't sexy! Fuck you, asshole, fuck you.

CHAPTER 14

"The Best Friend"

The cab ride back to my apartment after work was a lonely one, as I shifted on the worn out leather seat, missing my underwear, especially since the zipper of my pants was rubbing against poor Virginia. I normally took the subway home from work, since it was cheaper and faster, but in this state, I couldn't face the underground world of New York City.

I could feel myself start to slip into a dark vat of denial soup. I've spent a good portion of my life reading books about romance, and never once was I exposed to such a depressing reality that it wasn't as easy as it seemed, then again, Delancy and Henry seemed to have a pretty easy time when it came to obtaining a relationship. So, what it came down to was, I was cursed; there was no other reasoning for it.

Maybe I had high expectations, maybe I was setting the bar too high?

My phone started ringing in my purse, and without looking at the caller ID, I answered.

"Hello?"

"Rosie?" a familiar voice asked.

"Yes?" I couldn't quite place the voice, but I knew I'd heard it before.

"Hey, it's Lance."

"Lance?" I asked, a little surprised to hear him on the other end of the line. After my split pants situation, I thought we were done. "Wow, I wasn't expecting to hear from you."

"Why not? I said I was going to call," he said in a relaxed tone, but I was anything but relaxed, because frankly, I was beyond up tight when it came to men now. It was almost impossible for me to relax.

"Yeah, but not to get all girly on you, that was a few days ago. After not hearing from you right away, I kind of tossed the idea of seeing you again."

"I'm sorry," Lance said, while blowing out an exasperated breath. "I wasn't expecting to like you so much."

"Gee, thanks," I said, while rolling my eyes and looking out the window of the taxi.

"That didn't come out right," he tried to say. "I just, I got scared."

"After you said you wanted to date me? After you said you waited to be put on another photo shoot with me? Stop playing with me, Lance. I'm not stupid."

Yeah, I was being a bit of a bitch, but I didn't feel like dealing with anyone, especially men. I was crabby, irritated, embarrassed, and all I wanted was to put on a pair of sweats and drown my sorrows in a pint of ice cream.

"I'm not playing with you, Rosie. I'm sorry I made you think otherwise. I'm an idiot, and yes, I should have called earlier. I really hope you will forgive me and consider going out with me again. This time, just you and me, no bowling or opportunities to rip your pants open," his dash of humor eased the tension in my body.

"What do you say, Rosie? Can I take you for a boat ride in Central Park on Saturday?"

"Hmm, that depends. Do you plan on tipping the boat? With my luck, that would happen."

"Promise, there will be no tipping of the boat."

Did I really want to go out with him again? I thought about it for a second, and honestly, I did. Out of all the dates I'd been on, I really enjoyed Lance's company the most. Atticus was fun, but I cracked his nuts, so there was no shot there; Alejandro was a no-go with the whole wildebeest growing in his pants, and Phillip, well, pretty sure I wouldn't be hearing from him.

"I think I might be free on Saturday."

"Are you playing hard to get?" he chuckled into the phone.

"Maybe, is it working?"

"It is. I'm starting to get desperate here. I would love to see you again, Rosie."

"It would be nice to see you again, too," I conceded. "But I won't be paddling that boat."

"I got it covered. How about a picnic as well?"

"Depends, what do you bring on a picnic?"

"Um, how do you feel about bologna sandwiches? I make a mean one with mustard and I cut them up in little triangles."

"Triangles, well, I have to say yes to that. I don't even think I have a choice."

"You really don't," he laughed. "So, do you want me to pick you up?"

"I can just meet you, no need to come pick me up. Just let me know when and where."

"How about by the boathouse around noon? Does that work for you?"

"Works perfectly," I replied, feeling a little better.

"Good, I look forward to it. Before we get off the phone, tell me, how's the cat world?"

"How do you think it is?" I asked, while chuckling. "Pretty sure if I let my guard down today, the cats would have eaten me alive. They can sense when I'm having a bad day and my resolve has weakened."

"You had a bad day?" he asked softly, making butterflies float in my stomach. "What happened?"

Ha! Like I was going to tell Lance what happened. Yeah, no thank you. I wasn't about to tell a man I wanted to date that I just ripped a loud one on a guy's face. Pretty sure that was dating suicide.

"Just some stuff at work that I won't bore you with," I answered evasively. "Nothing that won't just go away, but thanks for asking."

"Well, if you want to talk, let me know."

"Thanks, Lance," I said, as I pulled up to my apartment. "Hey, I have to pay the cabbie, so I should go. I'll see you Saturday?"

"Yes, don't be late."

We hung up and I paid the cab driver, giving him a decent tip for not making me wait in traffic for too long during rush hour. He did some fancy maneuvering that, yes, had me peeing my pants a couple of times, but he got me home.

When I walked into the apartment, I was surprised to see Henry was home already, and I was surprised that there was Chinese food on the kitchen counter, a pair of sweat pants and a baggy shirt folded on the chair, and a smiling Henry in a pair of shorts and a tight fitting T-shirt waiting for me.

"Welcome home, love," he said, while walking toward me and picking up my change of clothes. "Thought you might want to change before we get our little date started. Delaney will be staying at Derk's place tonight, so we have the place to ourselves."

"You say that as if something's going to happen," I said with a sad smile and grabbed the clothes from him. "Thanks for this. I'll go change and then I'll be back."

"Hold up," Henry said, while grabbing my hand and pulling me into him. "What's wrong? Are you still mad at me? I want you to know I'm really sorry Rosie, and I'm sorry if I was acting like an ass to that lint roller guy earlier."

"It's not that," I said, while pulling away. "Just a bad day. I'll be right back. Fix me a plate?"

I left him to tend to the food while I changed. I stripped down, took off my bra and went panty-less since I already was. I didn't want anything constricting me tonight. Once I threw my hair up into a messy bun and put my fuzzy socks on, I walked out to the living room to find Henry starting the DVD player and placing two huge plates of food on the coffee table.

"Got us all set up," he said, while coming around to the couch.

I sat cross-legged on the sofa and placed a pillow on my lap. Henry sat next to me and was about to hand me my plate of food until he saw the tears that were welling in my eyes. Instantly, he had his arms around me, hugging me closely to his chest.

"Rosie, what's wrong? Why are you crying, love?"

"I'm sorry," I said into his shirt, trying to avoid getting snot all over him. I pulled away and wiped my eyes. "Just a rough day."

"You said that; do you want to talk about it?"

"Not really," I admitted. Even telling Henry what happened seemed like something I couldn't possibly do.

He quirked his mouth to the side while he studied me. "Rosie, you tell me everything. What's going on? Does it have to do with that lint roller guy?"

"His name is Phillip."

Taking a deep breath, Henry responded, "Fine, does it have to do with Phillip?"

"It might," more tears started to fall down my cheeks just at the thought of what happened.

Growing angry in an instant, Henry made me look up at him and asked, "Did he hurt you?"

"No," I choked out as a sob escaped me.

"Love, please talk to me. What happened? You're scaring me."

Sighing into him, I just blurted it all out. "I farted on his chin when he was pleasing me orally."

The soothing rubbing Henry was making on my back with his hand stopped, and I could feel him trying to comprehend what I just said.

"Wait, what?"

Wiping the snot from my nose, I elaborated. "Things escalated a little at lunch, and he took me back to his office, where he went down on me, something I've never experienced before, and I got a little too relaxed, so when he was down there, I kind of tooted."

Henry's face contorted and I could see him trying to be polite and not laugh in my face from what I just told him, but he held it together as he pulled me back into his chest and kissed the top of my head.

"Don't worry about it, love. That happens all the time."

"That is not true. You're telling me a girl has farted while you were going down on her?"

"Happened to me twice. I take it as a compliment, that I was able to relax a girl that much that she let all her inhibitions go. Granted, it's not the sexiest thing to ever happen in the bedroom, but it's not the worst either. What did Phillip do?"

Loathing myself, I said, "He backed away like I just lit a match next to my butt to spout off dragon fire and went to this bathroom. I booked it out of his office, minus my underwear, as quickly as I could run, and then hid in my office until the end of the day."

"Oh, love," Henry kissed the top of my head. "I'm sorry that happened to you."

"You're not going to laugh at me, poke fun at me?"

"No, you're clearly upset, and the guy should have been more of a gentleman about it. It's not an uncommon thing, love. It's hard to keep everything held in when you're having a good time, which I assume you were having."

"Honestly, I can't believe I even let it happen. What was I thinking? I mean, I didn't even know the guy and I let him stick his tongue down there. I think I was all caught up in the fantasy."

"And what fantasy is that?" Henry asked, kissing the side of my head and snuggling in closer.

"You know, the alpha male, business man fantasy. Where the guy wants you right then and there and you let it happen; you throw caution to the wind and let the man dominate you."

"Not familiar with that fantasy," Henry lightly teased. "But seems like something I might be interested in."

"Stop," I laughed and pushed him away.

"Made that gorgeous smile of yours come out, now didn't I?"

I was about to answer when my phone rang. Reaching over, I picked it up and saw my parents' phone number appear.

"Hello?"

"Hi, honey," my mom said into the phone. "How are you?"

"Doing good, Mom."

Henry perked up at hearing me say mom. He loved my parents and my parents loved Henry, sometimes it felt like more than me at times.

He grabbed the phone from me and squeezed my thigh as he said, "Hi, Mrs. Bloom. It's great to hear from you, too. I'm doing great, and how about yourself. Oh, is that right? Well, tell Mr. Bloom I would eat your spaghetti any day, even if you used tomato paste as the sauce."

I cringed at hearing that. My mom wasn't the best of cooks, and growing up, my dad and I made sure to have spare meals around the house for instances where she made spaghetti sauce with only tomato paste.

"Good talking to you as well, hold on." Henry handed me the phone and said, "It's your mom."

"Really? I had no clue," I said sarcastically, while putting the phone up to my ear. "Hi, Mom."

"Oh, I really miss Henry. Please tell me you both will come out to the house for brunch on Sunday. We would love to see you two."

"Brunch on Sunday? I'm not sure, Mom," I looked over at

Henry, who was nodding his head and giving me the thumbs up. "Are you cooking, Mom?"

"Aren't you a funny girl today? No, you know your dad won't let me near the kitchen for brunch, especially when he's making his famous baked French toast."

"Baked French toast, yeah, I'll be there."

"And Henry?"

Figures, my mom was more concerned about Henry.

I turned to the man who was smiling brightly at me, his eyes happy and his handsome face lit up only for me. No matter what was happening in my life, I could always lean on Henry; I could always count on him to make me feel better.

"Henry, would you like to go to brunch with me on Sunday at my parents' house?"

"Do you even have to ask?"

"He's in, Mom." My mom cheered on the other end of the line, making me roll my eyes.

"That's just wonderful, honey. I miss you two kids. When are you finally going to get together? You would make such a perfect couple."

"Alright, I'm going, Mom," I said, ending the conversation. Without fail, my mom always asked the question of my status with Henry. She was bound and determined to make sure we ended up together. She couldn't get it through her head that we were just friends.

"Okay, honey. I love you and tell Henry bye for me."

"I will."

I hung up the phone and tossed it on the coffee table. Feeling exhausted, I rested my head against the arm of the sofa and looked over at Henry.

"Did she ask if we were dating again?" Henry asked.

"Never fails to ask."

Laughing, Henry pulled on my arm and made me sit up so I was in his embrace again. He made slow circles on my skin with his thumb, sending chills through me.

"Why don't you just let it happen, make your mom happy."

It was the same teasing conversation we had whenever I got off the phone with my mom. Henry found out my mom asked about us as a couple, he said let's give it a try, and I just rolled my eyes at him because I knew he was only kidding. He had a different idea of women to spend time with, but right now, it didn't seem like he was teasing, he sounded more serious.

"Yeah, because that wouldn't be a mistake," I replied, trying to lighten the mood.

I felt Henry stiffen underneath me at my words, and for a second, I thought maybe I offended him, but I felt him soften again as he said, "Yeah, probably."

"I think our food is getting cold," I suggested, trying to change the topic.

"Should I reheat?"

"No, let's just eat."

Releasing me, Henry leaned forward and grabbed for the food. He handed me my plate and a fork, and then grabbed his own.

"You know me too well, beef and broccoli, my favorite."

"Our favorite," he winked while digging in, not taking a moment to breathe as he inhaled everything on his plate. With his mouth full, he asked, "So, what does this mean for your book? Are you still going to write it?"

"I am," I nodded, while covering my mouth with my hand as I chewed. "It's just going to take a while. Did I tell you it's a little ode to our friendship?"

"Really?" he asked, a bit surprised.

"Yeah, I wanted to modernize it a bit, so I'm writing a book about friends in college who find they have feelings for each other along the way."

"Any of this story true?" he asked, while wiggling his eyebrows.

I pressed my hand against his forehead and said, "You and my mom, you're going to drive me crazy."

"It wouldn't be so bad, you know. We know each other, we're comfortable with each other, and we're best friends…"

"Yeah, and we would ruin that friendship when things don't work out."

"And how do you know things wouldn't work out?" he said with a teasing tone, even though his eyes looked serious.

"Because we both know I'm not your type, Henry. Plus, I'm way too inexperienced for you. The furthest I've gotten is face farting."

Chuckling, Henry shook his head and said, "Sorry, I just had to let out a little laugh."

"That's alright. I was waiting for you to finally lose that veneer you were living behind."

Shrugging, he said, "I'm only human, but back to us." Shaking my head, I let him continue, "Think about it, love. My experience can help your inexperience. I can teach you everything you need to know." Softly, he looked up at me and said, "We would be perfect together."

My heart dropped in my stomach as I thought about the possibility. God, at that moment, I wanted him, I wanted to see what it would be like to be his, to have his lips on mine, to experience another side of Henry, the only side I didn't know.

Instead of throwing my arms around him, I brushed him off, not ready to throw away one of the best friendships I've ever had.

"Get out of here, not going to happen."

"Why?" he asked seriously, making me sweat. Was he for real right now?

"Seriously?" I asked, feeling nervous.

Silence fell between us as Henry looked into my eyes, searching for something from me, and I had no clue what it was.

"Forget it. I'm not up for a movie. I think I might just go into my room and watch some TV and go to bed. You're welcome to join me."

I could feel him pull away, and I didn't want that, so I said, "Slumber party?"

His face brightened again as he nodded and took my now empty plate to the kitchen. I turned off the TV in the living room and helped Henry pack up the rest of the Chinese food. We worked in tandem, not having to say a word, but getting the job done efficiently. I giggled to myself as I thought about it. No wonder my mom wanted us together; we already acted like an old married couple.

The kitchen was clean, the lights were turned out, so we headed to Henry's room, which was always immaculately clean, cleaner than my room, and a hell of a lot cleaner than Delaney's, since she decided living in a rat's nest was a lot easier than just cleaning it.

We snuggled into Henry's bed, both facing the TV, but with Henry behind me wrapping his arm around me. We started snuggling in college, and it was something we did often, so to have Henry wrapped around me was nothing new, but this tingly feeling that was developing in the pit of my stomach every time I was around him was new.

"Where's the remote?" he asked, looking around. "It was on the bed," he reached over me and started digging around for it.

"Hey, watch it," I said, just as his hand connected with my breast. We both sucked in a breath as he looked down at me from his position over me.

Time stood still as we searched each other, tried to figure out the electric energy that was passing between us. In that instant, for the first time I could remember, I saw heat in his eyes as he took in my rising chest. My nipples were hard from the small contact he made, as well as from the heated look he was giving me, and from the proximity of our bodies; it was all too much.

My mind was screaming at him to kiss me, to touch me again. I never thought I would have such feelings for him, such outrageous cravings for the man, but with him staring down at me, so close to my body, building a wave a heat through my veins, I wanted his touch…needed his touch.

Painstakingly, his hand slowly moved to the front of my shirt where my breasts were resting. I could feel my breathing start to pick up at his closeness. His head lowered down just enough so his nose grazed mine, barely touching me. My heart seized in my chest just as his hand lightly caressed my breast over my shirt. My heart pounded in my chest as he lowered the extra inch and his lips just barely danced against mine. It was subtle, but it was fucking electrifying, as if damn sparklers were shooting off between us.

All the nerves I experienced before with the other guys were gone, and all that was left was an overwhelming feeling of euphoria. But this was Henry, my Henry, my best friend, the one guy I could count on. Was I really just letting him kiss me? Was I really having these all-consuming feelings for him?

Not once did he press me nor push too hard, he kept his kiss light, his hand soft, and his body relaxed, which caused me to feel every inch of him, every ounce of sweetness he was pouring through me, every last bit of yearning he possessed for me.

I was so gone.

The minute he pulled away, I felt empty, and for some weird reason, I wanted more…and that was what scared me the most. I didn't want him to stop kissing me, or touching me. I wanted him to strip me down and take what I was offering to every other man in my life. In that moment, I wanted Henry to be the one to take my virginity.

His eyes glazed over as he looked down at me and said, "Sorry, love."

The smile that crossed his face told me he wasn't truly sorry, which only confused me even more.

He reached under his pillow and pulled out the remote control that was hiding and turned on the TV. He rested his head against mine as his arm pulled me in close to his body. He didn't say anything to me, but he didn't have to, his lips literally did the talking for him.

For the life of me, I couldn't figure out Henry's motives or what he was planning on doing with the situation he just brewed up between us. After the conversation we had about being together and probably the most amazingly fantastic kiss I ever experienced, I was more confused than ever, but damn was I satisfied.

As the TV played in the background, I thought about everything that transpired between Henry and me. Was this really happening? Were we really crossing the line of friendship?

I could feel him drift off to sleep while he held on to me, so I planned my escape as I turned the TV off after a while and just laid in his bed, in his embrace, thinking what tomorrow was going to bring.

I felt awkward; I didn't know what to say to him, what to do. Did we just ignore what happened and move on our merry way, or did we talk about it in the morning while enjoying a cup of coffee together?

Heat blazed through me at the thought of having that conversation. There was no way I would be able to do that. I was too much of a wuss.

Instead of staying the night with Henry, I slowly crept out of his bed and covered him up with his blankets. Before I left, I looked down at him and studied his handsome face. Ever since I could remember, I had crushed on him, big time, but I always knew we were better off as friends, and I was right. He was my best friend in the whole world, and I wouldn't give that up for a crush. I would never want to lose him.

Once I left his room, I started thinking about what his intention was with his kiss. Why would he do that and risk everything we had together? Was he really a cherry chaser like Delaney said? It would devastate me if he was.

I went back to my room and shut my door quietly, not to wake up Henry. I pulled out my Kindle and started reading to clear my mind, and get lost in other thoughts other than my own. I drifted off to sleep that night, ignoring the pressing feeling that was starting to build in my chest from the knowledge that, in fact, Henry and I crossed a line tonight that I was pretty sure was going to have a huge impact on our friendship.

The next morning, I avoided him at all costs, getting ready for work. Usually, we ran into each other in the bathroom, or he would come in my room while I was doing my makeup and check up on me, but that didn't happen. We kept our distance and that gnawing feeling grew bigger with every minute we weren't talking to each other.

I got dressed in a high-waisted black pencil skirt and polka dot silk top and paired it with black heels. My hair was in waves this morning, thank you curling iron, and I was wearing my signature red lipstick. I had no clue why I got all dressed up for work, since my coworkers were a bunch of fur balls, but all I could think was that getting dressed for the work day made me feel better about myself.

Because Delaney was at Derk's last night, it was just Henry and me in the apartment, making it that much more uncomfortable.

I walked out into the kitchen while buttoning my shirt up, deciding if I could get away with two or three undone buttons, when I spotted Henry leaning against the counter in the kitchen, dressed in one of his immaculate suits, drinking a cup of coffee.

"Good morning, love," he said casually over his mug of coffee, as if he hadn't given me the most passionate kiss of my life last night.

"Good morning," I replied, while looking down at the ground and over to my purse. I was ready to get the hell out of the apartment, even if it meant getting to work early.

There was no chance for me, though, as I felt Henry come up to me from behind and place his hands on my hips. He lowered his head to my ear, sending chills up my spine.

"You look beautiful, love."

Virginia squealed with delight as I tried to calm my raging heart. What was happening?

"Thank you," I squeaked out.

"Turn around," he demanded, and I did as he said, not even questioning it.

With a tilt of my chin, he had me staring into his beautiful eyes, wishing I could read his mind.

"I'm sorry if I caught you off-guard last night, but I'm not sorry for what I did. I couldn't help myself when you looked so gorgeous with your hair fanned out against my pillow and your blue eyes staring up at me. I had to taste you, love."

Umm, not something I expected to hear from my best friend.

"Okay," I said like an idiot.

Smiling, he pressed his lips against my forehead and said, "Have a good day, love. I'll talk to you later."

With that, he buttoned his suit jacket and put his phone in his pocket. I watched as he walked away with ease, as if the tension between us wasn't hovering over us like a giant pink elephant.

Once the door to the apartment closed, I let out the long breath I was holding in and leaned against the kitchen counter. What the hell had I gotten myself into?

CHAPTER 15

"The Melting Pot of New York City's finest Bodily Fluids"

"Where's Delaney?" I asked Derk, who was hanging out in our apartment, looking rather fidgety.

"Out shopping," he looked around the living room as I grabbed a lint roller and started lint rolling the sweater I was wearing.

I was getting ready for my date with Greg that I was semi-looking forward to now. It felt like more of a chore than anything at this point. I was excited about the pizza part though.

The last two days had been the most awkward of my life, thanks to Henry's spontaneous kiss. All day yesterday, I thought about how he treated me in the morning, and how it felt right but also so weird. When I got home last night, I faked sick and made sure no one came in my room by turning out the lights and practically hiding under my blankets so my Kindle didn't shine too brightly.

Was I avoiding Henry? Of course. I didn't know what to say to him, how to react to him, and the one person I wanted I talked to, the one person I worked my problems out with was the problem this time. I thought about talking to Delaney about it, but I didn't want to get her in the middle of our little roommate drama, especially because she probably wouldn't ever let us live it down.

That left Jenny, so when I got to work yesterday, I sat in her office and waited for her to come in. Unfortunately, she and Henry really don't get along, so she wasn't of much help when it came to talking it out. She kept telling me to forget about him and move on, that he was just playing me, which I didn't believe was the truth; at least, I hoped it wasn't. He would have no reason to do such a thing, except for…Cherry Chaser.

There was no way he was a Cherry Chaser. I couldn't believe the idea of such a thing, and I couldn't believe he would ruin our relationship for that, no way.

This morning, when I got ready for work, I slipped out quickly, avoiding him once again, and I knew he knew because later today, he sent me a text letting me know he was displeased with not seeing me in the morning. I felt guilty, so damn guilty, but I was a nervous wreck now whenever I was around him, and I hated that. I shouldn't be nervous around him, ever.

I pushed the Henry drama out of my head when I got home from work and started getting ready for my date. I was hoping for at least an enjoyable night with Greg. He seemed like a good guy. I got a message from him earlier that he wasn't able to secure us reservations at the pizza place, but he thought it would be fun to make pizza at his place, which I decided I was comfortable enough with. I gave Jenny the guy's information, normally a task for Henry, and told her if I didn't text her later tonight, he had abducted me.

I studied Derk some more and noticed he was really on edge, like bouncing his leg up and down, looking at his watch constantly kind of on edge.

Taking a moment, I sat next to him and asked, "Is everything okay, Derk? You seem a little, strange right now."

"Fine," he curtly said, still looking at his watch.

"I don't buy it, what's going on?"

Derk ran his hands through his hair, looked around again, and then pulled something out from his pocket. He held it out to me and I gasped as I saw what it was.

"Is that what I think it is?"

"Yeah," he nodded.

"Are you proposing tonight?"

"I was thinking about it, but she's taking forever to get home. I'm going to lose my nerve."

"Why? Do you think she's going to say no?"

"She might. We haven't talked about marriage or anything like that, Rosie. But I know I can't be without her anymore. I can't stand this her place and my place thing. I want us to live together, to share a life together."

My heart melted right there on the spot. I liked Derk, but I just grew a little bit fonder of him after his little speech.

"She's going to say yes, Derk. No doubt about it. She's crazy about you."

"You think?" he asked, clearly fishing for compliments, but I would give them to him, because he looked seriously distraught.

"I know, Derk. She is going to be so excited. How do you plan on doing it?"

He shrugged his shoulders. "I don't know really. I thought about doing something elaborate, but that's not the kind of couple we are. I was thinking about just meeting her in her bedroom and going down on one knee, keep it simple."

"It will be a total surprise. Eep! I'm so excited for you two," I clapped my hands.

"Thanks, Rosie."

I thought about Derk and Delaney's relationship over the years, and how they started off as friends, but found they were a lot more than friends as their time together went on. I didn't blame them; they were electric together.

"It will happen for you, Rosie," Derk interrupted my thoughts. "Just have faith. You're going to end up with some stud; I just know it."

"Thanks, Derk," I smiled at his choice of words. "I can't believe you two are finally going to get married. I feel like you've been together forever."

"We have, but I'm glad we started out as friends, because there is no relationship unless you're friends first."

"But, weren't you worried about losing that friendship, if things didn't work out?" I asked, trying to sound casual about the question, but by the way Derk looked at me, he could see right through my motive for the question.

"I was more worried about not having Delaney in my life, every second of the day. You know that feeling when something happens to you and there is only one person in the world who will understand you and who you absolutely just have to tell?"

"Yes," I responded, while thinking about Henry, he was my go-to.

"That was Delaney for me. I realized that, at some point, I no longer just wanted her as a friend, I wanted her in my life at all times."

"But, crossing over that line, from friends to…more than friends, wasn't it awkward?"

"No," he said matter-of-factly. "It almost seemed like it was meant to be, like it was crazy we hadn't been making out for years."

"Hmm," I twisted my hands in my lap as I thought about the other night, how my lips so easily glossed over Henry's, how his hand roaming my body didn't make me want to swat him away, more like pull him even closer.

I've read books where best friends got together, and it always seemed so easy. Was this what it was like, to start to see your best friend differently? Did he see me differently? Or was I just being a girl?

"You should go for it. Henry is a great guy and adores you."

"Excuse me?" I asked, feeling a little shocked that Derk could read my mind.

"Come on, the sexual chemistry between you two is so damn uncomfortable to be around. It would be great if you two did us all a favor and finally did the dirty deed."

"I don't want that, though, to just have a night with him. That would ruin everything, Derk."

"I don't think he just wants one night with you, Rosie. You can see it in his eyes, the way he looks at you, the way he's overprotective of you."

"That's him being a friend."

"Is that right? Well, he doesn't do the same thing for Delaney, now does he?"

I opened my mouth to answer, to tell him he did, but when I thought about it, he really didn't. Henry and Delaney were friends, but not as close as Henry and I were.

"He doesn't treat her the same because she has you; he doesn't need to be protective over her," I countered.

"That's crap and you know it." Derk got up off the couch and walked toward Delaney's room, where I assumed he was going to wait for her. "Just admit it, Rosie, you like Henry and he likes you. The sooner you two figure that out, the sooner you will be able to find what Delaney and I have, and believe me when I say, I would wish my relationship upon anyone; it's the best thing in my life."

With a smile, he walked in her bedroom and shut the door.

I slouched on the couch and tried to figure out where my heart rested. Instead of being able to calm the nerves floating in my stomach, they just continued to twist in knots, over and over again.

The image of my lead character in my book came into my head, and I thought about what she would do in the situation, what

I would want her to do. Given that I'm a romantic at heart, I would be beating my Kindle against my pillow, telling the girl to give up her stupid reservations and just go for it. Isn't that how all romantics are, give love a chance? That was the sole basis of every romance novel out there; give love a chance.

It seemed so easy, to just put yourself out there, to give in to the feelings you've kept hidden for so long, to put the most important thing in your life on the line.

If I ever lost Henry because I thought he might actually want to start a relationship with me, I would never forgive myself. He is too important to me.

Ugh, I was that girl. That girl who couldn't make up her damn mind. That girl in a novel that I wanted to shake uncontrollably, slap some sense into her. I could see the reviews now, God, Rosie is so annoying. Rosie is so wishy-washy. Rosie doesn't know a good thing when it hits her in the face.

Well from an outsider's perspective, love seems easy, but when you're the one in the hot seat, making the decisions, it's not that easy putting your heart out there, gathering enough courage to fall into the unknown. Love isn't easy and love isn't kind; love is something you sacrifice everything for in the hopes that maybe, just maybe, there is a person in this world who will accept you for who you are.

The front door to the apartment opened, and I knew without even looking it was Henry by the way his shoes hit the wooden floors.

"Rosie, I'm glad you're here. I wanted to see if you felt like going to that swing club with me? Friday night swing," he wiggled his eyebrows as he sat next to me.

I hated how casual he was with me, when deep inside, my gut was twisting.

"I can't," I said as I sat up and looked over at him. "I have a date with Greg tonight."

Henry's brow creased as he studied what I said.

"That's the guy with the dog?"

"Yes, I'm going to his place to make some pizza."

"Dressed like that?" he asked, looking me up and down.

"Yes, what's wrong with what I'm wearing?"

"Seems a little revealing, don't you think?"

I stood up and walked over to a mirror that was in the living room. I took in the black outfit I had on. It was black pants and a black top, but the top had some lace in the front neckline, not really showing anything.

"No. It's fine."

"I think you should go change, and while you're at it, change into a swing dress so you can go dancing with me tonight."

"Henry, I told you, I have a date."

"Cancel," he said, as he came up next to me and grabbing my hands so he could pull me in closer to his body. His head lowered to mine so our foreheads were touching. "Come out with me, Rosie. Let me take you on a date." The way he spoke to me was so vulnerable, like he was trying to offer me the world, but was nervous about it.

My lungs seized on me, and I knew I was going to start hyperventilating. Why was he doing this? He was changing the dynamics of our relationship. It made me so incredibly scared.

Trying to not hurt him, I said, "We have a date Sunday; we're going to brunch."

With the touch of his finger, he lifted my chin and gazed into my eyes.

"I want a real date, Rosie. I want a date with you and only you, not your parents and not our friends. I want to take you out, open doors for you, spoil you, and take you home. I want it all, Rosie."

Being honest, I replied, "You're confusing me, Henry. You're making it seem like, like…you like me."

He tilted his head to the side as he responded. "Would that be such a bad thing?"

Would it? Well, Virginia would be happy, but right about now Virginia would be happy with a lubed up turkey baster. My inner girl, the girl who's had a crush on Henry for so long wanted it, wanted him, but my heart wasn't ready to lose my best friend.

"I don't know," I answered honestly. "I'm just so confused, Henry. The way you're treating me, the things you're saying, I'm afraid I'm going to lose you."

"What do you mean?" he asked, genuinely confused.

"You're my best friend. I don't want something to happen between us and then I lose you. I would be devastated."

"You would be devastated? Hell, Rosie, I wouldn't know what to do if you were no longer in my life."

"Exactly," I added, while patting his chest. "Why mess with a good thing, right?"

His brow furrowed and he stepped back from me, clearly insulted, even though I didn't mean to.

He rubbed his chin as he scanned me. "You know, Rosie, it surprises me how dense and naïve you can be at times."

"Excuse me?"

"You heard me. Don't you see the way I look at you every day, the way I touch you and talk to you? Can't you see my heart beating out of my fucking chest every time I'm around you?"

"Yeah, but it's because you're my friend, right?"

Shaking his head, he ran his hand over his face, and then walked away.

Yup, I get the moron of the year award.

"Henry, I'm sorry."

"Yeah, me too, Rosie. Have fun with the dog lover tonight. I'll be out for the weekend. Mikey invited me to the Hamptons."

"Wait, does that mean you're not going to brunch?"

"Yes, that means I won't make it to brunch, since I'll most likely be wasted starting tonight and ending Monday morning."

"You're really not going?" I asked, feeling pretty sad and upset that he was starting to shut me out.

"I'm really not going, Rosie. I'm sorry, but I just don't feel like being around you right now."

"But, Henry," my voice choked on a sob that wanted to

escape. The minute he heard the tightness in my voice, he sighed, walked over to me and pulled me into his chest. "You can't just leave me. This is why I didn't want anything to happen. I can't have you mad at me, Henry. Please don't pull yourself away, I can't handle it."

Blowing out a frustrated breath, Henry nodded and then pulled away. "Sorry, love. Just give me some time right now, alright? I will see you Monday. Have a good weekend and have fun with the dog lover. Don't get into any trouble."

A weak smile spread across his face as he nodded and walked away.

I could feel it, it was the beginning of the end for Henry and me. I knew he said it wouldn't affect us, but it already had. He was already pulling himself away, and because of that, a little piece inside of me died. I wouldn't be able to survive without Henry. He was everything to me, absolutely everything.

***

My mood for my date with Greg was dampened, thanks to the awkward conversation with Henry, but I tried to put on a good face when I met Greg, who was just as handsome in person as he was in his pictures.

Along with Greg was his best buddy, Bear, who seemed to be a very loving but protective dog. The dynamic between the two was endearing, and I could appreciate the bond they had with each other, even though it might be weird that Greg practically made out with his dog every chance he got.

After some semi-awkward pleasantries and introductions, we jumped right into the pizza making, which was good for me because I was starving.

Greg lived on the Upper West side and had a small but nice apartment. If your apartment wasn't small in New York City, then you were raking in some good money. Greg was a young investment broker, but according to him, he was on the "up and up" with his company and was looking at a promotion soon. He spoke animatedly about his job, like he actually liked it, and it surprised me, to see someone so enthusiastic about their occupation.

Maybe it was because I despised my job. Delaney and Henry would occasionally talk about what they were doing, but for the most part, kept their excitement to a minimum.

"So, tell me, Rosie, what brought you to New York City?" Greg asked, as he popped a bottle of wine, something I would probably have to choke down because wine wasn't my favorite of all the alcoholic beverages.

"My parents live on Long Island."

"Ah, I never would have pictured you as a girl from Long Island."

"Yes, I break all the stereotypes," I joked. "When I was in high school, I wanted to get off the island and onto the real one, so I worked my butt off in school and was accepted into NYU, where I majored in English."

"English? Interesting. Tell me, what's your favorite book?"

"No doubt about it, *Pride and Prejudice*. It's the ultimate romance, in my opinion."

Nodding, Greg handed me a glass of wine and went to the fridge where he pulled out a bowl of dough that he must have made earlier, because it seemed like the dough had risen throughout the day.

"Who is your Mr. Darcy?"

"Is that even a question? Colin Firth, come on Greg," I smiled.

"Okay, just checking, because if you said the guy who was in the new version of *Pride and Prejudice*, you know, the one with Kiera Knightly..."

"Matthew MacFayden," I helped.

"Really? That's his name?" Greg asked with a confused look. "Huh, never would have guessed that. Anyway, if you said that guy, I would have had to end this date."

"I didn't know you were such a P&P fan."

"That Elizabeth Bennet is a strong-willed chick to stand up to Mr. Darcy."

A slow grin spread across his face, loosening the tension in my body. Maybe I had a rough conversation with Henry that truly hurt my heart, but sitting here with Greg, drinking wine, it almost seemed so natural.

"You really know how to win over a girl's heart with that kind of talk."

"I'm a Jane-ite, what can I say?" he said, referring to the name Jane Austen fans called themselves.

"Shut up, you are not. Next thing you're going to tell me you're a Brony."

"What's wrong with that? Frankly, Rainbow Dash is my favorite My Little Pony, but Toola-Roola really has my heart at times."

I spit some wine out of my mouth at his confession and grabbed for a towel to wipe my lips as he just threw his head back and laughed.

"Please tell me you're not really a Brony? How do you even know their names?"

"I have a six year old niece who is obsessed. I watch her occasionally for my brother, and can you guess her latest addiction?"

"My Little Pony?"

"Bingo," Greg said while tapping my nose. "I get sucked into watching the damn show and playing with her figurines. I have to be honest, some of those ponies are real bitches."

"I can only imagine; there's only so much sparkle in the world to go around."

"It's so true," he shook his head and smiled. "Enough pony talk, shall we get going on our pizzas?"

"Sure. Let me wash my hands real quick and then I can help."

I got off the bar stool I was sitting on and went over to his sink, where I washed up. I really admired his small but modern kitchen. It was clean and well decorated. The guy had his stuff together, that was for sure.

"How old are you again?" I asked.

"Wow, getting down to it, aren't we?" He chuckled and answered. "Thirty."

"Thirty? Wow, you're an old man."

"An old man? Really? Well, I guess I'll just be enjoying the pizza for myself."

"No, I didn't mean that," I said quickly, while drying my hands. "You're…cultured."

"Ha, alright, nice recovery. Here," he handed me half of the dough. "Start kneading it and stretching it out so we can put some sauce and cheese on it. I have some toppings in the fridge you can choose from as well."

"Did you make this dough from scratch?" I asked, seriously impressed.

"I can see from the awe in your eyes that impresses you, so I hate that I have to say no. The pizza shop around the corner sells their dough, so I thought I would grab some for us tonight."

"Smart idea. Whenever I make home pizza, I grab a box of Jiffy pizza crust and let's just say it always turns out like crap."

Laughing, Greg agreed. "Worst pizza dough mix ever. The only thing Jiffy is good for is their corn mix. That stuff is legit."

"You know every southern cook is swearing your name from that statement."

"Hey, I'm a city boy, I don't know any better. A little honey on that cornbread, and you're good to go. Doesn't get much better than that."

"Pretty sure it does," I teased, as I struggled to knead my dough. Greg didn't seem to be having the same issues as me. "Why is your dough getting all stretched out and mine is shriveling up like balls in a cold vat of water."

Did I just say that? I threw my hand over my mouth, shocked that I said such a thing on a first date. When I looked over at Greg, he was gaping at me as a smile spread across his handsome face.

"Oh, my God, I didn't know I was getting a little potty mouth with the package I invited over. I like it," he chuckled. "To answer your question, you need to knead the dough, make love to it."

Easy for him, I thought. He definitely wasn't a virgin, not with that body, that face, and those hands. Nope, he was experienced.

How do you make love to dough? Visions of me making out with the dough, thrusting my tongue at it and stroking the dough until it flattened ran through my mind. The whole idea was completely absurd, but then again, maybe it could work.

I leaned my head down for a second and then common sense kicked me in the ass and told me to be a normal human. Instead of making out with my pizza dough, I looked over at Greg and watched what he was doing and mimicked his movements.

"I think my fists are too small," I said, as I pounded on the dough.

Greg pulled away from his pizza and grabbed my hands. He brought them close to his face and examined them carefully.

"You know, I think you're right. These hands are too dainty. Here, take my dough and I'll take yours."

"What a chivalrous man," I joked.

"Don't you forget it."

We flattened out our pizza dough a little bit more, and once we were satisfied, we placed them on a baking sheet.

"Alright, this is the fun part, time to put on some toppings." He went to the fridge and started pulling out bowls with saran wrap on them. "I have diced peppers, peperoni, black olives and broccoli," he winked at me and continued, "some sausage and mushrooms."

"Black olives and broccoli, trying to win some brownie points, are we?"

"Is it working?"

"Remarkably," I answered, knowing it really was.

"Yes," he fist pumped the air like a nerd, making me giggle.

Surprisingly, I was having a rather enjoyable time with Greg, and was trying to figure out what was wrong with him. There was always something wrong.

After we put the toppings on our pizzas, we placed them in the oven and waited for them to cook. He invited me over to his couch, which I accepted. I sat down, crossing one leg under my seat so I was facing him. He turned toward me with his arms on the back of the couch. He was wearing a navy polo and jeans; he looked casual, yet very nice.

What had me laughing was his interesting printed socks. They were yellow with strawberry frosted doughnuts on them.

I nodded toward them and said, "Nice socks."

"Thanks, my mom gets me socks all the time with weird things on them."

"And you wear them? Aren't you the model son?"

He shrugged his shoulders. "She's made it a hobby of hers now. She likes to find weird socks from different places. Randomly, I'll get packages in the mail containing just a pair of socks."

"Really? That's cute. What's been you're favorite pair so far?"

"Hmm, that's a hard question. I have so many. Probably the pair that's honoring the Duke and Duchess of Cambridge."

"You mean Prince William and Kate Middleton?"

"The one and only," he smiled. "One sock has the Duke and the other has the Duchess. I can't tell you how into the royal wedding my mom was. She flew to England to stand outside and wave a flag with their faces on it while they rode down the streets of London."

"Your mom was there?" I asked, completely awestruck. I mean, I wasn't obsessed with the royal wedding, but I will admit that I might have watched it, and I might have picked up a couple of magazines, but that was only because Kate Middleton was living a commoner's dream. She was a peasant in the morning, but a princess in the afternoon. When does that ever happen?

"She was. She started saving for her plane ticket the minute William and Kate started dating."

"Seriously? But didn't they break up at one point?"

"They went their separate ways for a brief moment in time, but my mom held out for them and stayed positive. I wish I had a recording of when my mom called me to tell me they were back together, oh, and then when they were engaged, God, I really thought she was going to have a heart attack, the woman was screeching in my ear. It was rather intense."

"I think I love your mom," I laughed.

"Were you into the royal wedding?"

"I mean, I didn't get a commemorative coin to remember the day, but I watched, and I might have picked up a magazine or two. And, I don't care what people say, Pippa didn't steal the show."

"I agree, she was beautiful, but nothing beats Kate in that lace top dress."

I paused and studied him for a second with a quirk of my lips.

"Are you gay?" I asked.

A guttural laugh came from him as his head flew back.

"No, I just get to hear my mom talk about the royal family all the time. No joke, anything that happens, she calls to talk to me about it."

"How did she feel when Prince George came into the picture?"

"She made a scrapbook for the occasion. Printing pictures off the internet of Prince William as a baby and glued them next to Prince George. She swears they're identical, but they really aren't. To please her, I just agree."

"You're such a good son," I patted his cheek.

"I try to be, so obviously, when she sent me a package from London, mind you, I knew it had to be a pair of royal socks, and I was right. She also put some tea and shortbread in the package, stating it was the best she had ever had."

"Seems like maybe she was supposed to be born in London."

"Tell me about it. She would move there in a heartbeat if it wasn't for me and my brother. She is attached to my niece, so she would never live that far away from her. We're nervous though, because my mom has already started talking to my niece about the royal family and becoming a princess one day. She believes she could be Prince George's wife. She even tells my brother there is nothing wrong with his daughter being a cougar."

"Oh, that is amazing," I chuckled. "Your mom seems awesome."

"She is."

The oven beeped, indicating the pizzas were done, so I helped Greg take them out, cut them up, and plate them. I put a little too many toppings on mine, so I had to use a fork and knife to eat mine, because every time I picked up a slice, it just flopped over, letting all the toppings fall off.

We ate our pizza, which was quite good, and talked about small things, keeping the conversation light and fun. The date that I was dreading earlier on was actually turning out to be rather fun. I should have known Greg was going to be a good guy from the messages he sent me.

After we finished the pizzas, cleaned up, and wiped down the counters, Greg grabbed my hand and led me back to his couch. This time, he sat much closer, still wrapping his hand around the couch as his other hand held onto mine.

"Thank you for coming over tonight," he said, while looking me directly in the eyes.

My heart took off at a rapid beat from his proximity. It never ceased to surprise me what a little human contact could do to me. When a guy started to become intimate, my body started to tingle, and my mind almost turned into mush.

"Thank you for having me over," I responded, just as Bear took a seat next to us and started licking himself.

The loud slurp of his tongue hitting his privates echoed through the silent room, and it was all I could think about as he lapped up his junk.

Glancing down, I took a look at Bear to see him lightly nibbling on his crotch, apparently trying to dig deep into his dirty junk. The noise, smell, and look of him cleaning himself had me revolting and wanting to dry heave. I thought Sir Licks-a-Lot was bad when he cleaned his mini kitty balls, but this was one hundred times worse, because the noise was like a slurping whale trying to waft through shit. It was nasty.

"Doing your daily cleaning, bud?" Greg asked, while looking fondly at his dog.

I wiped the look of disgust off my face as I watched Greg admire his dog's cleaning tactics, and wondered how the man could possibly enjoy watching that, let alone hearing it.

"He's really getting in there, isn't he?" I asked, trying to be polite.

"Oh, yeah," Greg responded, almost proud of the damn dog. "Bear has to have the cleanest balls in the Upper West side, isn't that right, buddy?" Greg asked, as he leaned down and rubbed Bear on the head.

"Well, what an accomplishment," I said, trying to hide the sarcasm pouring out of my mouth, which I did a good job of, since Greg turned to me and smiled. He pulled me in closer to him and started playing with my hair.

Yup, he wanted to kiss me, I could see it in the way he kept glancing down at my lips and the way he was inching closer every second.

The thrill of someone leaning in to kiss me never seemed to diffuse, because each moment was the same. I grew nervous and excited all at the same time.

Closing my eyes, I leaned forward as well, just as Greg's hand wrapped around my neck and pulled me in that last inch. His lips softly hit mine and gently started kissing me as I reciprocated the motion.

The man knew how to kiss, I realized, as I let him explore me, while I very slowly opened my mouth, but not quite enough for him to get too frisky. It was an innocent kiss, a sweet kiss, and one that I thoroughly enjoyed.

Everything was perfect, except for the feeling of someone staring at us. Carefully, I opened up my eyes and glanced over at Bear while I continued to kiss Greg. To my horror, I saw Bear looking up at me as he ever so slowly licked his crotch, as if he was watching soft porn and pleasing himself. His eyes bore into my soul and I couldn't help but pull away from Greg. I was able to get over most things quite easily, but a dog pleasuring himself while watching me make out with his master was something I just couldn't handle.

"What's wrong?" Greg asked, confused as to why I pulled away.

Clearing my throat, I chanced a look at Bear and said, "Bear seems to have a staring problem."

"What?" Greg asked, a little insulted.

"He keeps looking at us and cleaning himself, while we're kissing. It's just a little weird."

"It's not weird," Greg laughed, as he leaned over and patted Bear on the head. "You're just curious, aren't you buddy?"

In slow motion, I watched Bear's long tongue with a black dot on the end—gross—fly out of his mouth and start licking Greg's face, lips and yup, even tongue, as Greg laughed from the onslaught of love from his dog.

My eyes turned into microscopes, taking in every last germ that was spread from Bear's balls to Greg's face in a matter of seconds.

After a few minutes, Greg pulled away and turned toward me. "He's just a dog, nothing to worry about."

With a smile, Greg leaned forward and puckered his lips, just as my hand flew up and stopped his approach by basically palming his head like a damn basketball.

"Uh, what are you doing?" Greg asked between my fingers.

I tried to see Greg, tried to see the man I saw earlier, but it was impossible, because all I could see was small dog balls hanging off of his face, dog feces and dog pee tainting those lips. Thoughts of how many times Greg made out with his dog before I even got to his apartment tonight ran through my head. Did he make out with Bear right before I arrived? Did I, in a roundabout way, end up kissing Bear's junk tonight?

"Eck," I said, while getting up and shaking my hand.

"What's wrong?"

"You have dog balls on your face?"

"What?" Greg asked, truly confused.

"Dog balls, you have dog balls on your face. Jesus, I kissed a man with a dog ball face."

"Where is this coming from?"

"From your dog," I said, pointing at Bear, who was in proper ball licking position, but looking at both of us with the picture of innocence all over his face. "First of all, your dog licks his junk as if he's digging through a basin of quicksand, and secondly, do you realize the last thing your dog licked was his balls and then he licked your face? Call me a prude, but I don't want dog balls on my face."

"You're serious?" he asked, confused.

"Yes!" I said, while pulling my hand away. "You can't possibly think I would want to kiss you after that display of affection with your dog."

"I feel like you're insulting Bear. I'm not cool with that, Rosie."

Jesus.

"Well, I'm not cool with your dog practically giving himself oral while he watches us kiss."

"Wow, talk about a one-eighty. You're a bit of a snob, Rosie."

"I'm a snob? Because I don't want dog giblets on my face? Okay, I just thought that was being sanitary."

"I think it's time for you to leave."

"You think?" I said sarcastically, as I grabbed my purse and stomped out of his apartment more angry than anything else.

June 12, 2014

Getting lucky in the city is proving to be quite impossible. If it isn't a pube in the back of my throat getting in the way, then it's man's best friend, and I'm not talking about the penis.

Really? Did he really think I was going to kiss him after he made out with his dog? Even if his dog wasn't licking his junk beforehand, I still would have required a wipe down of the face before we went back to our lip lock.

Its common sense. Dogs carry a gaggle of germs on one millimeter of their tongues. If they're not licking themselves, they're eating their poop, or they're eating someone else's poop, or they're drinking out of a toilet, or just licking the light post that every hobo in the city has peed on.

Note to self, don't date men with dogs unless you plan on making out with a melting pot of New York City's finest bodily fluids.

CHAPTER 16

"The Man Milk Shuffle"

"Delaney, I can't believe you're engaged?" I said, as I eyed the rock on Delaney's finger. Derk really went all out when it came to her ring.

"I know. I gave Derk the best blow job of my life last night as a thank you."

"That was him squealing?"

"Yes," she smiled as I cringed.

I heard some hideous sound come from their bedroom, and I just assumed it was Delaney, even though it seemed a little deep for her, but to find out it was Derk, I didn't think I could look at the man the same way.

Even though I was slightly disturbed, I was still a little curious, so I asked, "What did you do that had him making such awful noises?"

"Don't judge the noises," Delaney waved her finger at me. "Until you know what it's like to lose all sense of what's around you in the throes of passion, you can't judge."

"Fair enough."

She was right. I really had no room to judge, especially since I didn't have any experience. The one time I was even close to reaching that big O moment with Phillip, the man who felt my fart

THE VIRGIN ROMANCE NOVELIST

caress his chin—poor Phillip—I made noises only a feral cat would make while searching for their mate in heat.

"So, what were you doing?" I asked as my face heated up from just thinking about that afternoon with Phillip…what a disaster that was.

Leaning in, Delaney propped her chin on her hand and said, "So, Derk has this thing with his balls, he loves them to be touched, sucked on, licked, what have you, but the thing with Derk is his balls are huge."

"Ugh, gross, Delaney," I said, while pulling away.

"What? They're big, Rosie. You have to know this, not all dicks and balls are the same. Some are uneven, some are crooked, some are small but wide, and some are thin and long. They're all special in their own way. Derk just so happened to be born with the balls of a fucking Greek god, that's if Greek gods had massive balls. Have you seen balls before?"

"Yes," I said defensively.

"Okay, well picture those balls in your head."

The only real life balls I had seen were Alejandro's, and we know they were covered by his man garden, so I tried to picture what they were underneath all the weeds.

"Okay," I faked, because all I could envision was his pubic hairs…everywhere.

"Well, triple the size of those balls, no, quadruple."

"Umm…okay," I said, still not seeing it, which Delaney noticed, so she huffed and looked around our kitchen.

"Oh, I know." She went to the fridge and started rummaging around until she pulled out a grapefruit and then grabbed a banana off of the counter. She put them together and held them in front of me.

"This, Rosie, this is what I'm talking about. His balls are like this grapefruit, just enormous."

Studying the grapefruit, I shook my head. There was no way Derk had balls that big, where the hell did he put them?

"I know what you're thinking, he wears briefs, straight up. He tried boxers once and I had never seen such bad chafing in my entire life. Briefs are like a protective sling for his balls, keeping them high and tight to his body, so he's able to walk around without making it that noticeable. The first time I ever saw his balls, I'm pretty sure I blacked out for a second. When he took his pants off for the first time in front of me, I watched as his balls dropped heavily from his briefs and dangled between his legs like a damn kettlebell. It was the sexiest most intriguing thing I had ever seen. There's something to be said about a man with a giant set of nuts."

"Is that right? What's that?"

"The amount of cum that spews out of them when they orgasm could take down the *Titanic*. It's always a mess with us."

"A mess? What? What do you mean a mess?"

"Rosie, when a guy comes and he's not wearing a condom, where do you think it all goes?"

"In your vagina," I said, matter-of-factly.

"And once it's in your vagina, where does it go from there?"

"Um, I don't know. Don't your uterine walls soak it up? You know, like lotion."

"Are you saying jiz is the vagina's form of lotion?"

I shrugged, "Isn't it?"

"No!" Delaney said, while laughing. "Oh, my God, Rosie. First of all, vaginas don't need lotion, second of all, what goes in, must come out."

"So, what are you saying? Does it just…drip out of you?"

"Uh, yeah. Haven't you seen me run from my bedroom to the bathroom wearing only a bathrobe?"

"Yeah, but I thought you just had to pee."

"No. It's called the man milk shuffle. You keegle the shit out of your vagina, keep your legs closed as tight as possible, don't even dare to breathe as you shuffle to the bathroom and then flop on the toilet to let everything fall out."

My hand flew to my mouth as I racked my brain for such a scene to have played out in any of the books I'd read.

Nothing.

Nothing about the man milk shuffle.

Disturbed, I asked, "It just falls out?"

Nodding her head and taking a giant bite out of the peeled banana in her hand, she said, "Yup, just falls right out. The worst is when you get all sexy in the bathroom of a bar or something like that and you don't have enough time for gravity to work its magic. Then you find yourself back out on the dance floor, dancing your life away, and all of a sudden, you get a wave of man milk falling right into your underwear…"

"Nope," I shook my head. "Nope, this was never told to me. Where was this information in sex ed? Where is it in life?"

"In case you haven't noticed, it's kind of taboo, Rosie. No one wants to talk about how jiz falls out of vaginas."

"Obviously!" I planted my head in my hands. "The more I find out about this whole sex thing, the more I want to avoid it. It's supposed to hurt, even though books describe it as a 'pinch', you're apparently supposed to bleed everywhere—looking forward to that—and now you have to worry about cum falling out of you?"

"Well, you shouldn't have to worry about that at first, because you should be using a condom. Plus, Derk is the exception since he has such huge balls. With another guy with normal balls, you won't have as much cream to deal with."

"Don't call it cream, Jesus."

Laughing, Delaney finished off the banana and said, "Still, it won't be bad, Rosie. I promise. Once you get past the initial awkwardness of it all, you will actually love it. There is just something about sex that is so primal, so absolutely fan-fucking-tastic that you have to experience, that you need in your life."

"So, when writing my book, do I include the whole cum falling out of the vagina thing?"

"No, God, Rosie. First of all, from the sounds of your book, you need to have the people practicing safe sex, because that's being responsible, and then secondly, do you really think the waterfall of baby gravy is going to be something readers will want to read about?"

"You did not just call it baby gravy."

"I did, because that's what Derk has. It's so thick..."

"Stop, please, just stop. There's a line, Delaney, and hearing about the texture of your boyfriend's cum is way past that line."

"Why are we talking about my cum? Derk said with a goofy grin on his face and his hair sticking out in all different directions, most likely from Delaney's fingers.

"I was trying to tell her about what made you scream like a girl last night, but it turned into talking about your huge balls."

"Babe, you know I only keep the knowledge of my melon balls between us."

"Apparently not," I mumbled.

"Don't I have the most gorgeous fiancé?" Derk asked me, while wrapping his arms around Delaney and kissing the side of her head.

"You do. I'm really happy for the both of you. Good job on the ring too, Derk."

"Thanks. It was worth it, given the blowy I got last night."

"Most expensive blow job of your life," Delaney teased, as she patted him on his five o'clock shadow.

"What are you two up to today?" I asked, just as my phone rang. "Hold that thought."

I looked down at my phone and saw Lance's number pop up. "Hello?"

"Hey, Rosie? How are you this morning?"

"Good, please don't tell me you're calling me to cancel our date."

Blowing out a long breath, he answered, "I am."

My stomach sank. I could have really used the date with Lance today, not only to forget last night's mistake, but also to get my mind off of Henry. Like he said, he wasn't home and he wasn't answering his phone. He wanted his space.

"But, I still want to see you today. I just need to change our plans."

Perking back up, I asked, "Why's that?"

"I'm kind of an idiot and broke my wrist last night, so rowing a boat is kind of out of the question."

"Oh no, are you okay?"

"I'm fine, more embarrassed than anything."

"Why? How did you break it?"

"I can't tell you. The way I see it is if I tell you before our date, you might not want to hang out with me. So, if you still come see me, I will tell you how I broke my wrist."

"You drive a hard bargain, but I'll take it. What are the plans now?"

"Would you want to come over here and hang out? Maybe play a game? I have some pain killers running through my system, and don't really want to be navigating through the city right now."

"That's fine with me. Text me your address, and I'll bring over lunch as well."

"Now, what kind of date would I be if I let you do that? We can order take out. Just get your sweet butt here around noon, okay?"

"Sounds good."

"Looking forward to seeing you, Rosie."

"You too," I said shyly, just as I hung up.

"Oooh, who was that?" Delaney cooed.

"My date for today, Lance. Remember him, the guy I split my pants in front of?"

"The cat photographer," Derk said.

"He doesn't just take pictures of cats; he only did that a couple of times," I replied in an annoyed tone.

"Still…meow," Derk said while raising his "pretend" claw at me.

"I hate you," I laughed. Changing the subject, I asked, "What's the newly engaged couple going to do today?"

"Probably fuck all day long," Derk said with a hopeful look.

"No," Delaney shot him down. "We have lunch with our parents to celebrate, but we can fuck up until then."

"Really? Then what are we waiting for?"

"Go get naked," Delaney slapped his ass. "I'll be right in."

"Best fiancé ever!"

We watched as Derk leapt in the air and clicked his heels together while taking his shirt off. Delaney shook her head at him, but her eyes spoke of love. I was so happy for them. They really deserved each other; they were perfect together.

Before the ugly green monster of jealousy roared to life, I shook the thoughts out of my head and twirled my phone on the counter.

"What's going on with you and Henry?" Delaney asked, just as Derk clicked her bedroom door shut.

"W-what are you talking about?" I stuttered.

The last thing I wanted was to get Delaney involved in the melodrama between Henry and me. I didn't want her to have to get in the middle and feel the need to fix things, because, knowing Delaney, that was exactly what she was going to want to do.

"Henry called me last night when Derk and I were in the middle of getting busy, so I didn't answer, but he left me a voicemail and he was drunk off his ass, mumbling into the phone about you and not giving him a chance."

Crap.

My heart churned in my chest from the thought of Henry getting wasted and having a semi-heart to heart with Delaney. First of all, I didn't like that my actions led him to have such a night, and secondly, I hated that he called Delaney. I was always his drunk call; I was the one he talked to when he was upset, but now that I was the issue, I couldn't be the solution.

"Yeah, you don't need to get in the middle of it. We're just having some miscommunications at the moment," I answered, trying to be as politically correct as possible.

"I don't buy it," she saw right through me. "Derk said some strange stuff was happening between you two, and he also said he heard Henry ask you to go swing dancing last night."

"Derk needs to mind his own business," I mumbled.

"He's a nosy little bitch, you know that, especially when he's uncomfortable. Since he was proposing last night, just waiting for me, of course he was going to listen to your conversation. Now tell me, what's going on?"

"Nothing," I said, growing irritated. "Just drop it, Delaney."

"Is he trying to get with you? I told you he's a cherry chaser."

"He is not," I defended him. "He wouldn't throw our friendship away just because he likes to sleep with virgins, which isn't the truth anyway."

"Have you asked him?"

"No," I replied. "How would I even go about having that conversation with him? There really isn't a smooth segue into such a topic."

"You're right about that. I would just ask him."

"I'm not going to ask him, because it's irreverent. We're just having a disagreement right now."

"Okay," Delaney eyed me suspiciously. "I'm just going to tell you this, I don't like it when my friends are not talking."

"We're talking," I lied.

"Yeah, if you were talking, then Henry would have been dialing your phone number last night and not mine. Don't let whatever is going on between you two get in the way of your friendship, because what you two share is perfect. You don't want to lose that."

Duh.

Delaney wished me luck on my date and walked off to her bedroom, where I heard her squeal the minute she shut the door. Living with two very sexual beings was difficult, especially when they were on a high from getting engaged.

Since it was still early in the morning, I decided to tackle some pages in my book and listen to music to drown out the sounds coming from Delaney's room.

"You've never looked prettier," Brian said to Vanessa, who was wearing a bright yellow sundress that helped highlight her blonde locks.

"Thank you, Brian," Vanessa said shyly, wondering if this was truly the turning point in her relationship with Brian.

Secretly, she had been harboring feelings for Brian ever since she met him for the first time during freshman orientation, but she was just too nervous to do anything about her feelings. So instead, she became great friends with him, all the time watching him go out with girl after girl, slowly chipping away at her heart with each passing date.

She wondered why she was never one of those girls, strutting around on his arm. Why she wasn't the one who was able to hold his hand and walk through the lecture hall while he told jokes in her ear that only she could hear.

What she wouldn't do to be that girl, but now that she was faced with her dreams becoming a reality, she started second guessing the foundation of the friendship she'd built with Brian.

She wasn't second guessing the stability of it, no, she was second guessing her feelings toward Brian. She had a best friend who would be by her side through thick and thin. Did she really want to forfeit that for the possibility of love?

As she looked into Brian's eyes, she was at a standstill. Should she proceed? Should she take the leap?

"Damn," I mumbled, as I pulled away and looked at my book.

I rubbed my hands over my face and stepped away from my computer. I wanted to write an ode to my friendship with Henry, but what I didn't want to do was write an autobiography, and that was pretty much what was happening.

Instead of writing, I shut my laptop and tucked myself back in bed. A small tear fell down my cheek as I thought about Henry and what was happening. I was losing him, and I was afraid the only way to keep him from falling out of my life was tossing him my heart as a life saver, and I wasn't so sure I would be able to recover if he broke it.

CHAPTER 17

"The Worm with a Broken Neck"

I knocked on Lance's door and waited patiently for him to open it. I know he said we could order in, but I decided to bring cookies at least. I thought maybe the sugar would make his wrist feel better, at least that's what helped me get over an injury when I was younger. Lots and lots of sugar.

After a few locks moving around, Lance opened the door and smiled down at me. He was wearing a pair of worn jeans and a deep green T-shirt. He looked very casual but yummy with his styled hair and thick-rimmed glasses.

"Hey, Rosie."

"Hi, Lance, how's the arm?" I asked, while nodding toward his cast that was a fantastic neon orange.

"It's doing better now that you're here."

"Hmm, corny, but nice," I teased. "Awesome choice of color, by the way. I didn't know they allowed adults to pick cool colors like that."

"I had to suck my thumb and whine like a two year old to get it, but hey, I look cool now."

"Aw, no self-respect was lost whatsoever."

"Never," he laughed. "Come in."

His apartment was nice, small like every other apartment in New York City, but still nice. One whole side of his apartment was exposed brick with shallow metal shelves that held old fashioned cameras. The rest of his apartment was chic, modern, and welcoming. He definitely knew how to decorate, given the color palette of his place, as well as the knick-knacks and well placed black and white framed photos.

"Wow, I love your place," I admitted, while looking at a black and white picture of the Brooklyn Bridge. "This is exquisite, did you take it?"

"I did," he said, coming up behind me. His arms wrapped around my waist and turned me around.

When I met his eyes, all I could see was lust as his head dipped toward mine and his hands cupped my face. Lightly, he nipped on my lips until I reciprocated, deepening his nips into a kiss that had us both breathing heavily once he pulled away.

"God, why did I wait so long for that?" he asked, licking his lips, as if he was tasting me all over again.

Virginia was a happy camper.

"I ordered some deli sandwiches, if that's okay?" he said, as he walked me into his living room with his hand pressed against my back.

"Sounds good to me. I brought some cookies for you." He thanked me and put them on the kitchen counter, eyeing them carefully, like he wanted one right then.

Leaving him to his cookie staring, I sat down on his couch as he did the same and I turned toward him. "So, tell me how you hurt your wrist. I'm here, I want the details."

He linked my hand with his and said, "You can't leave, though, once I tell you."

"I can't make any promises," I shrugged.

"Then, I'm not telling you."

"Then, I'm afraid I have to go," I started to get up, but he pulled me back down, this time a lot closer. He grabbed my legs and swung them over his, so I was practically sitting on his lap.

"You're not going anywhere, now that I have you here."

That devilish grin was making Virginia clap her folds together in praise. This date was so much better already than the first one, because I had Lance to myself. I enjoyed just being with him, rather than a group of his friends.

"Alright, just tell me what happened, and then I can judge you after, is that okay?"

"I guess I have to take what I can get."

"Dish it," I said, while getting comfortable.

Playing with his hair, he looked off and started telling me his story.

"I was at a photo shoot for some stupid make-up products the other day. They're the worst kind of photo shoots because you have to place everything properly and take pictures of still products. The shoots pay well, but they are just boring as hell, so to liven them up, I play music for me and the other person the magazine sends along. I was hanging with this twenty-year-old intern…"

"A girl?" I interrupted, crossing my hands over my chest and trying out the fake pout. Didn't know how well it worked until he leaned over and kissed me. Maybe I should pout more often.

"Not a girl. It was a guy, and he was obsessed with Michael Jackson, so I thought, why not blast some MJ on my phone to make the shoot go by a little more smoothly?"

"They had a guy help out at a make-up shoot?"

"Believe me, we both wanted to shoot ourselves. It was awful. So, toward the end of the shoot, we started busting out our best MJ moves."

"Do you have moves?" I asked, eyeing him up and down, while his hand started to caress my thigh. I didn't even have to ask, he had moves alright, because Virginia was trying to suck in his hand and dance with it. Why did I bother with all the other guys? I should have just stuck with Lance. Clearly, he was the best choice out of all of them, even Greg, the dog balls guy.

"I have moves, baby. Just wait, I'll show them to you," he wiggled his eyebrows.

Cheesy, but I'd take it.

"So, then what happened?"

"Well, the intern, God, I can't remember his name, how awful is that? Oh well, the intern goes and lifts his knee and does this shaking thing with his leg like MJ does, and he grabs his crotch."

"Classic," I added.

"Very much so. So, of course, what did I have to do?"

"You busted out the moon walk, didn't you?"

"Did I even have a choice?"

"After the crotch grab? I'm afraid not," I said, while a grin spread across my face.

"That's what I was thinking. So, to add some pizazz, I turned in a full circle, grabbed my crotch—I felt like it was a given—and then started moon walking, right into the display of makeup, where I knocked over everything and landed on my wrist."

"Oooh, ouch, how was the makeup?"

Tickling me, he replied, "Is that what you really care about?"

Laughing, I replied, "If it was expensive, then yes."

"It was," he chuckled, as he calmed his tickling fingers. "I have some on my shirt still if you want to try to peel it off?"

"I'm good. So, that's how you did it? Trying to upstage a twenty year old with your MJ moves?"

"I mean, did I really have an option?"

"I don't think you did. At least you got a cool cast out of it."

He lifted it up for both of us to examine. "I really did. You can't believe all the girls that have come up to me, asking about my cast."

"Is that right?" I asked, backing away from him.

"No," he smiled and pushed me down on the couch so he hovered over me, utilizing his good arm. "There's only one girl I really care about."

"Well, aren't you just the charmer?"

"I like to think so," he said closely, just before his lips found mine.

I allowed the affection, because frankly, I wanted him. He was sweet, fun, and he liked me.

His body pressed against mine as he lowered himself down. My hands ran up his shoulders and into his hair, where I played with the slight curls that framed his face.

For a second, he pulled away, took off his glasses, and then found my lips once more, where he was more demanding this time. My stomach bottomed out as his tongue slipped into my mouth and started stroking the inside of it.

Holy mother of marmalade jars, he knew how to kiss, and my body recognized it, because instantly every inch of my skin was set on fire.

His good hand went to the hem of my shirt, where he lifted it just enough so he exposed a patch of my skin. His thumb found my exposed skin and started to stroke it ever so lightly, igniting something inside of me, something primal.

A moan escaped my mouth as his hand slid up just a little bit farther. Wanting to match his stroke, I moved my hand down to his jeans, where I felt his very excited bulge.

I gasped as my hand connected with his erection that was poking through his jeans. The thought of me being able to provoke such an attractive man was still a new concept to me.

"Sorry," he mumbled as he pulled away and started kissing my jaw. "I just can't help myself when I'm around you, Rosie. I've been waiting so long to get my hands on you."

I lifted my chin to give him better access, just as his doorbell rang.

Blowing out a heavy breath, he rested his forehead on mine and looked me in the eyes.

"Such bad timing," he said with a heavy breath.

"Do you want me to get it?" I straightened, as I looked down at his crotch. I had never seen an erection in the confines of jeans before, and it was actually a huge turn on.

"Might be best," he responded, while sitting up and adjusting himself. "Cash is on the counter, if you don't mind."

"Not at all," I said, while standing up and adjusting my shirt.

I was about to walk toward the door when Lance pulled on my hand and said, "Come right back here; food can wait."

Yup, food could definitely wait.

I opened the door to find a very short boy with a bag full of food with a deli's stamp on it.

"That will be twenty-four, eighty," he said in a high-pitched voice. I wanted to ask how old he was, since he was clearly still going through puberty and could hardly see over the bag he was holding, but there were more important things for me to tend to rather than bringing down a deli for violating child labor laws.

"Keep the change," I said, as I offered him the thirty dollars that was left on the counter.

"Wow, thanks!" he said, excited over a little more than a five dollar tip. Made me wonder what he normally got tipped.

Grabbing the food and shutting the door behind me, I walked back into Lance's apartment to see him stretched out on the couch, waiting for me with a sexy grin.

I was instantly hit with nerves as I saw him take in my entire body. Was he going to take the kissing and fondling all the way? Was I ready for it to go that far? Up until now, I had just done some exploring, or at least tried to, but this almost seemed serious, like this was the moment, the day I was going to lose my virginity. Did I want to lose it to Lance?"

As I set the food down on the counter, I looked him up and down and realized he was a good guy; he wouldn't hurt me and it seemed like he cared about me. He probably would be very gentle and kind if I told him.

Instead of coming out and saying, "Hey, Lance, before we get down and dirty, thought I would let you know, no one has ever been inside Virginia, so if we could take it slow, that would be great," I would just play it by ear, and if the moment sparked, if it seemed like we were going all the way, to the promised land where unicorns jumped over glitter rainbows, then I would give him a heads up.

"What are you thinking about over there?" he asked with his arms lining the back of the couch while his right leg crossed over his left knee. He looked so calm and collected, while I was fighting an inner battle, trying to decide if I should let the cat out of the bag.

Ugh, damn cats…

"Just looking at you," I said casually, trying to calm my voice.

Now that I had time to think about it, I was cracking, and I could feel myself starting to drift away.

Wanting to be a big girl, I strapped on my lady balls and decided to rip the Band-Aid off. Go for it. The first time was going to be awful, I got that, might as well just get it over with, see what the fuss was all about. Give Virginia some experience in the field of Cockland, and let her see what the wonder is all about when it comes to getting stuffed.

"Come here," he said, while beckoning me with his finger.

Casually, I walked over to him, trying not to stumble over my own damn feet. I could see it now, I trip over my own leg, fall forward with my arms out, punching him in the face and landing on his coffee table that breaks under my fall. It could very easily happen, given my luck.

"You're playing hard to get, aren't you?" he asked, as I eased myself closer.

More like trying not to trip like a doofus and ruin the moment.

Successfully, I made it to the couch, where Lance instantly was on me, grabbing my hand and making me straddle his lap. Instantly, Virginia had a visitor knocking on her door, and hell if the little hussy wasn't excited to see him.

"Mmmm…you fit perfectly on me, Rosie. I hate myself

for taking so long in asking you out and then taking so long to call you."

How was I supposed to answer that? Yeah, dumbass, good job? Nah, that seemed a little harsh, so I pulled out the little giggle I kept stored for occasions where I had no clue what to say.

"You're adorable," he complimented.

The giggle worked, so I made a mental note to keep that in my sexual tool box. Right about now, the only thing in that tool box was a giggle and the ability to properly put on a condom. Yup, I was a real mechanic when it came to the old horizontal tango.

Without warning, Lance wrapped his hand around my neck and pulled me in closer, where his lips met mine. I will admit this, if I had to pay myself a compliment, I knew how to kiss. I felt good kissing; it was something I didn't find too difficult. Keep your mouth clean, keep your eyes shut, and don't bump noses...pretty basic stuff.

As our lips danced together, I let my hands wander. Why not? If I had a fine specimen in front of me, I might as well let me hands do some exploring, especially when his hands were on my hips and starting to ride up my shirt.

Placing my hands on his chest, I felt the definition of his pecs and tried to calculate how many times he went to the gym in a week. It must have been at least three, because he had some nice muscles.

My fingers skimmed over his nipples by accident, but by the moan in his voice and the way his nipples peaked up, I could tell he liked the movement, so I let my fingers go back over the now erect nubs.

Erect nubs? Was that a term I wanted to use in my book? Seemed a little odd. Would you call a nipple a nub? It could be classified as a nub...

Focus, I chastised myself, as I told my hands to continue to explore further until they hit the waistband of his jeans. The minute my hands stilled, Lance thrust his hips up, letting me know he wanted me to go further.

I guess it was time to get serious, so I shimmied off his body and fell between his legs. I looked up at him briefly to see lust pouring through his face, just waiting for me to take action.

Jesus, I needed a drink.

With all the confidence I could muster, I looked down at his tented jeans, literally, tented, and undid them. Slowly, I unzipped his jeans and was met with a pair of black boxer briefs. Lance's chest heaved from how slow I was going, and he most likely thought I was trying to torment him, but in reality, I was trying to one, not get his penis caught in the zipper, talk about mood changer, and two, I was really freaking nervous.

With a deep breath, I grabbed his boxer briefs at the same time he lifted off the couch so I could pull them down with his jeans.

Once his clothing was pulled down and resting at his ankles, I shut my eyes for a second and then opened them to see his dick standing at attention.

Holy shit!

That wasn't right; there was something wrong with his penis.

Panic washed over me as I backed away and said, "I'm going to pee my pants! Where's your bathroom?"

"Seriously?" he asked, almost pained.

"Yes." I stood up and started dancing while grabbing my crotch.

"Umm, okay. Second door on the right down the hall, but hurry up."

"I will," I replied, just as I saw him look at me and start to stroke himself.

Eck!

I ran down the hallway, grabbed my phone from my purse, which was thankfully near the door, and locked myself in the bathroom.

Fumbling around, I finally was able to catch my breath and call Delaney.

The phone rang three times before she answered.

"Aren't you on a date?"

"Delaney, he has a crooked penis," I whispered.

"What?"

"My date, his penis is crooked, and I mean really crooked. Like someone grabbed it out of fury and bent it to the right."

"Rosie, didn't we go over this? All dicks are different shapes and sizes…"

"Delaney, this isn't like a dick that veers to the side, I'm talking like straight up, the man has a crooked dick. Like, if I let him impale me, the head of his cock would be tickling my ovary, winking at it."

"Seriously?"

"Yes! I'm not even sure how he has to go about getting inside a woman."

"Maybe he has a fancy swivel trick. You never know, it might feel really good."

"If I wanted to give him head, I would have to sit to his side to access his penis."

"It's not that bad," Delaney softly laughed.

"Delaney, I'm not kidding. It looks broken. What the hell do I do?"

"Take a picture?"

"That's not helpful."

"It's for science. I want to see it."

"Why did I even call you?" I asked, feeling exasperated.

"Because you and Henry are fighting."

"We are not," I lied.

"Whatever. Just go back in there and play around with it, but remember to steer clear of cum shooting to the right. You don't want to shoot your eye out."

"I hate you."

"No, you don't," she laughed.

We hung up, and surprisingly, I didn't feel any better after my phone conversation with Delaney. Remembering I had to "pee," I flushed the toilet and ran the water to make it seem like I was hitting all the marks of a bathroom visitor.

Dropping my phone off in my purse, I went back into the living room, where Lance was still stroking himself, but was harder than ever. I glanced down and couldn't help but notice that it looked like he was choking his poor dick, and its head was trying to spring free from his grasp.

What happened to his penis?!

"There you are, come back here."

It looked like a broken finger, a right hand turn sign, an Allen wrench, a drunk pencil, a worm with a broken neck, a damn garden hoe.

It was not a penis. I didn't have much experience with penises, but this wasn't right, it wasn't real. It had to be a prosthetic…that was melted in the sun.

Call me a bitch, call me stuck up, but I couldn't go through with this with him. I wanted to, damn did I want to finally rip the Band-Aid off, but I had zero experience touching a penis, so handling one that was proving the term "How you hanging," a little too seriously, was something I couldn't tackle.

"I'm a virgin," I blurted out, knowing that was a giant red flag when it came to guys. "I'm a stage five clinger. If you poke me with that penis, I will want to marry you tomorrow. I actually already love you. I didn't have to go to the bathroom, I was preparing my engagement speech to you, because I want to propose, and if we have sex, I guarantee you I will get pregnant, condom or not. My vagina eats condoms actually and my eggs are more than willing to pull your sperm into their sacs as hostages. We can make a baby today, just say the word. Marriage, babies, and I love you. I love you. I love you."

Yup, pulled out all the stops.

Lance's pants were pulled up and fastened as quickly as I could say deformed dick, and he was backing away from me.

"Rosie, I like you, but we just met."

"Yes, but don't you want a baby? Triplets run in my family."

Not really, but anything to get out of this apartment.

"This just got weird," he admitted.

No, buddy, shit got weird the minute your dick couldn't look me square in the eyes without me leaning over your lap to wink at him.

"Yeah, too bad it won't work out," I shrugged, while walking back down the hallway.

Without glancing back at Lance, I grabbed my purse and bolted.

It wasn't until I was walking down into the subway that I realized all the things I said.

Jesus.

I shook my head as I swiped my Metro Card and walked through the turn wheel. Stage five clinger? Really?

At least it got me out of his apartment and as far away as possible from the candy cane cock.

June 13, 2014

Note to self: When people say dicks come in all shapes and sizes, they are not kidding.

Dicks can be a grower, not a shower, they can be fat, skinny, long, short, brown, pink, white, black…purple. They have a mind of their own, and they are veiny with an eye on them that will stare you down, begging you to just lick them, taste them, satisfy them. They rest around in the dark, waiting to see the light, to be freed, only to be stuck, shoved and caressed in the dark once again.

Dicks are masochists.

They like to be plucked, tugged, slapped, and swallowed.

They are nudists, they only like to be naked; they prefer to be sheathed by a canal of flesh and that's all.

Dicks are sensitive, and if jostled too much, can spew in seconds. They prefer to do so on a woman, in a woman, anywhere near a woman, but even a sock will work.

The dick is a different species; it's a species all its own, and with a slight lift of its shaft, it's ready to party.

Virginia has been scarred. Any vagina would be startled after seeing such a bent cock wanting to come after them. She's not dumb, she knows how big she is and what can fit, and Mr. Dented Dick wasn't going to fit properly.

I don't know when she will ever be ready to make friends with another penis after being threatened by such a creature. She had such high hopes too.

Poor Virginia.

CHAPTER 18

"The Blooms"

I straightened my dress as I took in my outfit for the day. Yesterday was a mess. I just prayed I never saw Lance again, and that he kept his mouth shut about what I said. To say I brought crazy cat lady to a whole new level was an understatement.

Works for cat magazine, works with cats, writes about cats, is a virgin, confessed to being a stage five clinger, and professed love on the second date—yup, confirmed my single status for the next forty years.

Blowing out a heavy breath, I pulled my hair out of my curlers and ran my fingers through the strands. Pleased with my hair and white sundress, I put on a pair of my brown sandals, grabbed my purse, and headed out my door. It was time to have brunch with my parents.

I was halfway to the front door when someone cleared their throat behind me. I turned to see Henry leaning against our couch, wearing a pair of khaki shorts and a white polo shirt that clung perfectly to his chest. His hair was styled like normal, and he was wearing a pair of brown sandals as well. God, he looked beyond yummy.

"Good morning, love. Where do you think you're going?"

Shocked Henry was in the apartment, let alone talking to me, I turned to face him and replied, "What are you doing here? I thought you weren't coming home until Monday."

He shrugged his shoulders and started walking toward me.

"I was hungry, thought a couple plates of French toast would do the trick."

"You're going to brunch with me?" I asked, a little shocked at the turnaround in emotions from Henry.

"I am," he smiled as he stood right before me. He grabbed my hand and kissed the top of it. "I'm sorry, Rosie…"

The man was apologizing to me, when I was the one being an ass. How could I even think about turning him down the other night? I was so damn confused.

"No, stop, stop apologizing. I'm the one who should be sorry. I shouldn't have been so, so…"

"How about we don't?" he interrupted me. "Let's just drop it and go have a fun day on Long Island, eating French toast and playing Yahtzee."

"It's not a guarantee we'll play Yahtzee," I laughed.

"Love, when it comes to your parents, it's always a guarantee. I just hope I get the neon green dice this time. They're lucky."

"I'm sure if you make it known you're putting the neon ones on reserve for after brunch, you'll be able to play with them."

"I better, last time I had to play with the red dice, and we just didn't mesh well."

"Red is so not your color."

"It really isn't," he smiled that charming smile at me, and then pulled me into his chest and kissed me on the top of my head. "I missed you, love."

"I missed you, Henry. Especially after yesterday."

"Oh, yeah." He cleared his throat and said in a serious voice, "How's it hangin', love?"

"Ugh, I hate you and Delaney," I replied, while pulling away and walking toward the front door.

Henry caught up to me and turned me around while laughing.

"No, you don't. You love us."

"Unfortunately."

"Tell me, was it really that crooked?"

I nodded and replied, "You know how a giraffe's head extends perpendicular from his long neck?"

"Yeah..."

"Picture that, but in dick form."

"Oh, shit," he laughed. "Damn, did you take a picture?"

"No! What is wrong with you?"

"For science!"

"You and Delaney hang out too much," I responded, while finally making my way out of the apartment with Henry tailing behind me.

I started to head to get a taxi when Henry stopped me and said, "I got a car, love."

I turned to see him heading toward a black Ford Escape.

"Where did you get this?"

"Rented it, thought it might be nicer to drive then take a taxi and get ripped off. Plus, we can listen to Queen and sing our asses off."

My heart took off at how considerate Henry was. He was always thinking ahead.

"Henry, that's so sweet. Thank you, but you meant Britney Spears, right?"

"We'll see," he winked, while opening the door for me and grabbing my hand.

He helped me in the car and before he shut the door, he looked down at me with a spark in his eyes, something I never experienced from him before.

I could tell he wanted to say something to me, but instead of telling me what was on his mind, he leaned over, placed a kiss on my forehead and pulled away, shutting my door.

The rapid beat of my heart from his small gesture caught me off guard as I waited for him to get in the car. It was Henry; he kissed me on the forehead all the time. It was nothing to read things into.

But then why was I wanting him to do it again? Why did I want him to not just kiss me on the forehead, but on the lips again? Thoughts of the first time he kissed me on the lips ran through my mind. He was gentle, luscious, yet sexy. He felt right.

No, I chastised myself; we were friends.

"You ready to go, love?" he asked, as he placed his hand on my thigh, making Virginia come to life from the self-induced coma she'd put herself into after yesterday afternoon. Apparently, she didn't have any aversions to Henry.

"Ready," I gulped, as I watched his thumb slowly caress the inside of my thigh, next to my knee.

By no means was his hand in my crotch; it wasn't even close to it, but the fact that he was touching me in an intimate way had me sweating, shaking, and begging for more. It was going to be a very long car drive.

***

"I'm so glad you two could make it," my mom cooed, as she hovered over her French toast.

The ride from the city to my parents' house wasn't too bad, except for the fact that Henry's hand never moved from my leg, leaving me quaking in my seat, but his off-pitch singing helped ease the tension.

I was the DJ, so once I played a couple of Queen songs to appease my driver, I skipped through the songs of his playlist and was pleased to see he had every Britney Spears hit on his phone. The minute I started playing her songs, I watched as Henry changed from eighties rock band to nineties pop star, and I couldn't stop laughing. He hit every note, shimmied, and even popped a shoulder or two to the beat.

I was pretty sure he never sang and danced to Britney Spears for anyone else, and I was so honored that he shared his little hidden secret with me. I felt privileged to have such knowledge, and if I wasn't so distracted by his hand, I would have been recording his pop princess ass on my phone.

"Thanks for having us, Mrs. Bloom. When I heard baked French toast, I couldn't resist."

"You don't have to suck up to them," I whispered to Henry.

"You never know; I might just have to," he winked, making me wonder what that meant.

"Don't you two just look adorable, matching clothes and all. Did you plan it on purpose?" my mom asked, while my dad pulled his eyes off his plate for a second to look at us.

"No, just a coincidence," Henry replied, right before shoving a huge piece of French toast in his mouth, dripping syrup all over his white shirt.

"Oh, dear, honey, you got some syrup on your shirt."

"Oh, shoot," Henry replied while looking down. He grabbed his napkin and started smearing the syrup everywhere.

"That's not going to help; I'm sure Dave has a shirt you can borrow. You're about the same size, well besides the muscles. Have you been working out, Henry?"

"Um, just a little," he said modestly. "Do you mind, Mr. Bloom?"

"Not at all. Rosie, go help him find a shirt. Just don't give him my Bubba Gump shirt; that's my favorite."

"Wouldn't dream of it, Dad." I turned to Henry and said, "Come on, slob."

"Don't forget to soak his shirt," my mom called out. "I would hate to see it get ruined."

Grabbing Henry's hand, I led him upstairs and toward my parents' bedroom, but Henry stopped me in the hallway and said, "I want to see your room."

"You've seen it before."

"But not in a while. I always love looking at your pictures."

"No, you like making fun of me in braces and overalls."

"You were adorable, come on."

He pulled me toward my childhood room that was too embarrassing to have a guy in. Thank God I was comfortable enough with Henry.

The room was a mauve color with pale blue bedding, sheets and curtains. The furniture was an oak color, and if it wasn't for the Furby, Nanopet, posters of Jonathan Taylor Thomas, and other teenage knick-knacks, you would have sworn an eighty year old grandma was living in there.

On the bulletin board behind my desk was my wall of achievements, which was a pathetic assortment of made-up certificates. I didn't have much talent when it came to sports, so my mom decided to make up her own certificates and award them to me. I had a certificate of completion for a clean set of braces, for fitting into my first training bra, and successfully using my first tampon. Yup, big time achievements.

"I love it in here," Henry said, while taking in everything, as if he had never seen it before.

"Why?"

"It just shows me what formed you, why you are the perfect person you are today."

"I'm not perfect."

"Pretty damn close," he winked at me. "Ah, the certificate for inserting your first tampon. Such a great accomplishment. I really love how your mom used tampons as a border."

"Could we not look at that?"

"And it's laminated; she really excels at making certificates."

"Maybe she can make you one for being nosy."

"What I love most about you is that, instead of throwing away the certificates, you actually hung them up," he chuckled to himself.

"Well, that would have been rude. My mom spent time making them, even though they are slightly inappropriate and highly embarrassing."

"So adorable." Walking up to me, he grabbed my hands and said, "Want to make out in your bed?"

"No!" I practically shouted, as a wave of heat washed over me.

"Come on, it would be fun," he wiggled his eyebrows.

"We need to get you a shirt before you get us in trouble. Come on."

I dragged him out of my room and into my parents', where the mauve theme continued. My poor father. My mom was a mauve and frills kind of gal, where doilies were acceptable and muted colors were welcomed.

"Do you want a T-shirt or button up?" I asked, while I looked through my dad's closet.

"Whatever works," Henry responded.

Just as I looked up at him, I saw him take off his shirt and grip it in his hand. He wasn't wearing an undershirt or anything, so I was privy to stare at his well-defined chest and abs. He must be working out on his lunch breaks more often, because he was looking so fine.

Did I just say he was looking fine? When have I ever thought that about my best friend? Almost never, but now that he was in my head, all these thoughts about kissing and holding hands and whatnot, now I felt like I examined every last sexual aspect of him, and damn if he wasn't the sexiest guy I had ever met.

"Love, you can't just stare at me like that and get away with it."

"I'm sorry," I shook my head and turned around to look for a shirt, but for the life of me, I couldn't get my arms to function.

The strength of Henry stepped up behind me and placed his hands on my hips, sending Virginia into a frenzy. She was practically eating up my panties just to get closer to Henry.

My breath hitched as he leaned forward and moved his hands to my stomach, pulling me against his bare chest. The exposed skin on my back met his warm body, sending a thrill of excitement through me.

I shouldn't be feeling this way, I shouldn't be thinking naughty things about my best friend...like how I wanted him to press me up against a wall and finally take what I was trying to offer.

"Turn around, love," he said in a low voice, tempting me.

My mind and heart weighed against each other, trying to figure what was the best move. My mind was saying, no don't do it, you'll ruin everything, but my heart was beating at an alarming rate in my chest, letting me know if I didn't give in, I might lose at one of the most amazing opportunities of my life.

This time, my heart won out, so I turned in his arms and met his strong gaze.

His hands ran up my body until they were cupping my face. I stood rigidly, not really knowing what to do, how to blink, how to breathe, but the moment Henry lowered his head to mine, my body relaxed into his embrace and followed his direction.

My lips parted to his, and very slowly, he let his tongue slip into my mouth at just the right pressure so that I thought I was going to ignite into a pile of flames. He teased my mouth and caressed it, making me weak in the knees. With every movement he made, he turned me further and further into a pile of mush.

My hands found his waist and slowly started to creep up his chest, taking in every contour and ridge of his body. His breathing became just as labored as mine from my perusal, and it only encouraged me to move my hands up farther until they lightly ran over his pecs.

In a flash, Henry pushed me away and held onto my shoulders as he looked down at me, gasping for air, the same as me.

We stared at each other for a brief moment, wondering what the hell we were just doing, and what we were supposed to do next. I just hoped Henry wasn't looking for answers from me, because I had no clue how to handle such a situation.

Sparks flew between us, ignited like the damn Fourth of July. There was something different about Henry, something that felt so erotic, so wrong, but oh so damn right.

"Did you two get lost up there?" my mom called from the stairs.

Snapping out of the haze, I called back, "Nope, just picking out a shirt now."

"Okay, hurry up. Dad and I want to get in a couple of rounds of Yahtzee before you leave."

I rolled my eyes and shook my head as Henry chuckled to himself.

Trying to avoid the awkward conversation, I turned around and picked out a tye-dye T-shirt and handed it over to Henry.

"Here, this should be fine. I'll meet you downstairs."

I started to walk away, when Henry pulled on my arm and wound me back into him like a Yo-Yo.

"Oh, no you don't. You're not walking away from me like that."

"Like what?"

He didn't answer, instead he gripped my chin with his thumb and index finger and brought his lips back down on mine. Instinctively, I kissed him back, even though I probably shouldn't have.

Just as quickly as he kissed me, he pulled away again and put the shirt on that was one size too big and two decades too old, but he still looked good.

"Let's go, love," he said, grabbing my hand and entwining our fingers together. "Time to beat your parents at Yahtzee."

Stunned at his drastic change in mood, I whispered while we walked down the stairs, so my parents couldn't hear our conversation.

"So, you're just going to kiss me and then act like nothing happened?"

Before we were in plain sight for my parents to see, Henry turned and pinned me against the hallway wall.

His strong body pressed up against mine, while his hands found my waist again.

"There is no way I can act like nothing happened. Right now,

I'm on fucking cloud nine from that kiss, and instead of hashing it out like you probably want, I just want to enjoy it and play some Yahtzee. Sometimes, you just have to let things happen, Rosie, and not overanalyze everything. Live a little."

"I'm living," I said defiantly.

"That you are, but live a little with me, Rosie."

"What does that even mean?"

"Are you two coming?" my dad called out this time.

"Yup," Henry said, while pulling me behind him.

We met my parents out on their deck, where they had Yahtzee set up, and a special set of dice for each person.

"Look, honey, we found cat dice for you," my mom said excitedly.

No matter how many times I told my mom I didn't like cats, she still insisted upon getting me cat mugs, T-shirts, and calendars. She had it in her mind that since I worked at a cat magazine, I was in love with cats, when in fact it was the opposite. If I worked at a golf magazine, she would probably be stuffing golf balls in my stocking every year.

"Wow, thanks, Mom," I said, sitting down. Henry sat down right next to me, scooting his chair over, so he was practically on top of my playing space. He wasn't letting up anytime soon, and hell if I secretly wanted him to keep it up.

"That shirt is very becoming on you," my mom said to Henry.

"Thank you, Mrs. Bloom. I'm sure Mr. Bloom does it more justice than I do."

"I would say that's true," my dad said, chuckling.

"Oh, Dave, don't be jealous of the boy." She clapped her hands together and said, "Ready for the roll off? First to roll a six gets to go first. And, go!"

We all grabbed one die and started rolling until one of us got a six.

"Ah ha!" My dad called out, while fist pumping the air. "Looks like the old man has the upper hand."

It actually didn't matter who went first, but my mom insisted on a roll off at the beginning of each game. I wasn't as into it as much as my parents were, but looking over at Henry lightly smacking the table, I could see he was disappointed he didn't win the roll off. He was too damn cute.

"Next time," I whispered to him, causing his hand to once again find my thigh.

It was as if his hand to my thigh injected some kind of stupid serum, because my mind went blank, and everything around me went fuzzy. He had that effect on me.

"Honey, you're up," my mom said, just as Henry squeezed my thigh and leaned over into my ear.

"You're up love. Don't let me distract you."

Evil bastard, he was going for the win. Well, two could play at that game.

Puffing my chest out a little and adjusting the straps on my dress, I grabbed my dice and shook them up. From the corner of my eye, I could see Henry perusing my body, and even though it was making it that much more difficult to concentrate, I enjoyed hearing him clear his throat and shift in his seat.

The rest of the game was spent flirting shamelessly with Henry, trying to throw him off by bending to the side to pick up one of my dice that fell on the ground, showing off a great deal of thigh from my dress, as well as leaning over, showing off my cleavage to him every chance I got.

By the end of the game, we both had scores that were sadly unmentionable, and my parents took the win, blowing us both out of the water.

"Boy, what a good game, but I'm a little thirsty. Dave, why don't you help me in the kitchen? Rosie, why don't you take Henry down to the beach? It's only a block away; I'm sure he would enjoy it."

"That sounds great," Henry answered for the both of us as he stood up.

My mom winked at me as I got up too, making me roll my eyes at her matchmaking attempts. Once we were out of sight,

Henry grabbed my hand and walked with me down to the beach. There was a little walkway that granted people in the neighborhood access to the beach, which was nice, since beach access was quite hard to find.

"Did you go to the beach often when you were young?" Henry asked, as we took off our sandals so we could walk in the sand.

"Not much, but during the summers I would bring my books down here and read on occasion."

"God, that image is so adorable. Of course, you would bring your books down here. Did you have a spot?"

"Not really, just anywhere that I felt like sitting at the time."

"Do you want to sit and watch the waves with me?" he asked, while pressing his hand on the small of my back and guiding me to a little private alcove.

"I guess I don't have a choice," I laughed, as we sat down, gaining privacy from everyone else on the beach.

We sat in silence as we watched the waves crash against the sands of the beach. It wasn't the white sands of the Virgin Islands, but it was still pretty, even if there was trash here and there, thanks to the locals with no sense of protecting Mother Nature.

The sun peeked through the partly cloudy skies, warming us against the rocks we were sitting on and shining on the waves of the water rolling in. It was picturesque. I just wished I knew what was going through Henry's mind.

The way he'd treated me all day was weird, the way he touched me, talked to me…kissed me. Yeah, we'd never been kissers before. What did I do with that? Don't get me wrong, I would kiss him again, because how could I resist him, now that he'd broken that seal, that "we're just friends" seal? There was no going back from there, because I knew what he tasted like now, what it felt like to have my hands on his body, to have his lips pressed against mine. I couldn't just back away from that, but I also couldn't seem to gain the courage to move forward.

"I wish I grew up out here," Henry broke the silence. "It

would have been nice to have the beach in my backyard."

"But you got to have the concrete jungle as your playground," I joked.

Henry grew up in the city, born and raised, so to him, he didn't really get to escape away from his childhood home. But, he did know where all the good and cheap places were to eat while we were all in college. Him growing up in New York City was also a reason as to why he got such a great job right out of college, because he'd made connections growing up; he did internships in high school…he was set.

Me, I didn't have those opportunities, but who doesn't like working with cats, eating cat hair every day, and writing about the different clumping formulas on the market?

"It would have been nice to have a backyard, but I guess I can't complain," Henry said. "How's the book coming, Rosie?"

I shrugged my shoulders. "Alright, I guess. I still have yet to touch any kind of sex scene. I feel like I could write one, after all the books I've been reading and the research I've been doing, but I feel like there will be a lack of energy, or spark, you know? I feel like, in order to do my writing justice, I have to experience the real thing. I want there to be emotion, passion, and right now, the closest I've gotten to an orgasm is a fart on a face and a vibrator stuck in the vag."

Chuckling softly, Henry nodded his head. "I can understand that."

Feeling a little uncomfortable, I shifted on the rock I was sitting on and continued to stare out at the water, waiting for Henry to say something else, because I was at a loss for words.

My insides were all jumbled, my mind felt frazzled, and I wasn't the same person that I normally was around Henry. Henry literally flipped my world upside down the minute he kissed me, because even though I was sitting next to my best friend, someone I could tell anything to, I felt at a loss. I felt tongue tied, nervous, and sweaty, like I was on a first date.

"Let's get out of here," Henry said, after what felt like half an hour of just sitting. He stood up and grabbed my hand, leading me back to my parents' house, still in silence.

Was he feeling the same way? Was he feeling as anxious as me? As confused?

When we made it back to my parents' house, they were sitting out on the deck, enjoying a glass of lemonade, typical Blooms.

"Oh, there you two are. How was the beach?"

"Sandy," I muttered, as I tried to ignore the matchmaking gaze beaming from my mom's eyes.

"Oh, aren't you a card?" My mom waved at me and laughed.

"It was quite lovely, Mrs. Bloom. Good suggestion," Henry kissed ass.

"So glad you enjoyed it. Would you two like some more food? More Yahtzee?"

I was about to say no, when Henry started talking for the both of us.

"Actually, Mrs. Bloom, I think Rosie and I are going to head back to the city; we have some research to do for a project she's working on, and I've been dying to get some hands-on time with it."

With a squeeze to my hand, he winked at my mom, and gave both my parents a hug as I stood stiff as a board from his comment.

Hands-on time? What the hell did that mean?

My parents led us out to the car and gave me a hug good bye. Like a robot, I got in the car, buckled up, and looked out the window, while Henry said his last goodbyes.

I didn't know what to say, what to expect as we drove away.

Like clockwork, Henry's hand once again found my thigh, and when I looked up at him from his caress, he just smiled back down at me and turned up the music, ignoring my questioning eyes.

Just like the ride to my parents' house, it was going to be a long ride back to the city, and I thought the drive to my parents was bad, boy was I wrong.

CHAPTER 19

"The Fleshy Popsicle"

The apartment was empty when we arrived. On the way home, we got stuck in traffic, shocker, so when we got back to the apartment, we were met with a dark living room.

The ride back was full of sexual tension, something I never really experienced for such a long period of time. So, instead of trying to make up conversation, I turned my head toward the window and pretended to sleep. Pretended being the key word. There was no sleeping with Henry's hand lightly caressing my thigh for the entire trip.

Feeling anxious and unsettled, I followed Henry into the apartment as he switched on lights. Like a coward, I headed straight to my room, where I could debrief my day with my notebook, and possibly think about what kind of Chinese food I wanted to gorge myself with.

"Where do you think you're going?" Henry asked, as he came up right behind me.

Without turning around, I answered, "To my room, to change

and…"

"Nope," he cut me off. "We're going to my room."

"What? Why?"

Without answering, Henry led me to his bedroom, and then shut the door behind me. He turned me in his embrace and looked down at me with the most serious face I had ever seen.

His hand cupped my cheek as his body invaded every last inch of personal space I had. My back hit his door as he pinned me, making sure I had no way of squirming away, not that I wanted to. With the stroke of his thumb against my cheekbone, I started to melt on the spot.

His other hand gripped my waist just as his head lowered to mine. He was taller than me, so it was a little bit of a journey to have our lips meet up, but I didn't mind going on my tippy toes to meet him halfway, which was exactly what I was doing while my hand went around his neck.

Our lips connected and my stomach bottomed out from having Henry wrapped around me again. All the concerns I was feeling before, the tension, the uneasiness all faded the minute Henry wrapped his arms around me.

He was warm, strong, comforting, and sexy.

Damn, was he sexy, there was no denying that, especially when the moment his lips connected with mine, Virginia was celebrating.

Being a little adventurous, I opened my mouth and swiped my tongue against his lips, which caused a groan to rumble out of his chest. His hand that was once on my waist found its way down to the hem of my dress.

"I've been waiting so long to kiss you like this, touch you like this. God, Rosie, you're making my fucking dreams come true right now."

My heart stumbled at his words as he started to lift my dress up until his hand met my panty line on my thigh. Breath escaped me as his fingers danced along the seam of my conservative pair of panties.

Pulling away, he looked down at me, as if he was asking permission, permission to take off my dress.

Holy Hell, Henry wanted to take off my dress, and the strange thing was, I wanted him to do it. With a gulp, I nodded my head, eliciting a smile from him.

The hand that was on my cheek now went to the hem of my dress as well, and with precision, he took off my sundress, showing off my white strapless bra and my white cotton underwear.

The room felt cold as I stood in just my skivvies in front of Henry, my best friend. I could feel my nipples tightening, and I wasn't sure if it was from the room's temperature or if it was from the gaze coming from Henry as he looked me up and down. I did know the throbbing that started to come from Virginia was from Henry, definitely from Henry.

"You're so damn beautiful," Henry said, while his hands found my hips.

"Thank you," I said shyly.

Grabbing me by the hand, he led me to the bed and sat me down. This was getting serious, I thought, as Henry grabbed his borrowed shirt and pulled it over his head, revealing that perfect torso of his.

Leaning over, he pressed me against the mattress and hovered over me. I watched in fascination as his chest rippled from holding himself up. His skin was bronze, soft, and edible.

Did I just think edible? Good Lord, I was getting frisky, but hell, I couldn't help it if Virginia was begging me to lick every last orifice of his body.

Feeling a little brazen, I grabbed his head and brought it back down to my lips, where I continued to kiss him, something I knew I was getting damn good at.

He still hovered above me, but I could feel his bottom half relax against me, and that was when the bulge hit my thigh. Curious, I moved my leg to feel it some more, to explore without making it quite obvious.

Through his shorts, I felt how excited he was, how big he was, and it only made Virginia weep with joy. Moving my leg up and down, I lightly stroked him through his shorts, and after the fifth stroke, he finally caught on to my movement and started to press harder against my thigh, making the movement full of friction.

As I stroked his erection with my leg and made out with the sexiest guy I had ever met, I thought, was this dry humping? Or was it considered heavy petting? It was hard to tell, because I believed I was petting him—what a weird thing to say—but he was pressing against my leg in a hump-like manner so which was it? A hump pet?

"Hey, where did you go on me?" Henry asked, as he pulled away. "I feel like you just kind of vanished on me."

"Sorry," I said, as heat scorched through my body. Stupid brain. "I was just thinking."

"Thinking about what?" he asked, as his head was inches from mine, but from the corner of my eye, I could still see his muscular arms.

Ah, muscles, why have I denied myself such a treat for so long?

Clearing my mind, I decided to be honest and said, "I was wondering if what we were doing was classified as dry humping or heavy petting?"

The corner of his mouth twisted as he thought about it for a second. "I believe it was heavy petting."

"But, you were kind of humping my leg," I countered.

Still smiling, he shook his head. "No, I was pushing against your leg, this is humping your leg." With a few thrusts, he showed me exactly what a hump to the leg felt like.

"Oh," I said, feeling a little shy at how much his erection turned me on.

"See the difference?"

"I do." I scanned his eyes and then sighed. "I totally ruined the mood."

"No, you didn't, but I can see that this is going to be a learning experience, since you have so many questions, so we might

255

as well do it right. What do you want to know?"

Instead of hovering over me, he sat on the bed and placed his back against the headboard with his arms at his sides. His hair was slightly ruffled from me, and his eyes were full of lust. He was adorable, but also sexy; it was hard not to look at him.

"Come on, Rosie. Let me hear it. What do you want to know?"

"Seriously?" I asked, a little taken aback by his offer. What we were doing right now wasn't sexy, it wasn't passionate, it wasn't something I read in my romance novels, and I kind of wished I was able to have that all-consuming passionate moment with the guy who I couldn't take my eyes off of, but I had too many damn questions to let it happen.

Sitting up on my knees, I placed my hands on my thighs and said, "I want to touch it."

"Touch it? Rosie, if you are going to be a romance novelist, you are going to have to be comfortable with saying words like dick, cock, and penis, and you are going to have to ask for it, so try again. What do you want?"

Gritting my teeth, because I knew he was pushing my limits, I said, "I want to touch your penis."

If he laughed, I was going to throat punch him, because the words coming out of my mouth sounded so foreign, I had to replay them in my head to make sure they were English.

Being the gentleman he was, he refrained from teasing me, and instead, nodded his head as his hands went to his shorts and unbuttoned them. Nerves shot through me as he pulled them off, revealing his boxer briefs and his tented erection.

Tented erection, was that a phrase to use? Technically, it straight-up looked like a tent in his crotch, but was it sexy? Tented erection, tented erection…nope. Not sexy, more like a creepy analogy that makes you think of boy scouts. Eck, I should to go jail.

"Hey, Rosie. You still with me? It's a little alarming when you're about to take your boxers off and the girl who said she wants to touch your dick starts to drift off."

"Sorry. I was just thinking. Is tented erection something to write…?"

"No, nope, not something to write."

"Got it," I smiled, grateful that he didn't judge me. "I'm sorry about all this. Maybe we just forget it. Clearly, I can't focus on what I should be doing."

With a loving look on his face, Henry grabbed my hand and pulled me closer, so I was sitting on his lap, so his erection was poking against the back of my butt. It was odd, as if his cock was strapping me in against him, but I found it oddly erotic.

"Listen, I understand you're curious, that you will have questions, and I'm okay with that. I want you, Rosie, but I also want to help you, so do whatever you want, ask whatever you want; you're not going to scare me away. Fart on my face, puke on my dick, but just don't kick me in the balls," he teased, making me laugh.

Feeling the need, I pressed my lips against his while cupping his face and thanked him. His hands ran up my back to the clasp of my bra, making me gasp. I could feel his smile against my lips from my reaction, but he didn't ease up. With a flick of his fingers, he undid my bra and let it fall between us.

Instinctively, my arms went in front of my breasts, covering them from view, which, once again, made Henry smile.

"Hey, no covering up the goods," he chuckled.

"I'm nervous," I admitted.

"Why? Are you afraid I'll nibble your nipples right off?"

"No," I exclaimed.

"You should be. I'm kind of a nipple guy."

"What? Seriously?"

Laughing some more, he shook his head. "No, I mean, I love nipples, but I won't nibble them off; I'll just nibble. Believe me, it will feel good."

"But, I've never shown my breasts to anyone before."

"Then who better to inspect them than me?"

"You're going to laugh at them."

"And why would I laugh at them?" he asked, toning down his jovial spirit.

"I don't know. They're not all fake and perky; they're regular."

Looking me square in the eyes, Henry replied, "There is nothing regular about you, Rosie. You should know that by now."

Just like that, I was putty in his grasp. My hands went up to his face again as my chest pressed against his, causing an intake of breath to escape him from the contact, just as my lips met his. Softly, we pressed our mouths together, learning to move flawlessly together as we explored each other. His hands that were once on my hips found their way up to my ribcage where they rested for a short period of time, stroking my skin ever so gently.

Virginia screamed with joy as his thumbs slowly inched to right under my breasts. I could feel my heart pounding against his chest. My breasts ached for his touch, for just one little swipe of his thumb, but he wouldn't go any higher with his exploration, and after a couple more teasing swipes from his thumbs. I was squirming in his lap.

"Please, touch me," I said shyly into his mouth, making him smile.

"Thought you would never ask."

Still not looking down, he allowed his hands to go the extra inch and finally grasp my breasts. Instantly, my head fell back at the feel of his hands applying pressure where I needed it. He had a handful and squeezed with the right kind of pressure that had me rubbing up against his crotch, wanting more.

With just the light squeeze from him, he had me begging for more. Who knew getting your boob squeezed was such an integral part of being turned on? Hell, they were dangling milk sacs on a woman's body, but Jesus, Mary, and Joseph were they a pleasure button that shot straight to your lady cactus with a hydration mechanism.

He continued to squeeze my breasts, but slowly started to move his fingers to my nipples. My mind went blank as Virginia started to call the shots, allowing my chest to press into his hands, encouraging him to continue on his journey.

When my eyes opened to see why he wasn't gripping my nipples just yet, I saw the heated glare as Henry's eyes were glued to my exposed chest. Instead of covering myself up, I puffed my chest out more, allowing more of a view. Licking his lips, Henry's head dipped down and sucked one of my nipples in his mouth.

"Son of a saltine cracker!" I screamed from the pleasure rolling through me.

Henry looked up at me for a second with a questioning eyebrow, but went back to work.

I'll be honest, never did I think that sucking on a breast was something I would allow, since it seemed odd for a grown ass man to be sucking on me like a child, but hot damn, it felt like heaven.

His mouth pulled away, leaving me shaking in his hands, but like the fair man he was, he shifted to the other nipple and gave it the same special attention.

I wanted to scream; I wanted to wail; I wanted to go to church and thank God, Jesus, and everyone holy for the miraculous idea of sucking on a lady's boob.

Virginia tightened up and a deep pressure started to grow with Henry's tricky tongue that kept flicking my nipple in his mouth. My hands went instinctively to his head, encouraging him to do more, and when his hands traveled down my stomach, to the waistband of my panties, I grew stiff, and not in a good way.

"Whoa," I said, while popping my nipple out of his mouth.

"What's wrong?"

"You were getting close to my lady parts."

"That's kind of the point," he chuckled, while staring at my breasts. My arms covered my chest quickly, but were removed by Henry. "Don't cover yourself up in front of me. That's insulting. You should be proud to show me your body."

"It's just new for me," I said, resisting the urge to press my bare chest against the mattress, making sure only the mattress springs were able to get a sense of my upper half.

"Let go, Rosie. You're absolutely breathtaking."

Pure joy flowed through me as I accepted his compliment. I glanced down at his crotch, which was a little wet at the tip where his boxer briefs spread against his erection, and I studied it for a second.

"Did you...orgasm?" I whispered, looking down at his member.

"No, it's just a little pre-cum."

"Pre-cum, huh, didn't know there was such a thing. Can I touch it now?"

"Are we done with touching you for now?" he asked, looking a little disappointed. The sentiment made my heart soar.

"Just for a little, but I promise we'll get back to it because your mouth on my breasts was meant to be."

A full guttural laugh escaped Henry as he shook his head and put his hands on his waistband. In slow motion, I watched him pull down his boxer briefs and release his cock. The man had zero shame, turning me on even more.

Bologna pony was right. Holy hell, it looked like a slab of salami just sprouted between his thighs. Was that thing real? My hand reached out, inches away from touching it. It didn't look real.

Before touching it, I leaned forward some more and examined it a little closer. His penis was quite erect, and the skin almost looked taught, stretched from end to end. There were veins, no hair—good manscaping on Henry's part—and his balls, well let's just say my vision of a scrotum has come to fruition.

"I just want you to know, the way you're staring at my dick has me harder than a fucking light post right now," Henry admitted.

I looked up at him to see his hands gripping the sheets on the bed and his chest moving rapidly.

That's all it took, just a look, and he was about to burst? Men were so easy.

"I'm going to touch it now," I announced, as my hand hovered.

"You don't have to announce it; you can just touch it."

"Okay, I just wanted to give you a heads up. I'm going to touch my first penis. This is my first penis caress," I said nervously. "Here it goes, I'm about to touch it." My hand itched closer, but backed away for a second, wondering what it would feel like.

"It's skin," Henry said, "Not some slimy snake, although, after I'm done with you, it sure as hell will be slimy…"

"Ew, Henry!"

He chuckled and I watched as his body shook from the laugh. His dick moved with his movements. It was fascinating. I wondered if men thought the same things about boobs. Although, boobs didn't twitch on their own, and they sure as hell didn't have pre-cum, thank God.

"I dare you to touch it," he smiled.

"I'm going to. See," I said, while I poked the side of it. It moved slightly, but then came back to position. "Ahh," I squealed. "I touched it, I touched the penis. Oh God, it's like one of those blow up punching bags that you hit and it falls, but then comes back up."

"Pretty sure all dicks around the world don't want to be known as punching bags," he teased.

I ignored him and moved my hand back toward his penis, this time wrapping my fingers around him.

"Wow, it's pretty hard. I thought maybe it looked hard, but was squishy in the middle." I squeezed and tested out the strength of his cock. "Yeah, not squishy at all, but the skin is a little loose, only a little, which surprises me, given the fact that it looks like it's about to pop right out of its casing."

"Don't call it casing," Henry said a little breathlessly.

"I mean, look at this," I said while stroking him lightly with my fingers, running my finger along one of the veins. "It's like it has its own mind. Like, if I commanded it, it would do what I say because I have the vagina, and that's its ultimate goal." I dipped my head and looked underneath his dick. I ran my finger along the length of it, testing out all sides, that's when I saw Henry suck in a gasp of air.

I looked up to see that he had a light sheen of sweat on his upper lip. I sat up and studied him.

"Are you okay?"

"Yup, just trying to not blow you in the eye."

"What are you talking about?"

"Rosie, you can't just sit close to a dick, caress it, and examine it, and think the guy won't be affected."

"Am I turning you on?" I asked, slightly perplexed.

"Yes! I have an amazing view of your breasts, your lips are dangerously close to my cock, and you're stroking it with a feather like touch. Rosie, you're killing me."

"Oh, dear. I had no clue. Do you want me to do something else?"

"No, please, by all means, explore away, but if you see me panting, you know why."

"Fair enough," I smiled.

With a renewed confidence from the effect I was having on Henry, I ran my hand down his cock to his balls.

"Careful," he shifted in my grasp. "The balls are way different from the cock; you have to be gentle."

"Oh, right, I forgot. These little guys are sensitive. Noted."

With tender fingers, I lightly stroked his balls and felt the weight to them. They weren't giant, by any means, and he was cleanly shaven, so that wasn't a problem. They were actually kind of fun to play with, kind of like marbles in a Ziploc bag full of water.

Remembering what Henry told me about the perineum, I smiled to myself and glided my hand to the back of his balls, but came up short when I noticed he was sitting too upright.

"Can you slide down the bed a little and spread your legs more?" I asked.

"You're not doing a lady doctor exam or anything, are you?"

"No, why on earth would I do that?"

"I have no clue," he chuckled, as he did what I told him.

At that moment, I looked down at him while his hands went behind his head and his eyes landed on mine. He was giving his entire body up to me for my perusal, for my study, and I knew no other man would have been half as amazing, patient, and understanding as Henry has been through this whole process. He'd taken the role of best friend to a whole new level.

Just as I was about to run my hands up my thighs, my phone rang in my purse that was now sitting on the floor. I looked over at it, wondering who would be calling me, but with a tug to my arm, Henry pulled me back.

"Stay with me, Rosie."

Nodding, I positioned myself between his legs and lowered my head to his cock.

"I'm going to try putting it in my mouth. I can't make you any promises. Last time I did this, I threw up."

"Well, if you feel like throwing up, let me know. I'll hold your hair back for you." He winked up at me, making my heart stutter in my chest.

Gah, I instantly started to feel myself fall for the man, just like that, with a little wink I was his. I shook my head of the damning thoughts and focused at the task at hand…well, I guess mouth, now.

I grabbed ahold of his cock with one hand and lowered my mouth until it was a whisper from my lips. With a lick to wet my now drying lips, I opened my mouth and descended down upon his member. I could feel my mouth trying to stretch around him, and thought to myself how on earth did girls manage to hold their jaw open for so long? Mine was on his cock for a second and my jaw was already screaming at me.

I could feel my teeth against his skin, knowing biting the dick wasn't a good idea, so I took a deep breath, relaxed my face and opened wider.

To my surprise, I was able to move his cock further in my mouth. It wasn't gross like I thought it would be; it just felt like I was trying to suck on a warm, fleshy Popsicle.

Fleshy Popsicle, probably not the best of terms to use in my book, but spot on when talking to girlfriends. I filed that away for when I talked to Jenny or Delaney.

Breathing out of my nose, I lightly sucked on Henry's penis. I wouldn't say I was the best at it. I wouldn't even say I was subpar, as I couldn't control the drool that seeped out of my mouth or the constant gag reflex that threatened me every moment his cock was parked in my mouth, but I could see by the way Henry's muscles flexed that I was actually pleasuring him somehow.

Wanting to pull out some of my tricks that Henry had taught me, to impress him and show him that I was listening, I decided to try the hummer.

Now, I knew nothing about a hummer; I hadn't read about it in any of my novels, so I wasn't quite sure how to process such a sexual action, but from what Henry described to me, I just hummed while my mouth was on his dick. Simple enough.

Taking in some air through my nose, I started to hum.

"Hm, hm, hmm, hm, hm, hmm, hm, hm, hmm, hm, hmmmm."

In the middle of my humming, Henry sat up and looked at me with a quizzical eyebrow.

"Are you humming...*Jingle Bells*?"

"Yeah, wuts wung wi what?" I asked, dick still in my mouth.

"Hey, don't talk with your mouth full of dick," Henry scolded, while pulling my mouth off his dick and laughing.

"What's wrong? Did you not like the song? It's the first thing that came to mind. I can try some Britney Spears if that works better for you?"

"This isn't the game Cranium, Rosie. I'm not trying to guess what song you're humming on my dick. You're just supposed to hum, nothing in particular."

"Well, where's the fun in that? I think that's a new game we should introduce to the world, guess that song. The girl hums a song on the guy's dick, and he gets two guesses; if he guesses wrong, he has to hum on her nipples...damn, I bet that would feel good."

"I bet it would feel better on your clit," Henry said, while wiggling his eyebrows.

"Umm," I stuttered, making him laugh.

"Just hum, Rosie. No tunes."

"Got it," I said, as we both got back into position.

Not humming a song this time, I went back to business as Henry guided me.

"Now, when you have your mouth on a penis that you can't fully take in, you want to use one of your hands to stroke the base of the cock, that way the guy is fully pleasured. The tip is nice to be played with, but squeezing the base of the cock is…fuck yes, just like that," Henry praised, as I squeezed his base and stroked it while I hummed against his penis.

"Fuck, yes, Rosie," he said, his head moving against his pillow.

Feeling confident again, my spare hand started its journey back down south to find the perineum. I rolled his balls in my hand for a second, giving them a little love, until my fingers traveled a little further south, looking for that special spot. I watched with fascination as Henry's eyes closed and his hands that were once behind his head in a casual position were now gripping on to his headboard.

Going past his balls, my fingers slid into a warm area that felt like what Henry was talking about, until something clenched around my fingers and Henry practically flew off the bed. My mouth was ripped off his dick and my hand slid off as well as Henry backed up.

"Whoa, Rosie, what the hell are you doing digging around in my ass?"

The sheen of sweat that was once gracing his upper lip was now all over his delectable and corded body.

"That was your ass? Ugh, how embarrassing."

"What were you going for?"

"Your perineum," I said shyly, wishing I hadn't screwed up my surprise.

With a soft look, he nodded, and then laid back down on the bed. He spread his legs around me and took my hand. Guiding it under his balls, he pressed my finger right where he wanted.

"That," he breathed hard, "That is what you're looking for."

"Oh," I said, while I watched his dick grow harder.

Assuming positions, I placed my mouth back on his cock, my spare hand at the base, and in the perfect rhythm that I thought was appropriate, I moved my head and my hands. My tongue hummed against the underside of his dick, one of my hands played with the base of his cock, squeezing torturously, while the other hand played with that secret spot.

"Fuck, fuck, fuck," Henry said, while shifting on the bed and now gripping onto the sheets. "Damn, Rosie, I mean…fuck. God, I'm going to come, Rosie; you have to stop."

"Why," I said against his cock.

"Because I'm going to come," he said with a strangled voice.

I pulled away, but not soon enough, as my hand connected with his perineum one last time. I could tell he was going to explode, so to stop the flow from getting everywhere, I placed my finger over the hole of his cock and prayed that the ejaculation that was about to happen wouldn't get everywhere.

To my dismay, my idea of stopping the spurt of cum everywhere was countered by the high pressured hose Henry had in his pants, because what I thought was a good idea turned into a giant mess as my fingers assisted as a sprayer.

Cum flew everywhere, over me, over Henry, on the bed, and unfortunately, directly in my eye.

"Gah, you got me!" I said, as I covered my eye with my hand and fell back on the bed, wondering if the white, sticky liquid was going to blind me.

My eye burned from the onslaught of man milk that I wasn't expecting to have jab me, as I heard Henry chuckling in the background.

"What's so funny?" I asked, while still covering my eye. "I think I might be blind."

"You're not blind," he laughed. "But, damn, didn't think I would be doing the dirty pirate with you. Well, a dirty pirate, minus the blow to the kneecap."

"What's the dirty pirate?" I asked, starting to blink, hoping my vision would reappear.

"When a guy jizzes in your eye and then kicks you in the kneecap so you hop around and hold your eye, looking like a pirate. I'm supposed to say arghhh when I do it; I missed my cue. Didn't know you were going all out today."

"I hate you."

"No, you don't," he responded, while getting off the bed and running outside, naked. He returned quickly with a warm, wet towel. I watched as he leaned over me, dick still flopping around—good Lord—and wiped my eye. Slowly, my vision started to come back, and I could see once again; he cleaned us up the rest of the way.

Once we were clean, he pulled me into his chest and said, "When I say I'm going to come, you're supposed to pull away, love."

"But, don't girls usually swallow?"

"They can, but I would never ask you to do that."

"Does it taste bad?"

"Well, it's not like a milkshake going down your throat. It's salty, I guess, and warm, not the best thing in the world."

"Seems like it would be gross."

"It's like beer, you either like it or you don't."

"Have you ever tried it?"

"Can't say that I have," he laughed. "Not really into dudes. Kind of love the boobies," he said, while tweaking a nipple, waking Virginia up from her tiny siesta. "Now, I do believe it's your turn, love."

CHAPTER 20

"The Sacrificed Lamb"

"What are you going to do?" I asked, slightly nervous.

"Well, I plan on tasting you, and then, if you're up to it, I want to finally take that V-card from you."

The way he said it had me slightly cringing, as if it was a trophy he was waiting to grab and put on his mantle of sex, but I let it roll by, even though Delaney's voice kept ringing through my head.

Cherry Chaser.

No, Henry wouldn't be like that, not at all.

"You want to go down on me?"

"Yeah, I want to do a lot more than that, Rosie, but we'll take it slow." He rolled me to my side as he hovered above me. "First things first, time to get completely naked."

His hands found my panties, gripped the sides of them and pulled them all the way off my body, stripping me completely naked. I wanted to hide, curl up and cover up my bits, but after seeing the perusal Henry was giving me with the lust in his eyes, a new sense of confidence grew inside of me. He wanted to see my naked body, he liked seeing it, and it actually turned him on. It was a new concept for me, and I liked every second of it.

His hand ran over his mouth as he took me in.

"I'm such a dumbass," he confessed.

"Why?"

"For waiting this long. I should have done this the first day I met you."

With that, Henry lowered down his head and placed his lips softly on mine. Whereas, when I pleasured him, it was more of an experiment for me, a little learning experience, but this time, when Henry was in charge, it was more about passion, something I longed for.

While he kissed me, his hands ran up my body until they hit my breasts. With gentle strokes, his thumbs played with the underside of my breasts, something that Virginia absolutely adored.

His hands played my body like an instrument, sending waves of pleasure rolling through my body. He knew what to touch, when to touch it, and the kind of pressure it needed. When his thumbs stroked my breasts, his kisses grew heavy, and then his thumbs pulled away, so did his lips. It was pure torture, fantastically amazing torture.

Growing impatient from the pressure that was building up in my core, I was about to encourage him to suck on my nipples again, but I didn't get a chance, because he was so in tune with my body that he started making his way down to my breasts before I could say anything.

His mouth found one of my nipples, causing my back to arch off the bed from the light bite he applied.

"God, God that feels good," I said, voicing my pleasure, something I never thought I would do, but given the feelings running through me, I couldn't control what flowed out of my mouth. Delaney was right, when in the throes of passion, you couldn't control what came out of you.

Giving the other nipple attention, I writhed under his touch, his caress, his suckle, until I felt completely spent and in desperate need for him to ease the ache between my thighs.

Slowly, he lifted his head up, smiled devilishly at me and kissed my sternum, then my stomach, then right above my pubic bone. I gasped as he lowered himself completely below me and positioned my legs over his shoulders. He had me in position, and I should be nervous, I should be squirming under him, possibly sweating from the mere chance that I let a little flatus escape once again, but I wasn't; I was with Henry and I was safe.

Relaxing into the bed, I closed my eyes and allowed Henry to taste me, like he said. His fingers touched me, spreading me wide, and with one small swipe, his tongue ran right against my clit.

"Urrrrghhhhh."

God, I wish I could sound eloquent when a guy went down on me, but instead of being sexy, I sounded like a drowning seal.

Smiling, he continued his mission by burying his head between my thighs and his tongue inside Virginia. Clapping her folds, she celebrated the welcoming of Henry's tongue into her tight quarters.

There were times in a girl's life where she knew she would remember a certain moment in time, and right now, with Henry's head between my thighs, his tongue lapping at me like a damn dog licking peanut butter, I knew I would never forget this, because as the pressure built in my core, I knew Henry was going to be the first guy to ever give me an orgasm.

When I thought I couldn't handle his tongue any longer, his finger went inside Virginia, and his tongue hit my clit with a strong thrust.

In that moment, my vision went completely black, as it felt like every nerve that was in my body collected inside Virginia and exploded all at once, rendering me speechless. My body stiffened like a board, my toes curled, and this overwhelming sense of complete and utter pleasure overtook my body as Henry's tongue continued to move against my clit, making my body embarrassingly convulse in all different kinds of directions, until I knew I was starting to cut off the circulation from his neck to his head as my legs gave him a death grip headlock.

"Glah, glah, gibble me, me...fuuuuuuuuck," I screamed, as my body finally settled down and only little twitches ran through my body.

I watched as Henry slowly pulled away and traveled up the length of my body. His head lowered to mine, and with a grin, he kissed me, letting me taste myself on his lips.

    Now, I had read this in books before, and let me tell you, I wasn't turned on like all the other girls were. I was actually perplexed as to why Henry felt the need to have me taste myself, or have my taste on him.

When I kissed him, did I have dick mouth? Did he like the taste of his dick on my tongue?

Now that we were kissing, and his dick was once on my mouth and my vagina was on his, did that mean we were inadvertently having sex without penetration?

"I lost you, didn't I?" Henry asked.

"No, well sort of, I was just thinking about how you were kissing me after you just went down on me."

"Do you know what's more important than that?"

"What?"

"Was that your first orgasm?" he asked, almost desperate to hear the answer.

"It was," I admitted.

"And, did you enjoy yourself?"

Giving him a pointed look, I said, "You know damn well I did by the obscene gurgling I was doing. Jesus, could I sound any less attractive?"

"I liked it," he smiled. "How do you feel down there?"

"Wet."

"Good, do you think you're up for more?" he asked, while peeking down at his cock. I looked down at the erection he was sporting and gasped. Good Lord, he was ready.

Was I ready for this? I mean, I actually wanted it more than anything, but hell, I was nervous. Books said it was a slight pinch, but the girls loved it after the initial barrier was broken, so it couldn't be that bad, right?

Wanting to finally find out, I nodded and brought Henry's head down to mine, wanting to kiss his beautiful lips and sink into his embrace.

His body spread against mine, allowing me to once again feel his penis against my thigh, something I was starting to grow quite fond of...and fast. What a weird thing to enjoy, penis against thigh. Rosie Bloom, likes to write, hates cat, enjoys Chinese food, and penis against her thigh.

His hands wandered up my body, playing with my breasts and teasing me relentlessly, while my hands wandered just as much, but never really touching his penis. Two could play at this game.

"Don't tease me," he said into my neck as he kissed me up and down.

"Why not? You're doing the same," I said breathlessly, as he pinched my nipple. "God, my nipples love you."

"Good to know," he chuckled, just as his mouth wrapped around my breast and sucked hard. My back arched, my toes curled and my mind went blank as I pressed his head further down on my breasts. It was pathetic, I knew it, but the minute I found out my nipples controlled the be-all to end-all of pleasure, I wanted them played with at all times.

Like a professional, Henry sucked, nipped, licked and pinched them, never letting up, never paying too much attention to one single nipple. In five minutes, he had Virginia popping out of her dungeon, begging to be played with.

"I don't know how much longer I can last, watching you writhe under me like this," Henry said into my breast.

"Then don't," I breathed out.

He pulled away, gave me a questioning look, as if to say do you really want me to do this? With a curt nod, I gave him the go ahead.

With the green light, he leaned over to the night stand and

grabbed a condom. If I wasn't so sated, I would have offered to put it on, practice my condom skills, but I let him take care of it.

Once he was done, he positioned himself over me again and grabbed my legs so they hung over his shoulders.

"Wh-what are you doing?" I asked, feeling incredibly nervous.

"Making this as easy on you as possible. Do you trust me, Rosie?"

"More than anyone I know," I admitted honestly.

"Okay, then I'll be honest. This won't feel very good, it might hurt a lot, since I'm pretty big and you're very tight."

"Think pretty highly of yourself, don't you?" I asked, trying to lighten the mood.

"You know it's the truth," he grinned wickedly. He was right; he was sporting a tree trunk. "Ready? I'm going to go slow."

I nodded and braced myself. His hands ran to my breasts as he said, "Relax, love. The more relaxed you are, the easier this will be. Be in the moment with me."

Unclenching, I tried to take deep breaths, while one of his hands went to my right nipple. His other hand had ahold of his cock, which now rubbed against my entrance. Surprisingly, I was incredibly wet, so when he rubbed his cock against me, it actually pleased Virginia a great deal.

"Oh, do more of that," I said, while I braced my hands above my head.

Chuckling, he did as was asked, and I reveled in the feel of the smooth tip of his cock running the length of my core. It felt incredible, just incredible enough for me to forget the fact that Henry had inserted the tip of his cock into my vagina.

"Oh," I said, as I adjusted, but with each movement, he slowly went deeper.

"Don't move, love," Henry said, looking a little pained.

"Are you okay?" I asked, while trying to steady my breathing.

"You're so God damn tight, love."

"I'm sorry. Should we stop?"

"No! Don't be sorry; you feel beyond amazing. If it's alright with you, I'm going to go a little deeper. Are you alright with that?"

"I think so," I said cautiously, as I held my breath.

"You think so?" he questioned with a grin.

"Well, I guess since you're already pushing past the threshold, you should go all the way, right? I guess with you I can say, go big or go home."

Chuckling, he shook his head while looking down at me. "Remind me to tell you about bedroom talk later; we've blown past all bedroom decorum."

"Like what?" I asked, curious as to what I possibly said.

"Not now, Rosie," he said, a little pained. "Kind of having a hard time just tipping you."

"Tipping. Huh, is that a real term?"

"Not now, love."

I was about to say sorry, when his lips found mine once again, but this time, instead of being gentle, he was more demanding. He nipped my lip with his teeth, plunged his tongue into my mouth, and once again fondled my breasts. The onslaught of attention to my body had me forgetting what he was doing down below, and before I knew it, a sharp pain flew through Virginia, making my body arch off the mattress and a moan escape my lips.

"Are you okay?" Henry asked, as he stilled above me. His breathing was labored, and I knew this was difficult for him.

My eyes were tightly shut from the pain that ripped through me, but once the initial shock of what happened passed, I eased my body and opened my eyes. Henry's concern was reassuring, as he scanned me for any indication that he should stop.

Oddly, I wasn't hurting like I thought I would, besides the initial "pinch" that was talked about. I just felt full, in a good way. I felt stretched, yet satisfied, like Henry was meant to be shoving his penis into me. God, I shouldn't think things like that.

Coming back to the present, I nodded my head and said, "I feel full, but in a good way."

"Good."

Gently now, Henry started moving his hips in and out of me,

forming a kind of friction in Virginia that I'd never felt before, even when I got the vibrator stuck up there. His lips started caressing my jaw lightly, turning an awkward moment into an intimate one.

His hands traveled slowly up and down my body, sending goose bumps to my skin. His fingers traced the outline of my ribs and at a snail's pace, found their way up to my breasts, where I felt my chest press into his hand once he grabbed ahold of them. I was shameless now.

The movements of his lips and fingers, combined with the gentle thrusts going in and out of me had my body wanting more, needing more, craving more. I felt like whatever he was doing was just not satisfying the pressure that was starting to build in Virginia enough, until one of his hands ran down my stomach and hovered right above my pubic bone.

Desperately, I waited for his next move, wanting to see what he had in store, because so far, I was cursing myself for not partaking in sexual intercourse before now. With a slip of his finger, he pressed against my clit, applying just the right amount of pressure to make the world around me slip into a dull darkness and leave only Henry and me in view.

"I'm going to come, love," Henry gritted out.

I wanted to respond, I wanted to tell him it was okay, but the epic orgasmic feeling running through my veins took over, and I was left speechless. Two more thrusts, a pinch to the nipple, and pressure on my clit had me screaming his name, pulling his hair out, and curling my legs around his waist, thrusting my hips into him like a horny ass dog.

"Henry!" I screamed, just as I felt him stiffen above me, voicing a low groan of his own.

"God," he mumbled, as his hips flew into mine, eating up every last point of pleasure we were experiencing.

Once we couldn't extract any more pleasure from our coupling, we stilled and just stared at each other. Henry hovered over me just perfectly, granting me that sexy smile of his, and right then and there, I felt happy, truly happy.

"By the nipple hairs of a wildebeest, that was by far the best thing I've ever experienced," I confessed, while reaching up my hand and caressing Henry's hair softly.

From my touch, Henry switched to leaning on his elbows, so he was only a few inches above me. His hands went to my face as well and stroked my cheeks. I relished the feel of him on top of me, of him caressing me, being intimate in a completely different way. Was this what post sex was like? Probably not with everyone, some people probably just did the deed and went on with their lives, but I enjoyed this so much more. I enjoyed the sight of Henry's eyes soaking me in, loving me; it was a moment I would never forget.

My phone beeped, letting me know I had a message, and that was when I remembered I'd gotten a call in the middle of my passionate moment.

I thought about answering it to avoid an awkward moment, but held off when Henry asked, "Was everything okay?"

"It was perfect, Henry. It hurt a little at first, but you helped me forget. You're really good at kissing."

"I should say the same about you. You do this thing with your tongue that has me losing all my self-control."

"Really?" I asked, kind of proud of myself.

"Really," Henry chuckled. Stroking my cheek, he continued, "You're so beautiful, you know that?"

"Thank you," I replied shyly. "You're kind of crazy sexy yourself."

"Just kind of?" he teased.

"Only kind of," I smiled.

My phone beeped again, which had me wondering. No one would leave me a message unless it was important, which only led to my overactive imagination to freaking me out to the thought of my mom and dad dying in a ditch somewhere.

"Do you mind if I check my phone?" I asked, knowing I ruined the moment.

"That's fine," he said, getting off of me.

I sat up and looked down to find that the crisp and clean sheets we were once on were now covered in blood.

"Holy hell, it looks like someone sacrificed a lamb," I said, wondering if Virginia was okay. I knew if she wasn't, she would be sending me a keegle SOS, so apparently, from lack of communication, I assumed she was safe for now. She was really good at communicating through vagina Morse code, thankfully.

"Hold on, let me get a warm towel to wipe things up."

I watched as Henry shuffled off the bed, shucked his condom and threw on a pair of athletic shorts that were in his closet, all the while taking in the sight of his tight rear end. Never thought I would be checking out my best friend, but damn if I couldn't help it now.

Within seconds, Henry reappeared with a wash cloth. Taking charge, he spread my legs, making me blush, and started cleaning me up. To say I felt mortified was an understatement. I read about men cleaning girls in books, and how it was a kind gesture, which it was, but for a girl who just started spreading her legs for the man cleaning her, I felt like clenching my thighs shut, not caring if his hand was still in there or not, but I refrained.

"There, you're all set."

Wanting to cover my body, I leaned over and grabbed his shirt to shield his prying eyes that were staring at my breasts.

"Don't cover up on my behalf," he laughed, as I grabbed my phone from my purse and keyed up the voicemail. The missed call was a number I didn't recognize, so I grew even more worried.

The voicemail started up and I listened carefully while sitting next to Henry on his bed.

"Hi Rosie, it's Atticus, you know the guy you kicked in the crotch. Uh, I'm sorry it's taken me so long to call you. I've been out of town and also trying to gain the courage to call you again. Even though things ended on a crushing note," he chuckled, "I would still like to see you. I had a great time, minus foot to the crotch, so if you were thinking you might want to go out again, give me a call. Okay, see ya."

I sat there, motionless, as I listened to Atticus' voice on the other end of my phone. He still wanted to go out with me? After I took out his family marbles? Atticus was probably the last person I expected to hear from, especially after how everything went down.

Now, I was confused. I looked over at Henry, whose brow was wrinkled and he was staring at his hands that rested on his lap.

"Umm, that was Atticus, you know, the guy I kicked."

"Yeah, in the balls, right?"

"Yeah, he uh, wants to go out again."

Silence filtered into the room as Henry sat on the bed, contemplating what I was telling him. I was confused; I didn't know what to do. Obviously, if I had it my way, I would be lying back down with Henry, relishing the feel of his embrace, but I wasn't sure where we stood. From all his hints and the way he touched me and spoke to me, I figured he would want to start a more serious relationship with me, rather than be just friends, but by the way he was now distancing himself from me, maybe I was wrong.

Clapping his hands, Henry stood up and turned his back toward me.

"Sounds like you should call him back. I have to take a shower and then go out. I, uh, will see you around."

Time stood still as I watched Henry gather his towels and shower caddy, as if he couldn't wipe the scent of me off of him quick enough. I sat in silence, trying to figure out what just happened.

"Wh-what are you doing?" I stuttered.

"Taking a shower," he repeated, while facing me this time, his face completely expressionless, like what we just did wasn't this magical act of ungodly pleasure.

"You're just going to leave?"

"Yeah, I mean, you have stuff to do, things to write, now that you got what you wanted."

"What are you talking about?" I asked, a little thrown off by his tone.

"Your virginity, it's no longer a mystery. Go write about it."

I stood up and placed my hands on my hips, trying not to get worked up, but I didn't like the way he was talking to me.

"Why are you being an ass? Are you trying to brush me off?"

"No, just moving on with life, that's all."

"Moving on?" Delaney's words rang through my head, reminding me of his obsession. "Oh, my God, Delaney was right. You are a cherry chaser."

"Excuse me?" Henry asked, looking angrier than I had ever seen him, but I didn't let him intimidate me.

"You're a cherry chaser. You get fixated on virgins and bring them into your lair until you take what you want. No wonder you were so good at it; you knew exactly what you were doing."

The words hurt coming out of my mouth, but by the way he was brushing me off, I had to save my heart somehow, because what we shared together would go down in history as one of the best moments of my life, and I didn't want to tarnish it; too bad there was no way of stopping that from happening.

"Wow," he paused while he ran his hand through his hair. "Glad you think so highly of me."

"Tell me it's not true," I countered. Wishing he would tell me I'm an idiot, that I was wrong, that I am the most inconsiderate ass he had ever come across.

"Believe what you want, Rosie," was all he answered, leaving me to believe that what I was saying was true.

"You're a dick," I spouted off. "I can't believe you would sacrifice our relationship, our friendship for a roll in your bed because you have some creepy obsession. Why would you do that?"

My breath was getting caught in my throat as I talked, and tears threatened to fall down my face. I refused to cry, though, I didn't want to come off as an attached ex-virgin clinger, and if I cried over him doing the old stuff and go, then I would look like a serious clinger.

Taking a deep breath, Henry walked over to his door and turned toward me to answer my question. "Because, according to you, I apparently don't care about our friendship and would rather just stick you and throw away everything we ever had." He shook his head, and as he walked away, he said, "See you around, Rosie. Good luck with Atticus; hopefully he treats you better than I did."

With his last words, my tears that were building up finally fell. I took off to my room and slammed my door shut, wishing to take back the day from the very beginning. I never should have kissed him, I never should have let him touch me, and I never should have given into his seducing ways. Everything was ruined now.

I pulled out my notebook and stared at it for a while, until I wrote the one thing I would remember for the rest of my life.

June 14, 2014

Note to self: Never sleep with your friends. It never ends well, no matter how many romantic comedies you watch.

CHAPTER 21
"The Sexuals"

    The sound of Sir Licks-a-Lot's sand papery tongue echoed through the walls of my office as I watched him prop his leg up like a gymnast and go to town on his mini kitty balls. His favorite spot to clean himself in my office was on the top of my filing cabinet, where he could be spotted from around the office, and today, once again, he was taking advantage of the office view.

    Occasionally, he would pull his head away from his crotch and shake his head, as if his cat balls got stuck on his tongue, but then he would just go back to licking. It was like he was giving himself oral, just like Bear; it was unconfutable and odd to be around.

    I tried shooing him away, so I didn't have to hear his scratchy tongue cause an obnoxious friction against his private bits, but all he did was flip me off with his toes. Coincidence that his middle toe stuck up further? I think not; the little bastard knew what he was doing.

    It's been two days since I talked to Henry. He hasn't been around the apartment, and neither have I, to be honest. I've put in some extra time the past two days at work just to avoid him. Now that it was Wednesday, I was starting to get stir crazy from avoiding the apartment.

Yesterday, when I got home, Delaney tried talking to me, but I faked a headache and went straight to bed, avoiding dinner and any reason as to why I needed to go into the common spaces. I even brushed my teeth in my room with a bottle of water and spit out my window, not the classiest of options, but the moment I heard Henry's voice in the common space, I swore not to step foot outside my room.

To say going to bed with Henry was a mistake would be an understatement. It was probably the most colossal mistake I would ever make in my lifetime, because to my dismay, after just a couple of days, I saw that Henry was already looking for a new apartment, after seeing a listing tucked under his computer that was lying on the kitchen counter.

Not only did I put distance between us, but I practically put him out of his own home. Well, it was both of our doing, I guess. I couldn't take blame for everything that happened. He was the one who persuaded me, kept being all handsy and…perfect.

Damn.

I missed him. Why did things have to take a turn to Crapville?

I replayed the moment after I checked the message on my phone over and over in my head, trying to figure out where we went wrong. Was he mad about Atticus calling? Because, after I hung up my phone, his entire mood changed. The loving Henry who was once holding me and loving me turned into an angry man, full of nasty comments and hatred.

The misrepresentation of my best friend sent me to tears after I went back to my room. I still couldn't believe the way he talked to me, the way he looked at me.

A knock on my office door shook me out of my thoughts. Jenny was on the other side, and letting herself in.

"Hey, Rosie. I feel like I haven't talked to you in forever."

"How was your little mini vacation?" I asked, knowing she and Drew went on a little long weekend vacay up to New England.

"It was so beautiful up there, but I'm all fudged out. You wouldn't believe the number of specialty fudge shops up in the area. Every little town had their own fudge, and do you know who just needed to test every single one of them?"

"Drew?" I asked, clearly knowing the answer.

"Yes, it was a little obnoxious after the seventh stop, but the man needed to try every unique flavor he came across."

"What was your favorite? There must have been one that caught your eye."

"Neapolitan. It seems simple, but believe me, after testing flavors like Oreo, Maple Walnut, and S'mores, Neapolitan was the superior winner. The strawberry flavor just hit you, you know? Very smooth."

I giggled.

"I can see you've become a connoisseur of fudge on your time off. I'm impressed."

"Don't be. I now get to spend every spare minute I have at the gym working off every last calorie I ate this past weekend. Drew can eat whatever he wants and still have a perfect body, but me, if I eat a peanut, I have to work it off in the gym for hours."

Jenny had a perfect body, but to be fair, worked her butt off for it, and was paranoid that she was going to not fit into the same pants she'd worn since high school. She never wore them in public, given the bedazzled ass that was popular ten years ago, but she kept them around as a tester, to make sure she stayed on track.

"How are the jeans fitting?" I asked, seeing if she'd tried them on.

"Fine, but I swear they felt a little tight yesterday."

"You're insane."

"I know."

I loud sneeze escaped Sir Licks-a-Lot, as his head pulled away from his crotch and he sneezed again, nearly blowing himself off of the cabinet.

"Got some pussy dust in your nose?" Jenny asked, making me laugh.

Sir Licks-a-Lot stretched on the filing cabinet, then leapt off of it, onto my desk, knocking over my water, right onto Jenny's lap, making her spring up from her chair. Jumping off of the desk, Sir Licks-a-Lot walked out the door, but not before turning his head to look at both of us and kicking his legs behind him, as if he was covering us up with imaginary dirt.

"That little fuck," Jenny mumbled, while she waved her pants around.

"At least it was water and not coffee."

"Did you see the laughter in his eyes? He knew exactly what he was doing. Fucking demon pussy."

"It's like you expect something different from him. You can't insult him and get away with it unscathed. Come on, Jenny, you know better than that."

"You're right," she agreed. Clapping her hands together, she leaned forward and said, "Now, tell me why you've been working late. Marian over in editing has been keeping an eye on you for me while I've been gone."

"What? Why? I don't need a babysitter."

"You do when you've been going on dates with hunky men. So, tell me, why have you been staying late? Are you waiting for a midnight rendezvous?"

"I wish," I mumbled, while I focused my attention on my computer and let the words in front of me bleed together.

"Okay, this doesn't sound good. What happened?"

The excitement that was once lacing Jenny's voice now turned to deep concern.

I will not cry, I will not cry, I repeated in my head as tears started to well up in my eyes.

"Rosie, why are you going to cry?"

Crap. That's all it took. Tears started streaming down my face out of my control; it was no use, I was an emotional wreck and bottling up my emotions could only last for so long.

"We did it," I stated through tears.

"Who?" Jenny asked, confused, as she grabbed some tissues

off of my desk and handed them to me.

"Henry and me. We had sex."

Jenny sat back for a second as she studied my confession. She knew of our friendship and how much he meant to me, so it must have been a shock for her to hear such a thing come from me.

"Wow, I wasn't expecting you to say that. When?"

"Sunday, after we had brunch at my parents. He was really touchy and sweet, and I don't know, it just happened."

"I'm assuming the post sex party didn't go very well?"

"Nope," I sniffed. "I thought everything was good, he was stroking my face tenderly, took care of me like I was the most precious thing to him and then, like he was Dr. Jekyll and Mr. Hyde, he just switched. He became rude and detached."

"That seems weird. I mean, I don't like the guy very much, but that doesn't seem like him. Did something happen in between..."

Before Jenny could finish her sentence, my door burst open and Delaney stood in the door frame, looking rather angry.

Slamming the door shut and inviting herself in, she took the other seat that sat in front of my desk and dropped her purse on the floor.

"What the hell is going on?" Delaney asked, while she briefly looked at Jenny, waved, and then turned her attention back to me. "So, what is going on with you and Henry?"

"We were just talking about that," Jenny answered for me. "Apparently, they had the sexuals on Sunday."

"What?!" Delaney nearly spat, as her eyes bulged out of their sockets. "And you didn't tell me this because?"

Feeling guilty, I shrunk in my seat and said, "I didn't want to get you in between everything."

"What do you mean? Did things not go well?"

"The sex was good..."

"But post sex was bad," Jenny finished for me. "He turned into a bit of a dick afterwards."

"Really?" Delaney asked, a little confused. "That doesn't seem like Henry."

"That's what I said!" Jenny replied, while lightly tapping Delaney on the shoulder. "And I don't even know the guy that well, but I know that's not the kind of man he is."

"What happened after you guys did it?" Delaney asked, trying to get down to the source of the issue.

"That's what we were just discussing," Jenny added, as they both leaned forward and waited for me to answer.

Feeling a little overwhelmed, I sat up in my chair and replayed the moment for them.

"Well, after we did things, he held me for a while, talked to me, told me I was beautiful, stroked my hair, sweet things like that."

"Now, that's Henry," Delaney pointed out.

"But my phone kept beeping from a message, so to stop the irritating sound and make sure nothing was wrong with my parents, since my mind wanders, I listened to the message on the phone while Henry sat next to me. He was totally cool with it, but once I hung up, it was like he was a completely different person."

"What was the message?" Jenny asked.

"Remember that guy, Atticus?"

"The one you kicked in the crotch?" Delaney asked.

"Yes, him. He called me and asked to take me out again, which I thought was weird, because I for sure thought we were done after I used his crotch as a kicking bag. I was shocked and didn't know how to respond, and that's when Henry went all weird."

Blowing out a heavy breath and sitting back in her chair, Delaney shook her head at me. "God, Rosie, you're so dense at times. You obviously upset Henry with that voicemail. The guy has it bad for you, and right after you guys have sex, you talk about possibly going out with another guy. He was an ass because he was protecting his heart."

"Wh-what? No…"

Henry's face flashed in my mind when I started talking about

Atticus, and that's when it hit me. Delaney was right, Henry was upset about the phone call...that was the only explanation, because after that, his entire demeanor changed.

"Oh, God, I am dense," I said, while burying my head in my hands. "Do you really think he likes me like that?"

"God, I even saw that he liked you," Jenny said. "It's so obvious, Rosie."

"She's right. It's obvious, sweetie. Ever since freshman year in college, he's loved you, but you've always just wanted to be friends, so that's what he granted you, friendship. I can only imagine how much he wanted you as time went on, and after seeing you date all of these guys in a short time period, he snapped."

"I don't know what to say. I mean, what the hell do I do now?"

"Talk to him," Delaney suggested. "Are you going to go out with Atticus?"

"No, I haven't even called him back."

"Then let him know that. Do you like Henry? Do you have feelings for him?"

That was an easy question to answer. Of course I had feelings for Henry. I've had feelings for him ever since I met him, but I've always thought he was out of my league, that's why I kept him as a friend because, if anything, I just wanted him in my life, any way I could take him. But now, now I wanted more. I wanted to be the one he kissed good night, the one who slept in his arms, the one he sent flowers to on special occasions. I wanted every last inch of Henry all to myself, but was terrified to actually hand it over.

"I do," I admitted, making Delaney squeal. "I just don't know if he wants me still."

"Never know until you put yourself out there and ask. Time to take your life by the lady balls, Rosie," Delaney said, while Jenny nodded in agreement. "He'll be home tonight. Don't wait any longer; make it happen."

"I feel like I'm going to puke."

"Welcome to the world of love, Rosie. It sucks, it's nauseating at times, and nerve racking, but the reward is so worth it when you have someone by your side supporting you, loving you, and being your life support. There's nothing like it."

Life support, yup, that was what Henry was to me, because at the moment, without him, I could feel myself slowly deteriorating, losing the ability to be happy, to eat, to sleep. He was my life support, hands down; he was the reason why I breathed.

***

Later that night, when I got home from work, I stood in front of my apartment door, contemplating what I was going to say to Henry, how I was going to approach the subject without being incredibly awkward.

Usually, at this point in the books I read, the guy is the screw-up for the most part, and he goes about winning the girl back with ease, explaining that he was an idiot, and makes a grand gesture like proposing.

Well, that was out of the picture; there was no way I would be proposing, talk about an epic mistake. I would love to just jump his bones and make up that way; I read a book where that was completely acceptable, but my gut was telling me that wasn't the best of ideas.

Talking was obviously the clear cut choice, but how to go about talking to him was the question.

Did I just say something like, "So, about our post coitus relations…"

No, no one says coitus, unless you're a doctor in the fifties who likes to skirt around words like sex and fucking. I didn't even really say fucking, even though, there were times where people just fucked. Not that I've experienced that, I've only had penis insertion once, but in some of the books I've read, those characters fucked, holy hell did they fuck. Up against walls, in hot tubs, on desks, kitchen counters, chairs, and my favorite…on top of a horse. That's fucking, what Henry and I shared was…God, it was making love.

I'm such an idiot. I'm that girl!!

I'm that girl you read in a romance novel that you want to shake uncontrollably and say, "You idiot! He's the perfect man for you!"

There have been many times where I've read a book and thought, God, what was the author thinking. Well, duh, it's real life. People are idiots in real life, and don't see what's sitting in front of them until they lose it. Life really isn't a bunch of sunshine and rainbows. Nope, people make mistakes, they can't see past their noses to find that the one man that has been a constant in their life was actually made for them.

Sam Smith was right when he said, "Too much of a good thing, won't be good anymore," especially if you don't give it the attention it needs.

My stomach flipped as I thought about losing Henry forever, if I really couldn't patch up everything I messed up. I didn't think I could handle not having Henry in my life.

Not wanting to waste any more time, I charged through the apartment door to find piles of boxes scattered across our living room.

What the hell?

I walked around the boxes to Henry's door, which was closed, but I could hear voices on the other side. Lightly knocking, I waited for Henry to answer.

Were the boxes his? There was no way he found a place that quickly. Maybe they were Delaney's; maybe she failed to tell me she was moving in with Derk, or maybe Derk had moved in with us.

Henry's door opened, and on the other side was Tasha, his girlfriend from college. She was wearing one of Henry's shirts and her hair was rumpled. Just past her was Henry, lying in bed with the covers over his lower half, but showing off his bare torso.

My heart sputtered in my chest at what was in front of me. Henry and Tasha?

"Rosie! Oh, my God, it's been so long," Tasha said, grabbing me into a hug. Involuntarily, I felt my arms wrap around her and take part in the spontaneous hug. "I'm so glad you're here. I've missed you. Can you believe Henry and I are moving in together? When he called me Sunday, saying he wanted to get back together, I was shocked, but couldn't be happier. God, isn't this exciting?"

Swallowing the lump in my throat, I nodded my head, as I casually eyed Henry behind Tasha, who failed to make eye contact with me. Coward.

"That's great. I'm happy for you two."

"Do you want to help pack? We're aiming for a Saturday move, but we'll see. He's going to move in with me for a bit, and then we're going to try to find a place on the Upper West Side. Fingers crossed." She crossed her fingers up and down and bounced in front of me. The girl was perfect with her caramel hair, olive skin, and bright blue eyes. She was the girl you chose to hate just based off of looks, but was as sweet as could be. I despised the woman.

"Fingers crossed," I said, feeling like I was going to puke. "Um, seems like I caught you two in a bad spot. I will, uh, let you get back to business."

"You're sweet. It was so good to see you, Rosie."

"You too, Tasha."

She shut the door on me, leaving my heart broken and scattered on the floor. He called her Sunday? Sunday?!

He must not have felt what I felt to have called Tasha so abruptly after our coupling.

Every nerve in my body ached as I forced myself to walk to the kitchen for a bottle of water. Just when I thought I could fix things, it blew up in my face. I only had myself to blame.

As I was grabbing a water from the fridge, I heard Henry's door open and shut. I refused to turn around to see if it was Henry, but once I felt his chest against my back, I knew it was him; there was no mistaking it.

"Hi, Rosie," he said in that deep voice of his.

"Hey," I replied somberly, as I shut the fridge and started

walking away.

"Can we talk?" he asked, sounding a little desperate.

Gaining enough courage to look at him, I glanced up and saw that he was only wearing a pair of athletic shorts, the same ones he wore the other night, after we…

Damn it, my heart was ripping out of my chest.

"What, Henry?"

His eyes scanned my face, ripping every last part of my heart with those beautiful eyes of his.

"Why did you come to my room?"

To tell you I love you, to tell you I'm in love with you, that I want you more than anything. That I've dreamt of being held in your arms ever since I met you.

Even though those words were at the tip of my tongue, I couldn't say them, I couldn't risk the rejection. Clearly, he'd moved on; he was with someone else and escalating a relationship with her to a new level.

"Um, I saw the boxes and thought I should let you know the shirt I borrowed will be clean tomorrow for you to pack."

Damn, shit….fuck.

The sullen look on his face let me know that wasn't what he wanted to hear, but honestly, what was I supposed to say to him at this point? There were no options left for me. I wasn't one to break up a relationship, and by the looks of it from Tasha's expression, they were happy.

"That's all?" he asked in disbelief.

"Yeah."

He nodded his head as he looked away and ran his hand through his hair. I could see the frustration pouring off of him, but I didn't know what he wanted from me, what he wanted me to say.

"Are you going out with him?" Henry asked, sounding angrier by the minute.

"Who?"

"Atticus, don't play dumb with me, Rosie."

I stepped back from his attack of words. I didn't like this side of Henry at all. It scared me.

"That's none of your business."

"I thought we were friends," he said with a snide tone.

"Yeah, so did I until you started acting like a complete ass," I shot back.

"I'm the ass? You're the one talking to a guy the minute I remove my dick from you."

Fury lashed through me as I spoke. "I didn't speak to him, I just checked my voicemail, and I didn't say I was going out with him. I haven't even called him back, because in my head, I thought maybe there could be something between us, but clearly I was wrong. You only wanted my virginity."

"You know what? Fuck you, Rosie. Fuck you."

Tears fell down my face from his harsh words. In all the years I've known Henry, not once has he ever said that to me. His words hit me hard, hitting me directly in the chest, where it was hollow now.

Through sobbing tears, I faintly heard Tasha say something to Henry and him just tell her to go back in the room.

I shook my head and wiped my tears. With all the bravado in my body, I lifted my chin and looked Henry in the eyes.

My voice was weak, but I still tried to speak with passion.

"I'm sorry things had to end like this, Henry. Honestly, I wish this never happened, that we never were intimate, because what really suffers from all of this is our friendship, the one thing I valued most in this world. It makes me ill to think of us as no longer friends…that I won't be able to rely on you when I need you the most, but I guess that was all part of the gamble, of trying to make something intimate work between us. I knew the consequences, and still tried anyway. My mistake. Lesson learned."

I turned and started walking toward my room when Henry called out my name, making me stop.

"Rosie, please, let's talk about this."

"There is no talking, Henry. Good luck with your move, and I hope you and Tasha are happy together. I remember how good she was to you in college."

    With a broken heart, a hole in my chest, and a lack of purpose, I walked back into my room and rested my torn up body on my bed. This is what heartache felt like. This is what all those books were trying to describe, but never truly did justice, because I wanted nothing more than to crawl in a dark hole and never see sunlight again. The feeling of total emptiness encompassed me as darkness took over and I shut my eyes, allowing the world around me to move on while I lay, fragile and cracked.

CHAPTER 22

"The Smell"

From my window sill, I watched as Henry directed the movers, who were packing the moving truck with his boxes. The week had flown by in a blur. I took the rest of the week off, faking illness and just lying in bed, wondering when the pain in my heart was going to stop, but unfortunately for me, it never did; it only grew worse, especially since it was Saturday and Henry was moving out.

I hadn't seen Tasha since I saw her the other day, but then again, I'd only showered and left my room for the first time today since I found Tasha and Henry together.

The smell coming off of my body was too overwhelming this morning, so I gave in and took a shower, which was a bad idea since I just stared at Henry's razor in the shower and cried over the fact that I wouldn't see that razor in the shower anymore. I contemplated stealing it for my own sick purposes, but refrained from going bat shit crazy on him. Instead, I just emptied the remaining shampoo that was in my bottle and filled it with some of

Henry's, so I would at least smell him for the next couple of showers.

Pathetic? Yup, that was me, pathetic with a capital P.

When I wasn't lying around, I was writing, fixing the problem in my life through the words in my book. I made sure my two main characters were always together; no matter what they faced, they wound up together. There was no break up, no apex in the story where everything came crashing down, I was too raw to write such a thing. No, they were going to be together forever. If I couldn't make it happen in real life, than I sure as hell was going to make it happen in my book.

Currently, I was that wishy-washy girl who went back and forth between loving and hating Henry. I hated him because he moved on within minutes after we yelled at each other on Sunday, but then again, I was the one who started it all, so did I really have the right to blame him? No, I didn't.

Delaney tried to come into my room and convince me to talk to Henry, but after the second time of her hanging in, I started barricading my door with a chair. I didn't want visitors; I just wanted to smell, be lonely, and lay in the dark.

Derk came up to Henry and patted him on the back while giving him a handshake. I hated that Derk and Delaney were helping him. I mean, I got why, they were friends, but the bitter person living in my shell of a body wanted them to hate Henry, which was ludicrous. Henry hadn't done anything to them, no he only wrapped me around his finger, made me love him, and then just tossed me away.

That was a lie, he didn't toss me away…that was the bitter part of me talking. The bitter me made up lies in my head as to what happened, tried to convince my brain that all of this was because of Henry; he'd ruined everything, not me. But the sensible side of me knew Bitter Betty was just trying to get her revenge.

The movers closed up the back of the truck and started pulling away from the curb. Delaney gave Henry a hug and then shrugged her shoulders when she pulled away. All three of them, at the same, time looked up toward my window, making me duck behind my curtain. My stealth like moves were telling me I went undetected, but the way all three of them were shaking their heads after I took a peek told me I was slower than I thought.

I didn't care…if they saw me, they saw me. What use was it going to do now?

I watched as Henry took out his phone and started typing, probably calling Tasha to see if she wanted something to eat for lunch. That was the kind of guy Henry was, always thinking ahead and making sure you were well taken care of.

Damn.

My phone beeped with a text message, drawing me from my thoughts. I checked it and saw that it was Henry.

Henry: Rosie, come down here and say goodbye. Just don't stare at us from up there.

Mortification ran through me from him calling me out.

Come say goodbye to him? Yeah, no thank you. That was the last thing I needed right now. Even though I was smelling like Henry, thank you shampoo, there was no way I was strong enough to say goodbye to him and not cry, not cling on to his leg and beg him not to go. I've lived with Henry for so long now that not having him in the next room to me was going to be weird. I couldn't face reality just yet.

Instead of being a grown up and going downstairs. I texted him back.

Rosie: Sorry, can't. Probably not the best idea anyway. Happy house warming to you and Tasha.

Tears started falling from my eyes once again as I turned off my phone and went to my bed, where I buried myself once again in my comforter, separating myself from the world. It was the only way I knew how to currently live.

The shirt I borrowed from Henry was under my pillow. I never returned it because it was the one thing I clung on to, the one last piece of him that I would be able to hold onto and I would be damned if I would let it go.

***

"Rosie, I'm not kidding. If you don't let me in this room, I'm going to break down the door and you can explain to the landlord why your door is broken."

Groaning, I got out of bed and opened my door to find Delaney and Derk standing outside of it, casually dressed with their arms folded over their chests.

"What do you want?" I said, while my voice croaked and my eyes tried to adjust to the light. What time was it and what day was it?

"You smell!" Delaney said, while pinching her nose.

"Thanks, is that all you wanted to say?"

"No, it's Monday, and Jenny said if you don't show up to work tomorrow, Gladys is going to have a coronary."

"I have pneumonia," I fake coughed.

"No, you don't. Now, come on. We're going to get you showered because, damn, girl! And then we're going to go out for dinner. I don't think you've eaten for days."

"I had some saltines I found under my bed," I confessed.

Derk's nose crinkled at me as he studied my get-up. I was wearing long john bottoms, a purple oversized shirt, one sock, and my hair was plastered to my head since I hadn't taken a shower in two days. Not my finest hour.

"You're done moping around. Let's go."

Without my permission, Delaney gabbed my hand and led me to the bathroom, where she started the shower and stared at me. I held my hands up as I backed up into the wall.

"What the hell do you think you're doing?"

"Taking your clothes off. I don't care if I see you naked; you need to be cleaned."

"Well, I care," I squeaked.

"Then, be a big girl and take a shower yourself, or I will have to do it for you. I will have clothes picked out for you when you get out. Hurry up, because Derk and I are getting hungry."

"Fine," I succumbed and waited for Delaney to leave, but instead of exiting the bathroom, she sat on the toilet and covered up her eyes.

"Go on, I won't look."

"Why aren't you leaving?"

"Oh, so you can lock me out of the bathroom and drown yourself? Yeah, I don't think so."

"I wouldn't drown myself," I sneered as I quickly took off my clothes and got in the shower. "Ahhh! It's freezing!"

"Yes, I know. I thought it would wake you up."

Frantically, I turned the water to hot, knowing full well I couldn't hop out of the shower, because then Delaney would see me naked, that evil, evil girl. Once the water warmed up, I started going through my shower routine, trying to forget about the fact that Henry's razor was no longer hanging there. Nope, I would not think about it.

I showered like a boss, taking only two minute to cleanse my entire body, because the longer I stayed in there, the longer I felt myself start to weaken and want to crawl into a fetal position at the bottom of the tub.

I turned the shower off and grabbed the towel hanging right next to the shower.

"Did you even clean your lady cactus? That was a pretty quick shower," Delaney stated.

"Yes, I cleaned my lady cactus. God, I'm not a Neanderthal."

"Pretty sure Neanderthals cleaned their lady cacti."

"You're making this such a joyous experience," I said sarcastically, as I wrapped the towel around my body and pulled back the shower curtain.

"I thought you were going to have clothes ready for me."

"Oh, yeah, well come on, let's go to your room. You can comb your hair there and put on at least some mascara."

Rolling my eyes, I followed Delaney out of the bathroom and into my room, while Derk sat on the sofa, watching sports highlights. My mind went to many nights where I saw Henry and Derk watching highlights together, talking about their teams of choice and their wins and losses.

My heart ached.

"You're kind of depressing to be around," Delaney said, after moments of silence of me brushing my hair and her picking out an outfit.

"Thanks, you're really sweet."

"Well, I mean, come on, Rosie. You could at least give me a small smile."

"I don't feel like it," I said sadly. "You know, Delaney, I never realized how much one person could need another until Henry left. People always talk about having another half, but I never really understood it until now." I took a deep breath and looked at her. "Will the pain ever lessen?"

Delaney gave me a sad smile, but nodded her head. "It will, Rosie. I promise. It's just new right now. It will get better."

"I hope so. Can I just throw my hair up in a wet bun? I don't feel like doing anything special to it right now."

"That's fine, but at least wear a headband."

"Well, of course," I lightly smiled.

Delaney picked out a pair of my favorite jeans and a simple black top that was fitted to my upper half. I matched the top with a black headband that had a little red flower on it, put on some eyeliner—yes, crazy I know—and applied some mascara. That was as good as it was going to get.

"Might want some deodorant," Delaney added, as she saw me walking toward my door.

"Ugh, stupid arm pits."

I applied some deodorant and a little bit of perfume—things were getting wild—and grabbed my purse.

"Okay, let's go."

Derk met us out in the living room with his hands in his pockets.

"Ready?" he asked, while pulling Delaney into his side.

"Ready," I reluctantly replied, knowing already that I was the awkward third wheel on this outing. "Where are we off to?"

"How about Shake Shack? Simple but good, and the perfect cure for that little broken heart of yours," Delaney said.

"I could go for that, are you buying?" I batted my eyelashes, trying to work the whole pitiful card.

"I will," Derk winked at me. "But that means we get to stop at my buddy's place real quick to pick up my Ultimate Frisbee set. His place is right next to Shake Shack."

"Ugh, twist my arm."

Being the high rollers we were—not—we filed into a taxi and sidled up next to each other in the back, while Derk gave the cabbie our destination. I wasn't paying, so I wasn't going to complain about taking a cab. Derk had plenty of money; I wasn't worried about mooching off of him.

The busy streets of New York City passed me by as we drove in and out of traffic-filled roads, coming almost too close to other cars at times. Riding in a taxi in New York City was definitely a driver's version of Russian Roulette. Were you going to make it or take the bullet, aka, crash into the car in front of you, beside you, or even behind you? It was a chance you took every time you stepped into a taxi.

"Thinking about what kind of shake you're going to get? Strawberry?" Delaney asked me, while nudging my shoulder.

"Yeah, something like that," I responded.

The ride to Derk's friend's place was surprisingly uneventful. We pulled up to a building, where a doorman was standing outside, waiting to tend to new visitors of the building. Fancy.

I was jealous of the location; it was right next to the theater district, where I've always wanted to live. The history of New York City and the old time feel always called out to me, especially anything that had to do with Broadway. I was not the least bit good at singing, but place a musical in front of me, and I would be watching it for days. I had an old soul.

"Wow, I'm jealous of your friend," I admitted, as Derk nodded at the doorman, who opened the door for us.

The lobby of the apartment building was beautiful, full of white marble and pillars. It almost seemed too fancy, like Donald Trump should be popping out from behind a door any minute.

Derk led us to the elevators, where he pushed the button for the tenth floor, the middle of the building. His friend was fancy, but not too fancy, since he wasn't in the penthouse suite, but who was I to judge? I'd been using my sock as an eye cover for the past couple of days.

"Nice place," I said, while we traveled up.

"Yeah, rent was a steal. The guy has connections."

We walked to the end of the hallway, to a golden yellow door with an eight on it. Derk knocked a few times and we waited patiently for the door to open, but all we heard was a "Come in" from a far off spot.

Derk opened the door, and I followed behind him and Delaney, feeling slightly awkward that I was walking into a stranger's apartment.

The floors of the apartment were a deep oak, and the walls were a natural taupe color. Not my favorite, but it looked nice with the floors. The living room was the corner of the building, offering a beautiful windowed view of what was happening in the streets below. Yup, I was officially jealous. I scanned the living room and appreciated the bright red couch that looked like heaven to sit on and the white fireplace that sat in the middle of the room.

It wasn't until I spotted the framed pictures of me and Henry on the mantle that I realized I was standing in Henry's new apartment.

I started backing up, but didn't realize Delaney was being a tricky little bitch and stopped me from fleeing.

"Hey guys," Henry said, as he walked in, but stopped

immediately when he saw me.

I wanted to crawl into a hole, bury my head in the sand, do something to get away from the shocked eyes of Henry.

"Uh, what are you doing here?" Henry asked me.

My eyes floated from his mantle, where every single picture was of him and me, and they were the only decoration gracing the place, and then back to his eyes, those beautiful, mesmerizing eyes.

"Picking up Frisbees," I said, like an idiot.

"Frisbees?" Henry asked, now looking at Delaney.

"Gee, look at that, we have to go, Derk. We have that appointment with the sex and yoga guru. Sorry, we can't help unpack, but, oh hey, look at that, Rosie is free. Go on, Rosie," Delaney pushed me into the living room. "Help Henry. See you later."

Just like that, Derk and Delaney scooted out of Henry's apartment, leaving us completely alone.

I stood awkwardly, fidgeting with my purse, trying to think of any kind of excuse that would give me an option to leave, but my mind was drawing blanks. Complete blanks.

"It's good to see you," Henry said, walking closer to me, making my sweat glands work on overdrive.

"You too. Nice place," I complimented.

"Thanks."

"How's Tasha? Is she all moved in as well?"

Why would Delaney bring me here? Why was she being so cruel? I get it, I needed to move on, but to throw me in the shark tank while I was still bleeding...that wasn't a friend move, it was a straight up bitch move.

Henry looked down as he spoke. "Tasha was a mistake. I, uh, let her down earlier this week."

"Then, why did you move?" I asked, before I could stop myself.

"I've been looking to move for a while now, since Delaney and Derk were going to be finding a place together soon. This place became available, and I couldn't pass it up."

"Oh," I replied, feeling like my heart was going to fall right out of my chest in front of Henry, just so he could stomp on it a little bit more.

He was planning on moving all this time, no wonder why he decided to finally just have sex with me, because he was leaving anyway…there were going to be no strings attached for him.

Needing to get out of his apartment so I could breathe again, I started walking backwards to the door.

"Well, I'm not feeling very well. I think I'm going to go." Not a lie at all. I literally felt like I was going to throw up.

"Rosie, wait," Henry said, as he quickly walked over to me and grabbed me by the hand.

Instantly I felt the warmth coming off of him, making me want to buckle over and cry. I missed him terribly.

"Please, just sit down and talk to me for a second."

I was weak, I was pathetic, I would do anything to just spend a few more minutes with him, so I nodded and allowed for him to guide me to his red couch, which felt like heaven under my bum. I was right, it was supremely comfortable.

"Nice couch."

"Thanks, got it on sale. Loved the color, it reminded me of you."

Yup, I didn't want him to say things like that, because it only gutted me more.

"Okay," I said lamely.

At times, I really did wish I was more profound, more prolific, but when my heart was hanging on by a thread and my brain was mush from the man sitting next to me, I had no ability to form a sentence.

Running his hand through his hair, I watched as his muscles flexed under his shirt, the same muscles I once had my hands on.

Then it hit me…oh, my God, I was a virgin clinger.

No!

No, I was not a clinger, I was a girl who fell in love with a boy way before she got intimate with him. I just denied my feelings to save my heart. A lot of help that was, I thought, as I sat on Henry's new couch, contemplating whether or not I was going to have a heart attack from his proximity.

Softly, his hand grabbed mine, and he forced me to look him in the eyes. My heart pounded against my chest, making me very aware that he was holding me. Virginia stopped weeping for a second and took note that the man who stole our souls was now holding us.

"Rosie, I need to tell you something."

"Are you dying?" I asked, letting my mind wander to the worst thing possible.

"What? No," he said, confused, but then chuckled softly. "I'm not dying. I just...damn, I thought this would be easier."

"You're not pregnant, are you?" I teased, trying to ease the pressure in my chest.

"No," he laughed. "But I did have a scare for a second on Monday."

"Sounds frightening. Never been happier to see Aunt Flo, have you?"

"This is so wrong," he laughed some more, and then took a deep breath. His hand reached up and cupped my cheek, making me sweat even more. I was a hot mess. "God, Rosie, I'm so far in love with you, it's ridiculous. I don't just love you, I'm in love with you, like desperately, hopelessly, can't be without you in love with you."

Chills flew over my body as my stomach flipped upside down and Virginia started flapping in excitement.

"I know I was an ass, and I know I haven't been the easiest person to be around lately, but I blame you," he smiled. "You turned my life upside down the minute you decided you wanted to date. I couldn't take the thought of you with anyone else, because I knew deep down in my soul you belonged with me. Rosie, I'm sorry for everything, the way I treated you, for bringing Tasha into this; I was just...lost. I thought you wanted to go out with that Atticus guy, right after we shared one of the most amazing moments of my life."

"One of the most amazing?" I asked, while tears streamed down my face.

"Yes, the most amazing was when I met you."

I chuckled and wiped a tear away from face. "That was so corny."

"Yes, but true." Looking me in the eyes, he asked, "Do you feel the same, Rosie?"

His eyes pleaded with me, begged me to say yes, and that's when I realized the man truly adored me. He wasn't playing with me, he wasn't trying to just be kind, no, this man sitting next to me, searching my eyes for an answer, undoubtedly loved me with every inch of his being. The revelation was intense, heartwarming, and so damn overwhelming that the only thing I could think of was to throw my body at him and kiss those lips that I'd been dreaming of for the past week.

Without warning, I launched myself on his lap and grabbed his face with my hands.

"Henry, you have no idea how far in love I am with you."

A giant grin spread across his face, just as my lips found his. His hands went straight to my waist where he gripped me hard, as if I was going to float away. Slowly, I felt his hands work their way under my shirt, but not in a sexual way, just in a way that conveyed to me by touching my skin, he was getting as close to me as possible.

My lips danced with his as we both reveled in being with each other, giving in to all of the anxiety, the road blocks and misgivings our relationship had brought forward. Instead, we pushed past it all, put our hearts out on the limb, and took the leap.

I pulled away for a second and stared him in the eyes while I rubbed his face with my thumbs.

"I missed you so much."

"I missed you too, Rosie. Not having you near me these past couple of days has been torture. I truly thought I lost you."

"Me too," I said sadly. "But if you were in love with me, why did you move away? Why didn't you fight?"

He gave me a half grin and moved his hands up to my shoulders, where he gripped me tightly.

"This apartment came up on my radar, and I knew I couldn't give it up, because it's your dream apartment. If I couldn't win you back myself, I was hoping the apartment would."

"Wait, what are you saying?"

He kissed my nose and said, "Rosie, I want you to move in with me. Just you and me. No Delaney, no Derk, no subway rides out to Brooklyn. I want you here, with me, I want a life with you."

My heart soared and tears once again sprung from my eyes. This time, tears of joy.

"Are you serious?"

"Beyond serious, love. Live with me?"

"Yes!" I said, while wrapping my arms around him and hugging him tightly. "I can't believe this."

"Believe it, love. It's just you and me now."

"Does this mean we're boyfriend and girlfriend?" I asked shyly.

"It better," he nuzzled my neck. "You're mine, love."

"Wow. Aren't you just taking all my virginities? First boyfriend, first apartment I share with only a guy, first to visit my down below."

"Your down below?" he asked, laughing. "What about the elevator guy you farted on?"

"You know what I mean," I said, while playfully hitting his shoulder, making him laugh even harder.

"Do you think you have enough material to finish that book of yours now?"

"Hmm, I'm not sure. I might have to do some more research in the bedroom. Test some things out I've read in some of my books."

"I'm yours, love. Test away."

His cute smile hit me hard in the gut as I looked back at him. I was one hell of a lucky girl. How I'd snagged Henry to be mine, I had no clue, but now that he was mine, I wouldn't be letting him go.

Love is funny. It comes in all different shapes and sizes. Sometimes it's hard to find and sometimes it's sitting right in front of you, waiting to be recognized. What I learned from all the books I've read and from the book that I'm writing is that no matter what, you have to work to find love. It isn't a given and it isn't instantaneous. It's a privilege to find, and should never be taken lightly.

Everyone deserves a happily ever after; I'm just glad I found mine. Now, I just have to turn that happily ever after into a book. With Henry by my side, I have no doubt I'll be able to make it happen.

EPILOGUE
"The Insatiable Virginia"

"Henry, you have to sit still. You can't thread a needle if the needle keeps moving."

"I'm sorry, but the look on your face is so damn serious, it's hard not to laugh."

Henry and I have been living together for a week now, and we've spent most of the time in bed, exploring the ins and outs of each other. We bought a bed together, found the softest sheets available, and picked a neutral comforter we were both happy with. The bedroom was the only decorated room in the whole apartment, but we were happy with it, and frankly, it was the only room we spent time in.

In books, once the characters have sex, they tend to go at it like bunnies, and I always wondered if that was real life. Well, if those characters had a penis eating vagina like mine, then yes, it was true.

Virginia was insatiable and wouldn't quit. I didn't know how she kept up, but she was like an orgasm spitting machine. Henry went down on me, orgasm, henry fingered me, orgasm, Henry used a dildo, orgasm, Henry pulled down his pants...yup, orgasm. She was a randy little hussy, but I loved her.

"I'm just concentrating."

"It's not that hard, love. Just put it on."

"It's not going to fit. How on earth did you think this was going to fit?"

"Love, it's going to fit, just put it on."

I sat up on my knees, studied the cock ring in my hand, and then looked down at Henry's erect penis. The man could hold an erection for days, even when chuckling.

"You should have gotten a tire…that would have fit."

"Damn, love. You really know how to compliment a man."

Instinctively, he started stroking himself, making my mouth water.

So, I once was a virgin who would poke a penis to see if it was real, but now I was a horny girlfriend with the need to fulfill every sexual fantasy that came across my mind. My latest experiment stems from a sex scene I started writing in my book about a cock ring and riding Henry cowgirl style while the ring was on him, like my own personal dildo, but Henry-shaped. I don't know where the thought came from, but in order to truly write it out, I wanted to experiment with it first. Henry was very grateful for my writing, actually loving it, because he benefited from all of my experiments.

Please note, doing it against a wall, not as easy as it's written. There's a lot of fumbling involved. Also, shower sex equals awkward as hell, especially when the shower head starts to drown you. Sex doggy style while lying over a couch, exhilarating, but watch out for queefing.

"You're drooling," Henry pointed out, pulling me from my thoughts.

"I am not," I said, while wiping my mouth, realizing I was drooling.

"You so were. Don't be embarrassed; it's a turn on."

"Drooling? That's a weird turn on, Henry."

"The turn on is the fact that I could make you drool by just touching my dick, which, by the way, if we could hurry this along, that would be great. Poseidon is getting a little angsty."

Yes, Poseidon. That's the name Henry gave his penis. Unfortunately, Virginia was quite fond of the name and the member in question, so there was no changing it.

"Okay, but if this rips the condom, it's your fault."

"You lubed it; it will be fine."

I leaned forward and placed the cock ring on the tip of his cock and then slowly worked it down to the base, afraid I was cutting the circulation off from his dick.

"Holy hell," Henry moaned as his head fell back. "Love, please I need to be inside of you now."

That plea would never get old to me, ever.

Giving the man what we both wanted, I straddled him and positioned myself to take him in. Slowly, I allowed the tip of his dick to play with my already wet center, thank you Virginia. The vibration of the cock ring ran up the length of his shaft and hit me hard, made me weak, and made me collapse on top of him, not taking him in slowly like I wanted.

"Fuck!" he moaned, while he gripped my hips and started thrusting. "Never gets old, love. You were made for me."

I couldn't agree more. We fit perfectly together.

With small thrusts, Henry moved in and out of me as the cock ring vibrated us both. The feeling was intense, magnificent, and so overwhelming that my hands fell forward and clutched his chest as I felt my orgasm already starting to build up.

"Oh, my God, Henry, this feels so damn good."

"Fuck, it does."

Henry was cute, because whenever he was intimate with me, his tongue slipped up and he swore more often than he normally did. It was cute, that I could make him slightly lose his mind like that.

"Love, I'm so close."

"Me too," I gritted out, as my hair fell in front of my face, blocking my view of Henry.

"You're so beautiful," he squeaked out, just as he stiffened under me.

That was all I needed, together, we both fell over the edge and thrusted into each other, riding out our orgasm until there was nothing left.

My body flopped on top of his while he shucked the condom and cock ring to the ground. It was a habit I was not fond of, but that could be fixed by birth control or a waste basket next to the bed, simple.

Henry's hands ran up and down my back as he kissed my shoulder, slowly bringing me back to the present.

"Is that going to make the book?" Henry asked me, full of hope.

"That is definitely going to make the book."

"What else can we try?" he asked, making me laugh.

"How about we take a break for a second?"

"Come on, you know Virginia wants more."

He was right, because Virginia was sending me her keegle sign for yes at a rapid pace, but I tamped her down. She couldn't make all the decisions.

"She does, but give her at least a few minutes."

"Fair enough," Henry said, while kissing along my jaw. I knew exactly what he was trying to do, and damn if it wasn't working.

Pressing against his chest, I lifted myself up and looked Henry in the eyes. "I love you, Henry."

His eyes softened as he gripped my cheek with his hand. "I love you, Rosie. More than anything."

And just like that, I had my happily ever after, and so did Virginia and Poscidon.

The End

ABOUT THE AUTHOR

Born in New York and raised in Southern California, Meghan has grown into a sassy, peanut butter eating, blonde haired swearing, animal hoarding lady. She is known to bust out and dance if "It's Raining Men" starts beating through the air and heaven forbid you get a margarita in her, protect your legs because they may be humped.

Once she started commuting for an hour and twenty minutes every day to work for three years, she began to have conversations play in her head, real life, deep male voices and dainty lady coos kind of conversations. Perturbed and confused, she decided to either see a therapist about the hot and steamy voices running through her head or start writing them down. She decided to go with the cheaper option and started writing… enter her first novel, Caught Looking.

Now you can find the spicy, most definitely on the border of lunacy, kind of crazy lady residing in Colorado with the love of her life and her five, furry four legged children, hiking a trail or hiding behind shelves at grocery stores, wondering what kind of lube the nervous stranger will bring home to his wife. Oh and she loves a good boob squeeze!